Taming
Tom Jones

Margaret K Johnson

CROOKED
CAT

First Red Line Edition, Crooked Cat Publishing Ltd. 2015

Discover us online:
www.crookedcatpublishing.com

Join us on facebook:
www.facebook.com/crookedcatpublishing

*Tweet a photo of yourself holding
this book to @crookedcatbooks
and something nice will happen.*

For the commitment phobics and serial monogamists I've encountered in my life. You know who you are.

Acknowledgements

Thanks as ever to my wonderful beta readers: Ann Warner, Juli Townsend, Shani Struthers and Becky Bell, and to the members of the former Women's Fiction Crit Group on Authonomy. Also to the Crooked Cat community for making me feel so welcome.

About the Author

Margaret K Johnson began writing after finishing at Art College to support her career as an artist. Writing quickly replaced painting as her major passion, and these days her canvasses lie neglected in her studio. She is the author of women's fiction, stage plays and many original fiction readers in various genres for people learning to speak English.

Margaret also teaches fiction writing and has an MA in Creative Writing (Scriptwriting) from the University of East Anglia. She lives in Norwich, UK with her partner and their bouncy son and dog.

Taming
Tom Jones

Chapter One

I'm in the ladies toilets at my local superstore. Inside the one functioning cubicle, sitting fully clothed on the toilet seat, surrounded by overflowing carrier bags, a peed-on plastic tester stick clenched in my hand. Waiting for my fate to unfold.

Two minutes. The time it takes for Michael to go to sleep after we've made love if I don't do anything to stop him. The pee on the plastic stick is asking a question, and the chemicals inside it are working out their answer. And in two minutes I'll know whether their answer agrees with my instinct.

"I'm crazy about you, Jen," Michael said three months after we first got together. "I want us to be together. But I've got to be totally honest with you, if you want kids, you'd better find someone else, because I've already done all that. Don't get me wrong, I love being a father to Kyle, but it's enough for me."

Michael. We met at a fancy dress party nearly four years ago – my mate Rick's thirtieth birthday party. The theme was Pop Icons of the Twentieth Century, and the room was stuffed full of Elton Johns, Donny Osmonds and Mick Jaggers. I was Madonna, complete with pointy bra, and Marcia, my best mate, was Diana Ross.

"You look fantastic with all that long hair," I told her as we propped up the bar, preening ourselves and pointing out funny sights to each other.

"Thanks. I could get used to this glamour." She ran a hand over the sea-green sparkles of her dress. Perhaps we should start a band."

"Yeah, right." I hadn't forgotten our last spectacularly bad attempt at karaoke on holiday in Spain, even if she had.

Marcia never has liked to be reminded of her failings, even at school. "Your bazoomers aren't level," she told me stonily, jabbing an accusing finger in the direction of my breasts. "You need to go up a bit on the right."

I yanked dutifully at my right cone, wondering if Madonna had experienced the same trouble.

"Anyway," Marcia said, "who are you going to get off with tonight?"

"I'm not going to get off with anybody. It's only been three months since I split up with Luther."

"That's what I'm saying," she said. "Three months of freedom and so far you've done zilch to celebrate."

"I don't feel like celebrating." I was hurt by now, but Marcia never has been a girl to let my hurt feelings stand in her way when she's telling me something for my own good.

"Well, you should. Luther was a prize tosser. You are far, far better off without him, Jen."

"I loved him."

"You *thought* you loved him. That's about as different as Ibiza and the Isle of Man."

Marcia stood on diamanté sandal tip-toes, peering into the crowd, the dark river of fake hair flowing all the way down her bare back. "Him," she said, pointing. "That's who you'll get off with if you get off with anybody."

"Who?"

Marcia pointed again. "Him," she said. "Tom Jones."

"Mummy, I need to do a poo-poo!" In the supermarket toilets, a child's urgent voice interrupts my reminiscences.

"Excuse me, will you be long?" her mother asks.

There are two blues lines showing in the clear plastic window of the tester stick.

"Only the other cubicle's out of order, and I think this is an emergency," the mother continues.

I'm pregnant.

"Sorry. I...I'll be right out." I get up in a daze, flush the toilet, and begin to fumble with carrier bags, testing stick and door.

I'm pregnant. *Pregnant.*

"Too late, Mummy. Too late…"

One of the carrier bag handles snaps, and as I scrabble for control, a box of tea bags and the testing stick skitter onto the floor.

"Mummy, I pooed my pants."

The woman with the small child looks first at the stick, and then at me. "Good luck!" she says as her child begins to cry.

"Thank you." I pick up the stick, and make my way from the toilets and out to my car. Load the bags into the boot of my car. Unlock the driver's door. Get in. Just as if it's any ordinary day.

But then I just sit there, gripping the wheel, staring straight ahead at nothing. My mouth's numb and I've got pins and needles starting in my fingers. I want to cry because I've never felt so afraid and alone. And I want to laugh because I've never felt so excited and happy. It isn't possible to feel all of those things at once, and yet I do.

I do.

Finally I get it together enough to drive home. But by the time I've hauled the carriers out of the boot of my car, I'm still weighing up the pros and cons of telling Michael right away, as soon as I see him, or getting him drunk first. I still haven't come to any firm conclusion about it when a motorbike roars up the drive towards me.

I stop – my shoulders pulled down by the weight of the shopping – to see who the rider is. Taking his time, he cuts the engine, hoists the bike onto its stand and dismounts. I only realise that it's Michael when he takes the crash helmet off and stands there, grinning at me.

"What d'you think?"

I look from him to the bike and back up at him again. "Where's your car?"

"I traded it in. Isn't she beautiful?"

So somehow the 'tell him right away option' passes me by.

"I'm not sure motorbikes are female anymore," I say limply instead, but Michael doesn't hear me. He's gone back to run his hands over the new love of his life.

At the party, I asked Marcia, "Why him?"

She shrugged. "He's your type, that's all."

"Curly wig? Doormat chest hair?"

"Sodding great crowd of people laughing at his jokes. Throwing his head back when he laughs. Tall, loud and over-confident. Someone who thinks he is somebody."

"Who's getting the drinks in?" we heard 'Tom' bellow. "Another pint and you never know, I might sing you a verse of Delilah."

"Oh yeah, I forgot something," said Marcia. "He's obviously just as much of a tosser as Lucifer."

"Luther," I corrected her automatically, watching as one of the Eltons detached himself from Michael's group and headed for the bar.

"Whatever. Mind you, if that bulge in his trousers isn't a sock, he might well be worth a shag." Marcia looked at me sternly. "A *shag*, mind you. That's all I'm suggesting. He doesn't exactly look like marriage material."

"Marcia," I said, "I don't exactly look like the Business Woman of the Year myself tonight."

"Why should you?" she said with a typical Marcia lack of logic. "This is a fancy dress party."

"Come for a ride with me," Michael suggests. "Let me show you what she can do."

I've unpacked the shopping, and now I've started on tea. Michael's filling the kitchen doorway – a tall, broad-shouldered man with the same cheeky, teenage grin as his son. The familiar contours of his body are concealed beneath creased and creaky black leather, and his face lit by the thrill of his recklessness. Without warning, a huge rush of emotion washes over me, and I have to turn away, busying myself with the stir-fry I'm cooking.

"Jen?"

"No." My voice comes out funny, as if I'm trying to hide something. Which I am. "Not today. I'm a bit scared of motorbikes."

"You're mad at me," he says.

I add bean sprouts to the sizzling wok. "You're the one who has to travel all over the place for your job. The one who has to transport paintings to exhibitions all the time." I stir vigorously; too vigorously – bean sprouts scatter onto the hob and beyond. Somehow the activity provides me with enough control to look at him again.

Michael's cheeky grin has been replaced by an expression I've become all too familiar with lately; a blend of exasperation and disappointment that gives me the impression I don't quite come up to scratch. As I watch, he shrugs. "I'll hire a van when I need to," he tells me dismissively. "It's not a problem." Then he sighs and makes an effort to produce a persuasive smile.

"Come for a spin with me, Jen," he asks softly, reaching out to caress my neck just below my ear the way I like it. "Please."

And the thing is, I would do normally. That combination of caress and softly persuasive tone of voice would soon have me turning the gas off, abandoning the bean sprouts to their greasy decline. And Michael would laugh, grab hold of my hand and yank me triumphantly out of the door. Two minutes later I'd be wearing a helmet precariously too large for me and we'd be off, roaring down the street. A big man crouching forward over the handle bars like a boy racer, and a small woman with her breasts rammed into her man's back for warmth and a promise of security. Me and Michael.

But the blue lines on the tester stick have changed all that. "No thanks, love," I say once again, turning away to hide it from him. "Not today."

Michael's hand stops caressing my neck and falls away. I imagine that beguiling smile switching itself off. "Fine," he says. "Well, see you later then."

7

A slam of a door, a roar of the bike, and he's gone.

Marcia and I met at boarding school in North Norfolk when we were seven. She was the only black girl at the school, and as prickly as hell with her too-old-for-her-age sullen stares and snapped remarks. But for some reason, I could see beyond all that to the person she really was underneath, and I just tagged along determined to become her friend, ignoring all the put downs until I was accepted. These days I know Marcia loves me – in the only way Marcia knows how to love – fiercely, protectively; never afraid to speak her mind if it's for my own good.

But it isn't Marcia I phone after the motorbike roars off into the distance. How could it be? Marcia, who still thinks I should have kept Michael as a one-off shag instead of attempting to build a future with him. Marcia, who's been trying to make a baby with her husband ever since they got married three years ago.

"Hi, Marcia. Guess what? I'm pregnant. Michael would rather have a motorbike than a baby, and anyway, I think he's building up to ending our relationship. But I want this baby. I want this baby more than I've ever wanted anything. What d'you think?"

I think not, that's what I think.

No, I call Hannah, my other great friend. Hannah, who, at seventy, is technically old enough to be my grandmother. Hannah, Luther's mother. My almost-mother-in-law.

Michael dislikes both my best friends. He doesn't even know Hannah; it's enough for him that she's the mother of my ex – the ex I only discovered was doing the dirty on me on my wedding day.

"I can't understand why you still want to maintain that contact, Jen," he says periodically. "There's something very unhealthy about it."

"You wouldn't say that if you met Hannah," I explain gently, over and over again. "She's such a great person."

"She can't be that great if she managed to create such a

8

prawn as Luther," Michael says.

It's about the only thing Michael and Marcia have in common apart from a connection with me – a mutual loathing of Luther.

"Is everything all right?" Hannah asks when she hears my voice.

Dear Hannah. She's the mother my own mum never had the chance to be, dying young the way she did, and she's equipped with radar for my troubled emotions. She's also capable of reducing me to a pulp with just one caring word or look. I can hide things from almost everyone but Hannah.

"No," I say. "Not really."

"Has something happened?"

I swallow back tears. "Yes, sort of. But can I tell you all about it when I see you?"

"Well, let's make it soon then. How about tomorrow? I've got to come into Norwich anyway. I could meet you at Rainbow Restaurant at one o'clock, if that's any good."

"That would be fantastic, Hannah." I smile down the phone at her, already cheered just by the thought of having someone to get it all off my chest to. "How are you, anyway? Have you seen Luther lately?" *I can do this. I can still talk about other things as if my whole universe hasn't been turned on its head.*

"No, but I should do next week. It's his birthday."

"Of course it is." I'd forgotten, which is amazing. At one time I had a whole catalogue of our mutual anniversaries engraved on my soul. Is that what it will be like if Michael and I split up? Birthdays and anniversaries melting away into the slush of time?

But I can't think about the possibility of Michael and I splitting up. I can't contemplate never receiving one of his perfectly wrapped gifts on my birthday. Trying and spectacularly failing to wrap his present as neatly on his.

We talk a little while longer, and then I say goodbye. "See you tomorrow at Rainbow then, Hannah."

"Looking forward to it, dear. Bye for now."

If Marcia hadn't pointed out Tom/Michael to me at the party, it's likely nothing would have happened between us at all. Oh, I'm sure I would have noticed him, because Marcia was right; he was completely my type. A fairly quietish person myself, I always do seem to go for loud, charismatic men. "All mouth and insecurity," Marcia would say about them. "Got to keep talking and making people laugh in case they disappear forever."

But that night at the party I was still very down about my split with Luther, so I'd probably have left the party early and gone home to brood on my own. Instead I stayed, and when Rick, the birthday boy, came up to the bar for a pint, I asked him about Tom Jones.

"That's Michael Brandon," he said, downing half of his pint in one. "Lives out near the university. Had to consult me about a couple of chestnut trees in his garden once. Beautiful specimens, they are. Over a hundred years old."

Rick is the Council's Tree Officer, and works to maintain protected trees in the city.

"We got a particularly fine view of the trees from Michael's local pub." His smile was mischievous. "He's just been asking me about you, actually."

My heart began to race. "Has he?"

He nodded. "Want me to introduce you?"

"Yes," said Marcia on my behalf. "She does."

And that was that.

"Michael," Rick said half a minute later, "I'd like you to meet Jenny, a colleague of mine at the Council. She's an expert at making people happy."

Michael stood looking down at me through a pair of very dark glasses; an outsize crucifix tangling in what I hoped was false chest hair. "That's quite a way to be introduced," he said, giving me my first taste of that cheeky, teenage grin. "As an expert at making people happy."

I was embarrassed as hell. "It's Rick's way of saying I'm a community worker," I told him. "And I don't always manage it."

He whipped his dark glasses off, looking down at me

with seriously stunning green eyes. "Don't always manage what?" he asked.

"To…make people…happy," I said vaguely.

"Why not?"

He looked at me in a direct way that made it hard to concentrate on what I was saying. "Because everyone wants different things and you often end up having to compromise."

"Doesn't sound like a Madonna kind of thing to do, compromise."

"No."

It wasn't the most enthralling conversation in the history of conversations, I know. But words weren't important somehow. Our bodies were doing a very good job of communicating on their own, and that was without them even touching. It was just like in the trashy romance novels my gran devoured by the cartload before she died.

One hundred per cent chemistry.

I'm in the bath when Michael gets back from his bike ride, soaping my still flat stomach in the steamy atmosphere of the bathroom, and thinking of the life growing invisibly beneath my hand. Michael's child. My child. *Our* child. The essences of us both joined together to create new life.

It seems like a miracle, and of all the things Michael and I have done together in the last four years, the creation of this child is the best thing of all. We've never stopped using contraception, and I haven't resorted to Marcia's suggestion of pricking our condoms with a needle. "Selfish bastard," she's said on more than one occasion. "Why should you be deprived of a child just because he's already got a son?"

But in the end I didn't need to go behind his back. Fate has provided a dodgy condom and helped us to create a child together without any need for subterfuge on my part. The mush of emotion floods me again, stronger this time, and I think it's because I've been suppressing this yearning to have a child for so long. Even from myself. Especially from myself.

The bike revs up in the drive below the bathroom window. Once, twice, three times. Then the engine's cut and I hear it being yanked onto its stand. Imagining Michael dismounting, I splash water onto my face to make it uniformly wet. The front door opens and slams shut, and I clear my throat to call down to him. "I'm up here, in the bath!"

Seconds later he bounds up the stairs with all his usual energy. "Hi," he says, coming into the bathroom, hair sticking out at the back where he's dragged the helmet off, face wary as he tries to gauge what kind of reception he's going to get.

"Hi," I say back. "Good ride?"

"Fantastic." There's still a hint of rebellion in his voice, just in case I'm going to start making a fuss about the bike after all.

"Good." I smile, and he looks at me warily, but then enthusiasm gets the better of him. "You should see her go, Jen. Amazing acceleration. Only took me twenty minutes to get to the coast. The sun was just setting – a great, red ball of fire. It was as if I was riding right into it."

I've always loved Michael's enthusiasm and zest for life. When it was all directed at me, it was heady stuff. And I know that's what I want for this baby – for Michael's enthusiasm to warm it into loving life.

"That's great," I say, but too late, because Michael's already realised he hasn't got my full attention.

"Well," he says, turning away, "tell me when you've finished, will you? I need a shower."

My hand's still resting on my stomach. "Why don't you join me in here?" I invite him. "It's still nice and hot. You can tell me more about the bike."

We often shared a bath at the beginning, in the days when we couldn't bear to be parted from one another for a second, our various limbs contorting and wrapping to accommodate each other. Taking turns to have the end with the taps. "No," he says, "that's okay. I'm filthy. Besides, I need a cup of tea."

And suddenly I picture the box of tea bags in the supermarket toilets where I left them, lying half way under the door of the out-of-order cubicle.

"Oh. I...I forgot to get teabags. Sorry. There's...there's some wine though."

Michael pulls a face. "No, I might go out on the bike again in a bit. Ride down to the pub and show her off."

And that's what he does. So, somehow, when we're lying back-to-back in bed and I'm pretending to be asleep, I still haven't told him he's going to be a father.

Chapter Two

Michael, 1985

Michael and his mother were hiding behind the sofa. She was leaning back against the wall with her eyes closed, but he didn't think she could be asleep; there was far too much noise for anyone to sleep.

"Linda! Let me in!"

Crawling on his hands and knees, Michael peeped round the edge of the sofa. Through the window, he could see his father, one hand shielding his eyes as he tried to see inside, the other bashing on the dirty glass. The bashes were so hard Michael could feel the vibration of them through the floorboards. Any minute now the glass would break, and jagged shards like ice daggers would cascade from the window.

"Linda, I'm sorry, all right? At least let me see the boy."

Michael closed his eyes. Inside his head he could see two men; one was standing on a beach, wearing a blue shirt, open at the neck. The shirt was the same colour as his eyes, and his eyes were laughing. "Come on, kiddo," he said, "we're going to make an amazing sand castle. The biggest, grandest castle the world has ever seen. It's going to be so good; we're going to get in the Guinness Book of Records!"

The other man was sitting on the sofa – the very same one Michael and his mother were hiding behind now. It was almost dark, but the overhead light wasn't on yet, and the TV was sending flickering patterns around the room. Michael was on the rug, making a tower out of Lego. The light was so dim; it was getting difficult to see where to place the blocks. Suddenly the tower fell, sending bricks scattering all over the rug. "Shut the fuck up, won't you?" that man yelled, reaching out to give him a stinging clout round the ear.

The smiling man on the beach and the scowling man in the flickering darkness were both Michael's dad. The only thing was, he didn't know which one was outside right now, squashing the spring daffodils in the border below the window.

Suddenly the sun came out, sending a shard of light in his direction, picking him out like a searchlight. His father saw him. "Michael!" he yelled, the taps on the windowpane getting faster. "Let me in, son!"

"Get back here!" his mother growled, yanking him back behind the sofa by the arm. Michael's head made stinging contact with the wall, and he cried out with pain.

"And shut up."

Stifling his sobs, Michael rubbed his head and listened to his father banging on the window. Bang, bang, bang.

"Come on, son; let me in. It won't be like last time, I promise. Daddy's going away; he just wants to see you before he goes."

Suddenly Michael knew it was seaside Daddy out there. Happy Daddy. The person he loved more than anyone else in the world.

"Daddy!" he cried, trying to wriggle away from his mother, but she still had hold of his arm, and now she gave him a slap for good measure. "I said, shut up!"

Outside, his father gave the window one final reverberating slap with his open palm and turned away. "Sod you both then!" he yelled, and Michael heard the sound of his boots crunching away on the gravel path; the throaty blast of his old van starting up and pulling away.

Then nothing.

Chapter Three

"But what makes you think Michael's about to call it a day with you?" asks Hannah at lunch the next day.

We've been in Rainbow Restaurant for ten minutes – enough time to place our orders and for Hannah to say how well I'm looking. And for me, on the contrary, to ask with concern whether she's okay. Because although Hannah's dressed in cheery bright colours, and her hair and make-up are immaculate as usual, there are these dirty great big *alarming* black circles beneath her eyes; circles she's explained are a result of her increasingly nocturnal habits due to her penchant for watching live cricket from all four corners of the globe.

When I told Hannah about the baby, she was as thrilled as if it were her own grandchild-to-be. And you know, I so wish it was. I don't remember my mum because I was only three years old when she died, and I've never met Michael's mum – he fell out with his parents years ago and now they live in New Zealand. He doesn't even get a Christmas card from them – it's very sad.

"It's not just because he's bought a motorbike, is it?" Hannah asks me now. "Because lots of men do that, don't they? To reassure themselves they're still young. With Albert it was tractors."

"Tractors?" I laugh. I can't help myself. I never met Hannah's husband – he died before I met Luther. But from what I can gather, he was just as much in love with his tractor as he was with either his wife or his son.

"Tractors can be every bit as sexy as motorbikes, you know," Hannah twinkles. "At least, they can to Norfolk farmers."

"And to little boys."

16

It's an innocent-enough comment, but Hannah suddenly grabs my hands across the table, and we both stop smiling. Faces may become lined as people grow older. Hair may go white. But eyes never change. And Hannah's are a beautiful slate grey.

When she wants them to be, they can be very intense. "I'm so glad you're going to have that whole experience of being a mother, Jenny," she says, and my own eyes instantly fill up. "There's nothing to equal it in this life. Nothing. Hard, hard work, of course. The hardest work there is. But the only work that really counts. And I'm sure Michael knows that, deep inside of himself. You'll see. He'll forget all about his motorbike when he knows about the baby."

I want to believe it. I so want to believe it. "The thing is," I say, "I don't want him to stay with me if it's just because I'm pregnant."

Hannah sits back, and I know she understands. "You want to know he's with you because he wants to be with you."

"Yes. Anything less, well…" I shrug. "What's the point?" My voice breaks a little with emotion, and Hannah reaches across the table to squeeze my hand.

"So how can I tell him?" I ask her. "Because if I do tell him and he stays, I'll never be completely sure it's not just because of the baby, will I? Not a hundred per cent."

"I see what you mean."

"And isn't only the motorbike. He's just seemed… I don't know, restless lately, I suppose." I sigh. "You know what his track record is, Hannah. He's never stayed with anybody for longer than four years, not even Kyle's mother."

"He does seem to be something of a serial monogamist," Hannah says thoughtfully, and I nod.

"Yes, and it's our fourth anniversary soon. I can't help thinking I'm living on borrowed time."

The waitress arrives with our food, and Hannah lets go of my hand.

"Two tagliatelles in creamy mushroom sauce?"

"Yes, thank you." I summon up an automatic smile, and as I do, I wonder what else we do automatically in this life. Kiss our lover good night, maybe? Make love? Shop for two for the weekend believing there will still *be* two at the weekend?

"But four years... It's just a number, isn't it?" Hannah says. "It doesn't necessarily follow that he's planning to end your relationship just because you've got your anniversary coming up. If he's happy with you, then he won't be counting."

"But that's just it. I don't know if he is happy." I think about Michael, attempting to pinpoint exactly how I feel he's changed. "He's always on the phone, you know?" I say at last. "Talk, talk, talk to everybody but me. Sometimes it seems as if he finds it hard even to sit on the sofa next to me for a whole evening. Remember how he wanted to move house? Dragged me round loads of properties, and then changed his mind. Then it was an extension. Had the plans drawn up and everything. It just seems as if it's all grand schemes and searching for something."

"And now the motorbike."

"Yes." I look down at my untouched food miserably. "I don't know, Hannah, "I just don't seem to know what he wants from me these days. Everything feels like some kind of test. And I'm trying to pass the test; only I don't know what the questions are, let alone the marking scheme. Sorry, I'm going on. Don't let your food get cold."

Hannah picks up her fork and expertly winds some tagliatelle around it. "Have you ever talked to Michael about why all his other relationships broke down?" she asks.

I shake my head, picking up my fork. "Not directly, no. We talked about our old relationships a bit when we first got together, but he's not one to dwell on the past." I sigh, winding the pasta onto my own fork with considerably less expertise than Hannah. "I suppose until recently I've managed to convince myself the reason Michael didn't stay with all his exes was because they just weren't right for him."

"The way you're right for him."

"Well, yes…"

"Which jolly well ought to be the case, since you're beautiful, intelligent and extremely pleasant company!"

I want to be exactly like Hannah when I'm her age. Attractive, intelligent and caring. Only, I don't want to be attractive, intelligent and caring and alone, watching test cricket in the middle of the night. I want to be enjoying my retirement with Michael. Travelling the world. Spoiling our grandchildren.

"I think you might be a little biased, Hannah," I tell her. "And besides, if Michael has got doubts, then he isn't alone, is he? I wasn't enough for Luther either."

"No," Hannah says rather fiercely, "and love my son as I do, I still haven't forgiven him for being stupid enough to let you go out of his life."

We eat our pasta for a while, both busy with our thoughts, and then Hannah wipes her mouth with her napkin. "It's a shame we can't find out why all those past relationships of his ended, isn't it? If we knew that, then we'd have more of an idea of the pitfalls you might be facing."

Something sparks to life somewhere inside me. "You're right," I say. "It would be good to know that."

Hannah sighs. "Though I suppose there would be no easy way to find out, would there?"

Kyle, I think, my brain racing. Kyle, Michael's teenaged son, has kept in touch with most of Michael's exes. And of course, he's the son of one of them. I could ask him. I could do some investigating; set out to meet some of them. Why not? What have I got to lose?

At two o'clock, Hannah goes off to her dentist appointment.

"Don't worry," she says as we kiss goodbye. "Everything will be all right."

And, as I begin to make my way back to work, I feel as if just a little bit of the weight on my shoulders has been lifted. The more I think about it, the more I think the whole investigating Michael's exes thing is a good plan. Asking a few questions isn't going to do any harm, and if I'm careful, there's no reason why Michael should find out.

It shouldn't take me long to get back to work, because City Hall is only two minutes' walk from Rainbow Restaurant. That is, if you don't go via the market, and you really don't need to go via the market.

I plunge into the timeless world of narrow, striped-canopy corridors, past the cheap golfing umbrellas and suitcases, sterilised dog bones and feather boas. The Hoover bag man with the stall that looks as if it's been permanently ransacked. People eating chip butties shoulder to shoulder with people flicking through endless stacks of old records. It's easy to lose yourself in the market's archaic chaos, and that's just what I want to do for a while; lose myself.

Sitting on a free high stool at the chip stall surrounded by pungent chip grease and parfum de tomato ketchup, I order a mug of coffee and wonder if and when I'll start to experience morning sickness. If it does happen, it's going to be difficult to hide my pregnancy from Michael.

Hide my pregnancy from Michael. Suddenly the reality of it hits me. There was a time, not very long ago at all, when I wouldn't have dreamt of hiding *anything* from Michael. Why would I have wanted to? He was the other half of me – the part that made me complete. I've got no idea when that changed. When it started to seem right to use the past tense. He *was* the other half of me and not he *is*.

After Michael and I first danced together at that party, we couldn't get enough of each other. Two total strangers, we moved slowly around in the middle of the dancers in a sort of sexual fog. I expect we looked ridiculous in our fancy dress. No, I *know* we looked ridiculous in our fancy dress. A fake Tom and a fake Madonna with bits of our costumes slipping, pressed together like there should be a welding joint. But we didn't care about ridiculous. Ridiculous didn't enter our heads. I kept expecting him to go back to his friends, but he didn't. And though I knew somewhere on the fringes of the fog that I ought to go and check on Marcia, I just couldn't break away.

Looking back on that night now, I like to think the sexual fog wasn't just about lust and alcohol. I like to think it was about love at first sight.

As the evening went on and the music got slushier, we kissed and we fondled, forgetting everyone could see us. Like a couple of kids. Emerging startled and starry-eyed when the DJ finally packed up and the lights went on.

"Everyone's coming back to mine for coffee," Rick told us, but Michael had hold of my hand, and it didn't feel as if he was going to let it go.

"Thanks, mate," he said, "but we're heading back to mine."

I avoided looking at Marcia. "Just a shag, okay, Jen?" Her eyes would be saying to me. "Just a shag, remember?" And I didn't want to think it was 'just' anything. I didn't want to think at all.

Michael hailed a passing taxi and we kissed all the way back to his house. When he broke away to look down at me, I had no idea what he was going to say, but it certainly wasn't what he did say.

"Listen, I'm aware that this is a very un-Tom Jones kind of thing to say, but I have a son. And because I have a son, I have a babysitter. I need to pay her before I can ravish you. So, do you want to subject yourself to her laser-sharp scrutiny before you even know what type of underpants I wear? Or d'you want to wait round the back while I get rid of her?"

I blinked at him, suddenly wondering what I was getting myself into. I could almost hear Marcia saying, "Get out, Jen! Get out now!" But I was weak with desire, and anyway, before I could speak, Michael was encouraging me round the back of the house where I waited, alone and shivering in the dark, while he chatted to the babysitter. Then at last she was gone and he was opening the patio doors to let me in.

21

"Sorry about that; thought I'd never get rid of her," he said, and then he pulled me down onto the rug in front of the gas fire, his kisses hotter than the fake flames.

Later, when we went upstairs and he tossed me down onto the bed, I still didn't know what his hair was like because he was still wearing the Tom Jones curly wig. He sat astride me, and I looked up at him over my pointy cone breasts as he unbuttoned his shirt, revealing a foot-square mat of stick-on chest hair.

Reaching up, I tangled my fingers in it, making it flap slightly at the edges.

He clamped one strong hand down on mine. "Don't you be discovering all of my secrets now, girlie," he said in a fake Welsh accent, and as I laughed, he reached up to tear the wig off, tossing it over his shoulder before he kissed me. His hair was short and black as a raven wing, turning his eyes green as moss. He was the most attractive man I'd ever met, and I was here, in his bed, about to make love to him. The time for comedy was over. At least until the next morning, when I woke up to see the Tom Jones wig hanging from the lampshade along with my cone bra.

I don't get the chance to speak to Kyle about his father's exes straight away, even though I see him the very same day I get the idea. When I get back from work, he's outside the front of the house sitting astride Michael's motorbike.

"Hi, Jen," he says, and I kiss him.

"Hi, Kyle. How are things?"

"I'm okay," he says with a nod. "Surprised about this." And he looks down at the bike, stroking the fender. "D'you think Dad's going through an early mid-life crisis?"

Good question. "Because he's bought a bike?"

"Yeah, and the rest."

I frown at him. "What rest?"

Kyle shrugs, looking at me through his unnecessary sunglasses. "Dunno. Just a feeling. Clothes and stuff. And he's not coming to my play."

Now that does surprise me. Shocks me, actually. "He's

not?"

Kyle polishes the bike fender with his sleeve. "He just told me. Got to go to America or something."

Michael goes to America quite a lot. He runs a couple of art galleries and imports and exports original works of art. But he's known about Kyle's starring role in his college play for months now, and I'm amazed he's going to miss it. Usually he tries really hard where his son's concerned.

Kyle is an exceptionally nice boy. Somebody, somewhere, has done the right thing with him. Stacks of right things. Michael of course, every other weekend – which was all that was open to him after the divorce. But Diane, his mother, has to take most of the credit, I suppose.

"Mum's coming," Kyle says. "And you, right?"

I've met Diane several times since Michael and I have been together, when she's dropped Kyle off or we've taken him back to hers at the end of a weekend. The first time she let her gaze sweep assessingly over me for several seconds before she smiled. I wasn't sure whether she was impressed by what she saw or not. I tended to think not. Diane's tall and slim and blonde in a 'young enough to be a new hippy' sort of way, whereas I'm petite and brunette in a 'trying to look well-groomed and occasionally succeeding' kind of way. Not that Diane isn't young. She's just turned thirty-five. Only three years older than me.

Sometimes I think of the two of them, Diane and Michael, newly married, not much more than children themselves, parents of a new baby. I've got this picture in my mind, probably from some photo I caught a glimpse of once, of the two of them standing on a bridge, holding hands, with Kyle in a pram next to them. They look as if they sneaked out of school to pose for it.

Too young, too soon; that's the obvious answer behind that particular relationship breakdown.

"Jen? Are you coming to the show?" Kyle's looking less of the cool young biker by now and more the insecure teenager, so I quickly move over to kiss him on the cheek.

"You couldn't keep me away," I say, and he smiles again.

"Just as well Dad won't be there really," he says cheekily. "As well as you, there might be two other ex-girlfriends of his."

My heart starts to speed up with interest. This could be the opportunity I need. "Will there?" I say, seized by a sudden wave of emotion. Kyle's so nice, it's no surprise to me that all those exes want to keep in touch with him, and I know I'd want to too.

"Hi," Michael says to me, coming out of the house with two bike helmets. "Had a good day?" He gives me a quick peck on the mouth.

"Yes, not bad." I reach out, intending to pull him closer, but he's putting on his crash helmet, having handed the spare to Kyle, so it doesn't happen.

"Good. We're just going for a spin. Won't be long."

"Dad's riding pillion," Kyle jokes.

"In your dreams," his father tells him, and Kyle shuffles reluctantly backwards on the leather seat.

"D'you want to stay for something to eat when you get back, Kyle?" I ask, just as the bike roars into loud life.

Kyle shouts to me through the muffling confines of the crash helmet. "Can't tonight, sorry, Jen. Got a rehearsal. Dad's giving me a lift there. See you soon. At the show if not before."

Michael revs the bike up, shouts something unintelligible at me, and then they're gone, roaring up the drive to the main road to frustrate the stationary commuter traffic.

Chapter Four

Michael, 1986

His mother was talking to herself again. The first time it happened, Michael thought they had a visitor. But when he went to see who it was, there was no one there – just Mummy, in the kitchen, having a conversation with the wall. "No, you don't understand. You've got it all wrong," she said. Then she waited a moment, and shook her head. "What do you mean it's the same? You couldn't get anything more different if you tried!"

When she waited again, obviously listening, Michael looked at the wall. But it was just a wall, and he couldn't hear anything.

"You're not even trying – that's always been your trouble. You just don't put the effort in."

"Mummy?" Michael tried to get her attention, but she didn't seem to even notice he was there.

That had been the start of it, but eventually he got used to it, because it started to happen more and more often. And not only with the wall – it could be a plant, or the vacuum cleaner, or just nothing – empty space.

This morning, he didn't even bother to go and see. She was in the bedroom, and he knew she wouldn't be coming out to help him to get ready for school. So he dressed himself and went – without much hope – to see what there was for breakfast. Yesterday the milk had tasted funny. Today it had turned solid, left out next to the sink with the washing up.

He went into the bedroom. "I'm going now, Mummy." She was lying in bed, quiet now. He stood there for a moment, by the bed, but she didn't speak or turn to look at him.

Letting himself out of the house, Michael set off down the street. The school wasn't too far away, but there was one busy road to cross. Michael knew the lollypop lady would comment if she saw him on his own, so he waited around a corner until he saw two mums with five children between them approaching the crossing. Then he hurried to join them, doing his best to blend in. Two of the boys were jostling each other, taking the adults' attention, and this helped him to get across undetected.

At school, he hung his bag and coat on his peg and went into the classroom. Some mothers were in there too, helping their children with activities before the bell went. But other children were on their own like him, and he joined them at the drawing table, quickly becoming absorbed in a picture.

"It's time to put this away now, Michael," Mrs Sturridge told him after a few minutes. "The bell's gone."

Michael hadn't even heard it; he'd been completely absorbed in his drawing. He didn't want to stop.

Mrs Sturridge was looking at him. "Michael, will you come with me, for a minute? Mrs Clark, I'll be five minutes. Can you get them started on their worksheets? Come on, Michael."

Reluctantly, Michael followed her out of the classroom, wondering where they were going. Mrs Sturridge was still smiling at him, but somehow this didn't feel like a good sign. "That jumper you're wearing is covered in paint, Michael," she said brightly. "We got a bit carried away with our pictures yesterday, didn't we? I don't think the cleaners were very happy with me."

Michael looked down at himself. He didn't know what to say, so he said nothing.

"Anyway, I'm sure there's a spare jumper in lost property for you to wear until your mummy's had a chance to do some washing. Let's go and look, shall we?"

Michael's bottom was itching like crazy. He had an overwhelming desire to scratch it, but dared not in case she realised that his school jumper wasn't the only item of his clothing that was dirty.

Mrs Sturridge was rummaging through the forgotten water bottles, odd gloves and grubby PE shorts in the lost property box. She pulled out a jumper and held it aloft triumphantly. "Here we are. Right, Michael, let's get this painty jumper off, shall we?"

The lost property jumper was too big and smelled of the last person to wear it. Michael breathed through his mouth as it went over his head.

"How is your mummy?" Mrs Sturridge asked. "Did she bring you into school this morning? I didn't see her."

She was squatting down, level with him, her face close to his. Michael's eyes slid away from her. "She left me at the school gate," he lied. "Had to go to the doctors."

"Oh yes," said Mrs Sturridge. "When is your baby brother or sister going to be born? Do you know?"

Michael shook his head.

Mrs Sturridge looked at him and sighed. "Come on then," she said. "Let's get back to class."

Chapter Five

Marcia comes to Kyle's play with me.

We arrange to have something to eat first, and Marcia chooses a fish restaurant that's recently opened. It's called The Meeting Plaice, and the staff seem enthusiastic and eager to please. As do the smiling reliefs of lobsters and crabs that are mounted on the wall near our table.

"This is how Norwich does haute cuisine," Marcia comments sarcastically, and I laugh.

"It smells good, though."

Marcia's a nurse at the Norfolk and Norwich hospital, and she's been chopping and changing shifts lately to cover for staff sickness, so I haven't seen her for over a week – a week during which my whole world has changed forever. I know I have to tell her, but I just don't know how to do it, so instead, I stall for time.

"So," I ask, "anything new with you?"

She smiles, looking happier than she has done for ages. "Yes," she says. "A result."

My heart lifts. "A result?" Maybe she's pregnant too. Maybe we can do it all together – the antenatal classes, childbirth, cracked nipples, sleepless nights, the lot!

"Yes. Mum and Dad have given me the money to give IVF another go."

"Oh." My excitement crumples slightly, but I smile. "That's good." Marcia and her husband have already been through three rounds of IVF – the first two paid for by the NHS, and the other wiping out their savings. All were unsuccessful.

"Yes," she says. "Now all I've got to do is convince Gary about it."

Gary hated the IVF experience; and it wasn't even him

actually going through the treatment. The drugs. The 'procedure' to remove the eggs. The implants. The bated breath. And ultimately, the failure.

He hated being a helpless witness to Marcia's seesawing emotions – to her grief. The pitiful desperation of it all. He told me once that it was the worst time of his life.

"You haven't told him yet?"

"No. It just hasn't been the right time. He's a bit stressed at work at the moment. I'll wait till things have calmed down for him a bit. It's good though, isn't it? Oh, Jen, just think; I could be pregnant by the spring!"

Marcia's face is so aglow, she looks as if she's just told me that she's actually pregnant, not that she's probably going to try to get pregnant. So how can I tell her about my own baby?

Maybe that's why I decide to tell her the other part of my news – to compensate for withholding the most important news of all.

"Listen, I need you to help me with an investigation I'm starting tonight."

"Investigation?"

"Yes. Kyle says that some of Michael's exes are going to be at the play. I'm going to get him to point them out to me at the after-show party. But I won't be able to talk to them all. That's where you come in."

"Wait a minute," she says, frowning at me. "I'm missing something here. Why do you want to talk to Michael's exes at all?"

So I tell her everything. Everything except the baby bit. And by the end, she's even more cheerful than ever.

"Sounds cool. I'm up for it."

I look at her suspiciously. "I still love Michael, Marcia," I remind her. "I'm not doing this to try to find reasons why I should leave him. And I don't want you to approach it from that angle either. Understand?"

She smiles at me mischievously. "Would I do that?" she asks.

"Yes." I'm filled with a sense of treachery – a feeling that

I've somehow betrayed Michael by talking about all this. I've never believed in betraying our intimate, private business to anyone, not even my close friends. And until now, I haven't needed to.

"When you start poking around in Michael's past you'll probably hear so many horror stories you'll decide to scarper of your own accord."

"Marcia!"

"Well." She takes a good look at my face and sighs. "Oh, all right," she says reluctantly. "All right. I know he's the love of your life and all that."

"He is," I tell her. "The love of my life. He is."

Marcia looks more like her usual grumpy self now. Somehow it's reassuring, even though I'm hurting.

"Okay! I won't do anything you don't want me to do!" she says.

"Promise?"

"*Yes*. Promise."

There's a strained little silence between us.

"I promise, okay?" she says again, and I sigh, fiddling with my napkin.

"I still don't really know why you've always had it in for him," I say, silently admitting to myself that the way Michael 'accidentally' forgot her wedding, arranging a business meeting for that very afternoon, can't have helped a lot.

The waitress arrives with our food. "One salmon special, and one Caribbean-style snapper," she announces, and I think that just lately it seems as if all my important conversations are interrupted by the arrival of food.

"I hate the way you always jump when he says jump," Marcia says when we're alone again, sprinkling salt onto her dinner. "And he wants you to jump far too often."

"Does he?"

Marcia picks up her knife and fork, tucking into her food with the clear conscience of someone who's convinced they're in the right. "Yes," she says. "Look at tonight, for example. *His* son's play. Why isn't he here himself? Why is

30

it you going instead?"

And I don't know; that's the thing. Michael was evasive when I tried to find out more about his sudden business trip. "It's just work, that's all, Jen," he said. "Kyle understands. There'll be other plays." But I wasn't taken in by his casual attitude then, and I'm still not now. It's just too out of character.

But I don't tell Marcia any of that. "He had to work." I say. "Besides, I was coming anyway."

"That's beside the point," she says. "The way I see it, Michael takes you for granted, and he's got all the power. And you don't notice it because you can't see beyond the sex and dependency thing, which is what you think true love is about."

"Remind me again why you're my friend," I ask, and she sighs.

"Look, I've said I won't interfere, and I won't," she says, putting a big forkful of Caribbean-style snapper into her mouth. There's a pause while she chews and swallows, and then she continues relentlessly. "But don't be surprised if these women dish out a lot of dirt about him, that's all I'm saying. By the way, I saw Lucifer's mother the other day."

"Hannah?"

"Yes. She was just coming into the hospital as I was on my way home. Must have been about three o'clock."

I frown at her. "She had a dentist's appointment on Wednesday," I say. "We met for lunch."

Marcia shrugs. "Well, there are dental surgeons at the hospital," she says. "Must be serious though, if she's going there."

"Oh, poor Hannah," I say, and think how typical it is of my friend not to make a fuss. "I must give her a ring and find out how she is."

Kyle is superb in the play. It's Entertaining Mr Sloane, and he's Mr Sloane, so he gets to kiss the older woman and to swan around being sardonic in his underpants.

"He's too good to be true, that boy is," Marcia shouts to

me over the rapturous applause at the end of the performance. "Talented, handsome, charming. Something's got to be wrong somewhere."

"Can't you stop being cynical for one second?" I say, but she just laughs.

As people gather in one of the classrooms for the after show party, Kyle makes his entrance like a race horse into the winner's enclosure, make-up hastily removed, body still pump-charged with performance-induced adrenalin.

He goes over to Diane first, of course, and Marcia and I watch as he gets thoroughly hugged, kissed and congratulated.

"Is that his mother?"

"Yes, that's her."

Marcia gives Diane a good long stare before pronouncing her verdict. "I think she left her guitar and hymn book at home."

Then, while I'm still laughing, Kyle says something to Diane and starts to walk towards us. It's our turn to congratulate the star of the show, and I do it with as much enthusiasm as his mother.

"You were fantastic," I tell him, giving him a huge hug. "Really fantastic."

"D'you think so?" he says, and Marcia slaps him mateishly on the back.

"You were great, kiddo," she says. "And you know it. So don't fish for compliments."

Kyle laughs. "D'you think Dad would have thought I was good?"

My heart goes out to him because it's not fair. It's not. He shouldn't have to ask that question. Michael should be here.

"Definitely." And then, before he can dwell any longer on the subject, and before his rapturous public can claim him, I ask my own question. "So, Kyle. How many of your ex-stepmothers turned up in the end?"

He looks around, and waves at a tall woman with shiny black hair. "Just Nita, by the looks of it. I'd better go and thank her for coming. Catch you guys later."

"Nita, eh?" Marcia says. "I'll take her, shall I? You go for the mother."

I can't take my eyes off Nita. She's so pretty, and she's got these long, long legs that go on forever.

"Jen?" Marcia says again. "Is that okay?"

"Sorry, yes. Yes, that's fine. But don't mention Michael, will you?"

"Yes, I know, just get enough information about her so you can make contact if and when you want to. I know. You said. I'll use her boots as my opener. They are gorgeous."

As we watch, Kyle is claimed by some of his fellow actors, and Nita's left alone.

"Right," Marcia says. "That's my cue."

But I stop her. "She's stunning, isn't she?"

"Yes."

"Stunning and young, and obviously nice to Kyle."

"Yes... So?"

"So why did Michael split up with her?"

"That's for you to find out, isn't it? I'm just going to find out about her boots. See you later." And she strides purposefully off in Nita's direction, a woman with a mission. A *small* woman with a mission. Because, next to Nita, Marcia looks pocket-sized. Not that it matters. My friend is a match for anyone.

I only wish I felt as confident about speaking to Diane.

"Hello, Jan," Diane greets me, when I approach. "Everybody," she says loudly – far, far too loudly – to her circle of friends, "this is Jan, my ex-husband's girlfriend."

At least she didn't insert the word 'latest', though it definitely feels to me as if it's implied.

"Jen," I say unconfidently. "It's Jen, actually. Jenny."

Diane looks unconcerned. "Whoops, sorry," she says. "Of course it is."

Out of the corner of my eye, I can see Marcia and Nita laughing together as if they're old friends, but this isn't the time to feel envious of how well Marcia appears to be doing. Diane's looking at me, clearly waiting to find out

33

why I've bothered to infiltrate her cosy little group.

"Kyle was excellent, wasn't he?" I say, and her face lights up.

"Wasn't he? I'm so proud. My boy. A star in the making!"

This provokes some fond teasing from her friends, and general laughter. And I don't know if it's because the focus of the attention has shifted away from me, or if it's just that Diane's unselfconscious display of maternal pride has reminded me of my own baby and the reason I'm doing this at all, but suddenly I feel more confident.

"Actually, Diane," I say after a moment, "I wanted to talk to you about Oak View."

Oak View is the care home Diane manages. It's about a half a mile outside my working 'patch'.

"Oh, yes?" Diane looks surprised, as well she might.

Her friends are talking amongst themselves now, and I nod, smiling at Diane with the best community worker smile I can manage.

"Yes. I don't know if you know I work in the community organising various projects? Well, I have some money left in my budget that needs to be used up quickly, and I wondered if I could do something for your residents."

"Oh! Well, yes, it's possible. What did you have in mind?"

"Well, perhaps we could meet to discuss it further? I could come to see you at Oak View early next week if that's convenient for you."

"All right then," she says.

And it's as easy as that. When I meet up with her I still have to think of a way of shifting the conversation from the entertainment of her elderly residents to her break-up with Michael, but it's a start.

Marcia and I meet up again by a poster-sized map of the world that indicates this is a geography classroom.

"Nita works at Boots on London Street," she tells me, grinning. "Very appropriate, don't you think?"

And when it's time to leave, I make my way home with

the feeling that my first attempt at investigating Michael's exes has been pretty successful. Though whether that's a good thing or not, I'm rather less sure. Especially when I get home and press the 'play' button on the answer phone and the living room is filled with Michael's voice.

"Hi, love, it's me. Hope everything's okay and that Kyle's play went well. I'll give him a call myself tomorrow to catch up. Afraid it's looking as if I might have to stay a bit longer than I thought, maybe until Friday. I'll phone you again when I know for sure. Take care. Love you."

Love you.

I slump down onto the sofa, the room suddenly blurring.

Love you.

Why did he have to say that? Because now I feel completely guilty and ashamed and foolish. A stupid insecure cow who ought to know better.

But then I remember that Michael's always more affectionate when he's away. And that I can't remember the last time he actually told me he loved me face-to-face. And that I had no idea whatsoever that Luther was being unfaithful to me until that telephone call on our wedding day.

Maybe we only have one quota of trust in this life. Maybe we're only given this one quota, and when it's used up, that's it. And after Luther's treachery, maybe my trust quota is pretty much all gone.

Anyway, I've got an appointment at Oak View with Diane at eleven o'clock on Monday morning, right after my doctor's appointment, and I'm not going to break it. If nothing else, I'll make some pensioners a bit happier for a while.

Chapter Six

Michael, 1986

His mother was screaming. Michael tried hiding under the bedclothes to block the sound out. He covered his ears. He hummed. But nothing worked – the awful noise kept on coming, like an animal being torn apart.

The old lady in the flat above always banged on her floor with her walking stick whenever Michael had the TV on too loud, and she did this now – bang, bang, bang – but Michael could hardly hear it over the screaming. But maybe she would phone the police? Maybe the police would arrive with sirens and lights flashing and knock on the door to find out what was wrong?

Another, particularly loud scream rent the air, and Michael slid out of bed. Somebody had to come. If not the police, then somebody else. Sobbing with fear, he crossed the landing to his mother's bedroom.

"Mummy?"

She was lying on top of the bed, clutching at her stomach, not screaming any longer, but panting instead like the neighbour's dog that time it got hit by a speeding car.

"Mummy?" he said again, creeping closer. "Shall I get you an ambulance?"

Her eyes were wild, and even though she was in pain, she managed to twist to look at him, her teeth pressed together scarily. "You do, and I'll fucking kill you, understand?" she hurled at him, and then she turned her back and began to moan again.

With tears spilling down his face now, Michael returned to his room, not knowing what to do. He knew the screaming must be because of his baby brother or sister, and he hoped with all his heart that when he or she came, there would be no more screaming. Or talking to walls.

Sitting on his bed, Michael imagined him and his mother walking to the supermarket with the baby in the buggy to get something for their tea. In his imagination, they were all smiling – him, his mum and the baby. And when they got home from the shops, Daddy was here. He picked Michael up, swinging him high over his head the way he liked, and he said how much he'd missed him – how much he'd missed them all. And then he looked at the baby and said how beautiful it was, and Mum shut the front door and got on with cooking tea.

When the screaming suddenly stopped, the silence was somehow even more frightening than the noise had been. Michael crossed to the door again, waiting and listening. It was a good ten minutes before he found enough courage to tiptoe across the landing again.

"Mummy?"

She was lying on her side, asleep. Next to her, pressed against her tummy, was a baby. But it was like no baby Michael had ever seen before. Smeared with blood and white yucky stuff, it was a greyish-blue colour, lying still and unmoving. He knew it was dead, and his lip trembled at the realisation that there would be no new baby brother or sister, no trips to the supermarket with the buggy.

He moved closer to the bed, sobbing; and that's when he saw something even worse than the dead baby – a great, huge bloody thing between his mother's legs; something that was soaking the sheets red – a part of his mother that had come out. Whimpering with fear, Michael looked from the grizzly sight to his mother's paler than pale face and ran to the phone in the hall. He knew how to call for an ambulance because they'd learnt how to do it at school and, no matter what his mother said, she needed one now. Very carefully, Michael pressed the three nines.

"Which service please?" asked the woman on the other end of the line.

"A-ambulance," Michael said. "I think my mummy's dying."

Chapter Seven

"Can I get you a cup of tea while you're waiting for Mrs Brandon?"

It sounds stupid, but it's the first time I've actually thought about Diane having the same surname as Michael, and it startles me for a moment.

"Oh. Yes, thank you – that would be nice." The care assistant smiles. "If you take a seat in the conservatory, I'll bring it into you there."

My appointment with Diane was for eleven o'clock, and soon it's ten past, but I don't really blame her for keeping me waiting. I'd probably do the same in her place. Besides, it's nice to have a breathing space. Time to think.

Because my pregnancy has just been confirmed. Not only that, but the birth has been ascribed a likely date. The third of July. My baby's star sign will be Cancer. Just like its father.

Marcia is a star-sign fanatic. If she were in on my secret, she'd be able to give me the complete run-down on what its rising moon was going to be. But Marcia isn't in on my secret. Only me, Hannah and the doctor know about the life growing inside of me.

Suddenly I long to speak to Hannah. Speaking to her would make me feel so much less alone, and she was the one who unwittingly gave me the idea for this whole investigating the exes thing. Yesterday I tried several times to ring her, but her landline just rang and rang, and she didn't answer her mobile either.

Sitting in my easy chair, I rerun my appointment with the nurse in my mind; collecting all the information she gave me like items in a child's treasure box. The baby growing inside me is just over four weeks old. Its brain and spinal cord have begun to form, and its heart is beating.

This is what I've learned this morning – this miraculous information that for now I must hug to myself, but which makes me turn to jelly just to think about. I am so impressed. So totally awe-struck. And here I sit waiting for a cup of tea in a care home as if it's an ordinary Monday morning.

"Mrs Brandon's ready to see you now, so I've taken your tea into her office." The smiling care assistant returns, dragging me back to the here and now, and I blink, storing my treasures away until later and getting to my feet.

"Thank you."

"How can I help you, Jen?" Diane asks me.

We've had a tea and biscuit preamble, and I've looked at Diane across her desk, this woman with her hair neatly tied back for work, a woman with Kyle's chin and Kyle's nose. She's shared the very same experience I'm now experiencing. She's carried Michael's child in her womb, just as I'm doing, and it seems such a momentous thing to have in common, I'm seized by a sudden impulse to reach out and squeeze her hand. To tell her.

But I don't. Instead, with the teas drunk and the ice broken, I get down to business, describing various projects I've organised for the elderly on previous occasions.

"As I say," I wind up, "making a connection with a local school can be a very worthwhile project to both parties, and I'm very happy to help you to arrange that in the future. But for the purposes of using this particular pot of money…"

"It has to be a quick fix project?"

"Well, yes, something shorter-term. Still with measurable outcomes, of course…"

Diane's little frown tells me I've drifted into Community Worker speak.

"That just means there has to be some sort of learning outcome," I tell her. "But the term can be very broad."

"You mean we can stretch it to mean what we want it to mean?" she says.

I like her down-to-earth way of speaking. *Like*? I *like* something about Diane?

"Yes," I say. "Within limits."

Diane sits back in her chair and looks thoughtful. "And literacy skills might, perhaps be boosted by a perusal of a guide book?" she goes on to suggest. "For example, of a stately home?"

"I don't see why not," I agree, and we smile at each other.

Michael's ex-wife and his current girlfriend, not only having the shared experience of Michael's baby in our wombs, but actually on the same wavelength too. It seems too good to be true.

"A coach trip to Blickling Hall perhaps?" she suggests, and I nod.

"An excellent suggestion. I'll sort it out right away."

When I get back to work, Marcia phones for an update. "You're going to Blickling with Diane and a coach-full of old dears?" she repeats incredulously, when I tell her. "You must be off your head."

"Well, she's not likely to reveal the intimate secrets of her relationship with Michael unless she gets to know me and trust me, is she? Besides, I like Blickling."

"The gardens are okay on a summer's day, I suppose," Marcia says. "But summer's over, Jen. If the old dears wander around the grounds Diane will wind up with half her residents decimated by pneumonia. Then she's not likely to trust you very much, is she?"

"Always so cheerful, Marcia. That's what I like about you. Besides, Blickling was Diane's idea, not mine."

"Oh, well, I think you're mad, but it's your funeral. When's this crazyfest taking place?"

"A week today, if I can get a coach booked."

"No hanging around then?"

"No. No hanging around."

There isn't time to hang around. I still don't seem to be suffering from morning sickness, but I probably will soon.

41

And I can hardly wait until my pregnancy starts to show. The time available to me for my investigations is strictly limited. In fact, I tried to push for the coach trip to take place this week, but Diane said people needed at least a week's notice, and that the looking forward to it was all part of the experience.

On Friday night I rush home from work. Michael's due back from America today, and I want to get cracking on a special meal. But before I do, I decide to try and get hold of Hannah again. It's just not like her to go off like that without telling me, and if there's still no answer I'm just going to have to bite the bullet and phone Luther.

But fortunately I'm saved from such an unpleasant prospect because this time Hannah answers.

"Hannah! I've been worried about you! Where have you been?"

"To Paris," she says, as calmly as if she's saying Great Yarmouth. "To do a bit of shopping and to see the sights. I've just this minute got back. It was lovely. Really lovely."

"Paris! How fantastic!" I say. "But you didn't mention it last week."

"I didn't know I was going to go last week," she says. "It was an impulse. But I *am* sorry if you've been worried. There's a message from Luther too. I'll phone him when I've had a cup of tea and a bit of a sit down."

Through the living room window, I see a taxi pulling in up the drive. It's Michael, back earlier than I expected him to be.

"Oh, Hannah, I've got to go," I say. "I'll call you over the weekend to find out all about it, okay?"

"All right, love. I'll look forward to that."

Michael's getting out of the cab now, and by the time I reach the front door he's fumbling for his key. Michael. Creased clothes, tired circles beneath his eyes, hair all over the place.

"Hi, you." I move into his arms, and he drops his bag to hold me properly.

"Hi."

I nuzzle his neck and the skin behind his ear, re-familiarising myself with the places where he smells of him the most. Re-staking my claim. "I've missed you."

"Have you?"

"Mmm…" I kiss my way along his jaw line until I reach his lips, then fit my mouth to his, hitching myself up on tiptoes to get the best fit, my breasts pressing into their place against his chest.

"Seems as if you have."

"I'm cooking a special dinner for you. Later." There's an emphasis on the word later that can't possibly be missed, and Michael hauls his holdall indoors, closes the front door and allows himself to be led upstairs.

"I might be too tired to do this, babe," he protests half-heartedly when we reach the landing, but I'm not going to be deterred.

"You won't have to do anything," I say. "Well, anything very much anyway." And I lead him into the bedroom and proceed to strip his travel-crumpled clothing off, kissing and licking any exposed areas of skin as I do so.

I've cranked the heating right up, so after I've got him naked, it's warm enough for me to push him down on top of the bed. When he's there, he watches me through half-closed eyes as I strip off down to my pre-selected black silk vest top and French knickers. And as I peel off each layer, I watch him watching me, and I feel an easy sense of power and confidence. I don't think about the investigation. Or the baby. I don't think about anything.

Reaching for the massage oil from the bedside cabinet, I uncap the bottle and pour some into my hands to warm it slightly, and then I climb onto the bed and stand with my legs either side of him.

"Turn over," I command. "I'll do your back first."

He makes a sound that's almost a purr and obeys me, surrendering himself to my attentions, and I begin to massage his back, taking my time and putting some force into it. After his back, I work my way down his thighs and

43

his calves, right on down to his feet.

I once took part in a taster session of Shiatsu massage during a women's health event I'd organised for work, and in that hour I learnt how to do an excellent foot massage. Or so Michael's told me on many occasions. It involves circling the balls of his feet quite firmly with the thumbs, then spreading out his toes like petals unfurling, and finally, a brisk chaffing rub of the outside of each foot in turn by both hands.

Anyway, I put some concerted effort into massaging Michael's feet, by which time he's drifting on a cloud of bliss as he usually is. And then I move up his body again and squirt a good shot of the oil onto his buttocks. The oil from the bottle is cold, and he squeals, roused abruptly out of his sensual stupor.

I laugh softly, and he grunts in reply. Then I massage the oil into his buttocks, my hands moving in vigorous circles, before finishing off with a couple of resounding, insolent slaps that get him moving quickly to pin me beneath him. The bottle of oil flies from my hand and lies discarded on the rug.

Michael holds my arms effortlessly above my head, looking down at me for a long moment.

"Come here," he says, and then he bends to kiss me more hungrily than he's done for months.

Sex with Michael after the Pop Icons of the Twentieth Century Party was incredible, despite the fact that we were both pissed.

I was nervous at first, because I hadn't made love to anyone since splitting up with Luther, and Luther and I were together for five years, so it had been a while since I'd been with anyone new. I was aware that the cone bra made my breasts look bigger than they really were, and the tight corset had given me a tiny waist. What was this incredibly gorgeous man going to think when he unzipped my outfit and reality poured out?

But judging by the way his tongue seared its way across

my nipples, he was quite happy with the way my breasts looked, and soon my back was arching up to get me closer to the magic. His hand left a trail of fire down my body, gripping my buttocks, sliding between my thighs, and I felt wild – far wilder than I'd ever felt with Luther, wanting to taste and experience every part of him.

Yet there was still time for an element of humour within the intensity. "That Madonna outfit must have been a killer to wear; just look at the marks it's left on your skin. And such tasty skin too…" Michael said, making me giggle as he kissed a healing trail around my breasts and my thighs.

"Don't kick your shoes off yet; wrap your legs around me. That's it, hold me hard. Oh God, yes. That's it. That's it. You've got it, girl."

Love-making with Luther was a silent and serious affair. Michael was a whole different proposition, but then there were so many differences between Michael and Luther. Luther would never have gone to a fancy dress party dressed as Tom Jones, for a start. He'd have made some token gesture towards the fancy dress theme – dark glasses and his coat collar turned up perhaps, something like that. Something he felt made him look cool and sophisticated whilst preserving his dignity.

Michael was a bigger man than Luther – heavier, louder and ruthlessly confident in his caresses. The Tom Jones medallion swung above my face as he expertly judged the right time to enter my eager body, steadfastly resisting my clamours of *"Now! Please!"* choosing instead to torment me with slow, tantalising thrusts that slid through my wetness, before withdrawing almost entirely out again. Only when I thought I might go demented with desire did he finally thrust hard and deep right to the core of me, pounding over and over until a torrent of pleasure pushed me over the edge.

I'd never had an orgasm like it, and afterwards we grinned at each other like stupid kids before he collapsed, panting beside me.

I'm not going to have an orgasm this time, despite the fact that Michael's doing all the things he knows I like. Angles, places, amounts of pressure, timing – everything's right – and I feel so happy to be in my man's arms, sharing this familiar intimacy again. There really is nowhere on the planet I'd rather be at this moment. It's perfection.

But how can I be relaxed enough to have an orgasm when I've kept such an important piece of information from him? When I'm lying here beneath him and I remember the advice on one of the pregnancy information websites that in most cases intercourse is harmless to the baby? When my mind's busy processing this information but I'm not able to share it?

I can tell Michael's finding it difficult to hold back any longer.

"It's okay," I whisper. "Don't worry about me."

He glances quickly at me to check that I mean it, and then he takes me at my word, speeding up and quickly coming to a climax.

"Are you tired?" he asks a little while later when I'm curled up in my favourite place of all, my head on his shoulder, my arm and one leg wrapped around him.

"A bit, I suppose. Nothing that a nice dinner with you won't cure. I'll get cracking in a minute."

"I thought I'd pop over briefly to see Kyle on the bike before dinner. That okay?"

The bike. With it safely out of sight in the garage all week, I'd almost succeeded in forgetting about it.

"Yes, of course."

We both move at the same time, me to sit up in bed, Michael to swing his legs round and to reach for his discarded underpants.

"Bloody hell," he says. "That oil's ruined the rug."

Chapter Eight

Michael, 1986

The sitting room was large and so tidy Michael felt he was spoiling everything just by being in there. The sofa and the chairs were cream, the curtains golden-yellow, and the carpet a colour somewhere in between. Outside, instead of a jungle of weeds and brambles like at home there was a lawn, and borders full of flowers.

The woman – Mrs Clark – had very shiny hair. It was the colour of fresh conkers, and it swung around her face when she moved her head. Her lips were pink and plump; Michael couldn't take his eyes off them, even though they were saying things he didn't want to hear.

"How long will I have to stay here?"

The woman who'd brought him here had talked to him about it – the thin woman with the curly blonde hair the police had called to come to the house. But he'd been so upset about his mother and the baby; he hadn't really listened to anything she'd been saying.

Now, Mrs Clark's pink mouth smiled at him. "Your mummy isn't very well, Michael," she said. "You'll stay here until she's feeling better."

Not very well. That was a lot different to dead. The relief of it brought sudden tears to Michael's eyes, and he dropped his head, not wanting a stranger to see them.

But he obviously hadn't been quite quick enough, for Mrs Clark took him gently by the arms. "Oh, Michael, you didn't think…? Listen, your mum's going to be fine. All she needs is a good rest; I promise you."

He couldn't get the image of that red thing out of this

mind. Or his mother's still paleness. Suddenly it occurred to him that this woman might be lying to him, and his eyes flung open again. "She looked dead," he said, and the hands on his arms squeezed gently.

"How awful for you, sweetheart," she said. "But she's not, honestly. She's just very tired."

"So she just needs to sleep and then she'll be better?"

Something flickered over Mrs Clark's face. "There are different kinds of being tired, Michael," she told him gently. "Sometimes we need to rest our bodies, and sometimes we need to rest our minds. At the moment, your mummy needs to do both before she can look after you properly again."

And suddenly Michael understood that this wasn't just about the red thing and the baby dying, it was about the painty jumper and Mummy talking to the wall. "I will see her again, won't I?" he asked.

The pink lips smiled, and the lady stood up, holding her hand out to him. "Yes, of course you will. Now, come along, I'll show you where you're going to sleep. My son will be home from school soon. That'll be nice, won't it? He's called Edward. He's a few years older than you are, but he's got lots of toys you can play with together. I'm sure you'll have great fun."

She was still holding her hand out to him. He didn't want to take it, but he didn't know how to avoid doing so. Suddenly, he wanted to run. If he'd known where he could go, he would have done it too, but he'd seen the blonde lady lock their door behind her when they left the house, after Mummy had been taken to hospital in the ambulance. She'd slipped the key into a zip-up pocket in her handbag.

"Here we are; this is your room. I put a Spiderman cover on the duvet; I hope you like Spiderman? And here are some pyjamas and slippers for you. They're old ones of Edward's – he's too big for them now. They should be fine for you though, I think."

Mrs Clark paused, and Michael thought she was waiting for him to say something, but he couldn't think of one thing *to* say. And even if he'd been able to think of something,

48

despair was creeping up inside him, filling up every spare place.

"All right," she said in a bright voice, "so that's your room, and just here is Edward's playroom, where all the toys are. D'you want to go in and take a look? I'm sure you'll be able to find something that—" When she suddenly stopped speaking, it was a relief for a moment not to have that relentless talking firing at him, but then she was squatting in front of him, her eyes all wet and staring and his face went red, the despair threatening to overflow.

"It will be all right, Michael. I promise you. You'll be safe here with us for a few weeks, and then, when your mummy is well again, you can go home."

Something shifted in Michael's chest. He looked at her, wanting to believe it. She gave him one more smile, then she stood up and pushed open another door. Michael turned to look inside, and saw more toys than he had ever seen in his life – planes, cars, a wooden castle with knights, and boxes and boxes of Lego.

"Go on," Mrs Clark said, smiling now at his expression of awe. "You go and play. I'll bring you a drink up, and when Edward's auntie brings him home from school, he'll show you everything."

By the time Edward got home, Michael had almost finished building a house out of Lego. It had a door and a window that opened, a garden with a wall, and he was just finishing a tricky part of the roof.

The second introductions had been made and Mrs Jones had left them alone to play together while she made tea, Edward smashed Michael's house to pieces with his foot. Then he put his face right up close to Michael's and hissed at him. "These are my toys, and my Mum and Dad, got it? Don't you touch anything unless I say you can."

When Michael hit Edward with part of a wooden castle, giving him a cut above the eye and causing his nose to bleed, he was removed from number 59 Lawnsdale Gardens immediately.

For one glorious moment, he thought he was going home. But he didn't recognise any of the streets they were passing, and then the woman with the blonde curly hair – Sharon, Mrs Clark had called her – stopped the engine of her car to look at him sternly.

"Michael," she said, "I know this is difficult for you. No one wants to be away from his home and his mother. But everyone is doing their very best for you, and time will pass a lot quicker if you're a good boy. Now, this is to be your new home for the next few weeks – with Mrs Burrows. She's looked after a lot of children for us in her time, and she hasn't got any children of her own, so you won't have to share any toys. Okay?"

Michael looked out of the car window. There were no trees or grassy spaces in front of the houses like there'd been at Lawnsdale Gardens; the houses were all joined together with no front gardens, and there were cars parked all along the road. It was much more like he was used to.

When he didn't speak, Sharon sighed and opened the car door. "Come on," she said. "Let's go and meet Mrs Burrows."

The lady who opened the door was old – much older than either his mother or Mrs Clark. She was wearing an apron, and she had hard-looking hair that didn't move when she did.

"Hello, Irene," said Sharon. "This is Michael. Thanks for agreeing to have him at such short notice."

Mrs Burrows nodded. "Hello, Michael," she said. There was a large brown mole on her face, to one side of her nose. Michael couldn't help looking at it.

Sharon gave him a nudge. "Say hello, Michael."

His gaze dropped to the floor. "Hello."

"Let's take your things upstairs to your room, shall we?"

The room was small and dark, with only space for a bed, a chest of drawers and a small bookcase. There was no duvet cover here, Spiderman or otherwise – just neatly tucked-in sheets and blankets.

"Here," said Mrs Burrows, pulling something out from

beneath the bed. "Some toys for you to play with."

Michael looked wordlessly at the battered collection of toys in the box, but didn't move to pick any up.

"I'll leave you to settle in, okay, Michael?" Sharon said. "Be a good boy. I'll see you soon." She moved away towards the stairs. Mrs Burrows followed her, leaving Michael alone. Fragments of their conversation drifted up to him: *Just that one time… Not really violent… A sad case…*

Michael knelt down to sort listlessly through the box of toys. He thought of Edward's playroom and his mother's pink, smiling mouth and he began to cry.

Chapter Nine

After I've done my best to get the body oil off the rug, I cook us a meal while Michael goes to visit Kyle. He says he'll only be an hour or so, but it turns out to be much longer.

"Sorry I was a long time," Michael says when he finally gets back. "Kyle had a recording of his play. I stayed to watch a bit of it."

"That's okay."

The steak's leathery, the potatoes chalky, and the pepper sauce congealed. But the wine's definitely had a chance to breathe.

"Was the video good?" I ask.

"Good enough to get an idea of the production."

"It was excellent. Kyle was excellent."

"Yes," Michael agrees, gamely attacking his kept-warm-in-the-oven steak. "He was. Seems like his acting might become more than a hobby. Anyway, what's all this I hear about you organising a coach trip to Blickling Hall?"

I flush. "Diane told you about it?"

"Yes. I was a bit surprised, I must admit. I thought her care home was miles out of your patch."

"It's not that far. We've got some money to use up, so we've decided to extend the area in special circumstances. I'm going to be visiting all the other care homes too."

"Oh, I see."

There he is, chewing on his ruined steak with absolutely no suspicion that he's been lied to. It's shocking, really, how easy it is to lie. And how easy it must be to be lied *to*.

"Michael," I say suddenly, "what made you and Diane split up? You've never really talked about it."

He looks at me; fork half way to his mouth. "What makes

you ask that now?"

I give up on my food and lay my knife and fork across my plate. "No reason, just curious."

"Same things that make anyone split up, I suppose," he says, after he's finished his mouthful. "We grew apart. Wanted different things." He thinks about it. "That and the pressures of premature parenthood. And the fact that, beneath that do-gooder exterior of hers, Diane is really as selfish as hell. I can practically guarantee that you'll have discovered that for yourself by the end of Monday."

But at first I don't see it at all. It's true that Diane spends the whole of the journey to Blickling Hall chatting to Marco, the driver, but Marco's attractive, without the usual coach-driver's paunch, and she's currently single, so I don't blame her.

At Blickling Hall, two guides are waiting for us, and Diane clearly approves of my arrangements.

"Well done, Jen," she says. "We can leave them to it and take some time off."

"Oh," I say. "D'you think so?"

But she's already on her way outside again, waving a hand in the direction of her huddle of residents. "See you lot at eleven-thirty back here," she calls. "Be good!"

The guides are herding our group gently forward, and I wrestle with my conscience briefly before following Diane outside. Stately homes have never really been my thing, and guided tours make me positively claustrophobic. Michael, on the other hand, laps them up. Every minuscule detail of them. Always the first with his hand up, asking questions. The tour guide's dream, as opposed to me, the tour guide's worst nightmare. Besides, this could be my chance to talk to Diane.

Except that she's nowhere in view. At first. Then suddenly I do see her, walking briskly back in the direction of the coach. Or rather in the direction of the coach driver, who's lounging against a tree trunk and smoking a cigarette. He's all dark hair and biceps bulging out of unseasonable short sleeves, and somehow I don't think Diane's gone back to confirm our departure time with him. Feeling superfluous to requirements, I turn and walk in the opposite direction.

It's a beautiful, crisp, autumn day; one of those clear, blue-skied days that make you think winter's still far off. I button my coat right up to the neck, cram a woolly hat onto my head and sit on a bench and pretend to look at the gardens. Except that I'm really imagining the coach windows steaming up. The coach rocking. Suddenly it hits me that I'm envious. Not of Diane with the coach driver, but of risky, unplanned sex. Yes, oh yes; I'm envious of that.

I've had my fair share of risky, unplanned sex – Michael and I had a sort of compulsion for making love outdoors at one time. Beneath trees, against trees, under the stars, in bushes, night or day. Like the shared baths, it seems to be something that's petered out lately.

I sit in the garden for ten minutes or so, until my feet are pinched with cold. Then I head to the café to warm up, and to my surprise, there are Diane and Marco, sitting innocently at a table without, at first glance anyway, a hair out of place or a T-shirt or jumper on inside out.

Diane sees me and lifts a hand in greeting, and I wave back, joining the queue at the counter. By the time I take my mug of hot chocolate over to their table, I've just about managed to push the erotic images from my mind. Images that obviously say a lot more about me than about Diane and Marco.

"Wondered where you'd got to," Diane says to me. "Marco's been telling me all about his new bambino."

"Elena," Marco smiles proudly, and I smile to myself, wondering how wrong you can get. Because all of a sudden it's easy to imagine a tiny baby cradled tenderly against those T-shirt encased pecs.

Marco speaks of sleepless nights (very worrying for a coach driver), the regularity of feeds, and the importance to a young baby of establishing a routine, all with that gooey new-father grin. And I lap it up of course; asking questions to keep the information flowing, all the time aware of

54

Diane's increasing restlessness. I'm still pretty sure she wasn't expecting anything like this when she left her residents to it and caught up with Marco under that tree, and she looks a lot as if she's contemplating a return to the house to join the tour of the roped-off four posters.

Marco pausing for breath coincides with Diane looking at her watch for the fourth time, and I seize the opportunity to change the subject before she can leg it.

"Do you think everyone will be up to walking around the grounds before lunch?"

"I don't know," she says. "Shall we go and check them out before we make a decision? See you back at the coach, Marco."

"God," she says when we're safely out of hearing range, "parents can be such bores."

I smile. "But isn't it nice?" I say. "To listen to someone who obviously thinks his child is a miracle?"

"It was nice for about two minutes. I was there before you, don't forget. Where did you get to, anyway?"

"Oh, I was sitting on a bench in the sun. Just round here." I answer vaguely, thinking to myself that Marco's daughter is so lucky. She'll grow up with that sheen – the special coating confident people have. A coating that comes from a fundamental knowledge that they are deeply and unconditionally loved. A knowledge they don't need to think about, the way breathing is something they don't need to think about. It's what I want for my child; that special coating. I want my child to have everything I didn't have.

"Lead me to it," Diane says.

"To what?"

"To that sunny bench, of course!"

We find the bench and establish ourselves. Then we decide to let the group make their own decision about visiting the gardens or not, followed by lunch in the café and a visit to the gift shop for souvenirs.

"Sounds absolutely perfect," Diane says, and the sarcasm in her voice takes me by surprise.

"Don't you like your job?"

"Oh, it's okay," she says, "but it's hardly earth shattering, is it? Traipsing about with a lot of old biddies pretending to be interested in Queen Anne beds and Blickling Hall tea towels." She looks at me. "You know, you're not at all what I expected."

I flush, wary at being her sudden focus of attention. "What did you expect me to be like?"

She shrugs, reaching in her bag for her cigarettes. "Oh, I suppose I expected you to be the same sort of tart Michael left me for," she says casually.

Chapter Ten

Michael, 1986

Michael thought about his parents every day; especially his mum. He woke up missing her, and went to bed missing her. And in between, the missing her was a pain in his tummy that never quite went away.

But despite this, and despite the battered box of toys, he quite liked being with Mrs Burrows. His clothes were clean and there was always something nice for breakfast and tea. Michael began to look for her quiet face when he came out of school; she always stood slightly apart from everyone, not engaging in all the chatter around her. It was nice to feel her hand on his shoulder and to hear her ask, "Have you had a good day today, Michael?"

Sometimes, if the weather was good, they went to the park on the way home. And because Michael knew Mrs Burrows would be there, waiting in one corner near the big tree, he could forget all about her while he played.

She was always there when he had nightmares too, which was often. He knew now – because Mrs Burrows had told him – that the red thing he'd seen coming out of Mummy was something called the *afterbirth* and that it was the thing that kept the baby alive inside the mummy's tummy. But this new knowledge hadn't stopped him dreaming about it, especially since, in his mother's case, the afterbirth hadn't worked properly. His brother had died.

"Sometimes babies do just die, Michael," Mrs Burrows explained to him patiently. "It isn't anybody's fault; there's probably something wrong with them."

"Is there still something wrong with my mummy?" he

asked.

Mrs Burrows was making a cake, beating the eggs into the mixture. Michael loved it when she made cakes, because she always let him scrape out the mixing bowl, and he had never tasted anything quite so delicious as cake mixture, especially chocolate cake mixture, which she was making today.

"Actually," Mrs Burrows said, "I had a phone call from Sharon this morning. She says your mummy is quite a bit better. Sharon's going to take you to see her for a visit."

Michael didn't want to go to see his mummy with Sharon, he wanted to go with Mrs Burrows, but that wasn't allowed. Sharon's hand was thin and cold, not warm and comfortable like Mrs Burrows' hand. As they walked together along the street from where they'd parked the car, Michael tried to hold onto the warm, calm way Mrs Burrows always smiled at him; the reassuring feel of her hand on his shoulder.

Sharon had talked to him all the way in the car, but he hadn't said anything back, and finally she gave up. He felt sick, and he was putting all his concentration into controlling it, so he didn't throw up. Now, when they were almost at his home, Sharon paused to look down at him. "We're just going to stay for half an hour or so today, okay, Michael?" she said.

He nodded, but as he did so, the suppressed vomit rose up inside him and he was sick in the gutter. Unfortunately, some of it also splattered onto his jeans and trainers.

"Oh dear," said Sharon, sounding fed up. "Never mind." Michael stood there as she did her best to mop the mess up with a tissue from her bag, then they walked on and knocked on his door.

It opened. And there was Mummy. Only she looked different. Her hair was beautiful – long and almost as shiny as Edward's mummy's hair – and she was smiling at him. For a moment there was a rushing sound in Michael's ears. Then he snatched his hand from Sharon's and launched himself at his mother, clutching at her legs, vomit-splattered trousers and all.

"Oh," Mummy said. "Hello, Michael. God, what's that awful smell?"

"I'm afraid Michael's been a bit travelsick. Have you got a pair of trousers he can change into?"

The trousers were his, but they were too short now and they pinched his waist. Down the hall, he could hear Sharon and Mummy talking in the front room. Heart racing, Michael crept across the hallway to peer into his mother's bedroom. It was untidy, with clothes on the floor and the bed unmade. But there was no red afterbirth lying there like a monster about to come alive.

Sharon came out of the front room to check on him. "All right, Michael?"

The visit was the first of many visits. Sharon stayed with them at first, but gradually she began to stay for less and less time until she left Michael and his mother alone. The first time this happened, he wasn't quite sure how to behave. Sharon had warned him not to mention the dead baby or his mother being ill, but he couldn't help thinking about those things. And it didn't feel right somehow to mention Mrs Burrows and his life with her to his mother.

Finally, when the silence had gone on too long, she spoke. "Shall we put the telly on?"

He nodded, and sat down next to her on the sofa. And after a little while, he moved a bit closer to her. Then closer still, until they were almost touching. Later, Sharon said the visit had been a success and that if things continued to go so well, he'd soon be able to return home again for good. And a few months later, she told him it was time.

When the day came for him to leave, Mrs Burrows was her usual calm self. She didn't look sad that he was leaving. She was smiling as if it was a happy day. "Everything will be fine, Michael," she told him. "It's been a real pleasure to have you stay with me."

Michael felt something twist in his tummy. He didn't want to say goodbye to Mrs Burrows. It wasn't that he didn't want to go back to live with Mummy; he did – more than anything in the world. But he didn't want to stop seeing Mrs Burrows. He wanted both of them.

Mrs Burrows hugged him for a moment before very gently pushing him away. "Go on," she said. "Your mummy's waiting for you. Goodbye, Michael."

Within a month, Michael's mother had stopped taking the medication she'd been prescribed and was back talking to the wall. Alerted by the school when they saw signs of neglect, Sharon came to take him away again.

"Am I going back to Mrs Burrows?" Michael asked, trying not to cry.

"No, Michael," Sharon told him. "I'm very sorry. Mrs Burrows has another boy living with her now."

She hadn't waited for him; she hadn't waited to make sure he would be okay.

"The couple you're going to stay with are very nice, Michael," Sharon told him. "I promise you."

But Michael didn't answer. He'd already decided that, no matter how nice they were, he wasn't going to get close to them. That way, when it was time to leave, it wouldn't hurt quite so badly.

Chapter Eleven

At Blickling, I'm still reeling from Diane's words. Her blonde hair's stirring in the breeze like seaweed in water, and although I hardly know her, I can still tell she's gratified by the effect her announcement has had on me. There's an unkind little smile playing about her mouth; a smile that makes me do my utmost to rein my feelings back from my face. It's not easy to do though, because 'the tart he left me for' is definitely a completely new angle on 'we grew apart and wanted different things'.

"Was she?" I say at last. "A tart?"

Diane's mouth twists. "Well, let's just say she was into leopard skin in a big way and she made it abundantly obvious that *her* tits weren't sagging as an after-effect of childbirth."

"You're not bitter then?"

Diane laughs at my joking comment, sweeping some of the hair back from her face to reveal an earlobe that looks stretched slightly from the habitual wearing of heavy, dangling earrings like those she's wearing now. "Not any more. It was almost fifteen years ago. More than that, I suppose. But I was at the time. Very bitter. I hated Michael like I've never hated anyone before or since. But you don't want to hear about that." She looks at me craftily. "Do you?"

I don't answer straight away because I've temporarily lost the battle with my face – it's just impossible to hide the swamping rush of emotions her words have provoked in me. I've been with Michael for four years now, and this is the very first I've heard about the tart with the leopard skin. And suddenly I feel as if I'm standing on the edge of a pit – a bubbling, boiling pit, brim-full of details and secrets

Michael has chosen not to tell me.

"Jen?" Diane says, and somehow I manage to smile.

When I speak, my lips are almost tremble-free. "Isn't everybody a little compulsive where information about their lover is concerned?" I say with a pathetic attempt at coolness, and she sits there looking at me.

"Maybe," she says, and into the small pause that follows, I silently supply the words *if they're insecure.* "I take it he hasn't told you about Rachel then?"

Rachel.

"Oh, yes, of course!" I lie. "But I'm aware it's probably only half the story."

Diane frowns. "The half that gives the impression I totally lost interest in him, I suppose. That Kyle completely replaced him in my affections. Am I right?"

I try a small, non-committal smile, and Diane accepts this as her answer. "Typical," she says. "Oh, not just of Michael, but of men in general. They just can't see the bigger picture, can they? Asking them to see something from any point of view other than their own is like asking them to take the bus when they've got a Ferrari parked in the drive." She looks at me sharply. "By the way, what d'you think of Michael's new toy?"

"It's none of my business," I say quickly, and she smiles.

"Ah, I see I've hit a nerve." She's still got that that unkind little smile on her face, and now it's joining forces with her tone of voice to remind me of the reality of an ex-wife and a current girlfriend meeting up. This woman and I are never going to become friends. I am never going to go shopping with her or meet up with her after work for a drink. But that doesn't matter, because I'm after information, not companionship.

"So, how did Michael meet this Rachel?" I ask, getting back to business.

"She was an art student, in the same year as Michael," Diane says. "I caught them in a clinch at their degree show. He tried to kid me there was nothing going on, but I'm not stupid. There I am, struggling to keep afloat with a young baby, and all the time he's messing around with someone else. I told him to piss off."

I don't say anything, but I want to know what made her so sure Michael was being unfaithful with this Rachel if he denied it so strongly. Did she catch them together?

Maybe she can read the doubt on my face because she suddenly stubs out her cigarette, her tone of voice irritated as she speaks to me. "You haven't got children, have you?" she asks, and I flush, because she knows I haven't. *Yet*.

"If you had, you'd know that they change everything. They have to change everything. Take Marco; he's at the honeymoon stage. He's in love with the way his life's changed. But he's still got to get to grips – the way every parent has to – that his life has changed *forever*. And it's a long time, forever, believe me."

"Michael loves Kyle, though."

"Oh, yes," she agrees. "Of course he does. And he's a great father. *Now*. But then... Then, well, he just saw this tiny, demanding creature with its mouth constantly open, yelling, seeking, always wanting. A baby bird begging for food. Oozing filthy substances from every orifice. Turning its mother into an exhausted, hysterical pulp." There's emotion in her voice. Even now. "And the truth is, Michael could only hack it for short periods of time." Diane looks at me. "Michael likes to be the centre of attention," she says. "But you'll know that."

I know that when Michael's happy, I'm happy. I know that when he laughs and picks me up in his arms, twirling me around the room like a child, until I shriek out loud, I'm in paradise, pure paradise. And I know that when Michael's unhappy he takes off somewhere without telling me where he's going, or he shuts himself away in his study with the music blaring, leaving a wake of emptiness behind him. And I know that my world stops – quite literally stops – until the clouds roll away, the volume goes down on the music, and Michael comes back to me again.

"I suppose he was very young when Kyle was born," I say, searching for excuses, and a spasm of resentful anger

63

crosses Diane's face.

"So was I!" she says tersely. "Young and frightened and lonely and responsible. I needed Michael. I really needed him. But I needed him to be different. And he; well, he just couldn't accept that he couldn't come first for me anymore. I didn't have the energy to reassure him because I needed too much reassurance myself."

The demands of premature parenthood. That's how Michael summed all of that up. But would it be any different now? *Will* it be any different now?

Diane gets to her feet. "I'd better go and chivvy everyone along. It's almost time for lunch."

I let Diane and one of the care assistants organise everyone, tagging along at the back as if nothing's wrong. But inside, I feel completely churned up. My brain's just got too much information to process, and I'm glad when it's time to head back to the coach.

On the way back to Norwich, one of the residents tells Diane she needs to go to the toilet. This is at a point where Blickling is too far away for us to turn back, and the likely location of the next nearest toilet is uncertain. It also happens to be very shortly after we've passed a sign for the village where Hannah lives.

"Clara, you'll have to wait," Diane says a touch sternly, but even before Clara begins to voice her concern that this might not be possible, my hand's shooting up in the air to get Diane's attention. Just as if I'm back in Year Four with Marcia.

"Yes, Jen?" Diane enquires with a sarcastic little smile.

"A good friend of mine lives just near here," I tell her. "I'm sure she wouldn't mind if we called in there. I can give her a call; see if she's at home."

"Right," Diane says dubiously, but Clara strongly supports the plan, so I go ahead and try to call Hannah. But as so often happens in rural Norfolk, I can't get a signal. "I can't get through," I tell Diane. "But I'm sure Hannah won't mind if we just turn up."

So we make the necessary detour, and a few minutes later

we're turning into the farm track located conveniently opposite Hannah's house.

"I'll go and knock," I say, and the doors hiss as Marco opens them.

"Take Clara with you," Diane says, not quite softly enough. "If your friend isn't home, then try to persuade her to squat down in a corner somewhere, would you?"

It isn't a very kind thing to say, and I think she knows it, because she avoids my gaze as I wait for Clara to make her way along the coach, then help her down the steep steps.

"I'm sorry to be such a bother," she says as we walk up the overgrown driveway, which is bordered by laurel bushes. "I think I drank a cup or two too much tea."

"It's no problem, don't worry. Hannah will be only too happy to help out if she's at home."

When we reach the house, I ring the doorbell and we wait. Then, giving Clara a reassuring smile, and hoping for the best, I ring again, for longer this time, peering through the smoked glass. And eventually I see Hannah coming down the hall.

"Jenny! How delightful!" she greets me when she opens the door, her face breaking into a huge smile. "And you've brought a friend with you. How nice."

"We aren't disturbing you?" I say, concerned, because despite the smile, Hannah looks very tired.

"No, I was just in the conservatory. Actually, I was just having forty winks, but I was only being lazy. Come in, come in."

I explain about the coach and Clara, and Hannah instantly ushers the old lady inside.

"Second door on the right, Clara. Towel hanging on the back of the door." Then she smiles at me again. "Why not bring everybody in?" she suggests. "I'll make some tea. I'm sure we can find enough chairs for everyone, and I think I've got a couple of cakes somewhere."

So I go and put the idea to Diane, and fifteen minutes later we're filling almost the whole of Hannah's bungalow – eight around the dining room table, nine more in the living room, me and Hannah in the kitchen, and Diane and Marco on the front step, smoking.

"Isn't this nice?" Hannah says as the kettle boils for about the tenth time. "It's almost like a party."

"I'll do this next lot," I tell her. "You sit down."

When everybody's got tea and a sliver of cake, I return to the kitchen, bending to kiss Hannah's cheek as I pass by.

"What's that for?" she asks, but I don't tell her about needing to see a friendly, caring face.

"Because this is so nice of you," I say instead, sitting down and sipping at my own tea.

"It's fun," she says. "I've often thought I could open a teashop here. Not that I have any plans to do so now, of course. Anyway, how are you feeling?"

"Oh, I'm very well, physically. No morning sickness or anything like that. I have felt a bit vague, but I don't know whether that's connected to the pregnancy or not. I've…had a lot on my mind."

Hannah looks at me seriously. "I've been worried about you," she says. "This investigation business. I wish I'd never given you the idea. I'm not sure it's wise to stir up past history."

"Well," I say wryly, "there's certainly plenty of past history to be stirred up. It hasn't taken me very long to find that out." I lean forward towards her across the table, whispering. "Diane's Michael's ex-wife, you know."

"What?" Hannah whispers back. "Her with all the wafting hair?"

"Yes."

"Humph," is her verdict on that, and then she sighs. "I can be a bit of a meddling old fool, sometimes," she says. "I should learn to keep my advice to myself. But I suppose it's too late for me to learn anything new now."

I look at her. "What made you go to Paris so suddenly?" I ask.

She looks straight back at me. "I went there to say goodbye to it, I suppose," she says. "I adore Paris – always have. But I won't be going there again."

I sit back, startled. "Why not? You could go again next week if you wanted to."

"Ah," she smiles, "but then I couldn't go to Bucharest, or Havana."

"You're going to Bucharest and Havana next week?"

"Both of them in one week might be a tad ambitious," Hannah says dryly.

Before I can reply, a diversion starts up in the living room. Somebody has opened the lid of Hannah's piano and started to play. Hannah claps her hands, delighted. "Music! Now it will be a proper party!" So we rush next door to find Clara of the weak bladder tinkling the ivories, and with a slight pause for reassurance that it's okay from Hannah, she continues, and it soon turns into a bit of a singsong. Five minutes later one of the two men in the group has asked Hannah to dance and they're waltzing about in the minuscule amount of empty space in the middle of the room.

Diane comes in to watch. "You certainly do seem to know some interesting people, Jen," she says over the music and chatter, and there's something about the slight edge of sarcasm in her voice that makes me suddenly think – "I don't think I like you, lady. I don't think I like you at all, gorgeous son or not."

"But we'd better not stay too long," she's saying. "We don't want to get stuck in the rush hour traffic or poor Marco will be deprived of quality time with his bambino."

There it is again, that ugly judgmental sarcasm. Clearly Diane thinks she's better than everybody else. *"I told you so,"* I can hear Michael saying. *"I told you she was selfish."* But is Diane selfish enough to deserve being abandoned with a young baby for an artist called Rachel Dewing? And how can I ever find out for sure when Diane will inevitably give me one side of the story, and Michael will probably give me no side of the story at all?

Twenty minutes later, on Diane's insistence, the lid on the piano is closed, Clara is persuaded to use Hannah's cloakroom one last time to make sure, and the party breaks up. Except that I don't want to go. I've had quite enough of Diane's company for one day – if not forever – and I'm feeling the need to be with somebody who cares for me.

"Mind if I stay on for a bit?" I ask Hannah. "I can catch a bus later."

"Of course!" Hannah says. "How lovely. You can stay for dinner!"

So I go outside to where Diane is marshalling the partygoers' progress back towards the coach. "I'm going to hang around here for a bit," I tell her. "Thanks for a lovely day. I'll be in touch again if I ever have any more spare money in my budget."

"Oh." Diane seems surprised that our acquaintance is to end so suddenly. "Fair enough."

I call goodbye to everybody and go back inside to help Hannah with the washing up.

Later on, after a delicious meal of fresh fish and vegetables, Hannah and I are sitting on her cosy sofa with a cup of coffee.

"What sort of mother do you want to be, Jen?" Hannah asks me.

"The sort who gives her child the confidence that she's loved and wanted," I say with emotionally charged conviction.

"Of course you do," Hannah smiles, "though parents do tend to express love in different ways, I find. Some think it's loving to show their child how to behave by being stern, whilst others think it's loving to allow their child the freedom to make mistakes they can learn from. Rightly or wrongly, that's what I chose to do with Luther."

And there in Hannah's sitting room, my body feeling welded into the upholstery by the relaxing effects of good food, I think really for the first time of the huge task I'm shortly to be faced with.

"I think I need to tell Michael about the baby," I tell her. "But I'm afraid. No, I'm not afraid, I'm terrified."

"At least if you tell him, then you'll know what you've

got to deal with, I suppose," she says.

"That's exactly what I'm afraid of."

I end up staying the night with Hannah. Time goes on; I tell her about Diane, and Nita, and Rachel Dewing, and suddenly the last bus has gone. When I phone home, Michael's still not there, so I try his mobile, but it goes to voicemail. So I send him a text to tell him I'm staying at Hannah's, and then I go to bed in Hannah's comfortable spare room, ignoring the little voice inside my head that tells me I'm putting off the evil moment of telling Michael about the baby by staying here.

Next morning both Hannah and I manage to oversleep, so by the time I get to the bus stop, I'm already late for work, and I've just missed a bus. On impulse I phone in sick and catch a bus on the other side of the road to Sheringham instead. Once I would have felt guilty about doing something so wicked, but I've changed recently. Now it doesn't seem important. Work doesn't seem important. Nothing seems important. Except the baby and my future with Michael. If there is one.

Tuesday is his day for being at the Sheringham gallery, and I don't want to wait until tonight to see him. I'm tired of the whole 'investigate his exes' plan. I just want to see him and to be held in his arms. Even if he did leave Diane for Rachel Dewing. Even if anything. We'll walk along the seafront and I'll tell him about the baby, and everything will be all right. It will.

"Michael's not here today, Jen," June, the gallery assistant tells me. "Did he forget to tell you? He's got a meeting in London."

Did he tell me?

"Yes, of course. What an idiot. Oh, well, never mind."

I wander down to the sea front, my brain so fuddled I can't think whether Michael told me about the London trip or not. I can't remember him telling me, but with all that's been happening lately, he may well have done. Fishing my mobile out of my bag I call him, half expecting his phone to just ring and ring the way it did last night. But it doesn't – he answers on about the fourth ring.

"Hi, Jen. You okay?"

"Yes, fine. Sorry I didn't make it back last night. Hannah and I got chatting. Where are you? Just wondered whether you fancied meeting for lunch."

"I'm in Sheringham today," he says. "It's Tuesday. I'm always at the gallery on Tuesdays."

I'm speechless.

"Jen?"

I speak quickly. "What? Yes, of course. Of course you are. Look, sorry, got to go. Somebody wants me."

Ending the call, I go over to the sea wall to sit down. It's always a shock to find out you've been lied to, and if it's by somebody you love, I suppose you do your best to come up with crazy explanations for it. Within two minutes I've taken some deep breaths and convinced myself that June must have got it wrong. That Michael's been busy in the back office, and she just hasn't seen him yet. That she's telling him at this very minute about me calling in. So I scurry back up the High Street to the gallery.

When I first go in, nobody's there at all; but the ping from the door brings a surprised-looking June into the gallery from the back.

"Oh, hello again, Jen. Sorry, I was just in the office answering the telephone."

I stand there like a fool. "Er... Did Michael say if he'd be back today?" I ask, and she shakes her head.

"No, I'm not expecting him in until Thursday now, Jen. Sorry."

I take a train back to Norwich from Sheringham. After a few miles, it stops for several minutes by the side of a huge field of ploughed black earth. The sky above it is an ominous grey and that black earth goes on forever. It looks aptly like the aftermath of a nuclear disaster, and I stare at it, trying not to think about Michael lying to me, but unable to think about anything else.

Then my mobile rings, the cheerful tune wildly inappropriate for my mood. It's Marcia.

"Hi, Marse."

"Where are you?"

"No idea."

"Right. Must mean you're not home ill in bed as your boss suggested when I tried you at work then?"

"I'm on a train," I tell her. "I don't know where."

"Okay…" Marcia drags the word out in a way that seems to insinuate she's sure I've lost my mind, but as it so feels like the truth, I don't offer any other explanation.

"Well," she says, "d'you want to meet up? I've got a day off."

"Yes. Yes, that would be good."

"Okay…" Again that dragged out word, only this time she's attempting to use it like a sensor, to gauge what's wrong with me. She can tell something's wrong, because she's known me since we were six and she's had varied experience of things being wrong ranging from skinned knees to bullying to frequent catastrophes with my love life.

"Well, I'd better come round to yours, hadn't I?" she asks. "Presumably you're incognito in town if you're on a sickie."

"All right. I should be back about one." If we ever leave Armageddon.

"Right, you can give me lunch. See you at one."

The train cranks itself up and leaves again soon after I put my phone back in my bag, and it seems to me that the rhythm of its motion is saying, *Michael lied to you. Michael lied to you. Michael lied to you.* Then, as it goes faster, the rhythm says: *Whatyougonnado? Whatyougonnado? Whatyougonnado?*

I have no answer for it.

Chapter Twelve

Michael, 1991

The foster carer Michael was living with lived quite a distance from his school. Since she didn't drive, the local authority paid for him to travel to school in a taxi. Michael hated it. The shiny black cab was like a dirty great banner that said *Michael Brandon is in Care!*

When he'd been younger, the other kids had accepted each other's differences without much question. But with the onset of their eleventh birthdays, that all began to change. Belonging to the pack was key.

Things really began to get worse when a new boy started at the school. His name was Jason Gardiner, and his family had relocated to Norfolk because of his father's work. New kids had started at school before – usually they were shy at first, and then they settled down and made friends. But Jason Gardiner wasn't like that. Right from the start, he expected people to want to be friends with him. And they did too; he was cool and clever, and slightly exotic with his cockney accent – like somebody from EastEnders. He also had all the latest toys, and a glamorous mother who turned up to collect him in a shiny new Mercedes. Michael wanted to *be* Jason Gardiner.

Jason wasn't in the same class as Michael – there were two classes per year, and Jason was put in the other class. For the first few weeks, Michael observed the new boy from afar, watching his circle of friends grow every day. Then, one grey Friday morning playtime, Jason approached Michael in the quiet area of the playground.

"Tommy West says your mum's a loony," he said with a

smile, making a twisting gesture with his index finger at the side of his head. Behind him, his friends giggled. They were all boys Michael had known his entire school life; boys he'd never had any trouble with until now, and it hurt to have them laugh at him. It also hurt that, since he was being nasty, Jason Gardiner clearly didn't want to have him as a friend. There was a smirk on his face – a cruel droop of his bottom lip.

"Don't talk about my mum like that," Michael said, his hands clenching into fists.

Jason gave a careless shrug of his shoulders. "True then, is it? Your mum's in the loony bin?"

The truth was, Michael didn't know. For some time now, his mother had been in and out of Hellesdon Hospital, and he wasn't sure whether she was in there at the moment or not. It was a long time since he'd seen her.

"What's the matter?" taunted Jason. "Can't you speak? Or are you a loony same as her?"

Michael didn't know he was going to hit Jason until his fist made splintering impact with the other boy's nose, sending blood spraying everywhere. Jason fell to the ground, clutching his face. Some of his new friends took a horrified step backwards, but others advanced on Michael. Within seconds he was surrounded, and fists were pummelling any part of him they could reach.

"Fight!" the children nearby began to chant. "Fight! Fight! Fight!"

Staff came running from all directions, tearing the boys away from Michael and helping Jason to his feet.

Later, while Michael was waiting for his foster mother to arrive to take him home for his suspension, the head teacher spoke to him. "Listen, Michael," he said. "I know your situation is very difficult. But you're a bright boy, and you're old enough now to choose how you're going to deal with your circumstances. While you're at school, there are always likely to be children who make fun of you about it. You can either fight them, as you did today, which won't do you any favours in terms of your education, or you can do

73

your best to keep your head down and to stay away from the trouble-makers. If anyone's unpleasant to you, tell a member of staff right away, and we can deal with it, okay?"

Michael kept his head down, avoiding eye contact. His ribs hurt, his eye was sore, but worst of all he knew that, far from being a friend, Jason Gardiner was now a sworn enemy. It was a situation that was hardly likely to improve if he ran to a teacher every time some kid was unpleasant to him. Besides, there would be no teachers around after school and in the holidays, would there?

His last escorted visit to see his mother had been ages ago, and on that occasion she'd been almost totally silent. The escort that day was called Frank – Sharon having moved on years previously. Ever since her departure it had been someone different every time he'd seen his mum. Frank was the worst of the bunch by far, completely lacking any ability to jolly things on a bit the way Sharon always had, and the three of them just sat there in his mum's front room in a silence only broken by the corny jokes of the game show host on TV.

Don't you want to know anything about me? Michael wanted to scream at his mum, resentment and hurt filling him up further and further with every passing minute. *Don't you want to ask me anything?*

Now, in the head teacher's office, Michael remembered his mum's blank, disinterested expression and knew that the head teacher was wrong. There were more than two ways to deal with his 'circumstances'.

As soon as he could after he returned to school when his suspension period was over, Michael approached Jason Gardiner in the playground.

"I'm sorry I hit you," he said before the other boy could speak. "You were right; my mum is a loony. This is her; look." And he screwed his face up in the ugliest, craziest face he could manage, eyes crossed, tongue lolling out. Then he stretched his arms, making the wrists all floppy, and staggered drunkenly around the playground.

There was silence for a moment as the group of boys

watched this performance. Then suddenly Jason began to laugh, and suddenly they were all copying Michael, tottering around like crazed zombies, chanting "I'm a loony! I'm a loony!"

To Michael, as he earned his acceptance into the group, it was the best and the worst day of his life in one go. Shortly afterwards, he told his social worker he didn't want to visit his mother anymore.

Chapter Thirteen

When my train gets into Norwich station, I catch a bus almost straight away. There's still an hour until Marcia's due to arrive, so I make a cup of tea and drink it in front of the French windows, looking out at the garden. The chestnut trees that first brought Michael into contact with Rick are ablaze with autumn colour, every leaf standing out against the dark sky like a fire cracker. If someone hadn't planted them a hundred years or so ago, I'd never have met Michael. Rick's party would have been a non-event – yet another drunken night on the long road of recovery from Luther's treachery.

On impulse, I open the doors and step out into the garden. Besides the chestnut trees, there are tall privet hedges. In the spring and summer, they teem with chattering sparrows, but today they're silent. There's only the swishing rustle of the chestnut leaves and the distant drone of traffic. I run my free hand over the privet, wondering yet again why Michael lied to me, and right there and then, I experience the first symptom of my pregnancy. My stroking action has released the smell of the privet leaves, and it's as if a booster switch has been turned on in my nose. Never, ever, has a privet hedge smelled so intensely *privety*. It's disgusting. Unbearable. Gagging, I recoil from the hedge, covering my nose with my hand.

And suddenly it seems as if there are smells attacking me from all quarters – the privet, the earthy smell of the first fallen chestnut leaves; even my tea. Retreating inside, I lock the doors. It's a few minutes before I start to feel better, but when I do I make my way upstairs to do something I've never done in the four years I've been with Michael – namely searching his pockets. For evidence, clues, I don't know what; anything, really. Any illumination. Because suddenly I feel as if I don't know this man I live with at all. This man who trades in his car to buy a motorbike, misses his son's starring role and says he's in Sheringham when he's not.

Is he having an affair? Lining up my replacement in advance?

Not that I find anything. Not even a used tissue. Michael's always very particular about his clothes. In fact, just about the only time I haven't seen him hang everything up as soon as he takes it off has been when he was dressed as Tom Jones. Unlike me. Michael quickly discovered that the way I disposed of my clothes as Madonna was, pretty much the usual way I dispose of my clothes. All right, so I don't quite throw my bra onto the lampshade, but my side of the bedroom does always look like an explosion in a clothes factory, or so Michael's always telling me. I'm messy, and Michael's not. If I was doing something I didn't want Michael to find out, there'd be evidence to be found all over the place, I'm sure there would.

But I'm not, and I wouldn't. And only a week ago I probably would have thought it impossible Michael was too. But now he's lied to me, and everything's different.

When the doorbell rings signalling Marcia's arrival, I abandon my search and go downstairs to let her in.

"Hi," she says, giving me a hug. "You all right? You sounded all weird on the phone. What's up? And before you ask, I haven't told Gary about the money for the IVF yet."

"Hi, Marcia," I say with as much sarcasm as I've got the energy for, which isn't a lot. "How are you? Good to see you too."

Marcia doesn't deign to make any comment to that, striding instead into the living room, her arms folded across her chest. She's wearing a short red skirt, fishnet tights and black knee length boots, and she looks superb.

"Why not?" I ask. "Why haven't you told him?"

She sighs, her shoulders moving in a jerky little shrug. "Flippin' bad timing, that's why. He's been mega stressed at work all this week. They've got some deadline or other. But I have to talk to him soon, Jen. Otherwise I'm going to explode."

"Are you scared Gary's going to say 'no', do you think?" I ask her gently. "Is that part of the reason you haven't brought it up with him yet?"

She sits down on the edge of the sofa. "Pathetic, isn't it?" she says morosely, studying her fingernails, which, since she has a day off work, she has painted the same red as her skirt.

Her vulnerability stabs me with guilt. I have to tell her the truth, and have to do it right now. I also know just how much it's going to hurt her. "No," I say. "I don't think it's pathetic at all. It's so important to you. Believe me; I understand. I really do."

There must have been something revealing in my voice, because suddenly she's giving me a sharp look. "What?" she asks. "Come on, spill. Something's happened, I can tell."

Swallowing nervously, I look down at my hands, my mouth suddenly stripped of moisture. "You're right. Something has happened." I look up at my friend, licking my lips. I so don't want to hurt her, and yet I know it's inevitable. "Something... I haven't told you about because...well, I'm not sure how you'll take it."

The silence that follows this statement seems really long because there's so rarely any silence in our relationship. Marcia isn't a silent type of girl. When a spasm of pain flickers across her face, I know she's guessed.

"God, you're pregnant," she says. "Aren't you?"

I nod. "Yes. Yes, I am."

She takes in a shaky breath, and I know just how much it's costing her not to jump up and start cursing.

"I... I'm so sorry, Marse. I really am. I didn't plan it or anything; it just happened."

"Well, congratulations!" she says, leaning over to give me a kiss on the cheek. Then she gets up and starts walking around the room as if she can't bear to be still any longer.

"You are sure?"

"Yes. I did a test, and then the doctor confirmed it. I'm six weeks pregnant."

"Six weeks?" she says. She frowns. "How long have you known?"

I look down. "For about two weeks."

Her hands make their way up to her hips. "Then you must have known when we went to Kyle's play. Why didn't you tell me?"

Suddenly I feel like crying. I know I've been a rubbish friend. "I wanted to tell you; I really did. But then you told me about the IVF money, and somehow—"

"Did you tell *her*?"

"Who?"

"Lucifer's mother."

"Yes. Well, actually, she guessed."

When Marcia turns away, I speak quickly, anxious for her to understand. "Marse, the only reason I didn't tell you straight away was because I knew how much—"

"—it would rip at my guts." Marcia sits down. "Yes. Well, ain't that the truth." Tears fill her eyes. "Look, don't get me wrong, I'm pleased for you. I know how much you've always wanted a baby. What about Michael? What's he said about it?"

I fiddle with a cushion, avoiding her gaze.

"Don't tell me you haven't told him yet?"

"No," I answer miserably, and in the silence that follows, I can hear the tick of the clock in the hall. For the moment I can think of nothing – absolutely nothing – to say.

"You know where you've always gone wrong with your love life, Jen?" she says at last. "You always think men will change. But they never do. Michael always told you he didn't want a baby, didn't he?"

"I know. I know, I know, I know. Why d'you think I haven't said anything to him yet?"

"So, when are you going to, eh?" she asks. "When your stomach's out here and you can't quite convince him it's because you've developed a passion for cream buns any longer?"

I get up to go and stare sightlessly out at the chestnut trees again. This is precisely why I've avoided telling her my news. Because I knew how miserable we'd both end up feeling.

"This is connected to why you decided to find out about his ex-girlfriends, isn't it?" she asks, the penny dropping.

"Yes, I thought… I wanted to know—"

But Marcia's sudden sob has me breaking off to hurry over and hold her. "I know it's not fair," I say. "I know… And you can't imagine how much I wish we could be doing this together. It would be so fantastic to share the whole experience with you. It really would."

Marcia breaks away and rummages in her bag for a tissue. Then she blows her nose and wipes her eyes, and when she looks at me, the usual steel has returned to her face. It's a relief, frankly. "We will, if I can do anything about it," she says. "I'm going to tell Gary about my parents' money tonight. Sod his deadline; I'm going to tell him and I'm going to persuade him to say 'yes'. In fact, I'm going to the supermarket right now to buy something special for us to eat. And a bottle of wine to go with it. If I can create the right mood, I'll be half way there."

I try not to think of my ruined steak with pepper sauce of a few nights ago as I watch her thrust her arms determinedly into the sleeves of her leather jacket. "Good luck," I say. "Let me know how you get on."

"I will." She turns to leave, then looks back, a flicker of vulnerability returning to her face. "What's it like?" she asks me softly. "What's it like being pregnant?"

I remember my recent experience with the privet. "Weird," I say. "Like…like I've lost control of my body. But…also…well, liberating I suppose."

She frowns at that. "Liberating?"

I nod, smiling a little because I'm surprised by the word myself. I *do* feel liberated by the knowledge of my pregnancy, but I haven't realised it until now. "Well, I don't have to agonise about it any longer, do I? I'm pregnant. I'm having a child. There are loads of other uncertainties, but that much is certain. Or as certain as these things can be."

Marcia swallows, emotional again, but when she speaks, it's in her usual bossy voice. "Listen, lady, if I catch you consuming any alcohol, or anything remotely unhealthy at all, I will be down on you like the proverbial ton of bricks, got it?"

I smile at her gratefully. "Got it."

After she's gone, the house seems quiet and empty. It's somehow impossible to imagine it transformed by the noise and clutter of a baby. Where will it sleep? The spare room is Michael's office and games room. Will he consent to giving them up? Will he even be here?

Suddenly I experience an overpowering need to do something – anything – about my situation. If Michael were here right now, I'd throw caution to the winds and tell him. But as he's not, I open up my laptop instead, and within seconds I'm Googling the name Rachel Dewing. There are thousands of results, so I add the words 'artist' and 'Norwich, UK' to the mix, and that narrows it down a lot. Clicking on a likely link, I soon find myself staring at an image of an attractive-looking woman of the right sort of age, busy at work in her studio, in the act of painting a huge canvas. Is it her? She's not wearing leopard skin, but then she'd hardly be wearing it night and day for the past thirteen or so years, would she? There's no way of telling if it's the right Rachel Dewing or not, but something in my guts tells me that it is.

I carry on clicking, taking a look at her paintings. They're good – expressionistic and emotional paintings of people and interiors that get you thinking. It's as if something significant has just happened in the room, and the viewer is left observing the moment after. Like the room I'm sitting in now would look if Michael were to come in and I blurted out my news to him…

The titles of the paintings are poetic and clever – Significant Sea Change, Spring Aftermath, Cliffs and

Forests. I imagine the fictional painting of Michael in the moment after I've told him about the baby. What would that painting be called, I wonder? *After the News*? *A Pregnant Pause*? Smiling grimly, I click on a link called 'Archive' to find images of older paintings.

And there, on the third click, is a painting of Michael.

He's sprawled in an armchair, asleep; a younger version of himself in a cosy room with an open fire in the grate. His face is stern, as if he's having a bad dream. Had he left his wife and child at this point? Probably, if Rachel's painting him. The picture must have taken a while to complete. The idea of meeting Rachel and finding out more is beyond scary, but somehow I know I have to do it, and find myself clicking the 'Contact Me' tab. Quickly, I fill in my details and type in the message box. *Hi, Rachel, I'm interested in commissioning a painting from you. I wonder if I could visit your studio? Thanks and best wishes, Jen.* I click 'send' before I can change my mind and close the computer down. Then I go downstairs to watch some daytime TV, which is about all I feel capable of doing.

Michael gets home late; he doesn't explain why. He doesn't ask me anything about the Blickling trip, so I don't mention it. But he does put an arm round me while we watch TV. It might be just like the old days if there weren't that stonking great lie forcing us apart. And the fact that he falls asleep with his mouth unattractively open, his breath whistling close to my ear. I could forgive that if it weren't for the lie though, and I steal myself to confront him about it when he wakes up. But I soon fall asleep myself. We wake up hours later and drag ourselves to bed, and that's another day done.

At lunchtime the next day I leave City Hall and make my way past the market to London Street. A band's busking outside Jarrold's department store – there are a lot of musicians with a large brass section and they're playing salsa. It's a big sound, and I feel it tingle its way down my spine. Luther and I used to go to salsa classes a lot. We loved it.

London Street curves around a bend, and the salsa band becomes a distant sound – just like my relationship with Luther. He's only occupying headspace as a displacement activity anyway – because I'm on my way to Boots, and it isn't to buy toothpaste or to collect a prescription. I'm going to see Nita, the girlfriend Michael had before me.

I haven't formulated any plan, and I don't have much time either – I've got a meeting out in my patch this afternoon. So I grab something off the shelves and join the snaking queue at the checkouts. There are three sales assistants at the tills – Nita is the prettiest, with her shiny dark hair and perfect make-up, red lips smiling as she deals with her customers. I do my very best not to imagine those lips anywhere near Michael.

Obviously I can't insist on Nita serving me, and when my turn comes around she's busy with someone else. So after I've been served, I have to grab something else from the shelves and start all over again. And when I get to the head of the queue and I'm still not going to get Nita, I have to let someone go in front of me by pretending I have to make a phone call. Then while I'm pretending, my phone actually does ring, and I have to take it, because it's Michael.

"Hi, love," he says.

Nita's free, and there's no one behind me.

"Hi there," I say.

"You okay to talk? Not in a meeting?"

"No, just doing a bit of shopping." *Just about to be served by one of your ex girlfriends.* "What's up?"

"Nothing. Does there have to be a reason for me to call you?"

"No, of course not." Though it is extremely ironic that he has to pick now, of all times to do it.

Someone's coming up behind me. Still with the phone to my ear, I go over to Nita and place my items in front of her. She smiles at me then scans them – a packet of plasters, some hair conditioner, and a bunion pad. A *bunion pad!*

"I thought I'd cook for us tonight," Michael says.

"Bolognaise all right?"

"Lovely," I say sliding my debit card into the machine.

"Great. With garlic bread or without?"

I try to remember what meetings I've got booked the next day and can't. "With," I say. "Let's live dangerously."

"Careful," Michael teases as I tap in my pin number. "You don't want to get too carried away."

I laugh, enjoying his teasing, and as he ends the call, Nita's handing me my receipt and my bag of items, and my chance to speak to her has gone.

Chapter Fourteen

Michael, 1997

Senior school was a chance for Michael to reinvent himself. Most people – including Jason Gardiner – applied to a different school to him, so overnight Michael became the orphan child of a dead single parent, in care because his mother had died in a car accident when he was eight years old.

As the years went by and he didn't see his mother, Michael almost came to believe the lie himself. He'd lived with his current foster family for over four years and he was happy there, although Dave and Wendy Fenwick had never really become like substitute parents to him. But witnessing the grief his friends got from their parents if they were even ten minutes later getting home than they'd said they would be, Michael thought he was well off. Dave and Wendy gave him boundaries, and so long as he kept broadly to these and there were no complaints from school about missed homework, they were content.

In truth, Michael didn't really think about his foster carers very much – they were the providers of his food and clothing, and the people who asked him occasional questions about how things were going. Sometimes Michael went to a football game with his foster father, but when Dave's shifts changed and he couldn't make so many matches, Michael wasn't unduly bothered. It meant he could meet up with his mates; kick a football about the park or, as they got older, watch girls.

Michael, being tall with trendily long dark hair, was quite a magnet to the girls. His current girlfriend was called

Tessa; with her curvaceous figure and long, auburn hair she was the girl all the boys were crazy about, but he was the one she had chosen to be with. They held hands as they walked to lessons, wrote each other notes during lessons and found somewhere to kiss every lunch break. Michael loved everything about her; the way she twisted the ends of her hair as she spoke, the way she looked up at him through her eyelashes, the way she spoke with just a slight lisp... And her body; definitely her body. Just lately she and her friends had taken to wearing satiny clothes that looked more like underwear than dresses, with thin straps and scraps of lace designed to drive a boy wild. It was a look that had inspired Michael's foster father Dave to call Michael into the garden for an embarrassed chat about 'being careful', and a reminder that it was against the law to have sex with anyone under the age of sixteen.

Walking along Gentleman's Walk with his arm around Tessa one Saturday afternoon shortly afterwards, Michael giggled with her about it, imitating Dave's self-conscious tone of voice and embarrassed expression.

"From what the teachers say, I gather you're very talented at art, Michael," he said as Dave, loving the way Tessa put her head back to laugh with delight. "If that's the case, you don't want unexpected parenthood to get in the way of any future plans. You could go to art college."

"Is that what you want to do?" asked Tessa now. "Go to art college?"

"Maybe." Actually Michael hadn't really thought about it properly until his foster father had brought the possibility up. The idea was appealing, but all that was surely still miles away. Besides, he didn't want to talk about it now on a Saturday in the sunshine. Tessa had looked so gorgeous with her white throat exposed and her hair tumbling all over the place while she laughed, and he just wanted to kiss her and kiss her until she gasped for air. "Come here," he said, pulling her towards him and starting to do just that right away, with the Saturday shoppers milling all around them.

As Tessa returned his kiss, Michael could feel the swell

of her breasts through the silky fabric of her slip dress and he groaned silently, recalling Dave's words once again. It had been a right laugh to witness his stepfather squirming with embarrassment like that, but Michael didn't feel like laughing any longer. Because there were two more years to go until he and Tessa were sixteen, and Michael just wasn't sure they could hold out that long. Every time they kissed, it was getting harder and harder to pull apart. And who decided what was the right age to do it anyway? Surely it should be down to the individual. He felt ready now, and he was sure Tessa felt the same.

Finally, Tessa drew back slightly. When he looked at her to see why, he saw she was laughing at something she could see over his shoulder. "Look at that crazy woman!" she said in a hissed whisper.

"What?" asked Michael with a smile, turning to take a look, ready to be entertained.

There, walking towards them along London Street, was a woman dressed in clothes so old they were practically rags. The woman was speaking to herself loudly, but Michael knew it wasn't this that had so amused Tessa. It was the fact that every ten seconds or so, she was thwacking an empty carrier bag through the air, making a sound almost as loud as bullet fire.

"God," said Tessa with one hand over her mouth to stifle her giggles. "She really is a bag lady, isn't she?"

A feeling of dread and dull inevitability had spread into Michael's gut. The bag-thwacking woman was his mother.

Shit, he had to get out of there – before she spotted him or worse still, before she stopped to speak to him. Tessa must never know that he knew her.

"Come on," he said, dragging Tessa away. "Let's go to the music shop."

"All right," said Tessa, scurrying along. "What's the big hurry?"

Michael didn't answer. Thwack, thwack, thwack. All the way down London Street to Gentleman's Walk, the sound followed them. Why was she doing it? Shit; she'd really lost

87

it this time. How long had she been like this? And if she were like this, did it mean there was a chance he could get like that one day?

Suddenly, Michael felt guilty. All these years, he hadn't so much as asked any of the social workers about her. If he'd thought of his mother at all, he'd imagined her immobile in her armchair, staring at the TV. Not this raving, chuntering lunatic drawing attention to herself. Even though he and Tessa were some distance away by now, Michael fancied he could hear people laughing at his mum, just as he and Tessa had laughed. Did she know they were laughing at her? Was she hurt by their taunts? Afraid?

Oh, God. He didn't need to care about it. What had she ever been to him? She wasn't his responsibility; she wasn't.

"What's wrong with you?" Tessa asked, and it was only then that he realised he'd come to a suddenly halt. "You all right? You're acting all weird."

He managed to dredge a smile up from somewhere. "Yeah, I'm fine," he said unconvincingly, reaching down to give her a peck on the cheek. "Just remembered something I've got to do. I'll catch you up in the music shop, yeah? Won't be long." And he bent to kiss her once again, ignoring her piqued expression and hurrying off before she could suggest coming with him.

His mum was heading up Gaol Hill now, thwacking her way steadily towards City Hall. He caught up with her near one of the bronze lions flanking its entrance, but didn't approach right away. Now that he was here, he didn't know what to say, or even the best way to get her attention. She was so obviously in her own little world, oblivious to everything. He didn't want to shock her, and neither did he want to proclaim his relationship to her by shouting out 'Mum'.

In the end fate lent a hand, a sudden gust of wind snatching at her carrier bag when it was at its apex. Up it sailed above the striped canopies of the market stalls, on a sure-fire route to the battlements of Norwich Castle. Michael watched his mother stop stock-still to watch it go, her mouth hanging open, and her eyes wide. Then she blundered quickly forwards into the road as if to go after it, stepping straight into the path of an approaching car.

"Stop!" yelled Michael and grabbed hold of her before it was too late.

She wriggled and jerked like a fish on a line. "Let me go! Get your hands off me! I haven't got any fucking money!"

She was still trying to move towards the road, but Michael clung on, desperate to prevent her from killing herself, his nostrils rebelling at the stench emanating from the filthy clothes she was wearing.

"Help! Somebody!"

"I'm not going to hurt you," Michael said. "You didn't look before you crossed the road, that's all."

She was surprisingly strong, and they were both in the road now as Michael struggled with her. A taxi en route to the taxi rank hooted at them. The sound seemed to jolt her into her senses, and suddenly she stopped wriggling to look at him. Licking his lips, Michael gazed back into her clear, grey eyes and found himself thinking of a field, a stream; some long-ago location for a picnic – a rare childhood memory. She was there, somewhere, his mum inside this desperate creature, but buried so deeply Michael knew he would never be able to do enough digging to get her out.

"I used to know someone who looked just like you," she said. "Only he was a lot younger."

The tears in Michael's throat prevented him from speaking.

"Haven't seen him for a long time though. Don't know what happened to him."

He's here! He could have said. *I'm your son, and I'm here!* But the moment's awareness in the grey eyes was already closing down; timed out. "My bag," she said. "I must get my bag." And she was off again, wrenching herself from his restraining hands and out across the fortunately clear road.

Michael had bought some new socks and underpants that morning, and he took them out of the carrier bag, catching up with her by the war memorial where she stood, looking for her own long-disappeared bag. "Have, have this one," he said, holding the bag out.

She took it from him doubtfully before trying it out for size. *Thwack!* "It'll do," she said, and began to walk away from him.

He stood there for a moment, waiting to see if she would turn round; but she didn't. Two more thwacks and she had turned right up Bethel Street and out of sight. Like someone in a dream, Michael began to make his way down the steps to the market en route to the music shop, Tessa and sanity. But he'd only gone a short way when someone leapt on him by the side of the work boot stall. "Michael! How the fuck are you?" asked a familiar voice.

With his head in a vice-like grip, Michael couldn't turn to see who his assailant was; but he didn't have to anyway, because he knew. Jason. Of all the times to run into him, it had to be now, when he was still reeling from the shock of his recent encounter with his mum.

"Hiya, Jason, how are you doing?"

"I'm good, yeah. Got you then, didn't I?" He laughed, slowly releasing Michael, who rubbed his neck, hoping against hope that Jason hadn't seen him with his mother.

"Say, what were you doing with that old cow, up there? Wasn't your loopy mother, was she?" Jason was staring straight at Michael, face filled with amusement, one hand doing the old loony twisting sign at the side of his head.

Hating himself, Michael smiled. "What her? Give me a break. "Course not. Poor old girl just needed some help across the road. Listen, it's good to see you, but I've got to go. I'm late meeting my girlfriend."

"Girlfriend, eh? Lead on. Got to meet my best mate's girlfriend. Can't believe I haven't already. Where've you been keeping yourself all this time?"

Making up something about football and course work, stuff he knew Jason wouldn't be convinced by, Michael reluctantly led the way towards the music shop. There was no way he wanted Jason to meet Tessa, but every step they got away from Bethel Street the better.

Tessa wasn't inside the music shop, she was waiting outside, and she was looking well pissed off. Michael couldn't really blame her – he'd been ages and he'd run off without even saying where he was going, but even so, his heart sank. Crazy about her though he was, he'd had to deal with one of Tessa's sulks before, and he wasn't looking forward to doing it again, especially with Jason in tow.

"Sorry, Tessa," he started to explain, "I got held up."

"He had an important meeting with his mother," Jason joked, and Michael's heart sank down to his boots as he realised Jason obviously hadn't believed him.

Tessa was frowning prettily. "His mother? She died years ago, when he was eight."

Jason looked in Michael's direction, his eyes alive with mischief. *Please*, Michael willed him. *Please.*

"My mistake," said Jason, turning back to Tessa. "I'm Jason, by the way; one of Michael's very oldest friends. And you must be Tessa. It's very good to meet you." This last was said as he lifted Tessa's hand to his lips to kiss it.

Wanker! thought Michael, but surprisingly, Tessa was all smiles, lapping it up.

"Nice to meet you too," she dimpled.

Two weeks later, Tessa told Michael it was over. Shortly after that, he saw her and Jason with their arms around each other walking down the street.

Chapter Fifteen

When I get home that evening, Michael's in the kitchen. He has all the ingredients for the bolognaise, but he hasn't made a start on it yet. "Hi, babe," he says, bending over a recipe book. "Good day?"

The back of his neck is tanned. I go over and wrap my arms around him, planting a kiss just above the top of his T-shirt. Suddenly I can't live like this anymore. What I'm doing is wrong – I have to tell him about the baby. But first I have to get him in the best possible mood. When I checked my emails earlier on, there was a reply from Rachel Dewing. She said she's currently living and working in Cuba, and as a result, she won't be able to see me. But as interesting/frustrating as this is, I'm not thinking about it at the moment, because I'm more than ready to give up this whole researching the exes plan to get things out into the open.

"Michael?"

He doesn't look up from the recipe book. "Hmm?"

"It's a lovely evening. Will you take me to the coast on the bike?"

That gets his attention, and he abandons Delia Smith to turn and look at me. "You don't have to if you don't want to."

Somehow I manage to smile. "I do want to. Just as long as you drive very carefully."

He grins, wrapping his arms around me. "I'll drive like a granny going to the shops," he promises. "Until you beg me to go faster."

"I don't think that's very likely," I say, and he smiles.

"No? I bet you will. In fact, I bet you by the time we get to Cromer, you'll be so tired of my gentle teasing you'll be begging for the full experience. "Now, Michael," you'll be begging me. "Now!"

The sexual connotations make my smile genuine and I put my arms around his neck and stretch up for a kiss. "Just keep on thinking Granny with a bag on wheels, matey, and everything will be fine."

"Just so long as it's a leopard skin print bag on wheels," he jokes, and I try not to think of Rachel Dewing and her leopard skin print trousers as he gives my bottom a playful slap. "Go on, get changed. You'll need your thickest jeans, boots, and a warm jumper and scarf. I'll dig out my old leather jacket for you."

I'll tell him as soon as we get to the coast. When he's still on a high from the ride. On the cliff top with the sun sparkling on the sea and the bike making a metallic creaking sound as it cools down. And I'll know, just as soon as I look into his face, if it's going to be okay. But it will be okay. Listen to him now, singing as he roots through the junk in the cupboard under the stairs for his old leather jacket – so happy because I've decided to give the bike a try. If he didn't love me, it wouldn't be so important to him, would it? And if he loves me, he'll be fine about the baby. He or she is a part of me, after all.

But then I'm bundled up in all the clothing he's insisted I wear and it suddenly hits me. The theory of putting Michael in a good mood for my news by going on the bike is all very well and good, but now I've actually got to do it. Oh heck.

It will be romantic though, won't it? I'll be pressed against him, with my arms wrapped around his waist. Just him, me and the bike. And the traffic. And the odd deer running across the road. Puddles to skid in.

Michael's already got his helmet on. He turns to me with the spare, lifting it to put it on my head. "All right?" he asks, his voice changed by the helmet.

I give him a thumbs up. "Can't wait," I lie.

He laughs, and says something about leopard skin and Zimmer frames while he fits the helmet on me. It pinches my cheeks in and muffles the world a bit. I wish it would

93

muffle it even more. That the bike was some sort of time machine so we could just be in Cromer without having to do the journey at all.

We go outside and Michael gets on the bike and starts it up. "Climb on," he shouts over the racket. I do so, shifting until I feel comfortable, which is when every possible bit of me is pressed against the solidity of Michael's body. "Use the grab rail at the back," Michael shouts over his shoulder. "It's more stable than holding on to me. And I'll need to bank the bike over a bit when we go round bends. When you feel it banking, lean in that direction yourself. Whatever you do, don't fight it, okay?"

No! I want to shout. No! But it's too late. The minute I've taken hold of the impersonal grab rail, Michael moves off. Perhaps he senses I'm about to change my mind about the whole idea, I don't know, but before I can make any protest, we're off down the drive and out into the evening traffic. My stomach lurches as we accelerate away, and as a crazy image of a leopard skin bag-on-wheels race fills my mind, with a row of grannies flying out behind, all dishevelled perms and rippling dresses, I apologise silently to the baby. *I'm doing this for you,* I tell it. *See? I'm already doing things for you.*

And then I concentrate on staying on the bike. It keeps me from dwelling on the difficult conversation I need to have in Cromer.

"So? Go on, admit it; you loved it, didn't you?"

On the cliff-top at Cromer, everything is exactly how I imagined it would be. Well, I can't hear the metallic creaking of the bike as it cools down, because there's a bunch of seagulls squabbling over some abandoned fish and chips nearby. But the sun's glinting on the sea. It's not as bright as the light in Michael's eyes as he takes his helmet off and looks down at me though.

"That wasn't what I call bag-on-wheels riding," I say, pretending to be stern.

He laughs. "It was a formula one kind of bag-on-wheels.

94

But you felt safe, didn't you?"

I shrugged. "Ish." Actually, I'm not sure what I felt. The ride is a bundle of mixed impressions I'm still trying to make sense of. It was thrilling, terrifying, life affirming and surreal, all at the same time. And in any case the impressions are melting away quickly under the focussed light of the words I'm about to say.

"You loved it," Michael pronounces, then, decision made, he looks along the promenade. "I'm starving. Let's get fish and chips." And, typical Michael, he begins to walk away before I've had the chance to respond.

Afterwards. After the fish and chips. I'll tell him then.

We walk along, side by side, both holding our helmets. He's swinging his by the strap; I cradle mine like a baby. But I refuse to read anything into that.

Michael looks at me. "Remember when we went to Hunstanton that time?" he asks, and immediately I know what he's talking about.

"Ladybird beach!"

"That's the one." He reaches for my hand and I hold the helmet by the strap so that I can take it.

The summer before last, we'd gone for a day trip to Hunstanton. When we arrived there, we were puzzled to find all the cars driving in the opposite direction. We soon found out why when we headed down to the beach. The place was plagued by ladybirds – they were literally everywhere, and within seconds we were covered. Our faces, our arms, our necks, even our hair – it was like walking through a firing line of miniature red bullets.

"You were screaming!" Michael remembers, doing a girly-sounding imitation.

"Well, so were you!" I come straight back.

"Might have been," he admits.

God, I love that cheeky smile. I hope the baby inherits it. In fact, it will be fine by me if it's a little clone of Michael, looks-wise.

I snort with laughter, much as I did that day in Hunstanton. In fact back then I was helpless with laughter.

So much so, my stomach hurt.

Suddenly my stomach isn't feeling too good now either. But it's not because of laughing; it's because we've almost reached the fish and chip shop and a great waft of chip grease fumes has just billowed out of the door towards me, catching me off guard. Oh, God.

When I stop suddenly, Michael looks at me enquiringly. I speak quickly. "Sorry, love, need the loo. Meet you back here."

"Okay. What shall I get you? Fish, chips and mushy peas?"

No! "Actually, I'm not very hungry. Don't worry about me…" I blunder away, desperate to put some distance between me and that stink.

"You've got to eat something," he calls after me.

"No, really," I say. "See you in a few minutes."

I don't quite make it to the ladies' toilets – I'm sick on the side of the prom a few metres away. Fortunately, Michael's gone into the fish and chip shop, so he doesn't see. Shakily, I continue to my destination, and once there, I splash cold water on my face. Another wave of nausea washes over me, making me sweat. There's no time to get into a cubicle, and I'm sick in the washbasin.

I'll tell him while he's eating his chips, I think, rinsing the horrible yellow bile down the sink, and contemplating the journey home with dread. Why, oh why, did this ever seem like a good idea?

When I get back, Michael's sitting on a wall near the chip shop eating his fish and chips. A wall too near the chip shop.

"I got you some anyway," he says, offering me a warm, wrapped package. "I knew you'd be hungry when you smelt mine."

I experience a flicker of irritation at that, because Michael does this all the time – thinks he knows better than I do. Often I ignore it and do what I was going to do anyway – he doesn't have to know, after all. But this one's going to be a bit trickier to manage; since there's no physical way I can eat the fish and chips I'm currently taking off him. But it doesn't matter does it? I'm going to tell him about the baby while he eats, and when I do that, he'll understand.

"Let's have a sea view while we eat," I say, beginning to walk away, holding the package as far away from me as possible.

"There were a couple of really out of control kids in the chip shop," he says, following. "Parents both texting or playing computer games on their phones, totally oblivious. Can't tell you how glad I am that Kyle's older and I haven't got to deal with all that any longer."

Shit. I stop walking to look at him. "Kyle was always well behaved though, wasn't he? He wouldn't have run amok in a chip shop."

Michael shrugs. "I guess. He had his moments though. All kids do. I'm just saying, it's nice not to have to keep a piece of my mind permanently on child alert, that's all. That's what the bike gives me too – freedom. It's a very precious thing."

Sitting down on a bench, I curse the unruly family who have totally demolished the atmosphere I'd so carefully cultivated. The fish and chips are on my lap, sending grease-laden fumes in the direction of my nostrils. I feel like hurling them over the cliff.

"Are you seriously not going to eat that?" Michael asks.

I can't even pretend to smile. "I told you I didn't want any."

"Oh well, shove them over here," he says. "Can't let them go to waste."

He sets to, while I stare miserably out to sea, trying to decide whether to just go for it anyway with my news, or to wait for a better time. But what if there is no better time?

"You never know what life's going to throw at you, do you?" Michael says through a mouthful of chips. "Sometimes you just want to take off; get away from everything. You can't do that if you've got kids."

"You did, when Kyle was young though, didn't you?" The words are out of my mouth before I realise I'm going to

97

say them. The reaction is instantaneous – I know, because I'm looking at Michael's face, and I see a distant coolness come down like a cloak of mist, obscuring the sunshine we've been sharing.

"I didn't exactly swan off to the Pyrenees though, did I?" he says coolly. "I was still in the same town."

"That's the second time you've mentioned The Pyrenees this week," I babble, trying to restore the atmosphere.

He shrugs. "It's somewhere I'd love to go to. Why don't you come with me? I know it's a bit different to a twenty-mile trip to Cromer, but you'd love it; I know you would. Say 'yes', Jen. Just you and me; no plans, no commitments, just a month of freedom on the open road. It's be fantastic."

And just like that, I'm right back where I started from. I haven't told him about the baby, and even though it's me he wants to accompany him on this jaunt to rediscover his youth and his lost freedom, I'm not convinced he's going to want to stick with me when he knows the truth about what the future holds for us.

"Actually," I say, knowing my words are a prelude to a tense return to Norwich and a silent evening ahead, "I was thinking of going on holiday with Marcia and Hannah, if that's all right with you. We were talking the other day about going to Cuba. I really fancy it."

Chapter Sixteen

Michael, 2000

Diane was asleep in the armchair by the window, her blonde hair spread out against the worn upholstery, her face and the folds of her dress suffused with light. In sleep her face was less grumpy than usual, her features accepting of the new plumpness that surrounded them. There was no resistance in her clothes either, which were lovingly moulding the swell of her stomach and the fullness of her breasts. Awake, Diane was grudgingly pregnant, reluctant to speak about imminent parenthood; but asleep like this, she was glorious.

Michael was drawing her with quick, confident strokes of his charcoal stick, capturing the extra flesh at her chin, which was being pushed up by the cushion and her hand curved around her belly. He would have liked to paint her, but that would take too long – Diane would go mental if she saw even this sketch of her in such an unguarded moment.

The baby was an accident, conceived during Michael's final year at art college. He and Diane had met when she'd moved into the shared house Michael lived in just off the Earlham Road. Like the others in the house, Diane was studying social work at the university – he was the only one at art college.

Michael had the room that was the former dining room right next to the kitchen. It was large and light and had French windows out to the garden, and he often spilled out into the garden to paint. Sometimes he worked well into the night and one night he'd stopped work around two in the morning and had looked up to see Diane standing in the doorway of his room, watching him. He'd heard that somebody new was moving in, but this was the first time they'd met.

Michael was attracted to Diane right away with her mane of blonde hair and her cool blue eyes, and it hadn't taken them long to hook up together. But he had no idea if their relationship would have lasted if Diane hadn't got pregnant the very first time they made love. Now eight months later, they were installed in a rented terraced house courtesy of Diane's parents, far away from the land of student bedsits and house shares and somehow, unbelievably, they were *married*. Michael had sleepwalked through it all, responding to the demands of Diane and her well-to-do parents, and now here they both were, waiting for their new lives to begin.

"What the hell are you doing?" Diane was awake now, her eyes accusing as they took in his drawing. "Shit, I look gross, Mikey. Don't you dare show that to anybody."

"You don't look gross. You look beautiful."

"Oh, yeah. About as beautiful as a cow would look if it was wearing a dress. God, my back aches."

Diane shifted in her chair, her expression sour. Michael closed his sketchbook. "Want me to run you a bath?"

"Only if you've managed to get hold of a crane to hoist me in and out of it."

"I can help you get in and out."

He really ought to be at college, working on the paintings for his Degree Show; either that or upstairs completing his dissertation. But somehow it was easier to let the college work slide than to deal with Diane's resentment. She didn't even like it when he went to work at the art gallery at weekends, although she couldn't suggest he give that up. Her parents may be paying the rent on this place, but they still needed every penny they could get, which was why Michael had recently taken a job in a pub three nights a week as well.

"What I really hate is this feeling of fucking limbo," Diane said now. "That and having a bladder the size of a walnut. Help me up, would you?"

100

Michael put his sketchbook on the bookshelf and started to go over, but before he could reach her she drew in a sudden sharp breath and looked at him with wide eyes, one hand between her legs, clutching the fabric of her dress. "Shit! Either I wasn't quick enough going to the toilet, or my fucking waters just broke!"

The first flickerings of panic started up in Michael immediately – just as soon as he realised that Diane's dress was far too wet for it to mean anything other than the baby was on the way. As Diane screamed at him to get her mother, phone for an ambulance, pack her a bag; the enormity of what was about to happen suddenly hit him. He was about to become a father. But for that to happen, first of all there had to be a birth – a birth Diane fully expected him to be present for. And the last time he'd experienced a birth, the baby had died.

"Don't you fucking well dare to leave me here alone!" Diane screamed at him as he made for the front door, so he went back to her, taking her hand and doing his best to stay calm.

She was clutching at her stomach now, clearly in pain, sweat forming on her brow, and Michael felt sick. "Listen, I have to go out to use the phone, Di," he told her. "We need an ambulance."

"Mum!" she gasped. "I want my mum!"

Michael let go of her hand and went to the door. "Yes, I'll phone her too. I'll be as quick as I can, I promise."

Running down the road, thanking his lucky stars he had change for the phone Michael tried to decide who to call first. Ambulance or Diane's mother? And what if her mother weren't in? What if she were out playing golf or lunching with her friends or whatever else she did when she wasn't being a total pain in the backside interfering in their lives? It would be entirely ironic if, the one time he needed and wanted her interference, she were unavailable.

Nearing the phone box, Michael saw someone else also on their way to it and sprinted the last few metres. "Sorry," he said, almost wrenching the door handle from the man's hand. "Emergency!"

Quickly, he dialled the number of Diane's parents' home. "Yes, Michael, what is it?" asked Diane's mother. "I'm just on my way out to the hairdressers." Her tone of voice made it quite clear – as it always did – that she thought he was a useless idler and she only put up with him because he was the father of her grandchild to be.

"The baby's on its way!" he shouted. "You've got to come!"

"But it's not due yet," she objected, sounding put out. Then, "Have you called an ambulance?"

"Not yet."

"Well, do it! I'll see you at the hospital."

Shakily, Michael tapped out the three nines and said what he had to say, doing his best to stave off the memory of the other disastrous time he'd had to do the same thing. Then he ran home to Diane to find her screaming with her hands clutching her belly in agony. Something was wrong; he knew it. Something was wrong and the baby was going to die. It was happening all over again.

In the ambulance, he let the paramedics comfort and reassure Diane. One of them squeezed his shoulder and told him everything was fine, but he didn't believe them. He had no idea what to say or do, and in any case, he knew Diane would reject him if he tried to take her hand or offer any words of comfort. Any time she wasn't screaming, she looked furiously angry, and it was all too easy to imagine her flinging off his hand and yelling, "Of course it's not fucking well all right! I'm in agony here!"

So he sat silently, hands uselessly between his knees, and gradually the past came to claim him. The screams; his mother yelling at him. Then the long, sudden silence before he'd gathered enough courage to go to her room…

At the hospital, Diane's mother took one look at him and dismissed him to the relatives' lounge. Despising himself, Michael allowed himself to be dispatched. But as time went on he began to feel more and more claustrophobic, and more and more certain the baby was going to die.

102

Exhausted, he finally fell asleep in the early hours of the morning, and was immediately claimed by nightmares. The baby – a boy – was blue and still, but Diane and her mother didn't seem to realise it. Someone had dressed him in a white babygro, and Diane was smiling down at him as she held him in her arms and saying, "Look at him, Michael; don't you think he's got my eyes?"

But all Michael could see when he looked down at his son was the lifeless angle of his head, the stiffness of his little arms and legs. "He's dead," he told her. "Can't you see that?"

"Michael?" Diane's mother was shaking him awake, and slowly Michael emerged from the horror of his dream. "It's a little boy. He's here. Do you want to come and meet him now?"

She was smiling, and it looked odd because he'd seen her smile so seldom. "He's…all right?" he asked, getting groggily to his feet. "You're sure?"

"Yes, of course," she said, a flicker of irritation already affecting that smile. "Come and see for yourself."

It was just like his nightmare, with Diane smiling down at the baby in her arms, who was dressed in a white babygro. But there the similarity ended. Because the baby wasn't blue and it wasn't still; on the contrary, his flesh was a healthy pink colour, his arms and legs were moving, and he was making a noise – lots of it. Michael had never been so glad to hear somebody scream in all his life.

"He has a fine pair of lungs on him," said one of the midwives, holding her arms out towards Diane. "Shall I give him to Daddy?"

"Where've you been all this time?" Diane asked him accusingly. "You missed all the fun. Careful; don't hold him like that, you'll drop him."

But Michael knew he would never, ever drop his son. *His son.* How amazing; he was a father! His son was here and very much alive, and infinitely precious. At last he could banish those ghosts of the past because that's all they were now – ghosts.

"Jesus, Michael," said Diane. "What are you blubbing for? Anyone would think you'd done all the hard work!"

Chapter Seventeen

Michael's watching me pack. "I can't believe you're really doing this. It's Christmas next month."

I've counted out eleven pairs of clean knickers and they're at the bottom of my suitcase beneath my freshly ironed T-shirts and cool, floaty dresses. Now I'm rechecking my handbag for my passport, tickets and money and the taxi's due to arrive in ten minutes. Rachel Dewing emailed to say she'd be delighted to show me her paintings sometime during my holiday so yes; I really am doing this, and I'm not sure what Christmas has got to do with anything.

"It's just a holiday, Michael. I'll be back in ten days."

He reaches out to stroke my hair. It's the most intimate we've been since I broke my news about the trip. In fact, I've hardly seen him for the past few weeks. I don't even honestly know where he's been because apart from saying 'it's just work', he hasn't offered much of an explanation for his absences.

"Cuba," he says now. "Why Cuba?"

I give a lying little shrug. "The cars, the salsa, the uniqueness; it's like nowhere else in the world, let alone the Caribbean."

"You sound like a holiday brochure."

I put down my handbag and press myself into his arms so he can't see my face. "It's a chance to discover new things, that's all." This much is true. I've got an appointment with Rachel Dewing in her studio in four days' time.

Michael gives a long sigh then moves away from me, busying himself with putting on his motorbike gear. "Right, well, I'm not good with goodbyes, as you know. So I'm going to take off for Sheringham. At least it's not raining today. Might actually make a few sales. Have a good time. See you when you get back."

"Bye…"

Every time I begin to have doubts about the action I'm taking, something snaps me back on course. This time it's the reminder of that Sheringham lie. Standing in the doorway, I watch as he yanks the bike off its stand and kick-starts it. Then he raises one gauntleted hand to me before riding off down the drive to join the morning traffic. I'm still standing there hugging myself two minutes later when the taxi arrives.

Pulling myself out of my torpor, I start to go back inside for my stuff, but Marcia pops her head out of the window to issue instructions. "Don't pick up your suitcase – the driver will do it."

The taxi stops, and the driver's door opens in time for me to hear Marcia telling him, "She's pregnant." Just as well Michael's gone, or else this whole *keeping my pregnancy secret while I investigate his exes* plan would have been brought to an abrupt end.

"Congratulations." The driver smiles at me as he picks up my suitcase.

"Thanks." My smile feels distinctly wan. The truth is, I'm as bone weary as if I've already done the whole Heathrow/Milan/Havana long haul thing. What's more, the hollow inside me that's been there ever since I began to question the reality of my future with Michael feels larger than ever.

"Smile," Marcia orders me. "We're going on holiday!"

When the taxi driver turns out of the drive in the direction of the train station, a motorbike's approaching from the other direction. Perhaps it's Michael, forgotten something. If it is, I'll take it as an omen. I'll get the driver to stop – let Marcia and Hannah go to Cuba without me. I'll do what I should have done right away and tell Michael the truth. I've got to face doing it sometime anyway; no matter what the consequences.

The motorbike accelerates past us at about ninety miles

an hour.

"Idiot!" shouts the taxi driver. "You trying to kill yourself?"

It looks as if I'm going to Cuba.

"How did Gary take the news about the holiday?" I ask Marcia, and I look at her carefully, because I know I'm not the only one who's feeling fragile and fucked up. Marcia rang me the other week after Gary point-blank refused to discuss them trying IVF again. Naturally, she was devastated, and though I tried to reassure her Gary would come round to the idea, I wasn't too sure I was right. Marcia's husband is the strong, silent type. He lets Marcia have her way over almost everything, but then suddenly he'll put his foot down, and that's it; he won't budge. And even though this time his stubbornness is dressed up with loving protestations that he can't bear to see her go through the pain of it all again, the result is the same – Marcia isn't getting what she wants.

"Gary and I still aren't really speaking," Marcia tells me bleakly, but there's no time for me to reply to this because the taxi driver has pricked up his ears at the mention of Cuba.

"Off to Cuba, are you? Make sure you use tourist taxis. They're a lot more expensive, but it's illegal to use local taxis. Don't want to end up in prison, do you?"

I shudder. No, definitely not.

Marcia's interest is piqued. "Why's it illegal to travel in local taxis?"

"Because they're cheaper. Out there, the government's out to fleece you the whole time. But don't worry; it's just a small annoyance. You're going to love it. Amazing place."

And with that, he launches into a description of his Cuban holiday. Marcia asks questions, keeping the conversation going, and I can't tell if she's really interested or whether she just wants to avoid a conversation about her and Gary. As for me, I don't really take in what the taxi driver is saying at all. Instead, I think about the irony of me and Marcia both having dodgy relationships at the moment.

107

Because we've been so happy these past few years, we really have. But now Marcia's furious with Gary and I'm keeping a huge big truth from Michael, and I've no idea how things are going to turn out for either of us.

When the taxi pulls into Norwich station I can see Hannah at the front of the building, waiting where we've arranged to meet, her suitcase on the ground beside her.

"I still don't know why you had to invite her along," Marcia grumbles.

"Because she's always wanted to go to Havana," I explain for the umpteenth time.

"Just so long as she doesn't expect me to carry her suitcase," Marcia says, and I give her a look.

"What?" she asks, all big, innocent eyes. "I can hardly carry three suitcases, can I? And you're definitely not carrying yours. I'm amazing, but not that amazing."

But it turns out that Hannah doesn't need any martyr-faced favours from Marcia anyway, because she's already arranged to have her bags carried for her. "Jen," she greets me with a delighted smile, kissing me on the cheek. Then, "How lovely to see you again, Marcia. Isn't this exciting?" And no sooner has Marcia given her a brittle nod of acknowledgement, than a smartly uniformed man arrives with a luggage trolley.

"This is the rest of your party, is it, madam?" he asks, and proceeds to load our cases onto the trolley. We follow him as he trundles a path towards platform Two and the London train.

"However did you manage to find him, Hannah?" I ask, impressed.

"Ah," says Hannah with a twinkle. "Everything's possible if you know how to do it. I wasn't head of Social Services in Norfolk for nothing."

"What's Social Services got to do with train guards?" I hear Marcia muttering under her breath, but I can tell she's reluctantly impressed too. There are lots of other people manhandling suitcases along the platform, and all of them are looking at our cavalcade with envy.

At London Liverpool Street, it's the same thing – a guard's waiting to help with our luggage, and takes it all the way out to the taxi rank. And at Heathrow, someone else is waiting for us – this time with a motorised buggy.

"I hope you won't feel too embarrassed by me being in this thing," Hannah says. "Only you do have to walk so very far in airports, don't you? I promise I won't be a burden to you in Havana. I'm very good on my own, you know. I won't expect to go around everywhere with you young things."

Marcia looks distinctly relieved at this, so I'm grateful that Hannah has started to make conversation with the buggy driver so she doesn't see. Actually, seeing Hannah getting so much help has made me feel a bit sad. I rarely think of her as being old, but somehow now, with her in the buggy, I can't help it. She looks old and tiny and frail, and I wonder if I was right to agree so readily when she asked if she could come to Havana with us.

On the plane to Madrid, I sit between Hannah and Marcia, with Hannah by the window and Marcia in the aisle. As soon as we're airborne, Hannah plugs herself into a *Refresher Advanced Spanish Course* and is soon silently mouthing along.

"Is there anything that woman can't do?" Marcia asks, irritably turning the pages of her in-flight magazine.

"I don't think Hannah being fluent in Spanish is a bad thing, Marse," I say. "Given that neither you nor I can do very much more than ask for two beers and I'm not drinking at the moment."

Marcia just sniffs, so I don't say what I could say – that having Hannah along with us makes me feel safe, old and frail as she may be. Hannah's done things – and been to places. And she's focussed on the moment. Whereas Marcia, with all her angst about Gary's refusal to even discuss IVF, is all sulks and flirtatious smiles at anyone male who looks unattached. I know she just wants to punish Gary in some obscure way, but to be honest, travelling with Marcia right now feels a lot like travelling with a time bomb.

"Are you going to Madrid or Havana?" I hear the man across the aisle ask her.

"To Havana," Marcia smiles. "How about you?"

"Yes, me too. I love Cuba. This is my fourth time."

"Wow! You must love it. So, tell me, what do you recommend I take in to have the best experience possible?"

On the face of it, Marcia's words are innocent enough, but she's leaning towards the man, her hand resting on her chin, so they seem charged with innuendo. Poor Gary; I know he'd be upset if he could see Marcia now.

Poor Michael, a voice echoes inside my head, instantly stabbing me with guilt. *How upset would he be if he knew what you had planned?* Oh, God, am I going to spend the whole journey with my conscience haranguing me? I look over at Hannah, wondering if I can disturb her Spanish studies to start a conversation that will stop me thinking too much, but see she has fallen asleep. Her mouth is hanging open slightly, and I can hear a faint male voice speaking Spanish to her from her headphones. On my other side, Marcia laughs and the man across the aisle laughs right along with her, obviously captivated.

It's going to be a long trip.

When we change flights in Madrid, Marcia's companion – Timothy – isn't sitting near us, much to Marcia's disappointment. After she's grumbled about this for thirty minutes, Hannah offers to change seats with him, so then I'm treated to ten solid hours of their conversation about Cuba. To be fair, they both try to include me every now and then, but I haven't looked at any guidebooks, so I don't have a lot to contribute. I haven't thought much about being in Cuba at all in fact – I've only thought about the meeting with Rachel Dewing, wondering what she'll be like and what I'll find out from her.

It's early evening when we finally arrive in Havana. I feel crumpled and exhausted as I watch Marcia and Timothy exchange hotel information. She's still all smiles and batting eyelashes, and I have absolutely no idea what she's playing at. It's a real relief when Hannah joins me.

"Did you manage to get any sleep?" she asks.

"Not much. You?"

"A little, thank you."

Behind us, Marcia laughs another of those hearty laughs she's been belting out the entire flight. "It seems as if Marcia has made a friend."

"Yes, doesn't it?" I reply, my expression no doubt expressing my opinion about that.

Slowly, we move towards the exit with our hand luggage, giving the requisite thanks to the flight attendants; and then I make my way out to the steps and walk out into the Cuban evening. The warm, wet heat hits me like a wall; just gorgeous, after a long, wet Norfolk summer. I feel a sudden surge of excitement; maybe, just maybe, this trip can be about more than Michael and Rachel Dewing.

"Blimey," says Marcia behind me. "I'm going to be sweating buckets in seconds. Let's get into the airport building."

"Bienvenido a Cuba," says Hannah.

Any excitement I felt on arrival is severely put to the test by a hellish long wait in Havana José Marti arrivals lounge. Marcia's complaining after ten minutes, and while I don't blame her – since everyone from the plane is crammed into a room with nothing ostensibly happening and not even any sign of proper queues – I'm quite glad when she heads off in search of Timothy again and leaves me and Hannah to wait wearily on our own.

"Are you all right?" Hannah asks me. "You ought to be sitting down in your condition."

Bless her; it's *her* that ought to be sitting down. She looks exhausted. "I'm fine," I say. "Honestly."

Finally, our passports stamped by a severe-looking man with oiled black hair, we're out of the airport and boarding a bus to take us to our hotel. After another thirty minutes the bus leaves, and another thirty minutes after that, we're finally pulling up outside our hotel.

Even Hannah hasn't been able to arrange for someone to be waiting ready to carry her suitcase here, but someone's there right away anyway. So, with Marcia pulling her case and mine along like two recalcitrant dogs on their leads, we go into the hotel lobby. As we do so, a band breaks into a salsa tune, and someone hands us a drink of something in a plastic cup that has leaves floating in it.

"Mojitoes," Marcia says. "Tim told me about them. They're mostly rum and lime juice."

I lift the concoction to my mouth curiously, only to have it snatched quickly away. "Hey!" says Marcia, "That's rum as in alcohol – not to be consumed by pregnant women?"

"I was only going to have a sip," I protest, but it's too late. Marcia's already quaffed my drink and is making inroads into her own.

It's a relief to get into our room. Hannah's paid a single supplement to have a room on her own, but Marcia and I are sharing. The room is fairly basic, but pleasant, and I'm surprised to see we have a balcony. The doors to this are open, but after a quick look out, Marcia closes them and cranks up the air-conditioning, saying, "It's like a flipping furnace in here, I'll never sleep tonight. Okay if I have the first shower?"

When I'm alone, I open the doors to the balcony and step outside. There's a slightly rusting seat out there, and I sit on it, leaning forward to rest on the balcony and look out into the darkness. My brain's still fizzing from the epic journey and a multitude of images – Hannah in the buggy, Marcia flirting with Timothy, the greased-back hair of the stern passport control officer at the airport. Closing my eyes, I take a deep breath in an attempt to try and shut it all out, and suddenly I hear the sound of a bird singing. Toco-toco-tocoro-tocoro. It's such a loud, exotic-sounding song, that suddenly it really hits me. I'm in Cuba, two thousand miles away from home and Michael. Opening my eyes, I try to spot the bird, but it's in the trees somewhere, and the streetlights aren't bright enough for me to see it.

A group of brightly dressed women pass slowly by on the

street below, talking and laughing together. I smile, watching them in the dusky light, and as I do, I catch the smell of food cooking. Suddenly, I'm ravenously hungry even though the strong smell has my hand quickly pressing itself over my nostrils to try and block it out. My baby might be the size of a kidney bean, but it's still demanding. The in-flight meals obviously didn't cut it as far as she/he was concerned. When I get home, it will be time for my first antenatal appointment. Will I get to hear the baby's heartbeat then? Or will it still be too early?

Cars pass by. Disappointingly, none of them so far have been the American classic cars Cuba is so famous for. Then, in a break in the traffic, I see a couple walking along with their arms around each other. When they are almost opposite me, they stop to kiss. He's holding her just like Michael held me at Hunstanton at ladybird beach – the way I wanted him to hold me at Cromer before the fish and chip fumes got the better of me. And suddenly I miss him so much it hurts.

The balcony doors open, and Marcia sticks her head outside. "God, I hope that bird's not going to make that awful racket all night," she says. "Come on; get your arse into gear. I'm so hungry I could eat a salsa trumpeter's boxers."

Chapter Eighteen

Michael, 2000

Diane was asleep, upstairs in the bedroom. It was three weeks since they'd brought the baby home from the hospital and he seemed to be nocturnal, sleeping all day and awake all night. Diane, who was breast-feeding, was grabbing sleep whenever she could, and at weekends, when Michael was at work, she went home to her parents.

Now when the baby whimpered, Michael quickly hurried over to lift him from his Moses basket before his cries could wake Diane. Earlier, she had expressed some milk, and now he grabbed this together with the changing bag and manoeuvred the baby and the buggy out of the front door.

Behind him, he heard Diane call out groggily, but he pressed on anyway, wheeling the buggy away from the house, confident that she would go back to sleep if she had some peace.

They'd called the baby Kyle – or rather Diane had. Michael was finding it difficult to get used to it; it seemed like a wishy-washy kind of a name to him, but Diane had been so insistent, he'd let her have her own way. Just as he'd let her have her own way about going home to her parents at the weekends. It was strange being in the house on his own on Saturday nights, although it did mean he'd managed to claw some time to finish his dissertation.

As they reached the bus stop, Kyle opened his lungs and began to cry in earnest, so Michael carried on walking towards the city. When he'd left the house, he'd had no idea of his destination, but now he knew exactly where he was going. When Kyle didn't stop crying, Michael stopped on a bench to give him his bottle of expressed milk, but Kyle wasn't impressed, spitting the teat out in disgust and clenching his body to cry even harder. Too late Michael realised it was because the milk was cold. For a millisecond he considered returning home, but he was over half way there now, and he was pretty sure they'd let him warm the milk when he got there. It was either that or put up with a squalling baby in the waiting room, and he didn't think they'd want to do that.

By the time Michael reached Social Services, Kyle was red in the face and Michael's nerves were shot. This had been a big mistake. Why was he even here? After all this time, and after everything that had happened? It was the woman who was supposed to get all hormonal and irrational because of childbirth, not the man. This was madness. But he was here now, and there was no way he could make Kyle wait even longer for his milk, so in he went, bumping the buggy clumsily up the steps and making the baby even more indignant.

Kyle's cries were deafening now, and when he went in, the duty social worker looked at him warily from her office. Michael ignored her for a moment as he lifted the baby from the buggy. "It's all right, little fella; it's all right..." Only it wasn't all right at all; Kyle's nappy had exploded, and his bottom half was pasted with yellow-brown poo. "There isn't anywhere I can warm his milk while I change his nappy, is there?" he asked, desperate now, attempting to hold Kyle so he wouldn't come into contact with his own clothes.

"I'll do it for you," said the social worker. "You go and sort him out. The toilets are through there. Have you got an appointment?"

"No, but I was hoping someone would be able to see me. My name's Michael Brandon."

It took some time and a lot of wipes and loo paper, but finally Kyle was clean. Thankfully, there was a clean babygro in the changing bag, but Michael suspected the baby blanket – which had been made for them by Diane's mother – would have to be ditched.

With Kyle feeding hungrily on his suitably warmed bottle, Michael began to relax a little. Diane had hardly let him do any of this stuff – whenever he tried to, she said what he'd done wasn't up to scratch, the nappy too loose or too tight, the milk not the right temperature et cetera. Smiling wryly to himself, Michael recalled his son's reaction to the cold milk and relented. Okay, maybe Diane had a point – this stuff didn't come naturally to him. But if she never let him try, then he wasn't going to learn, was he?

"Mr Brandon? Would you like to come this way?"

"Oh, okay, thanks." Carefully, Michael got to his feet, managing not to interrupt Kyle's flow of milk too badly. He'd never been referred to as Mr Brandon by social services before, and it was a mark of how long it was since he'd had any dealings with them, cut loose at the age of sixteen and left to fend for himself. He'd done okay too, but then nothing could be worse than that year in a children's home when they hadn't been able to find suitable foster parents for him. It had been a lonely, frightening time, and coming here brought it all back.

"My name's Michelle," the social worker introduced herself. "What's your baby called?"

"Kyle."

"What a lovely name. Do take a seat. Can I call you Michael?"

Michael nodded, settling himself down carefully. The milk was almost gone now, and he knew he was probably on borrowed time before Kyle kicked off again. "Yeah, that's fine."

"And how can I help you today, Michael?"

Michael kept his gaze on his feeding son. "I'd like to find out where my mother is," he said. Then he risked looking up. "She doesn't know about Kyle, you see. I'd like to tell her about him – tell her she's a grandmother. If she's well enough these days, that is. We…sort of lost touch."

The social worker took some information from him and left him alone while she went to make some calls. Kyle finished his bottle, and Michael put him over his shoulder the way he'd seen Diane do, patting him on his back. When the baby burped loudly, Michael laughed out loud. "There's a good boy," he said, bringing Kyle round so he could smile at him. "There's a good boy!"

When the social worker came back, her expression quickly wiped the smile from his face. "I'm afraid your mother's in Hellesdon Hospital, Michael," she said.

Hellesdon. Still.

"She's been there for a few years now. You can certainly visit her; I'll write down the details for you. But I wouldn't recommend taking little Kyle with you. At least, not right away."

No, indeed.

It was gone five o'clock when Michael got home again. He'd been out more than four hours, and he knew Diane wasn't going to be very happy with him. But even he couldn't have predicted how very unhappy she would be, and, since she was under the impression that his mother had died years ago, he wasn't in a position to tell her where he'd been.

"You just don't give a shit about me, do you, Michael?" she stormed at him, snatching Kyle so roughly from his buggy he began to cry. "You didn't give one thought to me sitting here with my tits leaking waiting for you to come back! And where's his blanket? I bet you've sodding well lost it, haven't you?"

Chapter Nineteen

Havana is breathtaking, alien and amazing. Last night we ate in the hotel restaurant, but this morning the three of us take a taxi into the city. It drops us off at Plaza de la Revolucion where an impressive giant mural of Che Guevara transforms a dull grey building.

Marcia stands contemplating the bronze mural; her arms folded across her chest, while passing Cuban men contemplate her. She's wearing an eye-catching combination of red Lycra shorts and a tight black T-shirt with a plunging neckline, and her sunglasses are pushed back onto her head so she can get a better view of Che. In short, she looks gorgeous. Hannah and I have both opted for cool, floaty dresses and wide-brimmed hats, so I suspect I probably look a bit like Marcia's maiden aunt. The dress isn't doing a lot to keep me cool either, because it's hot, hot, hot. "Well," pronounces Marcia, "I'd certainly have given him one. More than one, actually. He was a handsome bugger, wasn't he?"

"I imagine his good looks contributed considerably to the success of the revolution," Hannah says thoughtfully.

"You mean if he'd looked like a cow's backside the people wouldn't have followed him so readily?"

Hannah nods. "I think it's a strong possibility, yes."

I smile at this because it's so nice to have my two best friends getting along for once. Not that Hannah is ever anything but polite and friendly to Marcia. Marcia's in a better mood this morning, thank goodness. We all are, after a good night's sleep. I woke up once to go to the loo and it was as cold as a fridge in our room with the air conditioning cranked up full, but after I'd weighted the bedclothes down with a bath towel and a jacket, I got back to sleep.

But I know from my brief experience of being pregnant that I have about a two-hour window before I'm exhausted again, so I'm keen to get cracking. "Shall we book on a tour?" I ask, and Hannah smiles her agreement.

"I'd like to visit the Museum of the Revolution at some point," she says, "but I'm happy to fit in around you girls."

At that moment, several amazing classic cars drive past us, their polished pointed wings glinting in the sunshine. "I want to go in one of those!" Marcia declares. "Museums can wait!"

Ten minutes later we're travelling along the Malecon next to the sea in fine style in a turquoise blue 1957 Chevrolet. Marcia's grinning from ear-to-ear, and I think even Hannah has to admit it beats a crusty old museum hands down, though I intend to make sure she gets to one later on if she still wants to go.

"This is so fabulous!" Marcia says. "I must get a pic of us to post on Facebook. Gary will be green with envy."

Sadly, I recall their wedding day, three years previously, with Marcia all smiles in her perfect dress and Gary looking like a man who'd won the lottery and found the crown jewels all on the same day. How things change.

"That will make him sad though, won't it?" I say, and she looks at me.

"Tough luck," she snaps. "He shouldn't be such a stubborn pig, should he? And it might make him wish he were here with me. Besides, what about Michael? He'd be sad, wouldn't he? If he knew you were going to see Rachel Whatsherface behind his back?" And she looks away from me to wave at a group of boys doing their stuff on their skateboards.

"Blimey, Marcia," I say. "Speak your mind, why don't you?"

She refuses to reply, and suddenly the classic car jaunt doesn't seem such fun, and the sunshine doesn't seem as bright. Unseen by Marcia, Hannah – who has heard this exchange – squeezes my arm. I smile at her before turning my gaze away from the seafront to the passing streets.

Somewhere in that maze, Rachel Dewing is going about her daily life. I wonder what that consists of, and what brought her here? Apart from the amazing subject matter all around us for an artist of course. And I wonder what, if anything, I will find out from her.

By mid afternoon we've done the Museum of the Revolution and immersed ourselves in the story of how this unique place came to be. We've also been on a tour of a cigar factory. As we re-emerge into the pulsing sunshine, I feel as exhausted as if I've done a twelve-hour cigar-rolling shift myself, and by the look of her, Hannah feels the same.

"I'm exhausted," I say. "Can we go back to the hotel for a few hours?"

Marcia has the guidebook open. She's still a bit snappy from our exchange in the car. "Don't be such a lightweight, Jen. It's only three o'clock."

"It's being pregnant," I say. "You can't imagine how completely exhausted it makes you..." And how completely tactless.

Marcia snaps the guidebook shut. "No," she says. "That's right. I can't imagine it, can I? Thanks for reminding me."

Hannah quickly intervenes. "If we have a siesta now, there's an event we can all go to this evening," she says, pointing at a poster. "A meal and salsa dancing. How about it? It would give us a real flavour of Cuba. I could do with a lie down right now myself, I have to admit. But I do love a spot of salsa dancing."

This fact is enough of a distraction to get Marcia to walk along with us to a place where we can catch a taxi back to the hotel, and on the way, Hannah fills us in on her salsa experience – it seems she did years of salsa classes with her late husband. As this was long before I knew her, I've never heard about it before. The thought of seeing her in action is enough to make me look forward to the evening ahead, despite the fact that right now it feels as if I'll never find the energy to get up again once I lay down.

I don't even really have the energy to dwell on my tiff

with Marcia, although the memory of it is there, all the same, taking some of the glitter out of the day. But the baby's demands on my body are more effective than sleeping tablets in blocking out life's insecurities and unpleasantness. Within seconds of Marcia leaving our room to go for a swim, I'm asleep, and I don't wake up again until she returns about an hour later. Yawning, I watch her, trying to gauge whether an hour of pounding up and down the pool has improved her mood or not.

"Sorry I was so tactless," I say.

Marcia sits on the edge of the bed to brush her wet hair. "Sorry I'm such a prickly bitch," she says right back at me, and I smile, taking her free hand.

"It's quite understandable that you're sensitive about the subject."

She lets go of my hand and frowns at me with what I know to be her nurse's face. "You have made an appointment for your first antenatal, haven't you?"

"The Monday after we get back, yes."

She nods, satisfied for now, and I prop myself up on my elbow.

"What about you? Are you going to call Gary soon?"

"Not till he's had the chance to really stew. I want the reality of life without me in it to really hit him. So he's begging to try IVF again."

Is that the way people who love each other behave? It doesn't seem right to me, but there's no way I'm going to say such a thing when we've just smoothed things over with each other. Besides, I'm in no position to judge. I don't suppose keeping the fact that your loved one is to become a father secret makes an appearance on some long list of acts of eternal love either.

"Now," says Marcia, changing the subject. "What are you going to wear tonight for this salsa fest?"

The food at the do is bland – but then so far we haven't managed to find anything but bland food since we arrived in Cuba. And tonight it doesn't really matter, because the food is not the main attraction – the music and the dancing are. All through the meal, the band plays a kind of laid-back jazzy salsa, but the moment the plates are pushed aside the beat of the music picks up, and everyone immediately abandons their tables for the dance floor.

Hannah has the biggest smile on her face. She's dressed in black and her dress has a swinging, tulip-shaped skirt, and she stands to survey the crowd, obviously looking for a suitable partner. I wish Luther were here to dance with her – he's a good dancer, but apart from that, it would make him see his mother in a different light.

But Hannah doesn't need Luther, because a Cuban man a good twenty years younger than she is comes over, says something to her in Spanish and whisks her away.

"Holy shit!" says Marcia as they begin to dance. "She wasn't lying about those lessons, was she? She's really good!"

Her comment gives me a warm glow, but I don't say anything. And in any case, Marcia's attention has moved on. Suddenly she's on her feet, waving. When I take a look I see it's Timothy, from the plane. Instinctively, my heart sinks as he comes over, all smiles, obviously delighted to see Marcia. "Hi, Marcia!" he says. "How great to see you!"

"Of all the salsa clubs, in all the towns in all the world, you walk into this one," Marcia says, misquoting Casablanca.

Timothy, who is obviously not a classic movie buff like Marcia, looks confused for a moment. "Well, obviously I knew you were in Havana, didn't I?" he says. "But it's certainly a coincidence that we're both here this evening. A very good one!"

Timothy's dressed in a white shirt and cream chinos, and his face is red even though he's not dancing yet. Marcia soon puts that right. "Come on," she says, grabbing his arm, and seconds later they're on the dance floor, where it soon becomes clear that Timothy has no idea how to dance salsa at all.

A smile springs to my lips – I can't help it. The poor man

just looks so uncool out there, surrounded by expert hip wigglers. It reminds me of the time some friends invited Michael and me to a holiday camp in Great Yarmouth for a weekend of Ceroc dancing. I'd never danced Ceroc in my life; neither had Michael. But he convinced me it would be fun, and Gemma, one of our friends, lent me a short black skirt and a red top which she said would be perfect for dancing in. The only trouble was, it was exactly the kind of thing all the experienced Ceroc dancers were wearing – a kind of Ceroc uniform. Consequently, all the men assumed I was experienced too. Even though I was there with Michael, everyone danced with everyone, so there were a lot of disappointed male Ceroc dancers with bruised toes out there by the time the weekend was over.

As I watch Marcia and Timothy on the dance floor, I remember how in demand as a dance partner Michael had been that weekend, Ceroc novice or not, and suddenly I wonder what Michael's doing now, this minute. Is he playing games on his computer? Watching TV? Out on the bike? And what exactly am I even doing here, without him? It feels so wrong, suddenly. Mad. If my phone worked in this country, I'd ring him. Blurt out the truth about everything. I just want to hear his voice. But my phone doesn't work, so I can't speak to him.

"Señorita?" I look up to see a young Cuban guy, his body language asking me for a dance. To hell with it. I'm here in Cuba, and if Michael hadn't been acting strangely, if he didn't have his four-year relationship habit, I wouldn't be. I'd be talking to him about nursery colour schemes and lounging on the sofa with my head in his lap and his hand stroking my hair.

So I switch on a smile and allow the young man to lead me into the throng of dancers, and I'm a bit rusty at first, but then my body begins to remember and soon it's pure magic. Stepping, swinging, smiling. I defy anyone to dance salsa with an expert partner and not smile. When the music and the rhythm feel as if they've made an electrical connection with your bones, you light up and there's no space for brooding thoughts and what ifs.

For ten minutes it's pure happiness and wild forgetfulness, but suddenly there's a bit of a commotion over near the band and I look over to see what's wrong, and that's when I realise something's wrong with Hannah.

"Excuse me," I say, letting go of my partner and pushing my way through. Hannah and her partner have stopped dancing. He's holding her, and speaking in Spanish, his expression one of concern.

"Hannah?" I say, having to shout because of the music, "what's wrong? Are you all right?" But I know she's not; her face is so grey, it scares me silly.

Hannah makes a poor attempt at a smile, but she can hardly keep her eyes open. "I'll be fine, dear. I'm just tired. Perhaps I'd better sit down?"

"Si, si," says her partner quickly, and helps her to move through the crowd.

My heart's beating like a steam train, and I wave in Marcia's direction, trying to get her attention. Timothy sees and says something to her, and they both start to come over. By the time they get to us, Hannah's sitting down. Marcia takes one look at her and says, "Somebody get her some water."

"Agua," I say, dredging the word from some distant school Spanish lesson.

"Agua, si," says Hannah's partner and hurries away, looking relieved to have some action to take.

"I'm so sorry about this, girls," Hannah says. She has her hand to her chest and her face looks greyer than ever. "I think I might have overdone it a bit today."

Her voice sounds weak and fluttery, as if it's coming from a distance, and Marcia's sitting next to her, holding the hand that isn't on her chest. "Do you have a chest pain, Hannah?" she asks, and tears begin to roll down my face. Oh, God. Hannah's ill. She's really ill.

When Hannah opens her eyes I can see she's doing her best to look calm and reassuring, and that terrifies me more than anything, because it's so obviously a big effort. "A little, yes," she agrees. "But I don't need a doctor. There's a spray in my bag. That might help."

She's wearing her small tote bag across her body, and Marcia grabs it and starts rifling through it. She knows what she's looking for, and soon pulls out a small spray. Meanwhile, Hannah's partner has returned with a bottle of mineral water, which he unscrews and stands waiting to administer.

"Here," says Marcia and helps Hannah to use her spray, and within seconds, the colour begins to return to Hannah's face. It's such a huge relief, my legs start to wobble. Marcia flicks a glance in my direction. "You'd better sit down, Jen. I don't want two casualties on my hands."

Hannah's dance partner holds out the water to her. "Agua."

"Thank you, Julio." Hannah smiles at him and takes it. Then she says something to him in Spanish. When he replies, I guess she's telling him she's okay and that he doesn't have to hang around. He argues for a moment, then shrugs and melts away. The band starts playing something quieter, and the couples on the dance floor move closer together.

"How long have you had angina, Hannah?" Marcia asks.

Chapter Twenty

Michael, 2000

Michael stood in the middle of his exhibition space, looking round at the collection of paintings that would determine what grade he got for his degree. They were mostly pictures of interiors with strong lighting and bright colours, and to him they looked rushed and unfinished. Since they had almost all been knocked out in the past few weeks, this wasn't entirely surprising. He was on to something, he knew it; he just hadn't quite got there yet.

"Knock, knock," said a female voice, and he turned to see Rachel, one of the other painters in his year. "How's it going? Finished?"

Michael sighed. He liked Rachel; liked her paintings too. They were two of the few figurative painters in their year; the rest producing more abstract work, and this had drawn them together to discuss art over stewed cups of coffee in the student canteen. Because of Diane and the baby, he'd hardly seen her this term.

"Hi," he said, putting a friendly arm around her. "I'm not happy, to be honest," he said. "But I think this is as good as it's going to get. I've run out of time."

They stood there, arms around each other, looking at the large canvasses. Unlike Diane, who was tall and could look him in the eye, Rachel was tiny; her head barely reaching his armpit, and always made him feel like a giant. She had a big personality though, and was usually forthright in her opinions, so he wasn't altogether surprised when she voiced them now. "I took a look through your stuff the other day when you weren't around. These are good, but they aren't your best work. Why aren't you displaying your paintings of Diane and the baby? They're so much stronger."

Michael moved away to collect his tools together, feeling embarrassed. "Because Diane would freak out," he said. "She hates me even drawing her – she hasn't got a clue I've painted her too."

"Most people would be flattered," Rachel said, but Michael wasn't sure about that. The paintings were based on sketches he'd done of Diane dealing with Kyle, and they showed her warts and all. There were some of her gazing lovingly down at Kyle as he fed, but there were a whole lot more of her exhausted, slumped in the chair, or almost screaming with frustration as the baby bawled, red-faced and inconsolable.

"My space is still clear," Rachel said, tempting him. "Why don't we arrange the paintings in there, just to see what they'd look like?"

It was tempting, if only to see them all together. "Won't that hold you up?"

"Not at all. I know just how I want to hang my show. You can help me afterwards if you like."

He knew he really ought to be getting home to give Diane a break. But maybe Rachel needed his help? Perhaps she wasn't quite as confident about her show as she made out. "Sure," he said. "Why not? But I can't be too long."

"It won't take long," Rachel assured him. "Right, where are they? I'll help you carry them."

Within ten minutes the paintings of Diane and Kyle were arranged around Rachel's exhibition space. There were six in all, and Michael had to admit they looked powerful all together like this.

"See?" said Rachel, watching his face.

Michael didn't get the chance to reply. Unseen by either him or Rachel, Patrick George, one of their tutors, had come into the studio.

"Is this your show, Michael?" he asked, studying the paintings keenly. "I thought you were up the corridor? These are splendid. Why haven't we seen them before?

Excellent job; really excellent."

Michael experienced a sense of pleasure and panic at the same time. "Thanks, Patrick," he said, "but I wasn't actually planning on showing these particular—"

"But you must," Patrick said. "You simply must."

After the lecturer had gone, Rachel looked at him. "He's right, Michael," she said. "You know he is. Just tell Diane; she'll understand."

But Michael knew she wouldn't.

On the evening of the degree show opening, Kyle was teething and was extremely fretful. Diane, who'd been up most of the previous night, was at her wits end. "I don't see how I can bring him to the show like this," she said.

"That's okay," said Michael swiftly. "I mean, I'll be disappointed not to have you both there, but if it's going to stress you out…"

Diane looked him. "I'm going to be stressed out wherever I am with him in this state," she said.

"I know," Michael said, dropping a kiss on the top of her head. "But at least if you're here you can crash out if he does decide to drop off, eh? And the opening doesn't really matter, does it? The show was mainly for the tutors to see, so they could mark our work."

The marks had been given out the previous day – both he and Rachel had received a First: something that hadn't quite sunk in yet for him.

"If the opening's not that important, why do you have to go to it?" Diane asked, sounding suspicious.

Michael shrugged, trying to keep it casual. "Because people might want to ask me questions about my work, I guess. Look, do what's best for you, Di. If you want to come, that will be great. All I'm saying is that I'll understand if you don't."

When Michael set off for the art college alone half an hour later, it was with a huge sense of relief. Diane had decided to stay at home, and, since she would be going to stay with her parents for the weekend as usual the next day, this meant she was unlikely to see his show. All he'd need to do was find somewhere to stow the paintings when the show came down so that she never saw them. Perhaps John could find him some space at the gallery. Or, even better still, perhaps someone would even buy some of them.

At the exhibition opening the wine flowed, and the people mingled. It didn't matter for very long that Michael was the only student not to have any visitors, because the invited guests toured all the shows. And John, his boss, who had never seen any of his paintings, arrived.

"These are very strong, Michael," he said. "I'm impressed. Next time you're at the gallery, we must schedule in an exhibition for you."

"Really?" said Michael, delighted. "That would be fantastic!"

"It might not be for a few years though," John said quickly. "You know what a waiting list we've got."

"That's okay," said Michael, his spirits undampened. "There's no hurry."

When Rachel heard about it, she was thrilled for him. "That's fantastic, Michael!" she said. "I'm so happy for you!" And she reached up to give him a kiss.

"Thanks," Michael beamed, bending down to hug her, and he was so happy he lifted her clear off the ground and whirled her around.

She squealed with delight, clutching hold of him, and that was the exact moment that Diane arrived, having arranged for her mother to babysit.

"Diane," said Michael, putting Rachel down. "You came."

"Yes," spat Diane, her gaze raking over Rachel in her tight leopard skin print trousers and moving on to the paintings of her on the walls. "I thought I'd better see for myself exactly why you were so keen for me not to be here tonight. And now I know, right?" And with that, she tossed her glass of red wine at Rachel's face and turned away, her high heels clip clopping as she walked down the corridor.

"Diane!" Michael shouted after her, but she didn't turn

back.

"Fuck off, Michael," he heard her say before she turned the corner. "Go back to your little tart. You and I are finished."

Chapter Twenty-One

"I'm so sorry I worried you, Jenny," Hannah tells me next morning.

We're sitting up in her bed together, propped up on pillows against the headboard.

"Why didn't you tell me?" I ask, because as well as being worried sick, I'm also slightly hurt that she's kept me out of the picture. "I hate to think of you worrying on your own."

Hannah sighs. "I expect I've been in denial, darling. I haven't even told Luther. Silly, isn't it? Because it's not really any big deal. So long as I'm sensible and take the medication they've given me, I'll be fine, honestly."

I look at her searchingly, and she takes my hand. "Listen, I don't want your holiday to be spoilt because I'm a stubborn old fool who can't accept that her salsa dancing days are over. Please, you go and have a lovely day with Marcia, and I'll stay here and rest. I've got a very good book I'm reading at the moment, and if I feel too lazy to venture down to the restaurant, I'll order room service."

"But we can't just leave you on your own," I protest, but she's not having any of it.

"I'm used to spending time on my own though, aren't I? And all I want to do is laze about. Go on; please. I promise we'll talk more about my stupid health this evening if you want to. And I shall look forward to hearing about your adventures. You're bound to have some; Cuba seems to be that kind of place."

Sighing, I reluctantly allow myself to be convinced. It's true that Hannah does look better than she did last night, but since she looked utterly grim last night, that's not saying much. "Okay then, if you're sure. But promise me we will talk this evening."

"Of course," she smiles, drawing me close for a kiss.

I go to join Marcia in the restaurant, feeling uneasy.

"So," Marcia says as we eat breakfast, the guidebook open in front of her. "Shall we go to the craft market? It looks amazing. Or there's a tour that takes in the mysteries of santeria."

"What's santeria?"

"Black magic. Voodoo. That kind of thing."

I shudder. "No, thank you. That sort of thing creeps me out. Besides, don't they do all sorts of unspeakable things to chickens?" The thought of it puts me off my breakfast. Not that I feel very much like eating it anyway. I never want to eat very much first thing in the morning any longer, and besides, I'm still worried about Hannah.

"Do you think Hannah will be all right on her own all day?"

Marcia nods reassuringly. "I'm sure she will. She's doing exactly the right thing; taking it easy. And you'll see her later." She's busy with her napkin suddenly, wiping orange juice from her mouth. "It will be just the two of you then, because I said I'd meet Tim tonight."

"Right." It's only a little word, but I guess I've still somehow managed to charge it with my opinions, because Marcia suddenly looks defensive.

"We're just going to have a few cocktails, that's all. Tim knows this place with a great view of Havana. It's completely harmless, honestly."

I give her a look.

"It *is*," she says, sounding annoyed now.

"Marcia, I didn't say anything," I say, and she screws up her napkin crossly.

"You didn't have to. Disapproval's coming off you like a tsunami."

This sets the tone for a sulky taxi ride into the city, with both of us looking sightlessly out of the windows at the passing view. I honestly don't know what's going on with Marcia, or what she even sees in Tim. He's pleasant enough,

132

but he seems a bit dull to me, and after last night I know I'm always going to think of him as all white and pink – a bit like an ice cream with strawberry topping. Unfair perhaps, but true.

But maybe I'm worrying needlessly. Tim's hardly sweep-a-girl-off-her-feet material. And Marcia loves Gary. It's just that his standoff about the IVF issue seems to have inspired my friend to be all 'sod it' and reckless.

I reach out to give her a friendly shove, the way I used to do at school when she was sulking, and she looks at me warily. "Marse," I ask, "will you come with me to meet Rachel tomorrow?"

She smiles, clearly delighted by the prospect. "Of course. Just try and keep me away."

The craft market sells everything from portraits of Che Guevara to African style figures, musical instruments and jewellery. It's huge, and since Marcia wants to look at everything, totally exhausting for me. I've never been so bone-achingly tired, and it seems incredible that something the size of a kidney bean is making me feel this way. My sense of smell is still working overtime too, and there are about a zillion different scents, perfumes and stinks in the market. I don't want to spoil the morning, so I hide how I feel for as long as I possibly can. But when we reach a juice bar, I just have to sit down.

"That's why you should actually eat your breakfast instead of pushing it around your plate," Marcia tells me sternly. "You already need something else to eat, don't you?"

"No, I so don't," I protest, but she ignores me.

"Let's try and find somewhere really good to have lunch. I haven't enjoyed anything I've had to eat since I arrived in Cuba."

"You look for a good restaurant?" asks one of the juice bar guys in heavily accented English.

He's wearing a vest top that displays his fit, muscular body to its best advantage and a baseball cap the wrong way round. "No, thank you," I say, smiling politely.

"Yes please," says Marcia. "That's just what we want. My friend's pregnant, you see, so she needs to eat well."

Thanks, Marcia. Tell the whole market, why don't you? But juice bar guy doesn't seem to understand. "Pregnant?" he repeats with a frown.

So Marcia helpfully demonstrates a ginormous swollen stomach with her hands and repeats the word, pointing in my direction. "Pregnant." Then she mimes eating. "Hungry. Good food."

"My sister has a good restaurant," he says. "I take you?"

"No," I say. "Thank you."

But once again, Marcia drowns out me and my protests. "Yes please, that would be great."

When the man immediately starts a quick-fire conversation in Spanish with his juice bar colleagues, I seize the opportunity to whisper my protests. "Marcia, we can't just go off somewhere with that guy! We don't even know him. He could take us anywhere! We could end up getting mugged or something!"

But she just shrugs and smiles in a way that makes me want to kill her. "Chill out, Jen. It'll be fine."

Before I can say anything else, juice bar guy is at our side. "You come now?" he says, and Marcia goes off with him straight away, beginning a conversation about the craft market, her back blocking me and my protests out.

I follow behind reluctantly, feeling nervous and resentful. I suppose I don't really think the guy's going to mug us both the second we turn into the maze of crumbling streets, but the thing is, I'm not entirely certain he isn't going to either and it's just so annoying, the way Marcia thinks she can make decisions for me all the time. I know this is Havana, and things are different, but I've got a bad feeling about this, and there's already enough on my mind what with Hannah and my meeting with Rachel tomorrow. Why doesn't Marcia ever listen me?

Very quickly we've left tourist Havana behind us and we're walking through streets of crumbling, once-grand buildings. Everywhere there's peeling paint, boarded up windows and piles of rubble alongside weeds growing out of brickwork. It's all so dilapidated, but there's also a feast of utterly amazing colours – terracotta and pink, blue and green of every hue imaginable – and incredible Art Nouveau beasts carved out of stone. In other circumstances I'd definitely get sucked into the wonder of it all, but there are people everywhere, sitting on steps, propping up walls, watching us as we go past and making the odd incomprehensible comment in Spanish, and frankly, it's a bit scary.

Juice bar guy replies to people when they speak with a shrug of his shoulders and a laugh, but as I don't understand a word he's saying, it isn't reassuring.

"Do you really think this is a good idea?" I ask Marcia when I can catch up with her.

"I'm sure it's fine," she replies briskly, but I can tell from her voice she's starting to get the jitters herself now. "Besides, we'd never find our way back out of here now if we tried to turn back."

Precisely.

Just as I'm desperately trying to memorise landmarks in case we do have to run for it, juice bar guy turns to us. "This the shop of my uncle."

We pause at what appears to be a barber's shop, where an elderly man is bent over a young boy in an old-fashioned barber's chair. Behind them, in the darkness, I can see stacks and stacks of paintings. "He is artist," says juice bar man. "You want buy paintings?"

"Not now," Marcia says. "Food first."

Juice bar guy smiles. "Si, food. Next street."

We turn a corner and he stops in front of a house. "Here," he says. "The paladar of my sister."

Marcia and I exchange glances. "But it's just a house," I say.

Juice bar guy makes shooing gestures with his hands to usher us inside. "Many Cubans make restaurants in houses," he tells us. "Good food."

"It does smell good, Jen," Marcia says, her tone persuasive.

In for a penny, in for a pound. "Go on then," I say.

Inside we find four tables covered in crisp red and white tablecloths and a smiling woman who looks so much like our guide, she has to be his sister. Perhaps everything's going to be okay after all. Juice bar guy says something to his sister, and she smiles some more, indicating that we should sit down. Then she comes over and uses her two words of English on us: "Fish? Chicken?"

In our minds these past ten minutes, we've put our lives recklessly at risk, following a total stranger to who knows where through dilapidated streets. And all for the sake of fish or chicken, no doubt served with rice and beans – the very same food we've had ever since we arrived in Cuba. Somehow I manage not to laugh out loud, but it's a close run thing.

Marcia stifles a sigh. "Fish, I think," she says. "I had chicken yesterday."

Our guide – who tells us his name is Pedro – sits at a neighbouring table and Marcia speaks to him while we wait for our food.

"So," she asks, "are Cubans happy? Do you like living here, the way things are?" She'll never win a tact competition.

Pedro shrugs. "It gets better in the last two years. Raul Castro, he says we can start some businesses, like this one of my sister's. Before this time, we can only work for the government."

Marciá is amazed. "Really?"

"Si. The young people, when they leave school, the government tells them what job they will do. In Cuba, sometimes we are like children. We do not make our own decisions. We do not even decide where to live. The government tells us this."

I think of my job and how much I enjoy it. What if I hadn't been able to make up my own mind about what I was going to do?

"Does the government repair your houses?" I ask, and once again, Pedro shrugs.

"If a building is going to fall down, they repair. But we wait for that. A long time."

Pedro's sister comes in with our food at that moment, rapping out something in Spanish to Pedro as she does so.

"Fish," she says, placing our plates of food in front of us. "*Buen appetit.*" She smiles at us again, then disappears, with another sharp word or two in Pedro's direction.

"What did she say?" asks Marcia, and Pedro looks slightly embarrassed. "She reminds me that it is not safe to say bad things about the government. Sometimes people listen."

"And what if they did? What would happen?"

"Then maybe the soldiers come and take us away. Put us in…jailoso. Prison."

"Jeepers," says Marcia, and for a while we eat our food – which, incidentally, is delicious – in silence.

I search for a change of subject and settle on an image from our walk to the restaurant. "Why were there so many paintings in your uncle's barber shop?"

"My uncle is an artist who cuts hair," Pedro says simply. "He makes much money from tourists for his paintings. Tourists are money. This is why I learn to speak English – I want to be a tour guide."

"Your English is very good," I say. "Did you go to classes?"

But before he can answer, someone comes to the door. He's a big man, and he fills the entire space, blocking out the light. And he's a soldier – dressed in army fatigues. Marcia and I exchange worried glances, and my appetite suddenly deserts me.

When the soldier rattles something off in Spanish, Pedro gets up and goes over to him, saying something in reply. Soon, both men are shouting, and I feel completely terrified. Marcia's fork is frozen on its way to her mouth and I lay my own across my plate, feeling sick. Did the soldier hear what we were talking about? Is he going to cart us off to prison?

And why is Pedro being so antagonistic towards him? Surely that will only make things worse?

The soldier begins to advance into the restaurant, moving past Pedro, his gaze sweeping over us as he goes. Oh, God, I wish we'd never got into this. I don't want to spend the rest of my holiday in a Cuban prison. Come to think of it, I don't want to have my baby in a Cuban prison...

Pedro follows the soldier into the back room, still talking in that loud voice. We hear the clump of the soldier's boots as they take the argument upstairs.

"Shall we run for it?" I whisper to Marcia, reaching down for handbag, but at that moment Pedro's sister comes in, still all smiles, as if absolutely nothing amiss has happened. She asks us something in Spanish – something we don't understand. Then she mimes, and I realise she's asking if we're enjoying the food. Just like any regular day, in a regular restaurant. *Everything all right for you? Very nice thank you.*

I pick up my knife and fork. "Si," I say. "It's very good."

Pedro's sister nods and smiles at us. "*Bueno*," she says. "*Bueno*." And she leaves us to it again.

"I feel like I'm going crazy," says Marcia, and I pounce, taking out all my stress on her.

"I think you must be, insisting we go off with a total stranger like that!"

"Don't take it out on me," she spits right back. "This whole coming to Cuba plan was your idea!"

True, but not the point. "You always manage to get us into trouble, whenever we go away."

"How did I know that woman's angelic-looking little boy in Florence was going to steal our money?" she protests. "The trouble with you is you hold grudges."

"Oh," I say furiously. "And you don't?"

"I don't think I do, no."

"How about the way you're behaving with Gary at the moment?"

"Leave Gary out of this! It's none of your business."

Pedro comes back downstairs. "You ladies are slow at

eating," he says, taking his place at his table again as if nothing untoward has happened. Marcia and I exchange glances.

"Where's the soldier?" she asks at last.

"Taking a shower," Pedro says with a casual shrug of his shoulders. "He is my cousin, Raul. It is not his day for a shower, but I say he can have one anyway." Then he sees the relief on our faces. "Oh! You did not think...? Sorry, sorry, ladies!" He laughs then, and calls out something to his sister, who comes into the restaurant. After an exchange of words, she lifts apologetic hands to us.

"Phew," I say to Marcia, but she just shrugs, not bothering to answer. Clearly, she's cross with me for my remark about Gary. Normally I'd probably apologise and try to jolly her out of her sulk, but today I don't bother, because despite the fact that the scary soldier has turned out to be cousin Raul intent on a wash, I still remember how genuinely frightened I was. And besides, I do think she's treating Gary badly at the moment.

When Raul comes down, dressed in different clothes, his black hair wet and gleaming, Pedro says something to him and it's clear from the way Raul puts his head back to laugh, that Pedro has related the whole dragging us to prison misunderstanding to him.

In broken English, Raul starts talking to us, asking questions about our lives in England. I let Marcia do the talking, and smile at Pedro's sister when she comes to collect our plates. When she says something to me, Pedro translates. "Elena asks if want to see her baby. He is sleeping upstairs. I tell her about yours."

Suddenly, I want nothing more. "Si," I say, smiling at Elena. "Si, por favor."

Elena indicates that I should follow her, and together we walk through the back room and up a staircase that was, at one time in its life, extremely grand. Upstairs there is a large light-filled room with a battered-looking sofa and chairs, and peeling paint on the walls. It may be tatty, but someone has made an effort to make it homely, with hand-made rag rugs and shelves of books. There's an ancient TV in the corner and several paintings that might have been painted by Pedro's barber/artist uncle. But it's the crib that draws me, and the baby Elena's lifting from it.

"Luis," she says, holding him out to me.

I've held many babies in my time, as part of my community worker role – at mother and toddler groups and baby rhyme-time sessions, at breakfast clubs and crèches. I've admired newborns and had cuddles while mum takes her toddler to the loo. I've smiled and cooed and remarked on growth spurts. But that was work, and it was nothing like this. "Hello, Luis," I say, then change that to, "*Buenos dias*, Luis!"

Luis is golden-skinned and warm from sleep, wearing nothing but a nappy. He has one tooth, which shows when he smiles, which is straight away. I smile back – that big, gaping smile people smile at babies – and Luis kicks his legs and waves his arms about with delight. He smells of milk, sleep and complete deliciousness, and suddenly I know that the big difference between him and all those work babies is that I wasn't pregnant then.

When Elena returns, I look up from the baby to say, "He's beautiful, Elena. Really beautiful." Then I look back at the baby, saying, "You are, aren't you? Yes, you are!"

He laughs at me, and I laugh back, feeling happier than I've felt in a very long time. But then I look up to share the moment with Elena and see Marcia, at the top of the stairs. Pain and fierce jealousy are etched on her face – just for the most fleeting moment, because she quickly rearranges her features to hide it. But it's too late – I've seen her expression, and I wonder, if Marcia never gets pregnant, whether we'll we still be able to be friends after my baby arrives.

Chapter Twenty-Two

Michael, 2000

Drinking a glass of chilled wine, Michael stood in front of a large portrait of himself displayed in the gallery where he worked. In it, he was asleep in an armchair, and it reminded him of the sketches he'd done of Diane when she was pregnant. Diane had been relaxed in sleep though, whereas it looked as if Rachel had caught him on the way to one of his frequent nightmares.

"It's a very revealing picture of you."

Smiling, Michael turned to John, his boss.

"Yes. She certainly caught me at an unguarded moment, that's for sure."

"You look as if you're having a bad dream," John went on.

"Yes," he said his tone non-committal. "I do, don't I?" It was always the same dream – starting with the sound of screaming, and an intense feeling of helplessness. He knew he needed to get urgent help for his mother, but he couldn't move his legs. When he looked to find out why, he saw that someone had tied him to his bed.

"You're a man of secrets, aren't you?" John said, and Michael forced a laugh.

"Because I'm frowning in one of Rachel's pictures?"

"Not just because of that, no," said John, his eyes still on the painting. "I've always had the feeling you keep a piece of you hidden from the world. Maybe I'm wrong; maybe you share everything with those you love."

And with that John turned his attention to Rachel who was standing on the other side of the busy gallery, speaking animatedly to a tall man in a smart suit.

"It looks as if the show's going to be a big success for her," Michael said, deciding it was time to change the subject. He liked John a lot and was very grateful to him for all his kindness, but he didn't need a father confessor, and he had no intention of telling him about his nightmares, his continuing lack of contact with his mother or anything else he kept firmly to himself.

"It was very good of you to give her the slot."

The opportunity for the exhibition had come about when another artist had pulled out at short notice. John had initially offered the exhibition slot to Michael, but Michael hadn't been confident enough about his paintings to accept it. The only work of his he really liked were the paintings of Diane with Kyle he'd shown for his degree show, and in the circumstances it just hadn't felt like a good idea to put those in an exhibition.

"Rachel's undoubtedly talented," John said. "But not as talented as you are. I still wish you'd agreed to the show."

Michael didn't answer. He was working full-time at the gallery now, trying to save the money to get a place of his own, and he just didn't have the energy to paint in his free time. Besides, Rachel was always there; wanting to do something with him after being cooped up on her own painting all day.

He wasn't really sure how they'd become a couple – he could never remember making a concrete decision about it. It had just happened. The night of the Degree Show opening, Diane had gone totally crazy, locking him out of the house and slinging his belongings out of the bedroom window onto the pavement below, all to the accompaniment of Kyle screaming in the background.

Michael had tried reasoning with her, protesting his innocence as regards Rachel and apologising for displaying the paintings of her, but Diane wouldn't listen, and it wasn't long before one of the neighbours called the police.

Forced to depart with only the belongings he could carry, Michael found himself outside Rachel's flat, ringing her doorbell. Rachel welcomed him in, offering tea, sympathy, and, to his surprise, her bed. The former he accepted gratefully, the latter he resisted until it became clear – after repeated attempts to speak to Diane – that she meant what she said.

"Go back to your little tart! And don't think for a moment you're seeing Kyle after this!"

Sex with Rachel was a revelation. Since Diane had either been pregnant or recovering from giving birth to Kyle for practically the entirety of their relationship, hormones and fatigue had governed their sex life. It had certainly never been very energetic. But Rachel was always up for it; initiating sex in every room and on every surface in the flat, as well as in the countryside, on the beach, up dark alleyways, and even in the store cupboard at the gallery. Sex became like a drug to Michael, allowing him to find forgetfulness and release, if only temporarily.

"Do me a favour, Michael," said John now. "Get yourself a solicitor; finalise things with Diane and gain access to your son. Start living again. Then you'll want to paint."

Michael flushed, grateful when John gave his shoulder a squeeze and moved on so he didn't have to answer. Ever since the split, Diane had been a total cow about letting him see Kyle, and it killed him to think his son was growing up without him, the way he'd grown up without his father. He'd hoped Diane would come round in time, but it didn't look as if that was going to happen any time soon.

John was right; it was time to act. He'd do it – hire a solicitor, set the whole divorce train in motion and get access to Kyle. He'd also find a place of his own – somewhere suitable for Kyle to stay. Rachel wouldn't like it, but her place was too small for a baby, and her paints and paintings were everywhere. Besides, their relationship wouldn't last forever. Despite the mind-blowing sex, and everything they had in common, Michael knew he just wasn't in love with her. They were drifting along, helping each other to block out loneliness. The day she fully realised that as well would be the day their relationship was over.

Suddenly, she was there, at his shoulder. "Hi, Michael, I'd like you to meet Sean Frobisher. He's just offered me an exhibition in London, isn't that great?"

"Congratulations." He was genuinely pleased for her. She worked really hard, and she deserved this success. And if she was getting it in a sense at his expense – because he hadn't been in a position to accept John's offer – then that was hardly her fault.

No; working as an artist was a risky way to make a living, exhibition in London or not. If he was going to buy a house of his own, he needed something steadier. And he could always return to painting later.

Chapter Twenty-Three

While Marcia's off having cocktails with Tim, Hannah and I eat in the restaurant together. She's reassured me she feels much better after her relaxing day, and I've entertained her with stories of our encounter with Raul. But now I'm determined she's going to stick to her promise to tell me the complete truth about her health. "Hannah, you keep saying the angina's nothing, and yet somehow I'm not feeling reassured. Is there something else wrong with you?"

Hannah looks down into her rum, swishing the dark liquid around in the glass, and something about her face tells me I'm about to hear something I'm not going to like. "Yes, there is. I have a heart tumour. It's benign, so please don't worry. But it does need to be removed. I'm booked in to have surgery when we get back."

I stare at her, the blood draining from my face. "Hannah, please don't tell me you delayed surgery so that you could come to Cuba with me?"

Her delay in answering my question is answer enough. And suddenly I feel so utterly selfish. I've been so wrapped up in my own problems lately – what else might I have missed? And what exactly are the problems I've thrust centre stage? I'm expecting a baby – a beautiful baby who might not look too dissimilar to Luis, bearing in mind that Michael and I are both dark.

"It was my decision to make, Jenny," Hannah insists. "And a week or two is neither here nor there. They assured me of that. I just wanted to forget about it for a while, that's all. And I did – it was such fun sailing along in that old car and dancing salsa in that club! But I didn't want you to find out like this, and I certainly didn't want to be a burden for you." She sighs. "I really ought to know better at my age,

145

didn't I?"

I make her tell me everything about the tumour and the treatment and the prognosis, and store the information away to talk to Marcia about when she gets back later. *If* she gets back, that is, for the way my other friend is behaving, it wouldn't surprise me if she doesn't come back tonight at all.

Lying in bed alone a short while later, I so hope she doesn't stay out. It isn't just that I want to talk to her about Hannah, it's because I care about her and Gary as a couple. If we were in England right now, I know I'd go round to speak to Gary; try to do something to help sort the situation out. But I'm not at home, I'm in Cuba. And suddenly, as exciting and as exotic as it is here, I don't want to be here at all. I want Hannah safely at home having her treatment at the earliest possible opportunity. I want Marcia to be talking to Gary, trying to sort things out. And I want to be with Michael, facing up to whatever the reality of my future is going to be once he knows about our baby.

I don't know what time Marcia gets back because I fall asleep waiting for her. But I know she does get back, because at some time during the night I wake up to go to the loo and she's a dark hump beneath the bedclothes in her bed across the room. It's a relief, frankly, and one less thing to worry about. And in the morning, when I tell her about Hannah, she's reasonably reassuring.

"If they said she'd be all right to come away, I'm sure everything will be fine," she says as we go down to breakfast. "The cardiac department is excellent at The Norfolk and Norwich, Jen; they know what they're doing."

This morning Marcia's wearing dark glasses, but I refrain from asking her what time she got in or for any information about her evening. I can't cope with it, frankly, and Marcia never has taken my advice, so there's no reason to suppose she'll start doing so now. Besides, I have my imminent meeting with Rachel Dewing to think about.

A part of me would like to cancel it, since it hardly serves any purpose now I've decided to tell Michael about the baby as soon as I get home. Whatever I find out from

Rachel, it's not going to make much difference in the scheme of things. But I've come all this way now, and seeing Rachel was the whole purpose of the trip. So I may as well go. At the very least, it will be interesting.

When Marcia and I leave the hotel, I'm in a right state. I don't know why the prospect of meeting Rachel Dewing feels so much more nerve-wracking than spending time with Diane, but it does. Perhaps it's because Diane's always been a part of the fabric of our lives with her hand-written instructions slipped into Kyle's bag with his clothes or her reminder texts – *Football practise 2.30, don't forget!!*

Until our expedition to Blickling, this was about the limit of our contact apart from the odd front-door meeting for handovers, but Diane's like a bunion on your foot, ever-present but ignored until your favourite shoes begin to rub.

Rachel's different. I don't know anything about her for a start, apart from the fact that she once liked to wear leopard skin print trousers and she's an artist. Oh, and the small fact that – according to Diane, anyway – she broke up Michael's marriage.

Marcia's no help to me – she spends the entire taxi journey slumped against the window and it's obvious she's got a hangover to end all hangovers this morning. Either that or it's guilt that's clamming her up, but I prefer to cling on to my five-mojitos-too- many-theory.

Frankly, it's a little uncanny not to know what's going on in Marcia's head when she usually makes me only too aware of it, and I can feel myself getting tenser by the second. This whole idea is crazy. What am I going to say to Rachel Dewing when we get there? I really haven't thought it through at all, and consequently I have no plans about how to steer the conversation round to Michael.

Suddenly I really wish Hannah were next to me in the taxi driving past the inevitable crumbling buildings instead of Marcia. Hannah would be calm; she'd take my hand and say, "It will be fine, Jenny." And when we met Rachel, she'd know exactly how to engage her in conversation to give me a little breathing space while I get myself together. But Hannah has angina and a heart tumour and she's resting back at the hotel.

"I was thinking it might be a good idea to fly Hannah back early," I say to Marcia, partly to break the silence between us. This isn't strictly true, because I've only just thought of it. But now that I have, it seems exactly the right thing to do.

When Marcia turns her head in my direction, I can see my anxious face reflected in her sunglasses. "She'll be fine, Jen," she says. "Even if you went back early, they couldn't bring the date of her surgery forward. Anyway, have you even asked her if that's what she wants? I was under the impression she wanted to be here. I know I do. It's ages since I've had this much fun."

"I take it you had a good time last night then?" I say, unable to quite suppress a slight note of accusation in my voice.

For once, Marcia refuses to be provoked. "Yes," she says, smiling, "I really did."

There's no chance for me to say anything else – which is probably just as well – because we've arrived at our destination.

"How do I look?" I ask when we've paid the driver.

"Like someone on the way to the scaffold," she says. "Lighten up. At the very worst you'll buy a painting you don't want and find out Michael routinely cheated on her as well as on Diane."

Oh, I do so wish Hannah were here with me instead of Marcia.

"Come on," she says, relenting a little. "It'll be fine. *You'll* be fine." And she knocks on the front door, dislodging some of the peeling paint as she does so.

We wait for what seems like an eternity but is probably only a few seconds, and then we hear footsteps approaching from inside. My heart starts pounding like the proverbial steam train. The door opens, and there she is – Rachel Dewing. At least, I assume it's her, but she looks a lot different from the photo on her website. In that photo her hair was shorter, not down to her waist like it is now. Also, her feet weren't bare, and she most definitely wasn't pregnant.

Beside me, I sense rather than hear Marcia's intake of breath. Rachel's wearing a loose skirt and top, but somehow the loose clothing is accentuating her condition rather than hiding it, and my heart goes out to my friend whose fate at the moment it seems, is to be surrounded by fertile women.

"Hello, ladies," Rachel says brightly, pretending she isn't aware of us ogling her baby bulge, "I'm Rachel; welcome. Which one of you is Jen?"

I step forward, collecting myself enough to smile. "I am. And this is my friend Marcia. Thanks so much for seeing us." Good, I can string words together. I can even hold out my hand to be shaken without it trembling too much. It's a start.

"You're very welcome," says Rachel, shaking Marcia's hand too and holding the door open for us. "It's good to meet up with some fellow Brits. Sometimes I wonder if I'll forget how to speak English!"

"How long have you been here?" I ask as we follow her along a long hallway to the back of the house.

"Getting on for a year now," she says, turning to smile at us over her shoulder. "I came here to do a language course and ended up meeting my partner. The language course was just a front to get a visa though; I really came here to paint. But obviously my language studies ended up coming in very useful when I hooked up with Miguel... He's an artist too – he paints scenery for the Gran Teatro. Here, come in; I'll fix you both a drink. Iced tea okay?"

Rachel Dewing might be pint-sized – apart from her belly – but she still manages to be pretty overwhelming. It's quite a relief when she pauses for breath and goes off to get our drinks, giving us the chance to look around at our surroundings. Not that I take very much in; I'm too busy trying to imagine Michael and Rachel in a relationship with each other. In *our* relationship, Michael's the one who does the majority of the talking, or at least, until recently he was. I'm thinking that a Michael/Rachel household must have been off the Richter scale, with both of them competing to get in a word edgeways.

"You do realise Miguel is Spanish for Michael, don't you?" Marcia informs me casually, looking up at the ceiling where a highly elaborate chandelier speaks of long-ago sumptuosity.

I hadn't realised any such thing, and the knowledge makes me shiver. Hell, that is spooky: really spooky. Straight away, I look round the room, searching for photos – anything to reassure me that the similarity between my Michael and Rachel's current one ends right there. But Rachel returns with the iced tea before I've managed to find anything. She's still smiling, and I wonder if she's always this happy. It's quite a contrast to Diane. And me too lately, come to think of it.

"How much longer are you in Cuba for?" Rachel asks, handing us our drinks.

"Another week," Marcia says, giving me a pointed look.

"Lovely," babbles Rachel. "You must make sure you get to one of the beach resorts. Playa Baracoa and El Salado are both very good. D'you want to bring your drinks to the studio? Actually, studio is a bit of a grand word for it, as you'll see. I usually beg a space in Miguel's workroom at the theatre if I want to do anything of any size."

Rachel's paintings are in a box room about the size of Michael's office, stacked against the walls. Since there is a distinct smell of damp around the place, I wonder if that's an entirely good idea. They are mostly vibrant paintings of old Havana and I look through them with careful appreciation as Rachel commentates on painting techniques and where they were painted. I like them very much, but they aren't leading me any closer to finding out anything about Michael.

"Have you got any paintings of people?" Marcia asks, interrupting Rachel in full flow.

"Do you mean portraits?" Rachel asks, frowning slightly,

and I cut in swiftly, deciding it's now or never.

"There was one painting on your website I particularly liked," I say, giving Marcia a 'leave it to me' look. "It was of a man asleep in an armchair. I loved the light and the colours in it." I take a deep breath to give me courage before plunging on. "It particularly attracted me because it said it was painted in Norwich. That's where we live."

Marcia replaces a painting of a tumbling down cathedral against the wall and turns to face us. "The guy in the painting also happens to be a dead spit of her boyfriend," she says. "It's uncanny, actually; they could be twins they're so similar."

God.

Rachel's looking from one to the other of us as if she senses something's a little off but can't quite guess what. Then she shrugs. "I know the painting you mean," she says. "But, I'm sorry, that picture's in the UK. Just as well really – it's a portrait of an ex, and I know Miguel would never tolerate me having a painting of a former lover lying about the place. Particularly one I had such a passionate relationship with. We just couldn't keep our hands off each other…" Her voice trails dreamily away, stabbing me with jealousy.

Rachel comes to with a blink. "Sorry," she says, with a smile. "I hope you have a relationship as passionate as that with your boyfriend."

My face flushes bright red, and she laughs, touching me apologetically on the arm. But before she can speak, Marcia cuts in again.

"Sometimes I think they'll go up in smoke the pair of them," she says. "Puff." When she moves her hands to indicate an explosion, my cheeks grow redder still. But this time it's with hurt, because I know full well what Marcia means. She doesn't think my relationship with Michael is so hot we risk conflagration, she means it will soon burn itself out.

Once again, Rachel looks doubtful, as if she's missing something. Then she shrugs. "Good," she says. Then, "But no, I'm sorry, I can't help you with that painting. Not for a while, anyway. I'm not planning to return to England for a while. Miguel and I are going to get married next month, you see. And then the baby will be putting in an appearance." She looks down at her belly as she speaks, and one look at Marcia's face tells me she's thinking, *lucky cow,* so I speak quickly. "Congratulations."

Rachel smiles a smile of genuine happiness. "Thank you." Then she turns once more to the paintings. "Let me see if I can find something similar to that picture for you."

We watch her rifling through the paintings for a few moments, then Marcia asks, "Why didn't it work out with the man in the armchair then?"

Rachel turns in surprise, as well she might since it's a plain nosy question.

Marcia smiles, all innocence. "Sorry, I'm just interested in why people break up. I recently separated from my husband, you see."

This is news to me, and I'm not really surprised when Rachel looks distinctly wary. Someone about to get married hardly wants to hear about break-ups. "I'm sorry to hear that," she says, then shrugs once again. "Oh, Michael had a kid who visited a lot, and that made things difficult for us." She wrinkles her brow with distaste, remembering, and I'm suddenly sorry for the child she's carrying as well as aggrieved on poor Kyle's part. I can honestly say that I've never resented him being a part of our lives. Why would I? He's gorgeous, and he's a part of Michael.

"And of course, I was much more successful with my art than he was. I always thought he was jealous of that. It's not easy, is it, when you're both ambitious? Fortunately, Miguel's quite happy with his work at the theatre, so it's never an issue with us."

I don't know how to reply to this, because I can't tell if it's true or not. I've never known Michael as an artist. But it doesn't seem quite right to me; I can't imagine him being jealous of her success.

But Rachel hasn't finished her list. "Then there were his

constant disappearances," she continues.

"Disappearances?" Marcia says the second before I can say it myself.

"Yes," says Rachel. "He was always going off somewhere or other, and he would never say where he'd been. Of course I thought he was having an affair, but he always denied it. Anyway, I'm sure you don't want to hear about all of that." She looks at us and this time it's a different look: challenging as well as questioning. "You came here to buy a painting, right?"

"We did," I say, picking up the nearest picture to me – a painting of a courtyard in Habana Vieja, with brightly coloured flowers growing up the ruins of a once-grand villa. "And, since the portrait isn't available, I'll take this one."

We're almost out of the door – with me having handed over considerably more American dollars than I expected to for the painting – when Marcia stuffs up. We've done the smiles, the handshakes and the thank yous, and Rachel's wished us a happy holiday. Then Marcia goes and asks, "That passionate relationship you had; who decided to leave? You or Michael?"

Rachel Dewing's smile instantly evaporates, and she freezes, one hand on the doorknob, her eyes suddenly suspicious and searching. "I never told you he was called Michael," she says. "What's going on?"

It is yesterday with the Cuban soldier taking a shower incident all over again, but this time it isn't prison I'm afraid of, but total humiliation. We can't make a run for it because Rachel's standing between us and the outside world. Besides, that would be cowardly and childish.

I so wish I could reach that door.

Marcia's quiet – *now* she's quiet. I guess she's leaving it up to me to decide whether to come clean or not. Nobody speaks, but Rachel's body language says *well?* better than words could. I lick my lips. "We know because…Michael's my partner now." My voice comes out really quietly but I can tell she's heard. I can also tell she's having trouble believing what she's heard, but that's not surprising.

"You're going out with Michael?" she says. "I don't understand."

Marcia finds her voice again. "It's simple," she says. "Jen's with Michael now, only she's afraid he's going to dump her or do the dirty on her. So…"

"So while you were in Cuba, you decided to look me up? Find out how it was for me?" Rachel frowns at us for a moment. Then I see the penny drop. "No," she says, "it's more than that, isn't it? You came here specially to see me."

"Well," says Marcia with a shrug, "we are having a holiday too."

"And I do really like your paintings," I add, and I'm not surprised when both Marcia and Rachel give me a look at that little gem.

"I think you'd better come back in," says Rachel.

The return taxi journey is every bit as quiet as the trip out was.

"Look, I'm sorry, okay?" Marcia says at last. "I wasn't thinking. His name just slipped out."

"Well, maybe if you hadn't got such a colossal hangover, you *might* have thought." God, oh, God. Humiliation's still washing over me in dirty great big waves. The walk back down Rachel's dark hallway was a walk of shame, it really was. There was no iced tea or polite chitchat for us this time.

"Don't have a dig at me just because you didn't like what she had to say," Marcia shoots right back at me, and although a part of me knows she's right, I still can't help feeling cross with her. I know she's going through a hard time at the moment, but so am I. God, so am I.

Here's what I learned – in baldly stated terms – from Rachel. That Michael always kept a part of himself locked away, out of reach. That he would never explain his absences, or, if forced to do so, he would come up with something that was clearly a lie. That as soon as Rachel suggested that they'd coasted along in their relationship for

long enough and it was time to put it on a permanent footing
– ie to get married – he couldn't dump her fast enough. That
she, Rachel, did so much for him, and he shoved it all back
in her face without so much as a thank you. And that, in her
opinion, Michael is an emotionally deficient commitment
phobe who will never stick to a long-term relationship.

And after I've sat there and listened to this heart-felt
tirade for almost twenty minutes and feel as miserable and
as fearful as it's possible for a girl to feel, what does my
best friend do? She goes and compounds it all.

"Jen's pregnant too," she says. "Twelve weeks gone.
That's why she's here, looking for answers."

I still can't believe she told Rachel about the baby, and
now, in the taxi, I turn to her again. "Why did you tell her
about me being pregnant?"

Marcia's shrug is so casual I feel like slapping her. "Well,
she knew everything else, didn't she?" she says.

I close my eyes against both her and the retreating
buildings of Habana Vieja. "D'you know how humiliating it
was to see the look of pity on her face?"

"Look," Marcia snaps. "I'm sorry, all right? But you
were the one who wanted to come here to sniff out the truth.
If she looked at you with pity, then in my view, that tells
you everything. She doesn't think Michael's going to be
there for you, and I'm sorry, but neither do I. But in my
opinion, that's good. You're better off without him."

"You know what?" I say, swiping at the tears running
down my face. "I don't want your opinion. I'm sick of
hearing your opinions."

"Fine," she says, folding her arms, and we don't speak
again until she informs me later that she's meeting Tim
again and she's likely to be back late.

I can't get to sleep that night, which means I'm very
much aware that Marcia's bed remains empty. And suddenly
I've had enough. Marcia can stay here to put a death seal on
her marriage if she wants to, but if I can change our flights
and persuade Hannah to see sense, then I'm taking her

155

home. I can't leave this place soon enough.

As it happens, Hannah's happy to fall in with my suggestion to curtail our holiday, and I manage to get us a flight for the following morning. It costs extra money, and what with everything I've already paid out for lately – including an exorbitant amount for a painting I'm never going to hang on my wall – my bank balance is going to be pretty challenged for some time to come. But none of that matters.

When the time comes, I don't know how to say goodbye to Marcia. We still haven't apologised to each other, and I can hardly say 'enjoy the rest of your holiday' when I know she'll probably move Timothy into our hotel room the second the airport bus has driven down the road.

So in the end I just say 'see you' and she says 'yeah' and we embrace awkwardly before I turn to go. And it almost breaks my heart, because Marcia and I have been best friends for so long. We've always been there for each other and now – because of the way she's behaving and because I guess she can't cope with me being pregnant – it feels as if that friendship is sliding over a cliff. And I can't even talk about it all with Hannah, because she's ill.

All the way home I'm aware of her concern for me; I can't help but be, because she keeps giving me worried looks and asking if I'm all right. But I just can't pour out all my insecurity and unhappiness to her any longer. At some point during our time away our roles have reversed. She needs me to look after her now.

I only hope I'm up to the job.

Chapter Twenty-Four

Michael, 2001

Diane was working full-time now, and often had weekend shifts. So what with her mother having recently been diagnosed with Parkinson's disease, Michael's desire to maintain contact with his son was suddenly useful to her. But he was far too delighted about this turn of events to be bitter, although handover times were still frequently fraught. This morning was no exception.

"We've started potty training," Diane announced on the doorstep, "so I haven't sent any nappies. And I don't want you to use them either please. The potty's under the buggy."

"What about at night?" Michael asked, his mind racing as he contemplated the logistics of this new development.

"I've been waking him up to have a wee just before I go to bed myself," she said. "If you set your alarm clock, you can get him up early in the morning too. You'll manage. I have to."

And with that, she kissed Kyle goodbye and was gone.

Sighing, Michael cuddled his son, who had automatically wound his small arms around his neck. Poor kid; he was only two years old. Surely that was too young for toilet training? But what did he know? And anyway, since Kyle lived with Diane for the majority of the time, Michael didn't get to take part in decisions about such matters. But surely common sense said that if Kyle was potty training, Diane ought to have dressed him in something a little easier to get off than a pair of dungarees?

The second the thought entered his head he became aware that Kyle was trying to tell him something.

Something that sounded a lot like *potty*.

"Come on then," said Michael, sprinting for the toilet, but it soon became very clear it was already too late.

"I'm sure she does it on purpose so we have a rubbish time together," Michael complained to Rachel when she emerged sleepily from the bedroom. "We need tracksuit bottoms and lots of them – something easy to pull off. And toys. The poor kid hasn't got anything to play with here. Let's go shopping."

"Great," she frowned. "The perfect Saturday. Trudging around kid's clothes and toy shops."

More and more lately, Rachel had been sulky and discontented; making no secret of the fact that she resented the increasing amount of time Kyle was with them.

"Well, listen," he said, trying not to sound too keen, "Why don't you take off? Get on with some painting or something?"

"But I haven't seen you all week," she objected sulkily, coming over to press her breasts into the small of his back, her hands ranging over his chest. "Why don't we put the TV on for him and go back to bed? You know you want to." Her hand dropped lower, searching for an arousal that wasn't there.

Michael sighed inwardly. Rachel had been insatiable lately. They'd made love the previous night until the early hours of the morning, and again this morning. There hadn't even been time for him to shower before Kyle arrived, and he certainly wasn't in the mood for another session now, even if he wanted to leave Kyle in front of the television, which he didn't.

"If we don't hit the shops now, we won't be done by lunch time."

"So," she said. "We'll eat out."

Michael turned round in her arms to dislodge her groping hand. "You know how you hate eating out with Kyle."

"Only because Diane's made him so fussy about what he eats," she said, her expression sour.

Michael shrugged. "He's two. All two-year-olds are fussy

158

about what they eat." He moved away, trying to think what he needed to take out with him, and when Rachel still stood there, her arms folded, he glanced over again. "Go on; treat yourself with a nice child-free day. It'll be hell in the toyshop; you don't want to put yourself through that. Come back later, and we can have a nice meal together. Kyle will be ready for bed about six o'clock, I bet."

But Rachel refused to take the bait. "No, it's all right," she said with a sigh. "I'll come. I could do with buying some new shoes anyway."

In the end they split up in town, arranging to meet in the Castle Gardens in an hour. When Michael got there at the appointed time, Rachel hadn't arrived yet, so there was time for Kyle to play in the play area for a bit. There was only a slide set into a grassy bank and a few bouncing bugs, but the little boy immediately made friends with a girl around the same age as him.

Listening to the happy sound of his son's laughter, Michael marvelled at how quickly his moods could change. In the clothes shop, Kyle had gone into a full-on tantrum when Michael strapped him in the buggy to stop him from rampaging around amongst the displays. Kyle had been having the time of his life among the dresses and trousers, and hadn't taken kindly to having his fun curtailed. The resulting screams almost pierced Michael's eardrums, and he was sincerely grateful that he'd managed to persuade Rachel to go off on her own for a while.

But now, with Kyle happily playing, a languorous peace was stealing through Michael's body. He was tired, and the sun was extremely pleasant. If he closed his eyes, it would be all too easy to slip into sleep.

"Hi, lover," a voice broke into his half doze, and he opened his eyes in time to see Rachel zooming in for a kiss. Automatically, Michael responded, expecting it to be a peck, but the kiss went on, turning into a lengthy snog. As gently as possible, Michael pulled away. "Did you get the shoes you wanted?"

Rachel pulled a face. "I saw quite a few pairs, but

159

couldn't decide between them. I need you to help me."

Michael suppressed a sigh at the thought. He really didn't care what shoes she bought, and he could think of lots more things he'd rather be doing with his precious time with his son.

Suddenly, he heard the mother of Kyle's playmate speaking. "Amelia," she said, "we don't put stones in our mouths, do we?"

Immediately alert, Michael looked over and was just in time to see Kyle pick up a stone, clearly intending to copy the little girl.

"Put the stone down, Kyle," said Michael, but too late – it vanished into Kyle's mouth as he spoke.

Instantly panicking, he hurried over. "No, Kyle! Open your mouth!"

Startled by his father's urgency, Kyle took a step backwards and bashed his head on the edge of the slide. As he opened his mouth to scream, the stone toppled safely out, but there was blood in his hair, and when he took an anxious look, Michael could see he'd gashed his head open.

Shit. Diane was going to go mental.

"Oh dear," said Amelia's mother. "That looks like a trip to Accident and Emergency to me. Poor little chap."

"Oh, no!" groaned Rachel, "that will mean us waiting there for hours!"

Michael turned to look at her, clutching his screaming son to him, his resentment unhidden for once. "D'you know what?" he said, "don't trouble yourself. You go off and buy your shoes." And then he strapped Kyle into the buggy and headed out of her life at a run.

Chapter Twenty-Five

At Norwich station I hold Hannah tight at the taxi rank. "I'll ask at work about taking the time off next week for your operation," I say, but she pulls back slightly to smile at me.

"There's really no need for you to do that, Jen, honestly. I'll be out for the count most of the time anyway, won't I? Just a visit will be good, when it's all over. I'll see if I can find out what ward I'm going to be on and let you know."

"And you will tell Luther about your…condition?" She hasn't yet, which might seem incredible unless you know Luther. He doesn't do bad news very well.

Hannah nods. "Yes, I will – just as soon as I get home. I promise. Don't worry about me; you get home. Sort things out with that man of yours."

Immediately, tears spring into my eyes. I really wish I hadn't gone to Cuba to meet Rachel Dewing. If I was insecure about Michael and me before I went, then that insecurity is multiplied by a factor of at least three now. But I can't say that to Hannah, because I know she'll just feel guilty because she first gave me the idea about investigating Michael's exes. So I smile instead, blinking the tears back, and hold open her taxi door for her. "I'll call you very soon. Take care."

Waving to her one last time, I get in my own taxi and give the driver my address. "Been somewhere nice, love?" he asks, and my heart sinks, because I'm so not in the mood for a chatty cab driver just now.

"Not really; just away with friends for a few days," I say, and then, spotting an air freshener in the shape of a Norwich City football shirt, I ask him how the team's doing and it works like a charm. Within seconds he's off; moaning about the manager and a dodgy refereeing decision, and all I have to say is 'yes', 'no' and 'really' every now and then to keep him happy.

If only all conversations were that easy.

By the time we pull up outside the house, the cab driver's sacked the manager and put forward a selection of three possible replacements for him. "Well," I say, paying him, "I hope they start to win some games soon."

"Would do with me in charge, wouldn't they, eh?" he laughs. Then he drives off with a cheery wave, leaving me to face my fate.

I let myself into the house. "Michael?"

I don't know why I'm calling out really because it's obvious he's not at home. If he were home, the bike would be outside for a start, and there'd definitely be some kind of noise on the go. But there's nothing but muted birdsong from outside and the distant hum of traffic on the ring road. Having spent the whole journey back from José Marti airport psyching myself up for a big reveal, I'm going to have to wait to deliver it.

Suddenly feeling utterly whacked, I sit down and look around me, refamiliarising myself with my home. It's so quiet, after the bustle of Havana, and the walls are so smooth and perfect – no crumbling plasterwork, no peeling paint here. I close my eyes, seeking peace, but my head's still a mad jumble of sights, sounds and information, and anyway, I'm never going to find peace with my impending conversation with Michael hanging over me. I might as well do something useful like unpacking.

But my suitcase is heavy, and there's no Marcia or magic porter to help me with it this time. So I leave it at the bottom of the stairs and take my phone from my bag. It's dead as a doornail because I haven't bothered to charge it, so I plug it in, waiting impatiently until it has enough charge to do something, hoping for a message from Michael. Which is really loopy, considering he doesn't even know I'm home.

I should call him; let him know. The sooner he gets home, the sooner we can talk, and the less chance there is of me going demented. But before I can, the phone springs to life, whistling and beeping with notifications for me, and when I take a look, I see that half of the messages and missed calls are from Gary.

Great. So, because Marcia hasn't bothered to tell him where she is, am I expected to lie to him now? Marcia's my friend, but so is Gary. And he doesn't deserve to be treated this way. Very reluctantly, I dial his number, and he answers straight away.

"Jen?" he says, "are you calling from Cuba?"

"No, I'm home. Hannah was ill, so we came home early. Marcia didn't though; she's still there."

"Jeez, Jen," Gary says. "What's going on with her? D'you know she didn't even tell me she was going? She left me a bloody note! Didn't even tell me where she was going."

I'm shocked. "I'm sorry, Gary, I had no idea."

"What's all that about?" he says, sounding agonised.

Stubbornness? Desperation to have a baby? Going out of her mind? All of the above? Poor Gary.

"If I hadn't called Michael, I still wouldn't have a clue where she was."

"You called Michael?" I'm surprised, because Gary and Michael aren't really friends. They haven't got anything against each other, it's just that with Michael and Marcia loathing each other the way they do, he and Gary don't get the opportunity to meet up.

"Well," Gary says, "to be more accurate, I called you, but Michael answered." His voice gets more distant, and I realise he's speaking to somebody else; somebody in the room with him. "It's Jen; she's home."

Is Michael there with him right now?

"Michael wants to speak to you, Jen," Gary says, confirming it. "I'll put him on. But first, do you know when Marcia's due back?"

"On the fifteenth." My mouth is suddenly dry.

"Right," Gary says, and he sounds so sad, my heart really aches for him. "Oh, well, let me know if you hear from her,

163

won't you?"

"Of course," I tell him, though I don't expect to hear from Marcia at all.

"I'll put Michael on for you."

"Thanks, Gary."

"Hi," Michael says, and he just sounds like my Michael – not some two-headed monster with a phobia about being tied down and a tendency to do disappearing acts. "You're back early. How come?" God, I love him.

Eyes up screwed up tight; I put all my energy into keeping my voice steady. "There…were reasons. I…I'll tell you when you get home. When will that be? Michael, we… we need to talk."

I expect him to make some crack along the lines of 'that sounds ominous' or something like that, but he doesn't. Instead, after a short pause, he says, "Yes, we do. I'll be home in thirty minutes." Then he's gone.

He wants to talk to *me.* Oh, God; this is it. He's going to dump me, two weeks before our fourth anniversary. And I haven't even told him I'm pregnant yet.

Every one of the thirty minutes creaks past agonisingly slowly. After ten minutes my nails are bitten down to the quick, and I've practically walked a trail in the carpet with all my pacing up and down. Needing something – anything – to fill the time before Michael arrives, I fire up the computer to check my emails. There's a whole lot of junk, but also one from my Head of Department marked Important Information. I click on it, expecting some boring meeting details or a reminder about putting in any leave requests by the end of the month. But it isn't anything like that; it's an official notice that redundancies are to be made in the department. Fifty per cent of us are to lose our jobs.

Shit.

With my heart sinking, I read on, discovering that we are all going to have to reapply for our jobs and that three of us are to be made redundant. *Three* of us. Which could mean no maternity pay, if it's me.

I'm still recovering from this blow when I hear Michael's

motorbike coming up the drive. Quickly, I shut the computer down. The prospect of redundancy is certainly bad news, but it's nothing compared to what Michael might be about to tell me.

"Jen?" He comes in and I hear him call up the stairs.

"Up here; just coming," I call back, and take a few calming breaths before heading out to the landing.

"Everything okay?" He's at the bottom of the stairs looking up at me, bike helmet under one arm, hair sexily tousled where he's just taken it off, looking gorgeous. When I hurry down the stairs and straight into his arms, the helmet falls to the floor with a thump. His arms close around me and I hold on tight. Even if he's about to dump me, I want to pretend just for a few more moments that everything's okay. To smell the *Michaelness* of him. To fit my face into its familiar place against his neck.

Oh but, God, I can't do anything to stop the tears, almost as if he's already spoken the words I'm dreading.

"Hey," he says, moving ever so slightly back to look at me. "What's wrong?"

"Hannah has a tumour in her heart. She's having surgery next week…"

"God!" he says, moving back in to continue our hug. "I'm so sorry, babe. That's terrible. Is that why you came back early?" He leads me to the sofa and we sit close together, his arm around me while I tell him about it. But all the time I'm talking, I wonder if I'm just delaying those fatal words of his; that he's thinking he can't dump me just now, not when I'm so distressed.

"And what about Marcia?" he asks, after he's assured me that surgeons can do wonders these days and Hannah will be all right. "Gary's in a right old state. I felt sorry for the bloke. Even more sorry than I normally do."

I know he means he feels sorry for Gary for being involved with Marcia, and normally I'd probably rise to his bait. But there's nothing normal about today.

"Marcia just wants him to change his mind about trying for a baby again, that's all."

165

"Well, my guess is, if she'd just stuck around here instead of swanning off to Cuba, she'd have talked him round by now. He wants a family as much as she does. They need their heads knocking together, those two."

"You're right," I say, "they do." It feels good to be in agreement with each other about something. But then he goes and spoils it all.

"I did my best to convince Gary that not having kids has its definite upside," he says, "but I didn't get the impression he was exactly lapping my words up."

I can't believe Michael's just said that when I'm just about to tell him about the baby, I really can't, and I stare at him, not bothering to try to hide how I feel for once.

"What?" he asks, sounding defensive. "You know I love Kyle, but—"

No, I'm not having this conversation again. Not right now. "Michael, please; listen for a moment. There's... something I have to tell you."

"It's all right," he says, "I already know about the possible redundancies. But don't worry; you know how much they think of you. I'm sure it won't be you who loses their job."

Rick, I think, blinking at him. Rick must have told him about the redundancies.

"At least," he goes on, "I hope it's not you. That really would be a blow. But then when shit happens, it really happens, doesn't it?"

I can't think what to say; it feels as if I'm missing a piece of information somehow. But in any case, a noise suddenly starts up outside, distracting us – a loud banging sound.

"What the hell's that?" Michael asks, and gets up to take a look.

I follow him. Which is why we both see the man with the big hammer; the hammer he's using to put a sign up outside the house. A sign that reads: *For Sale by Auction.*

I stare, utterly aghast. "What's he doing? Michael, stop him, for God's sake!"

But Michael just stands there holding the curtain,

watching the lump hammer thump down onto the post, and a dreadful feeling seeps into me like rot. "Please tell me it's a mistake, Michael? He's got the wrong address?" And I begin to move, heading towards the front door.

Michael puts a hand on my arm to stop me. "Don't go out there," he says, and the utter brokenness of his voice tells me what the lump hammer really told me right away. And suddenly I'm very scared.

"That's what I wanted to talk to you about. Though I didn't expect…" He breaks off, sighing heavily, and when he runs a hand through his hair, it accentuates the widow's peak that's started to form in the last year or so, making him look suddenly vulnerable. "The business has folded, Jen. I've gone bust. They're repossessing the house."

My heart feels like it's outside my body, lying exposed and vulnerable on top of my chest. I know about repossession from my work. There has to be months of non-payment of the mortgage. Solicitor's letters. A court hearing. "But they can't be… It takes months to get to this stage of the process…"

Michael can't meet my eyes. "I'm so sorry. I really thought I could make it all right before it came to all that. I had a potential backer, you see – this guy I met in America. He was really keen to come on board when I flew over to speak to him."

And suddenly everything falls into place. "That's why you missed Kyle's play, isn't it?" I say slowly, and he nods.

"Yes. Then, last week, the deal fell through. I've been trying to convince the guy to change his mind, but it looks like it's no go."

Outside the thumping suddenly stops. We hear the lump hammer being stowed away again in the back in the van, and the van doors closing. Then the passenger door opens and closes, and the engine starts up. The van crunches its way down the gravel, and then there's silence.

"Why didn't you tell me you were in trouble?" I ask. *Before I booked an expensive holiday to Cuba and spent a fortune on a painting by one of your ex lovers?*

"Because I thought I could fix it." Finally he looks at me. "Because it was my problem to sort out, and I didn't want to worry you if I didn't have to. Jen, I'm so fucking ashamed, I can't tell you."

The way his voice shakes squeezes my heart and I go over to put my arms around him. "Listen," I say with a confidence I don't feel, "it will be okay; you can get a job. And I might not lose mine; nothing's decided yet."

Michael holds me at arms' length. "Or we could just take off somewhere," he says with an excited light in his eyes. "See this as an opportunity rather than a tragedy. Why not? Kyle's sixteen now, and he's sorted with that course of his. We haven't got any ties. We could just—"

"No!" I wriggle away, turning my back on him. I can't, can't, *can't* hear this again, and even if this is the worst moment in the history of moments, he has to know now. "Michael, I'm pregnant."

The birds stop singing. There's a lull in the ring road traffic. Or so it seems to me, standing there waiting for Michael's response.

"Jesus." Out it comes in a whoosh of despairing profanity, and with it the rooks begin to caw in the beech trees and an ambulance goes past on the ring road, siren blaring. "It can't be true."

Already I'm crying. "It can. It is. The baby's due next July."

His eyes are searching my face, and I steel myself for the question I know is coming. "How long have you known?"

I could lie. Except I can't. "A month or so."

"Christ, Jen, and you didn't think to tell me? You just jetted off to Cuba?"

Since I can't tell him the truth, there's no answer to this, so I keep on staring at the carpet, the tears sliding down my face. Finally Michael takes pity on me. "Oh, shit," he says with a big sigh. "Come here." He holds me for a while, then he says, "Seems we can both keep a secret, eh? What a pair."

His hand strokes its soothing way down my back, and it's

just too much, him being nice, and I begin to sob properly, my body shuddering, and his arms tighten, holding me close. We stand there like that until I begin to calm down. Then he drops a kiss on top of my head. "It'll be all right, Jen," he says. "We'll get through this. And at least it's early days; it's not too late to do something about it."

What the fuck? Freezing, I move back to look at him. "What do you mean?"

"Well," he says, "we can't keep it, can we? Not with all this on our plates."

My tongue feels like it's stuck to the roof of my mouth, but I force it to work because I have to be absolutely one hundred per cent sure what he means. "Are you saying you want me to have an abortion?"

He doesn't answer. But he doesn't have to – the expression on his face is enough.

My suitcase is where I left it, at the bottom of the stairs. I move towards it like a sleepwalker and click up the handle.

"Jenny…" he says. "Don't be like this." But I trundle past him on my way to the front door.

"Please. We can work this out together. You know I love you."

I turn to look at him, the suitcase half way out of the door. "It's all just words, Michael. I don't know any such thing. Not when you can—" Tears are obscuring my vision, but I can still make out the hunched way he's holding his body. "I don't know anything anymore."

He begins to move towards me and my heart lurches because I want him to grab the suitcase from the doorway and forcibly bring me back. "Jen," he asks, "did you get pregnant on purpose?"

I look at him for a long, disbelieving moment. Then I shake my head and push the door open wider. "Goodbye, Michael."

Chapter Twenty-Six

Michael, 2011

"Dad, you're not seriously going out like that, are you?"

"It's a fancy dress party, kiddo. Humiliation and making a total tit of myself are essential ingredients for a good night out."

"Should be the night of your life then. If you don't get attacked by a bear who thinks you're invading his territory on the way."

Michael had made a real effort with his fancy dress outfit. Rick was a good mate, and turning forty was a big milestone. Besides, Michael had always enjoyed dressing up as someone else. "It's just a chance to let my hair down," he told Kyle now. "You're only jealous because you're not coming."

"Yeah, right, Dad. And you haven't let your hair down. You've spread it all over your chest. It'll need a mower on it soon."

Sometimes, Michael thought, his son sounded so much older than almost twelve. God only knew what he'd be like in another four years' time. He was already supremely serious about the way he looked, preening in front of the mirror and rejecting cheap trainers and clothes. Michael often felt distinctly scruffy beside him.

Mrs Graham will be here soon," he said, looking at his watch.

Kyle groaned. "I'm too old for a babysitter."

"Nice try," Michael said, just as the knock at the door came. Mrs Graham was their neighbour; a totally reliable retired schoolteacher who'd insisted they call her Barbara,

170

but who had stubbornly remained Mrs Graham to both of them.

"Hello, Michael," she said now, coming into the house with her knitting and a large bag of Murray mints. "Or should I say *Tom*?" She gave him a playful shove, and Michael backed away quickly in case she felt tempted to stroke the fake chest hair revealed by his open-necked shirt. Behind him he was aware of Kyle sniggering, and Michael shot him a warning look.

"What's Nita going as?" Mrs Graham asked, looking curiously past them both to see if she could see her.

"Ah," began Michael.

"Dad and Nita have split up," supplied Kyle. "Thank goodness."

"Kyle," warned Michael.

"Oh," said Mrs Graham, her eyes lively with interest. "I am sorry to hear that."

"I'm not," said Kyle.

With a feeling that it was time to leave, Michael shot his son another warning look.

"What?" asked Kyle, all innocence. "I'm only telling the truth. That's what you're always encouraging me to do, isn't it?"

Embarrassed, Michael lifted his eyebrows in a *kids, what can you do with them?* kind of way and grabbed his leather jacket from the end of the banister. "He has some homework to do, Barbara. And bed by nine-thirty at the latest please."

It felt strange to be going to the party on his own. Walking from the house with the clunky crucifix swinging against his fake chest hair, Michael tried to think of someone he could invite to go with him. The trouble was, with it being a fancy dress party; no one was going to be able to sort out a costume, even if they were free to go at the last minute.

The break with Nita had come suddenly, the previous night. He knew he shouldn't be surprised; with hindsight, they'd been building up to an ultimatum for months now

171

with all Nita's hints about her friends' wedding and honeymoon plans. The trouble was, Nita never shut up – she could talk for England, and somewhere along the line Michael's hearing had gone on a mini break to get some peace and quiet. Not that a marriage proposal was strictly an ultimatum; it was an honour to receive one, he guessed. Or if not exactly an honour, then certainly something that didn't deserve the look of horror Michael knew he'd probably worn when Nita had proposed.

When she'd left shortly afterwards in floods of tears, Michael had felt bad for her. But he'd also been relieved, and he knew he ought to have ended their relationship a long time ago.

When he arrived at the party, Rick – who was dressed as Roy Wood from Wizard, complete with long brown wig, a false beard and glasses – asked about Nita straight away. "Where's Nita then?"

"We broke up."

Rick's expression was knowing. "Don't tell me; she got broody."

Michael shrugged, looking around the party. "Sort of. She asked me to marry her."

"Poor, misguided fool," said Rick. "Mind you, you know you should never have got involved with her in the first place."

"You sound just like Kyle."

"Well, it's true, isn't it? If you ask me, you can't hack being alone."

Fleetingly, Michael recalled the dark space in the house following his previous girlfriend Sandy's departure and silently agreed his friend was probably right. Nita might have grated on his nerves with her constant chatter, but it beat having space for bad memories to creep in. Not that he had any intention of letting Rick know he'd hit the nail on the head.

"And you're too good at being on your own," he teased, diverting attention away from himself. "When did you last have a relationship? When Wizard was at Number 1 with

Merry Christmas?"

"Fuck off," Rick said good-naturedly. "I wasn't even born then. Anyway, I'm surprised you thought you had to wear that fake chest hair. Should think you've got enough of your own already!"

But Michael wasn't even really listening; his attention had been caught by two girls standing over at the bar. Both were exceptionally beautiful, but they were as different to each other as it was possible to be – it wasn't just their skin colour and their costumes, it was their expressions. The one dressed as Diana Ross looked bored and hostile, while the one dressed as Madonna looked...well, vulnerable.

"Oh, no," said Rick, following the direction of his gaze. "They're not for you. Marcia would eat you up for breakfast if she wasn't already taken, and Jen... Well, Jen's special. She's not the type who deserves to be chewed up and spat out by some lothario like you."

"I'm not a lothario," protested Michael, though he wasn't completely engaged in the conversation, being too busy watching the two girls. It was easy to pick out which one was Marcia from Rick's description of her, and briefly he wondered what had happened to turn her into such a prickly-looking creature. Then his interest moved on to Jen, in her Madonna cone bra. Rick had called her special, and she *looked* special. She also looked hot as hell.

The girls were glancing in his direction now; he could see Marcia was saying something to Jen, and Jen listening. Then they both looked straight at him.

"Come on, Michael," Rick pleaded. "Jen's so lovely, and she's just split up with somebody. Be kind and leave her alone."

"You fancy her yourself, don't you?" Michael said, nudging his friend.

Rick quaffed some of his beer, hiding his face. "Makes no difference if I do. I'm just Uncle Rick as far as Jen's concerned. Not stupid, am I? And I wouldn't want to risk our friendship in any case."

Michael's attention had returned to the girls at the bar.

173

Beside him, Rick sighed. "I can see it's no use. Whatever I say, you're going to go over and talk to her, aren't you? With Nita's perfume still on your sheets. Bastard."

Michael was beginning to feel irritated. "God, Rick, I'm only going to speak to the women. I'm not exactly going over to offer my hand in marriage."

"And never likely to either, that's the problem." Rick sighed. "Actually, I've got to be honest, she was just asking me about you too."

"She was?"

"Yeah. I said I'd introduce you. But let me make it clear; you hurt a hair on her head, and it's chainsaws at dawn, clear?"

"As crystal."

So they went over, and Rick made the introductions. "Jen, I'd like you to meet Michael, a mate of mine. Michael, this is Jen, a colleague of mine. She's an expert at making people happy."

"That's quite a way to be introduced," he said, smiling at her. "As an expert at making people happy."

He liked the way she blushed, obviously embarrassed. "It's Rick's way of saying I'm a community worker," she said. "And I don't always manage it."

Michael took his dark glasses off, wanting to see her better. "You don't always manage what?"

"To make people happy."

"Why not?"

"Because everyone wants different things, and you end up having to compromise."

"Doesn't sound like a Madonna kind of thing to do, compromise."

"No."

Rick had taken the other girl – Marcia – off somewhere. A slow song began to play. Without asking if she wanted to dance, Michael took Jen into his arms. It felt right; more than right.

"Why did you choose to be Madonna?" he asked after a while. "Apart from the fact that it's a good reason to wear a seriously hot costume?"

Her face was close to his shoulder, and he could smell the subtle scent of her perfume. "I always liked her music when I was a kid," she said. "Plus, I've got a photo of my mum dressed something like this, at the time."

"Is that your mum's original outfit then?"

She shook her head, her dark hair shining under the disco lights. "No, I made this myself."

"Is that because your mum still wears hers and didn't want you to borrow it?" he teased, and saw a shadow pass over her face.

"No. My mum died when I was young actually. I can't remember her."

He took his hand from hers to cradle her face. "God, I'm sorry. That was tactless of me."

"No, it's okay; you weren't to know."

But Michael could sense that it was not okay; that there was a part of her that still missed her mum, even though she couldn't remember her.

"My mum emigrated to New Zealand years ago; I don't see her either." Michael trotted out the old lie, but as he did so, there was a part of his brain that sensed he could have told this woman the truth; that he could have said, *My mum has a history of mental illness,* and it would have been okay. But old habits die hard, and it was too late now anyway – the lie was already out there.

"Don't you ever visit her?" Jen sounded genuinely interested, and Michael thought of all the visits to mental hospitals and squalid bedsits over the years. The times when his mother hadn't even known who he was.

She was looking up at him with compassion, sensing his emotion, and Michael knew suddenly that Rick was right; she was a really special girl. And once again, he was swamped by a feeling of lost opportunity. This, he sensed, was a girl he could be truly himself with. Except that he'd lived behind lies and half-truths for so long, he wasn't entirely sure who that person was anymore. "It's complicated," he said.

175

"Families so often are, aren't they?" she said. "My father remarried a year or so after my mum died. My stepmother couldn't pack me off to boarding school quickly enough. That's where I met Marcia actually; she was a day pupil. We helped each other to survive." She laughed suddenly, looking up at him. "Listen to us!"

"A little too serious for a conversation between Madonna and Tom Jones?"

"Maybe." Her smile was warm and shy at the same time, and had an underlying layer of vulnerability that made him want to hug her.

"So, why did you decide to dress as Tom?" she asked, and he recognised it for the conversation-changer it was – an attempt to lighten the mood and to get away from the heavy stuff. Just for a moment, he paused, and then he smiled, taking the bait.

"I thought I might get lots of pairs of knickers thrown at me."

Jen put her head back and laughed out loud, and he joined in, pulling her close to him and consigning the truth about his mother to the back of his brain where he'd so often tried to keep it.

"Listen," he said to her much later, "I'm aware that this is a very un-Tom Jones kind of thing to say, but I've got twelve-year-old son. And because of that, I have Mrs Graham, the babysitter. I need to pay her before I can ravish you. So, d'you want to subject yourself to her laser-sharp scrutiny before you even know what type of underpants I wear? Or would you prefer to wait round the back while I get rid of her?"

Despite his bantering tone of voice, Michael felt slightly vulnerable as he waited for her to answer. It was light enough beneath the street lamp to see a flicker of uncertainty crossing her face, and he quickly pulled her in for another kiss, shaping her to him the way he'd done for half the night on the dance floor until she went quite limp in his arms, her mouth responsive, her breasts in their hard cones pressing against him.

His fingers itched with the need to unzip, unclip and de-buckle – whatever it took to feel her naked flesh against his – and he pulled away, giving her a final kiss on the lips. "Go on; go round the back. I'll put the light on for you. See you in a mo."

She went, and he let himself into the house, switching on the outside light and reaching into his pocket for the money to pay Mrs Graham, finding only a twenty pound note.

"Hello, dear. Did you have a good time?" Mrs Graham was knitting in front of the TV, and didn't stop as he came in.

"Yes, yes thanks. Very good." It was always a pain, having to make conversation when he came in – to pretend that he wasn't slightly under the influence. This time, with his Tom costume no doubt looking exceedingly bedraggled and with Jen waiting outside, the process seemed more excruciating and drawn out than ever.

The knitting needles were still click clacking – Mrs Graham was in mid row, and didn't look like stopping until she reached the end of it. Through the French windows behind her, Michael could just make out the golden figure of Jen in her Madonna outfit. The poor girl would freeze to death out there if he didn't get a move on.

"What was everyone else wearing?"

"Oh," said Michael vaguely. "There were lots of Eltons, a few Marc Bolans, a Freddie Mercury…"

"I always loved David Essex myself." Finally, she'd come to the end of her row, but she still wasn't making any move to get up, her eyes all glazed and dreamy as she remembered her youth.

Michael held the twenty-pound note out. "Here," he said. "Thanks ever so much."

Finally she stirred herself, pushing her knitting into the knitting bag and standing up. "That's too much, Michael," she said, looking at the money.

"It's all right, Barbara," he said. "I haven't got any change."

"I've got some next door," she said. "I'll get it, shall I?"

"No, really, it's quite okay," he said quickly. "I've an urgent phone call to make actually."

Jen was moving around on the patio with her arms wrapped round herself over her pashmina. Jen dived back into the shadows, but too late; Mrs Graham had seen her.

"I'll leave you to get on with your...er phone call then," she said, her tone ever-so-slightly less friendly, but Michael couldn't bother himself about that. Normally he was very careful about introducing his girlfriends to Kyle, but somehow tonight he just couldn't help himself. Ever since they'd first spoken, he and Jen had been wrapped in a bubble of attraction, and he didn't want that bubble to burst just yet.

"Thanks again!" Michael called after Mrs Graham as she made her way down the drive, then he closed the door and rushed to let Jen in.

"God, sorry it took so long. I practically have to file a Guardian Arts review every time I go out. That's the trouble with having to have babysitters. Come on, I'll switch the gas fire on."

"How old did you say your son was?" she asked.

"Twelve."

"And where's his mother?"

Clearly Jen had had time to think of a long list of questions to ask him while she was waiting. He didn't blame her, but he wished they could wait. "Probably on a wild night out, as I've got Kyle. We're divorced. I'm single, I promise you. Now, shut up and come over here so I can warm you up."

In the glow of the gas fire he'd never got round to having removed when he'd had the central heating installed, Michael took off his leather jacket and put it, still warm from his body, around her shoulders. She hugged it to her, smiling up at him.

"I thought you brought me here to take my clothes off; not to put more on me," she said, and he laughed, pulling her down onto the hearthrug. "All in good time," he said

178

against her mouth, and then they kissed until the smell of cooking leather finally drew them apart.

"Hmm. Let's go upstairs before we get barbecued," he said, and she giggled as he pulled her to her feet.

In the bedroom, things quickly became frantic, with Jen's hands at his belt buckle causing him to moan with lust. He picked her up and laid her down on the bed, gazing at her in all her golden gloriousness.

"How the hell do you get that thing off?" he asked of the Madonna outfit.

"Undo the belt, then peel," she said, smiling up at him and reaching up to tangle a hand in his fake chest hair.

He laughed and tore his wig off, tossing it over his shoulder and giving his liberated hair a shake. "Don't you be discovering all of my secrets now, girlie," he said in his best Welsh accent.

Then they were kissing again, and she was all silken smoothness, her bare legs moving against his body, her luxuriant breasts finally falling from their cone confines to fit into his palms. Hell, she was gorgeous. What a wonder life could be. You went out with nothing but the thought of having a laugh and a few drinks and you came back with an amazing girl like this, a girl that seemed to get you. A girl that could do incredible things with her mouth and tongue… Oh God…

"What time does your son wake up?" she asked much later, wrapped tightly against him, the sheets tangled around their legs.

"Not usually before seven."

"I'll try to wake up before then," she said. "If you want me to."

"It doesn't matter if you don't," he said, for somehow it didn't. "Kyle will like you."

"Kyle? That's his name?"

"Yes," he said sleepily. "Not my choice."

"I like it," she said.

It was the last thing he heard before he fell asleep.

179

Chapter Twenty-Seven

I call Hannah from a lay by on the outskirts of Norwich.
"Hannah, it's Jen."

"Jenny!" Since we only parted an hour ago, she's clearly
surprised to hear from me. "Is everything okay?"

"No." My voice wobbles. "I told Michael about the baby
and…well, let's just say he wasn't happy. I know it's not the
best time for me to be asking you this, but can I come and
stay with you for a few days?"

"Oh, Jenny, don't be silly, of course you can." Her voice
holds sadness for me and also infinite love. "I am so very
sorry, my dear. Please drive carefully, won't you?"

Without the baby as an anchor, who knows how I might
have driven with everything that's on my mind? I can't
believe everything that's happened in the past twenty
minutes, I really can't. The house on the market,
repossessed. The next time I go there, it will be to collect
my belongings, and then that will be it. Not that it has ever
really been *our* house. It's Michael's, in his name – his to
take care of, his to lose.

What does it say about our relationship that he wasn't
able to tell me his business was in so much trouble? Or that
the very first thing he thinks of when I tell him we're having
a baby is how quickly we can get rid of it?

Suddenly an image of golden-skinned Luis fills my mind;
kicking his legs joyously about in his crib in that dilapidated
former mansion, and indignation rises up inside me, every
bit as strong as my despair. This isn't a *thing* inside me to be
got rid of like the junk in the attic when the house goes to
auction, it's a baby like Luis. A baby with potential and a
future. Only that future doesn't look as if it's going to
include a father.

For a moment, driving towards the Norfolk Broads and the comfort of Hannah, I harden my heart, trying to convince myself the baby will be better off without Michael, the way Marcia thinks it will. But then I think of Kyle and the easy relationship he has with his father and I know this isn't true. *Kyle.* The baby will be his half brother or sister. Whatever Michael feels, I'm determined to make sure Kyle has a relationship with him or her if he wants to. And I'm not going to be just another name on his long list of ex stepmothers; I'm really not.

When I finally arrive at Hannah's house, I've never been so glad to reach anywhere. My head's pounding from the strain of holding back emotion, and my whole body aches with tension. I desperately need the sanctuary and support I know Hannah will offer me.

But then I drive round the side of her house to find that a familiar car – Luther's Porsche – occupies my usual parking spot.

Hell. If I'd had anywhere else to go, I might have driven off again. But I don't, and in any case, Hannah's waving to me through the sitting room window, having heard me arrive. So I wave back and walk slowly round to the front door. When I get there she already has it open and she's waiting, ready to fold me into a hug.

"I'm so sorry to turn up like this," I say, going into those arms. She feels as fragile as a bird, and the quick glimpse I have of her face shows me how exhausted she is.

"Shh," she says. "Don't be silly. Where else would you go? And I'm sorry I didn't tell you about Luther being here when you called; I was afraid you wouldn't come if I did. But I've warned him to be on his best behaviour, so you mustn't worry. Come on, come in."

I hesitate for just a moment longer, then I take a deep breath and follow her inside. I may not want the man who once broke my heart to see me like this, with my heart broken all over again by someone else; but the future's set to be filled with challenges I don't want to face, so I might as well get this one over with.

"Come on," says Hannah. "I'll put the kettle on. I think Luther's out in the garden."

He is. I can see him through the kitchen window, seated on a bench by the pond, facing away from the house. "I'll go and say hello," I say reluctantly, and Hannah puts a hand on my arm.

"Leave it till tomorrow if you don't feel up to it today. Go up to your room and try to get some sleep. I can bring you some supper up later."

It's a very tempting offer. Except that I can't let a dear friend with an imminent date for serious heart surgery wait on me or even look this concerned about me. So I smile and cover Hannah's hand reassuringly with mine. "No, I'll go and speak to Luther. Don't bring my tea out. I'll come back in for it."

There's a gravel path down the garden, so Luther must be realise I'm coming, but he doesn't turn to greet me. He's looking into the pond as if there are fish to watch, but I know for a fact that a passing heron ate all Hannah's fish last summer. I go to stand by his bench, wrapping my arms around my body. There's a sharp wind whipping in from the surrounding fields, reminding me that Christmas is almost upon us. It feels very cold after Cuba.

"You know I'm furious with you for dragging Mum to Cuba," he says. "Except that apparently I'm not allowed to be furious, because Michael's just dumped you."

This is so very typical of Luther; he's always believed in coming right out with the truth as he sees it. Unless he's having an affair behind my back of course.

I sit down on the other end of the bench and stare bleakly with him into the empty pond. "I'd no idea at all that your mum was ill, Luther. If I had, I'd never have agreed to her coming to Cuba with us. You know how much I care about her."

He looks up briefly. "So I'm not the only sap she's kept in the dark?"

I shake my head, reaching out to squeeze his arm. "No, honestly. It came as just as much of a shock to me."

He sighs, looking at me. "And now you've come home to another shock."

"Yes."

"Want to talk about it?"

"No."

"Good." When I glance at him, I see he's smiling – a little boy let off the hook – and I smile back – if a little shakily – relaxing slightly.

"Are you going to stay here with Mum for a while?" he asks. "It would be good if you did. I'll come and visit as often as I can of course, but it would put my mind at rest to know someone was here with her."

Since my immediate future is a blank book apart from the final chapter where I give birth to a baby, I'm happy to nod. "If Hannah wants me here, then I'll stay."

"Good."

Suddenly, although nothing in particular has sparked them off, tears fill my eyes. My whole researching the exes plan has been a disaster right from the start. It has done absolutely nothing to help; Michael and I have quite simply broken up because he doesn't love me enough. He can't do, if he wants me to kill our baby.

Luther takes my hand in his. "Look," he says awkwardly, "just because Michael's met somebody else, it doesn't automatically mean you have to split up with him. For a man, sex can just be sex, you know. It doesn't have to mean anything; that's what you women just don't understand. Take you and me; I can't even remember the name of—"

"What makes you assume Michael's met somebody else?" I interrupt, angrily swiping at my tears.

He looks taken aback. "Well," he says, "because…" He breaks off. "Hasn't he then?"

"No!" At least, not to my knowledge anyway.

"Well then, why have you broken up?"

I might as well tell him; he'll know soon enough anyhow. "Because I'm pregnant with a child he doesn't want."

The words sound so bleak when they're out there, but I'm still surprised by the strength of Luther's reaction.

"Jesus! Then he's a bloody idiot!" he says, and suddenly the tears explode from me in great shuddering, messy sobs.

"Oh, Jen," Luther says. "Come here." And he gathers me into his arms, where I sob and sob and sob. Eventually, when his shoulder's soaking wet and there are no tears left to cry, I become aware of Luther caressing my back. Since his mouth is also buried somewhere in my hair, I draw back quickly, my gaze wary as I blow my nose.

Luther laughs. "Sorry; it always did make me as horny as hell when you cried."

This is such an outrageous thing to say, and it has the affect of breaking the tension. "You do realise how sick that sounds, I suppose?" I tell him, shaking my head. "What is it with you men? Why can't you just appreciate what you've got?"

"I put it down to not getting enough love from our mothers," comes Luther's flippant reply, and, since his mother is Hannah – who has showered him with love his entire life – even when he didn't deserve it; I give him a shove.

But then, while he laughs, I wonder whether this could be true in Michael's case. Did he get enough love from his mother? There's no way for me to tell, since I've never met her. If she lived in the UK instead of New Zealand, she'd definitely be on my research list. But then I remember it's pointless me having a research list any longer since Michael and I have split up, and I begin crying all over again. I'm still at it when Hannah comes out with our cooling tea.

"Oh, come on, Jen, dear," she says, taking one look at me. "Let's get you into bed. You're exhausted. Help me, will you, Luther?"

I try my best to pull myself together. "No, Hannah. I should be the one looking after you!"

"She's right, Mum," Luther says. "You do look tired."

"I am a little, I must admit," she says. "I didn't manage to get to sleep on the plane. There was this family with a young baby…" She breaks off, embarrassed by what she's said. "Oh, I'm sorry, Jen…"

"It's all right," I say, blowing my nose again and wondering if I ought to find myself a retreat for the next few months – a hermit's hovel, or a nunnery; somewhere I don't have to pretend to be anything but heartbroken. A place where every little thing people say to me isn't like a butcher's knife slicing through my heart.

Later, lying in my borrowed bed waiting for sleep to come, I think about the other big break up in my life – from Luther, on my wedding day. Marcia comforted me then. Well, I could hardly seek Hannah out, could I? Not since Luther was her son. In fact, I might never have seen Hannah again if she hadn't sought me out and insisted we keep in touch.

But it was Marcia who picked me up and kicked me back into touch that time; not allowing me to be alone for a second, taking me out for cocktails, watching wallowy girly films with me and buying me wine and chocolate.

Marcia has her own problems this time though. Besides, she's still in bloody Cuba, wrecking her marriage.

Chapter Twenty-Eight

Michael, 2011

Squeals of laughter drifted back to Michael over the sound of the rustling autumn leaves in the trees as he followed Jen and Kyle through the park. They were both on roller skates – it was Jen's birthday, and the skates were his present to her. She'd never had any as a child and had always wanted some.

Three months had passed since their first meeting at Rick's party, and the time had flown by in a breathless rush of dates and glorious sex. They saw each other four or five times a week – as often as their work allowed really – and as Michael had predicted, Kyle adored her. Watching his son race along with Jen on his skates now, Michael smiled. His son's voice was on the verge of breaking, and the days of being able to persuade him to come to a park were severely numbered. It was good to see him acting like a kid, even though it did make Michael nostalgic for years gone by.

As he watched, Jen moved in wobbling circles around Kyle, laughing as she did so.

"Yeah?" said Kyle, "that all you got?" And he began to circle her so quickly he was almost a blur.

"You're such a show off, Kyle," shouted Jen, and Michael laughed. It was a real shame Kyle hadn't had Jen in his life earlier; she was so good with him. Not that the other women in his life had been *bad* exactly, but Michael had always felt they were waiting for the moment Kyle returned to his mother so that they could be alone together. And if he'd sensed that, then sure as hell, Kyle must have done so too.

It wasn't just Kyle that Jen was better with either. She seemed to get *him* better too. Without Michael ever saying anything, she instinctively understood what a wrench it was for him every time Kyle returned to Diane's – even after all these years.

"You should marry Jen, Dad," Kyle had told him the previous evening before she'd arrived for dinner.

Michael was taken aback. "I was thinking about asking her to move in here," he said. "But I don't know about marriage."

"Why not?" Kyle asked simply. "She's perfect. You should make sure she doesn't get away."

But Michael knew it didn't work like that. His father had been married to his mother, but he'd gone away and Michael had never seen him again. And look at him and Diane. Marriage was a guarantee of nothing.

"Are you okay?" Jen had asked him the previous evening when Kyle had gone to bed. "You seem a bit…well, serious I suppose. Nothing's wrong, is it?"

She was so beautiful, so sexy; so incredibly warm and loving. And Kyle was crazy about her. Kyle was right; she was perfect. Things were perfect between them, right here, right now. If only it were possible to capture this moment, these feelings – to make them last forever. But it wasn't, and they wouldn't. Inevitably, things changed.

"I'm just a bit tired, that's all," he said, pulling her close to hide his thoughts from her.

"Well, let's have an early night," she suggested. "Not an *early* night, but an early night. Just to sleep."

They hadn't, of course. They'd gone up to bed and made love for hours, effectively driving everything – including all the doubts and insecurities – from Michael's mind.

This morning he'd given her the roller skates and something about the way her face lit up made him imagine her as a child, lonely at boarding school, opening her birthday presents with strangers, and the shaft of love this image inspired was enough to make him ask, "D'you want

187

to move in here with us?"

She froze, looking at him, still holding the roller skates. "Really?" she said, then she dropped the skates on the bed to throw herself into his arms; her look of pure delight almost enough to make him take Kyle's advice and to take the invitation one step further. Almost.

"Yes please! That'd be fantastic! Wow; that's the best birthday present ever!"

Teasingly, he reached for the roller skates. "So, you won't be wanting these then?" he said, and she laughed, whipping them out of his reach.

"Oh no you don't! We're going to the park this morning to give these big boys an outing!"

Now, in the park, Jen and Kyle had been joined by a little girl, also on roller skates. The girl's mother was pushing twins in a buggy and smiling at Jen and Kyle as they interacted with her daughter. When Michael caught up with the group, Jen skated towards him, her eyes bright. "Kimberley here's been giving me skating lessons."

"Yes," he joked. "But she's still way better than you."

The little girl giggled, demonstrating a turn to show exactly how good she was. In the buggy one of the twins – both boys, to judge from the colour of their clothing – called out excitedly.

Jen went over. "What is it?" she asked. "D'you want a turn?"

"Please!" laughed their mum. "Give me a few years before I have to cope with all three of them skating at the same time."

After the family had departed in the direction of the play park, Jen was still smiling. "Weren't those little boys gorgeous?" She was rosy-cheeked, the happiness glowing from her as she looked at him. "What a lucky women, having two of them!"

Suddenly a hundred different films began to play in Michael's mind. Kyle, as a tiny baby; inconsolable at Social Services. Blood pouring from his head wound at Accident and Emergency. Diane screaming out in pain, her face blurring and transforming into that of his mother. The dark red stain on the bedclothes.

He couldn't go through any of that again. "Jen," he said, "you know I'm crazy about you, don't you?"

"Well," she said, her smile not faltering yet. "I should hope so, since you just asked me to move in with you!"

She was still skating, and he reached out to take her hand, stopping her. "I want us to be together," he told her softly, watching the lovely smile begin to falter at the seriousness of his voice. "But…look, I've got to be totally honest with you; if you want to have kids, you'd better find someone else, because I've already done that."

In the distance, Kyle was doing another loop on his skates, whooping noisily.

"Don't get me wrong;" Michael pressed on; "I love being a father to Kyle, but…it's enough for me."

"Dad! I'm going on the climbing frame!" his son yelled, oblivious to the seriousness of the moment, and it was excuse enough for Jen to turn her face away. But not before he'd seen all that birthday zest and vibrancy drain away from it, like a flower closing up for the night.

Suddenly swamped by a deep sense of loss and guilt, Michael reached out to cup her face with his hand. "Jen…" he said, but she broke away and skated quickly off out of his reach.

"See you in a minute. I'm going to practise some speed skating."

When, a few minutes later, she hit a tree root and went flying, she cried. And Michael comforted her, pretending he believed her skinned knee to be the source of her pain.

Chapter Twenty-Nine

On my first day back at work, my boss Julia is in the office to greet me. "How was your holiday? I'm sorry you had such bad news to come back to."

I stare, wondering how she can possibly know about me and Michael, then realise she's talking about the redundancy programme. "Oh, yes. It was a bit of a shock."

"I'm calling an emergency meeting this morning at eleven o'clock. Can you cancel any unnecessary appointments? I'd like everybody to be there if at all possible."

"Actually, Julia," I say, "I've got a doctor's appointment this morning."

She frowns. "Is it urgent? Could you postpone it?"

I need this job, and I should be fighting tooth and nail for it. But since it feels very much like my teeth and my nails have already been ripped out with pliers, and the thought of the baby is the only thing keeping me sane at the moment, I need to keep my antenatal appointment even more. "Actually, it's a first antenatal appointment, Julia," I say, causing her to slosh too much milk into the cup of coffee she's making.

"You're pregnant?"

I nod. "Yes. But I'd rather everybody else didn't know just yet."

For just a moment, Julia looks as if she doesn't know whether to smile or frown. "Of course. Well, that's... Congratulations!"

"I realise the timing's not great."

She smiles properly at me then, putting down her mug to give me a hug. "It so rarely is with babies, is it? Well! What lovely news. Of course you must keep the appointment. And do pass on my congratulations to Michael, won't you?"

Michael and I have only spoken once on the phone since I've been at Hannah's. Neither of us really knew what to say, but the imminent auction of the house means we can't avoid making arrangements to clear it. I'm going to fetch my stuff at the weekend. I will break my heart.

When Julia releases me from her hug, her expression's more serious. "Jenny, I must tell you, your pregnancy won't have any affect either way on the outcome of the redundancy review."

I know what she means: that equal opportunities works both ways – the baby mustn't be allowed to mean that I am given more of a right to a job, just as I don't have any less of a right to one either.

"Yes," I say. "I understand that."

Later, sitting in the doctor's surgery for my appointment, I read the posters on the wall. This time two months ago I probably wouldn't have noticed all the ones connected to children, but now they are all I can see.

Busy Bees Nursery – your child's happiness is our priority! Are your child's immunisations up-to-date? Three telltale signs of meningitis.

Across the room, a woman with a belly so huge she looks as if she might produce right here and now, keeps an eye on her toddler who's playing with the bead sorter. He's pushing the beads along the twisted wire and making brm brm noises, and every now and then, when he comes into range, his mother strokes his hair. It's an entirely unconscious gesture – I can tell she isn't even aware she's doing it, and it speaks of love and of care and commitment – a whole style of life, her days and her thoughts mapped out for her. I can see the woman's wedding ring as it catches the light, and I imagine the little boy laughing as he's hoisted onto his dad's shoulders. What his look of wonder will be like when he's introduced to his new baby brother or sister.

The woman smiles at me and I smile back, my gaze

moving on in case I look like a child-hungry stalker. Another poster catches my eyes. *One Parent Family? Benefits advice here at the Surgery every Friday.* Will that be me? No job, no man, not even a proper home? Existing on benefits and agonising about how to make ends meet?

Just for a millisecond, I allow myself to imagine a different future – a future where there is no baby, and Michael and I are free to take off to Spain the way he wants to. I imagine the bike parked up somewhere in the mountains and me and Michael dressed in matching bike leathers, holding hands as we watch a glorious sunset.

"Ms Bright?" A nurse summons me from my fantasy and as I stand up I somehow manage to drop my bag, sending its contents scattering everywhere.

"Sorry," I say, flustered, hastily scrabbling around for everything – used tissues, car keys, trolley pound, mirror, phone...

"No, Michael, that belongs to the lady. Go and give it to her, there's a good boy."

I sit back on my heels as the curly haired cherub brings me my Forbidden Fruit lipstick. That he is called Michael seems more than a little harsh, but even so, I manage to smile and thank him as I take the lipstick from his chubby hand.

Then it's on along the corridor after the nurse to answer questions about when my last period was and the way I'm feeling. It all takes place as if I'm in a dream; as if I'm watching myself giving the answers from a place near the ceiling. But then the nurse gets me to lie back on the bed, covers my tummy with cold gel and holds a probe against it, filling the room with the shockingly loud sound of my baby's heartbeat. And, just like that, I let go of Michael's hand and zap right back from the sunset in the Pyrenees. Into my life – that of a woman who will have a baby next July.

On the day of Hannah's surgery, Hannah and I sit together in her conservatory while we wait for Luther to arrive. He's taken a day off work so he can take her to hospital. Hannah and I are holding hands on her cane sofa and looking out at the dark garden. I'm desperate for my morning kick-start cup of coffee, but I'm staying dry out of sympathy with my friend, who is nil by mouth.

We don't say a lot, because there seem to be so many things *not* to talk about – today's surgery: how it will go and what else they may find; my imminent need to remove my belongings from Michael's house, the fact that I haven't as yet heard from Marcia even though she was due home from Cuba two days ago… Lots and lots of heavy stuff. But it doesn't matter that we don't speak because silences between Hannah and me have never been awkward, and I allow my thoughts to drift, remembering the way Hannah sought me out after my split with Luther – how she dealt so efficiently with Marcia, my fierce gate-keeper – because she was so determined to see me.

I was in my bedroom, still wearing my wedding dress, my make-up smudged by tears. The dress was my fantasy dress – the one I'd drawn pictures of over and over as a child. It was perfect; beautiful And now it was never going to see the inside of a bridal car or a church; was never going to be swathed in plastic and hung reverently in a wardrobe in some spare room of whatever house Luther and I bought together in the future. The thought of all those wedding guests turning up to be told the wedding was cancelled filled me with hot shame, and I wanted my mother, even though I couldn't remember her.

I certainly didn't want my stepmother – the women who'd persuaded my dad boarding school would be a good idea for me because she didn't want me around, a constant reminder that my father had once loved someone else. But it never occurred to me that Hannah could be my comfort, and I was surprised when Marcia told me she'd come. "Luther's mother is here. I tried to get rid of her, but she won't budge. Says she only wants five minutes. Cheeky cow! She doesn't deserve five seconds! Got to be partly her fault Luther turned out to be such a snake."

193

"Send her up," I said, blowing my nose, inspiring a scowl from Marcia.

"You've got to be kidding me, right?"

I shook my head. "No, I'd like to see her. Please, Marcia."

"All right. But you're off your head, if you ask me."

I was entitled to be off my head though, wasn't I? I'd just had a telephone call from my fiancé's lover on my wedding day.

So Hannah came upstairs and into my bedroom, still wearing her fuchsia pink wedding outfit. There was a jaunty pink feather in her hat. As if in acknowledgement of its inappropriateness, she took the hat off and placed it on the bed.

"I can't forgive him," I told her quickly. "So don't ask me to. I know he says it was just a fling, but—"

"Shh," she said. "I wouldn't dream of asking you to forgive him, my darling. You deserve so much better than this, and I'm so deeply ashamed Luther can't see that. I shall have to see him again, because he's my son. But, Jenny, I can't tell you how sad it makes me that I won't be a grandmother to your children."

We clung to each other then, both sobbing, and that's how Marcia found us a few minutes later when she came to check up on me.

Now, with the first glimmer of daylight beginning to show through the trees at the end of Hannah's garden, I squeeze my dear friend's hand. "Will you be my baby's grandmother, Hannah?"

She turns quickly to look at me, her pale face transformed by delight.

"Oh, my dear!" she says. "Of course I will! Thank you. How lovely." She covers my hand with hers to seal the deal, our eyes communicating what we don't say with words – our hopes that the operation will be a success, with no further complications; and that Hannah will live to take up the role she has just accepted.

Out in the hall the front door opens. "Ma? Jen?" Luther

calls to us. "I'm here."

It's time.

The day drags by slowly. My work used to be so important to me. How many times have I worked through lunch at my desk before going straight to a meeting about funding for a new community centre or a funding application for new play equipment? I've begged people to sponsor youth projects, and I've argued the case for legal graffiti areas. Time and time again I've taken the initiative to get things off the ground.

But now – at least today anyway – I don't give a shit. God knows, I ought to do because with the baby, and everything crumbling around me, I really need to keep my job. But all I can think about is Hannah under the surgeon's knife. And of course Michael's face as I walked away from him. Or at least, these things are all I can think about until Diane phones to give me something else to worry about.

"Jenny?" she says. "It's Diane."

"Oh," I say. "Hello."

"I gather from Kyle that you and Michael have split up." Typically, she goes straight for the jugular, and it almost makes me gasp out loud with shock. It's one thing for me to know I've split up with Michael, but quite another to hear the words from someone else. Hearing the words makes it a definite, irrevocable thing.

"He said that?" I ask weakly, hiding my face from Julia, who's looking over.

"Yes, Michael told him apparently. Look, I realise it might seem as if it's nothing to do with me, but Kyle's really upset about it, so that makes it my business. Apparently Michael refused to tell him what went wrong, but Kyle's saying he hates Michael, and never wants to see him again."

I find my voice with difficulty. "Can I speak to Kyle?"

"No, he's at college at the moment. And in any case, if you're upset, then it's probably not appropriate for you to speak to him, is it?" She pauses before making another attack at my jugular. "*Are* you upset?"

What the flipping hell do you think? I want to yell at her, and suddenly I want to cry so badly it's like there's a bucket of water poised above my head ready to tip over and soak me. Across the room, Julia's still casting sneaky looks in my direction, and I know I have to get out of the office fast if I want to preserve any dignity.

"Can I call you back please, Diane?" I gabble, then slam the phone down and make a run for the door. Unfortunately, the emotion bucket tips before I reach the toilets, meaning I have to pass several people with tears streaming down my face. The building houses various different council departments including the Tree Officers, and as luck would have it, one of the people who witnesses my soggy flight is Rick.

"Jen!" he says, looking horrified. "Are you all right?"

Since I'm quite incapable of speech, I just shake my head and press on, and, once inside a closed cubicle, I put my hands up to my face and proceed to sob my heart out. This is how it all started, in Tesco – with me and a tester stick in a locked toilet cubicle waiting for my fate to unfold. Now I'm in another toilet cubicle dealing with the aftermath and it sucks, it really does.

When the outside toilet door opens, I make a futile attempt to rein my sobs in, but only succeed in reducing them to noisy, coughing hiccups.

"Jen? Are you all right? Rick told me you were upset. He was worried about you."

It's Julia – Julia who's a sort of friend, but who is, most of all, my boss. Julia who's a key part of the team who will be making decisions about redundancies.

"Come on, Jen," she says, "unlock the door. Let's go somewhere quiet to have a chat."

I so don't want to do either of those things, but I know I don't have a choice about it, so five minutes later I'm sitting in an interview room with an unwanted cup of coffee opposite Julia, who has an equally unwanted expression of concern on her face.

"Isn't that just what life's like?" she says after I've told her everything. "Or at least, in my experience it is. If something bad happens, it seems to attract other bad things. You get all the bad stuff in one indigestible dollop."

It's no surprise to me that Julia thinks this, because two years ago, she had breast cancer. While she was recovering, her rat of a husband ran off with someone else. Then her mother died.

"Look, Jen," she says now. "Why don't you take the rest of the day off? Go and visit your friend in hospital. We'll see you tomorrow."

I blow my nose. "All right," I say gratefully. "Thank you."

Julia fetches my bag so I don't have to face everyone, and soon I'm outside, near the market, wondering what to do with myself. It's far too early to visit Hannah; she'll still be in surgery. Finally I go into Jerrold's Department Store and up in the lift to the restaurant on the third floor, seeking anonymity amongst the refill coffees and the echoing chat of the shoppers. Without making any conscious decision, I buy a cheese scone and take it over to a table by the window. But when the waitress comes to fill my empty coffee cup I realise there's no way I can drink it. I can't eat the scone either; unconsciously I've ordered what I always order when I come here, but that Jenny has gone for now. This Jenny feels tired and sick, and it's time she stopped living in the past. My life's changed forever, and I need to face up to it.

Reaching for my phone, I call Diane back. "Sorry about rushing off. Is it a good time to talk now?"

"I've a got a meeting soon, but I'm okay for a few minutes," she says, and I take a deep breath.

"Well, I don't know what Michael told Kyle, but the truth is, I'm pregnant."

"Ah," she says. "And I'm guessing a baby wasn't Michael's choice?"

I really don't like Diane, I decide, listening to her cold, interrogating voice. She doesn't have any right to information about my life, unless, as she says, it affects Kyle. But my hesitation has been enough to answer her question in any case.

"Listen, don't take it personally," she says. "This is a man who totally freaked when Kyle was born. The whole thing just seemed too much for him. Anyone would have thought he was the one being sliced open to accommodate a bowling ball. He didn't have to say 'never again' – I knew it from the look on his face. But that suited me just fine."

I close my eyes, uncertain what she's getting at. "Surely lots of men feel that way, don't they? I mean, childbirth must be a bit frightening for them."

Diane's laugh is humourless. "Poor things, eh?" she says sarcastically. Then I hear her sigh. "Look, I'm telling you, his reaction was extreme. Really phobic. But anyway, this pregnancy – can I tell Kyle about it?"

I imagine the way she might do that, saying something tactless like, 'Your dad's got Jenny up the duff', and decide this is most definitely not what I want. "No, that's okay. I'd like to tell him myself. What time does he finish college today?"

"Two o'clock, I think."

"Okay, I'll go and meet him. I've got the day off. Goodbye, Diane."

I end the call, and when a couple with a baby ask if they can share my table, I abandon my scone and coffee and leave.

At two o'clock I see Kyle's group of friends emerging from the drama studio – a laughing, scuffing clique blinking as they emerge into the winter sunshine. Kyle isn't with them, and when I ask where he is, they say he's been kept back by the drama teacher for misbehaving in class. Feeling illogically as if this is somehow my fault, I perch on a low wall to wait for him. Finally, he emerges.

"Kyle?" I say, though I know he's already seen me, there on the wall.

"Hi, Jen." His eyes are down, avoiding mine.

"Have you got yourself into trouble?" I ask, but he just shrugs lanky shoulders, toeing a stone with his foot.

"Mum sent me a text to say you're pregnant. Is it true?"

Bitch.

"Yes," I sigh. "It's true."

He looks up. "So, what? Does dad hate being a father so much he can't stand the idea of doing it all over again, is that what this is about?"

I want to pull him into a tight hug. "Of course not, Kyle, don't be silly. He loves being your father. You know that."

"So, why have you split up then? Don't tell me it's because you two don't love each other, because I know you do."

It's my turn to hang my head. "I don't know, Kyle." I really don't want to cry in front of him, but try as I might, the tears start to seep from the corner of my eyes.

As soon as he sees, Kyle dumps his bag on the ground and comes over to fold me into a teenage boy hug. "Dad's an idiot," he says, his voice choked.

We cling for a while. Then I blow my nose. "His business is in trouble, Kyle."

"Yeah," he says, "like that matters compared to a new life; to my actual brother or sister. He's a dickhead."

"No, he's not."

He looks at me. "Why are you sticking up for him when he's treated you like shit?"

I don't know, except that despite everything, I still love him, and I don't want Kyle to hate him. He needs his dad, and Michael needs him.

"Look," I say, "whatever happens, I'll always be there for you, okay? You can see your brother or sister whenever you want to."

He nods. When he looks up, there's the slightest glimmer of a smile on his face. "I hope it's a boy. I always wanted a brother."

I try for a smile. "I'll do my best."

By the time I reach the hospital, I'm feeling completely

wrung out. It's not just the exhaustion of the pregnancy; it's all the emotion. But I'm glad I've seen Kyle, and I really hope he and Michael are going to be all right. It's out of my hands now though, because I can't influence Michael if we're not together. And maybe I never could anyway.

Suddenly I spot a familiar figure up ahead – it's Marcia, walking briskly from the staff car park, head down, arms folded, obviously on her way to start a shift. It feels so strange to see her here, I don't know why. After all, this is where she works. But last time I saw her, we were in Cuba, and although that's only a week ago, it feels like light years away. She hasn't been in touch since she got back, and since we're normally in touch by some means pretty much every day, I know she's probably still cross with me. Either that or she feels guilty.

But whatever the reason, because we haven't been in touch, she has no idea about the huge changes in my life, and I really don't feel like filling her in right now. For about a millisecond I consider pretending I haven't seen her, but then I realise how weird that would be.

"Marcia!"

She whirls round. "Jen? What are you doing here?"

"Hannah's had her surgery today. I'm just going to visit her."

"Oh, right," she says. "Of course."

"So," I say. "You got back okay then?"

A nod. "Yeah. Sorry I haven't been in touch. Me and Gary have been a bit caught up since I got back."

I sense there's more to come, and wait. Suddenly she smiles, her face transformed by excitement. "Oh, Jen, he's agreed to give IVF one more try! Isn't that great? I just know it's going to work this time."

"That's so great, Marse," I say. "I'm really happy for you." And I *am* happy, but somehow I just don't have the heart to put much energy into my reply, and her smile quickly vanishes.

"You don't sound very happy."

"Marcia…"

"This isn't still about Timothy, is it? Only that didn't mean anything; I told you. It was just a fling to cheer myself up, that's all. Gary never needs to know about it. You won't say anything, will you?"

I feel unutterably sad. "No, I won't say anything."

"Good." Marcia looks at her watch. "Look, my shift starts soon; I've got to go. We'll get together for a proper talk soon, yeah?" She starts walking, then turns back. "How's Michael? You told him about the baby yet?"

"Yes."

She stops. "You did? And?" But there's no need for me to answer – one look at my face is enough. "Shit, he didn't dump you, did he? Christ, what a bastard! I'm so sorry, Jen!" She pulls me into a quick, tight hug. "Shit, poor you. Oh, god, I wish I had time to talk now. But I was late yesterday, and I'll be for the high jump if I'm late again. You're all right though aren't you? Are you staying at Hannah's?"

I nod. "Yes."

"But Hannah's in here," she says.

"Yes," I say. "But I'm all right; honestly. You get off. We can speak later."

"Are you sure? I'll phone you after my shift. But look, you'll be all right, Jen. I promise you. Speak soon, okay?"

"Sure."

She gives me another hug, then hurries off towards the hospital entrance, and I follow more slowly, not looking forward to her phone call. I know Marcia; she'll offer me tough love, and that just isn't what I want right now. I don't want to hear over again that Michael's a bastard and I'm better off without him.

Because he's not, and I'm not.

But if that's true, then why aren't I fighting for him? Why aren't I trying to convince him that we should bring this baby up together? Why am I just passively letting my relationship with Michael slip through my open fingers? Suddenly I have a desperate need to see him. To make absolutely sure there isn't a chance for us.

But first of all, I have to see Hannah.

Luther's already at Hannah's bedside when I get there. He's holding her hand, and speaking in a relentlessly cheerful tone I've never heard him use before. "Look who's here, Mum!" he says. "It's Jen."

I take Hannah's other hand, doing my best to hide my shock at how very pale and frail she looks. "Hi, Hannah. How are you feeling?"

"As if I could sleep for a thousand years," comes the weak reply. "But I understand the operation went well. I'll soon be salsaing again."

"Er, I don't think so, Mum," says Luther sternly, and it hits me all at once that their roles have changed. Mine too. Hannah's always been the one to listen and to offer us both advice even if, in Luther's case, that advice has usually been ignored. But now she's the one who must be protected and cared for.

A nurse comes over. "Excuse me," she says. "I just need to check Hannah's vitals."

Luther and I both shift to give her room. "How nice for you to have both your children here with you," she says, her eyes on the machinery.

Luther and I exchange glances, and Hannah smiles. None of us correct her. "It's lovely to have my two favourite people here, yes," she says.

The nurse finishes her checks and writes something on Hannah's notes. Then she looks at us. "Just a few more minutes, please. Hannah needs to rest." And indeed, by the time Luther and I get up to leave, she's almost asleep.

"Fancy going to the canteen?" In the corridor, Luther has his hands in his pockets, jingling his loose change about. His hair's flopping boyishly over his face.

"I'm not sure I could cope with all the food smells in there," I say and he nods.

"How's that all going?"

"The pregnancy? Fine, thanks. They say I ought to stop feeling queasy in another month or so."

A family passes by, the mother and father each holding one of their daughter's hands. Luther watches them go. When he speaks, his voice sounds a bit emotional. "You know, I wish you and I had children to bring to visit Mum. I wish we'd never broken up."

I stare at him. "Oh, Luther…" I sigh. "It's all such a long time ago now."

"That doesn't mean I don't regret the way things turned out."

"You're just feeling a bit down because your mum looked so…tired."

He pulls a face. "Ill, you mean. She looks ill. And yes, maybe, you're right. It's so easy to take parents for granted, isn't it? Then suddenly, wham, they're gone, like my dad. Have you seen your father lately?"

"No."

"He doesn't even know he's going to be a grandfather?"

I flinch, looking away. Luther of all people ought to know how difficult my relationship with my father and stepmother is.

"You should probably tell him, Jen," he says, then, when I still don't answer, he breaks eye contact, looking round at the hospital signs. "Right, well I'm going to try to find the canteen. Thank you for coming to see Mum." And he kisses me on the cheek before lifting his hand in farewell as he strides off down the corridor.

Marcia rings just as I'm letting myself into Hannah's house. "Hi, Marcia."

"Hi. I'm on my break. I just thought I'd give you a ring to tell you I popped along to see Hannah."

I experience a tiny flicker of alarm. "She's all right, isn't she? She was asleep when I left her."

"It might take her a while to recover at her age; you have to expect that. But as far as I can tell, she's fine. Listen, about earlier – sorry I couldn't talk for longer. Are you okay?"

I shrug out of my coat, sitting down on Hannah's sofa,

suddenly feeling very alone. "No, not really," I say bleakly, the events of the past week swooping down to crush me, as they always do whenever I give myself any time to think. "I just can't believe it's all real; that Michael and I are really finished and on Saturday I'll be going to fetch my things." Tears start to stream down my cheeks.

"Oh, honey," says Marcia, "I so wish I were there with you. Dratted shifts! But look, I know it seems hard now, but as time goes on, I'm sure you'll come to see—"

"Don't," I interrupt; because suddenly I just can't bear to hear the words I know she's going to say. "Please don't try and tell me I'll come to see it's all for the best, because I won't! I love Michael."

"Well, maybe it's time you stopped loving him," Marcia says, and although her voice is gentle, there's an edge to it too. "Jen, he just isn't good enough for you; he never has been, and I think you should just—"

"You always do that," I say, despair breaking down any usual barriers. "You always think you know what's best for me."

"Well, sweetie, those outside can just get a better view of things, can't they?"

"Not when their view is shaped by prejudice, no," I retort. "You never have liked Michael."

"Well," she comes back, slightly more cool now, "if that's the case, then maybe you ought to ask yourself why."

"I don't know, Marcia," I say, "I really don't. You've never given him a proper chance. You decided you weren't going to like him before you even met him."

"I hate to remind you, but I'm not the one who's just dumped you; he is." There's a pause, and then she sighs and says. "Look, you're bound to be upset; it's only natural. Anyone would be in your situation, what with the baby and everything. But don't let that get in the way of you getting what you're entitled to. You've given four years of your life to that man, and you've been there for Kyle time and time again. That deserves a bit of financial recognition."

"Anything I've done for Kyle has been done out of love,"

I say. "I don't need paying for it."

"Well, I know that," she presses on, "and Kyle's a great boy; but you know what I mean. It's not right that you should just walk out of here with nothing when—"

I just can't face giving her more ammunition against Michael by telling her about the failure of his business. "I'm sorry," I say. "I know you mean well, Marse, but I just don't think I'm up to having this conversation right now. It's been a very long day. Mind if I call you back another time?"

But after we've hung up and I've got the peace I wanted, there's just me, alone in the dark in Hannah's sitting room – no Michael, no Hannah and not really any Marcia, if I can't bear to talk to her. I'm alone, and suddenly I feel it as strongly as I did at boarding school all those years ago; as if I'm staring out into a dark, empty wilderness with nobody in sight for as far as I can see.

Then, suddenly there's a fluttering feeling in my tummy and I quickly place my hands on my belly, trying to capture it. Surely, it's far too early to feel the baby move? It must just be because I haven't eaten properly today. But oh, how I want to believe it is the baby moving – reaching out to me from the womb; reassuring me I'm not alone at all.

Chapter Thirty

Michael, 2011

She looked like Grace Kelly with her sunglasses and her bare shoulders, singing along to the radio as they drove towards the coast with the top down on the car. He wanted to tell her she could enter a talent competition with a sweet voice like that, but he knew she wouldn't believe him because of what that shit father of hers had done for her self-belief a long time ago, choosing his new wife over his daughter.

Parked up at Hunstanton, he took her hand and they headed for the beach.

"Why's everyone walking in the other direction?" she asked, and she was right, they were.

Then a blizzard of flying red insects hit them. "Bloody hell!" he said, trying to swat the things off without killing them. "They're ladybirds!"

Jen was shrieking out loud, the ladybirds all over her like spots he'd like to guess she never had as a teenager, a red crawling rash, turning her polka dot.

"They're everywhere!" she cried, and she was right, they were, a plague of the things. He held out his hand to her to keep her safe, but there was no safe; nowhere to run to. No escape.

"Over here!" a man shouted to them from down on the beach, and they looked out to see a family marooned far out in the tidal mud. "There aren't any down here!" The man's voice reached them faintly from his island, and for Jen and Michael, with ladybirds in their hair, and ears and clothing, it was enough.

"Come on!" he shouted, pulling her along, and he could see the ladybirds crawling inside her shoulderless top, right down into her cleavage. Amazingly, she was still smiling. Squealing, but smiling, and Michael felt a sudden burst of love for her. She was the sunshine in the rain. Whereas Diane, Rachel, Nita and the rest would have been the thunder in the rain, blocking out all chances of rainbows.

When she stumbled and fell, he stopped to help, holding out a hand to pull her up. But she laughed up at him and pulled him down instead.

"Why, you little minx!" he said, and if it hadn't been for the family, he'd have ripped off her top to brush the ladybirds from her breasts with his bare hands. But the family was there, and besides, Jen was reaching out to grab a handful of mud. Next thing he knew, she was slinging it at him, and it made slapping contact with the side of his face like a wet flannel, stinking and oozing and no doubt full of fishermen's lug worms.

He laughed, throwing her back into the mud and kissing her as the mud dripped down his face, as passionately as if it was Tom and Madonna all over again. Sod the family, sod everything; he had to have her. He would have her – if not here, on this beach, then down some alleyway, or on some nearby heath.

He loved her so much, and there was nothing to be afraid of when her arms were like this, curling around his neck, and he could feel the gentle points of her hipbones as she pushed her pelvis up towards him. Something as good and as strong as this had to be forever. Just him and her with their love. Nobody else. No past, not even any future. Just the glorious, amazing present.

Chapter Thirty-One

"Jenny, as you know a detailed examination of the work of everyone in the Department has been carried out as part of the assessment process."

It's January. I've got through a bleak Christmas without Michael, sharing the festivities with Hannah and Luther, and now I'm back at work to fight for my job at the Assessment Panel. Ever since I entered the room, I've been trying for a calm, co-operative smile, but suddenly the atmosphere seems to have changed, putting the smile distinctly at risk. For a start, Julia's not looking at me as she speaks; she's looking at her notes instead, and every instinct screams at me that my boss feels as uncomfortable as hell.

"As part of this process, certain…anomalies have come to light."

Anomalies? My heart begins to race.

Graham Barker, the other panel member, fixes me with a penetrating gaze. Graham is the Community Safety representative for the area I work in, and we've never got on. He's a stickler for the rule book and totally lacks any creativity, and although I've always done my level best not to show I think he's an annoying, self-important busy-body, I'm reasonably certain he's quite aware of my true feelings towards him.

"Julia's referring to the trip to Blickling Hall you organised for the residents of Oak View Care Home last month," he says.

Oh, shit. Suddenly I remember the way I lied so casually to Michael about that trip. *We've got some money to use up, so we've decided to extend the area in special circumstances. I'm going to be visiting all the other care homes too.* Why did I ever do it? It's just not me to be so underhand, or to twist the rules as far as my work's concerned. The fact that I did so is a mark of how desperate I was feeling. And it didn't even do me any good – Michael and I have split up anyway, and now it seems as if my actions might lose me my job.

"Oak View is, I'm sure you will agree, a considerable distance from the boundaries of your agreed work area," Graham Barker continues. "Perhaps you'd care to explain why you initiated the trip?"

Can I lie? Say that Diane approached me? That she practically begged me to help her out?

"We know it was you who started the ball rolling, so to speak, because we've had a conversation with Mrs Brandon."

No, I can't lie. God knows what Diane may have said. And even if she hasn't said anything bad, there's no reason for her to lie to help me. She doesn't know the reason why I decided to approach her about the trip to Blickling. Besides, even though we got on tolerably well that day, I'm reasonably certain she still dislikes me. Just as I dislike her.

"Yes," I agree, my throat as dry as sandpaper. "I'm sorry about that. I...I let my personal feelings cloud my judgement there. You see I...I knew how low people can feel in such care homes, shut indoors day-after-day..."

"Did you have any reason to think this situation was any worse in this particular care home?" It's Julia who speaks, trying to help me out, I'm sure; bless her.

"No... It's just that... Well, Mrs Brandon is known to me, so I suppose I was more aware of that care home than I was of others."

Graham Barker snaps up my words. "You say you know her?"

"Yes."

"How? How do you know her?"

"She's..." *The ex-wife of my ex-partner.* Oh, God. "She's my stepson's mother."

Graham Barker frowns, and I sigh. "It's complicated."

"Evidently."

209

"Look," I say, with a rush of desperate energy. "I'm really sorry. Financing the trip was an error of judgement; I freely admit that. But it was a one-off, and if you speak to the people in the community, I'm sure they'll tell you how hard I work for them. I've helped a considerable number of people get back into to work by various routes, and I've made several very successful funding applications recently..." My voice tails off because Graham Barker's stacking his papers together as if to say 'Case closed' and Julia's looking at me with big, doleful eyes like someone preparing to give very bad news.

And later that week, she calls me into her office, and that's exactly what she does. It's official. I'm being made redundant.

"I'm so sorry, Jenny. You know this is the last thing I wanted to happen; especially bearing in mind your circumstances. But with everyone else having an exemplary record, it was just felt that—"

I interrupt, not wanting to hear it all. I've lost my job, that's all I need to know. A job I love; a job that's shaped my life ever since I started at the council eight years ago. "It's all right, Julia. It's my own stupid fault."

She reaches out to take my hand. "Is there anything else you want to tell me? I still feel as if I don't entirely understand about that trip you organised for Oak View."

"No," I say. "There's nothing. It was just a mistake."

Julia nods. I know she doesn't believe me. "Well," she says. "If you're sure. There will, of course be a redundancy package for you. I've made an appointment with Personnel for you tomorrow morning to go through the details of it. And obviously I'll write you a reference. There won't be any need for me to mention...what happened."

"Thanks, Julia. That's good of you."

It *is* good of her, although I'm not sure how much use it will be. Jobs in community work are like gold dust these days. I let those golden grains slip through my fingers and there's nobody to blame but myself. Hannah may have inspired me into investigating Michel's exes but she would never have suggested that I fiddle the books at work, which was basically what I did. And even though none of this is her fault at all, I know she's going to feel bad about me losing my job, and feeling bad isn't something Hannah needs to do right now.

Marcia was right about Hannah taking a long while to get over the surgery; she's as weak as a kitten, and nobody but me and Luther seem to be concerned about it. To the medical professionals, I suppose Hannah's just an old lady. And the thing is, she *is* now that much of her verve and spark have gone. She hasn't been out of the house for ages, and she can't even get stuck into her beloved gardening. I'm really, really worried about her.

Still, I suppose at least that's one good thing about my redundancy – I'll be able to take better care of her. Suddenly I have an image of me and Hannah sitting and chatting in her conservatory, her with a cosy blanket pulled up to her chin, me with the swell of my stomach getting bigger by the day. In limbo together.

"Why don't you take the rest of the day off?" suggests Julia. "Go and do something nice. I'll take a look through your diary and sort out any appointments."

I don't remind her that I was having the afternoon off anyway to go to hospital for my first scan. Instead, I blink myself back into the room and dredge a grateful smile from somewhere. "Okay, thanks, Julia."

"And, Jen, I really am very sorry."

Outside, it's raining. People have their heads down and their umbrellas up, moving quickly from A to B. Nobody's chatting or browsing today; half the market stalls haven't even bothered to open. It's a rainy, droopy day in Norwich, the buildings still weighed down by redundant Christmas lights. I haven't got an umbrella, and the rain's soon dripping down my neck from my soaking hair.

All at once I miss Michael so much it hurts. I long to be able to call him; to take the train to Sheringham, turn up at the gallery and throw myself into his arms. To hear him tell

211

me, "You'll soon find something new, sweetheart. Something better. Sod them!"

But the gallery at Sheringham's closed down along with the Norwich one, and I've no idea where Michael's working anymore. Or even if he *is* working. Michael's living another life now – one that doesn't include me. I know he's staying with Rick since the house sold, but that's about it. I haven't actually seen him since I went to collect my stuff from the house. And as for talking to him, one look at his closed-off expression that day was enough to silence me.

When I go to hospital for my scan, the nurse asks me, "D'you want to know the sex of the baby?"

I knew they'd ask this of course, but somehow I still don't know what my answer is. Do I want to know? Or is it best for it to be a surprise? Instinctively I know that if Michael were on board with all this; if we hadn't split up and he was a doting prospective father, then he'd have wanted the baby's sex to remain a secret. I guess that's why I feel so indecisive about it; there's still a part of me that wants to please him.

So when I look straight at the nurse wielding the ice-cold, jelly-smeared paint-roller-like thingie on my belly, it's something of a momentous decision when I answer "Yes, please. I'd like to know."

"It's a girl," she announces. "You're going to have a daughter."

Instantly a great wave of love swooshes through me. A *daughter!* I'm going to have a daughter! The sheer wonder of it makes me smile and cry at the same time. It's so amazing, so fantastic, and the only thing that would make it better would be having someone to share this moment with. I can't wait to tell Hannah. She'll be so pleased for me. Already I can picture the way her face will light up with love at the news, all her tiredness brushed away.

"Oh, Jenny!" she'll say. "That's fantastic! I'm so happy for you! What will you call her?"

"One step at a time, Hannah," I'll laugh or something

very similar. "I've got to get my head round it first!"

The nurse smiles. "I can see you're pleased to hear that."

"Oh, yes," I say. "Though I'd probably have been just as pleased to have learnt I was having a boy."

She nods, still smiling, her eyes fixed on the monitor. "I'm sure you would," she agrees. "It just makes it all more real, doesn't it? Knowing the sex and seeing the baby."

"Yes," I agree, smiling at the blurred image on the monitor as she shows me the various parts that make up my daughter.

"Look," she tells me suddenly. "She's waving at you!"

I peer where she's indicating, and laugh out loud with delight. For it does, indeed, look exactly like that. Foolishly – uncaring that it is foolish – I wave back. "Hi," I say. "Hi there."

And for just a moment, I forget all about the absence of Michael in the room. It's just me and my daughter communicating; sending each other promises for the future. I may not have a job, I may not have anywhere permanent to live; I may not even be able to promise her contact with her father. But I can promise her what she needs, and that is endless love. The rest will sort itself out.

Chapter Thirty-Two

Michael, 2012

"Mr Brandon? This is Karen Davies from Social Services. I'm just phoning with an update on your mother. She's been discharged from Hellesdon Hospital and she's relocated to Great Yarmouth."

"Great Yarmouth?"

"Yes. Apparently she made a good friend while she was at Hellesdon this time, and they're flat sharing together. I think she particularly wanted to live by the sea."

The call came through when Michael was at the Norwich gallery, and he had a sudden mental image of his mum shuffling along Yarmouth seafront, searching for old chips in the bins, in competition with the seagulls.

God, he hoped it wouldn't be like that. "Is she well?"

"Yes, she is, while she continues to take her medication. She was asking for you. I think she'd like you to visit if you have time. Would that be okay?"

It had been a very long time since he'd seen her, and a big part of him wished he could find it in him to say 'no'. Life was a lot simpler when she wasn't in his life, that was for sure. But he just couldn't do it.

"Yes, that's fine. Is this Saturday any good?"

"I'll contact her to ask, shall I?"

"If you would."

"All right, I'll let you know as soon as I've been in touch with her. Goodbye, Mr Brandon."

The social worker phoned back quickly. Saturday afternoon at one-thirty would be fine, and she gave him the address. He only remembered when he caught sight of Jen's bridesmaid dress on her side of the wardrobe the following morning, that it was Marcia and Gary's wedding on Saturday.

"Shit!" he said, and phoned the social worker back as soon as he could to try and rearrange the visit. But the social worker had gone on annual leave, and nobody seemed to have his mother's details. There was nothing for it but to disappoint someone.

Jen was annoyed. "What? You've arranged a meeting for Saturday afternoon? But you've known about the wedding for months! I can't believe it."

He couldn't either, if he were honest. After all, he'd listened to enough angst about bridesmaid dress designs. The prospect of seeing his mother again had just wiped everything else from his mind; but he couldn't tell Jen that.

"Look, I'm really sorry. I promise you, I'll be as quick as I can. You'll hardly miss me." But she didn't look convinced, and he couldn't say he blamed her.

En route to Great Yarmouth on Saturday, Michael wondered about the friend his mother had hooked up with. There'd never been any mention of a friend when he'd visited her over the past few years. He hoped it was someone who'd be good for her.

Edward Street was just off the seafront behind an amusement arcade – a row of dilapidated terraced buildings that had once accommodated tourists in the holiday heyday of the town. Now it was home to an assortment of bleak bedsits and boarding houses aimed at benefit claimants. Scanning the house numbers for 47B, Michael thought his mother had probably lived in worse places. She'd also lived in better places too, and if her health was really improved, then maybe it was time to help her in some way? He'd thought about doing so before, but it was difficult to help someone hell-bent on self-destruction. And she hadn't always seemed to know who he was when he visited her. Besides, there was no guarantee she'd accept help from him anyway. The only predictable thing about his mother was her unpredictability.

215

The paintwork on number 47 was cracked and blistered by the elements. There was a line of yellowing plastic doorbells on the wall next to the door, and all but Flat B had names written beside them – Allen, James, Carter. Not very hopefully, Michael pressed the bell for Flat B and heard it ringing in some distant part of the house. At least it was working – that was something.

The sound of footsteps clumping on wooden floorboards reached his ears – surely too heavy to be those of his mother? The door opened, and a heavily built man with tattooed arms looked out at him.

"Yes?"

Michael was disconcerted. Surely this couldn't be the flatmate? Had he come to the right address?

"Sorry, mate," he said. "I'm not sure if I've rung the right bell. I'm looking for Linda Brandon?"

"She does live here," said the tattooed hulk at the door in a broad Norfolk accent. "But she don't want to buy anything."

This *must* be the flatmate. Blimey. What had his mum got herself into now?

"I'm not here to sell anything; I've just come to visit. I'm Linda's son. She's expecting me."

Uncertainty crossed the man's features. "Son? Linda hasn't got no son."

"Well, actually," he started, but the hulk turned his head away to yell down the hallway.

"Linda! There's someone here says he's your son!"

A door opened, and Michael heard the sound of shuffling feet approaching.

"You never said anything about having a son," the man said, his face still turned away from Michael, letting the door go so that it swung open.

Feeling about twelve, or maybe even six, Michael looked down the hallway towards his mother, trying to assess her the way a stranger would. She'd put a little weight on since he saw her last – her jeans were straining over the swell of her stomach. Her fingers were, as always, nicotine-stained, and her hair was over-long and needed a cut. But…it was washed and brushed, and there was a pink hue to her cheeks instead of the usual unhealthy pallor. As unlikely as it seemed, maybe this man was good for her?

"Hello," she said, and when she smiled at him, a tidal wave of emotion shoved everything else away. It was so rare to see her smile, and he certainly couldn't remember the last time she'd smiled at him.

"It's good to see you," he said, his voice cracking a little with emotion, and, stepping into the hallway he gave her a hug.

Despite the extra weight, she felt frail, and despite the smile, she held her body stiffly away from him. Stupid; so stupid, to be hurt. What did he expect, after all? He could barely remember ever being held by her, not even when he was a small child. And she was still her; albeit a happier version of herself. He ought to be grateful for that. He *was* grateful for that.

"You didn't say you had a son," the hulk said again, and Michael drew back, expertly hiding his feelings of disappointment and vulnerability.

"Don't always remember I have," his mother stated simply, and Michael nodded.

"She doesn't," he confirmed. "But you look great, Mum; you really do."

She smiled again, reaching out to take the man's hand. "Got Ronnie here to thank for that," she said coyly.

Ronnie grinned, a huge open-mouthed grin that showed a few missing teeth but what looked like a good heart. "Linda and me made a deal," he told Michael. "She takes her pills, and I take mine. Regular as clockwork."

"That's great," Michael said. And it was. Maybe if this state of affairs continued, his mother would stay healthy and happy. Maybe she'd always remember who he was when he visited.

That minute or so on the doorstep proved to be the best part of Michael's visit. Inside the flat, sitting in one of the mismatched armchairs while Ronnie made tea for them all,

217

Michael struggled to think of something to say. As usual, his mother seemed to feel no inclination to start a conversation with him; there were no questions about any aspect of his life. But why would there be? She didn't really know him. She'd never met Kyle, she didn't even know about Jen, or his work. Everything had always been about her.

And if he brought any of those parts of him up, then it would be natural to follow it up with introductions. And that would involve the unravelling of a lifetime of lies and untruths. So instead, Michael made conversation about Great Yarmouth and his mother's plans for the flat, and told himself it was best to wait. Hopefully her improved condition would last, but there were no guarantees this would be the case – he should know that better than anybody. He'd wait and see. And if things continued to improve, he'd think about what to do.

After half an hour, with all his conversational gambits used up, and his mum and Ronnie silently holding hands on the sofa, Michael told them he had a wedding to go to. She didn't get up to see him off, and he didn't attempt to hug her again. It was just, "See you, son." "Yes, see you very soon, Mum. Goodbye, Ronnie." And then he left.

Outside, he stood on the pavement, closing his eyes and taking a deep breath, hands shaking as the emotion returned. Why did she always have this affect on him? Even happy, as she was at the moment? Would it always be like that? Maybe not, if he saw her more frequently.

"You all right, mate?"

Startled, Michael opened his eyes to see a grey-faced man in a hoodie addressing him. He was over-thin, eyes dark in his gaunt face – a drug-user, by the look of him. There was something familiar about him, but then Michael had seen plenty of people like him over the years. Wasted, hopeless, washed-up. And to have such a person ask after *him* with concern; it was ironic in the extreme, but it also inspired hope in human nature, he supposed.

"Yes, thanks for asking, I'm fine," he said, but the man was narrowing his gaze, staring right at him.

"I know, you, don't I?"

Michael shook his head. "I don't think so, no," he began, but then the man smiled and it was as if the sun had come out from behind dark clouds, revealing an image of him as he'd once been. "Jason?" Michael said, incredulously. "Is it you?"

"Michael Brandon, as I live and breathe!" confirmed the man, slapping him on the back and making himself cough in the process.

"Jeez! It's good to see you!" Jason said after the coughing fit had subsided.

Michael felt his blood run cold. There was nothing good for him about seeing Jason again, and certainly not here, like this.

Jason was fumbling in his pocket, bringing out a dog-eared packet of cigarettes. "Christ, I can't believe it! Michael Brandon! Haven't seen you since I don't know when. Got narked with me, didn't you? When I started going out with Tessa."

Unwelcome memories crawled back into Michael's brain; Tessa breaking the news to him, her face sullen, refusing to make eye contact. The way he'd seemed to bump into her and Jason whenever he went into town, almost as if they'd got some sort of inside information into his movements. Seeing the pair of them kissing in the Memorial Gardens. At a music festival. In a pub.

"How is Tessa?" he asked now, repressing a desire to shoulder Jason out of the way so he could get to his car, parked on a meter on the seafront. "Didn't I hear you two got married?"

Jason's cigarette was alight now, its tip glowing as he inhaled on it deeply, his cheeks concave with the force of the suck. "Yeah, we got married. She died though, a while back."

Michael couldn't believe it. "She died?"

Another long suck as Jason nodded. "Yeah. Overdosed on heroin. Coroner said it was an accident." He shrugged. "Never know if he was right, will I?"

Michael remembered kissing Tessa in the city, the day he'd seen his mum with that carrier bag; the day Tessa and Jason had first met. How warm and alive her body had been, pressing urgently against him, returning his kisses kiss for kiss. And now she was dead? Had been dead for years? How was that even possible?

"What brings you to these parts anyway?" Jason asked, the subject of Tessa and her early demise obviously concluded as far as he was concerned.

Michael, still struggling with his thoughts, looked at him. Jason was the worst kind of low life; he always had been. What part had he played in Tessa's death? It was all too easy to imagine that he *had* played a part, getting her hooked on heroin in the first place.

"I know," said Jason suddenly with a delighted smile, "it's your crazy mum, isn't it? She lives round here!"

"No," said Michael quickly, but Jason laughed.

"Go on, I bet she does! Only druggies and loonies live in this street!"

Michael moved past him. "I've got to go, Jason," he said.

"Or maybe she's both, eh?" Jason called after him. "A druggy and a loony?"

At the wedding reception, Michael saw Jen before she saw him. She looked beautiful in her violet-coloured dress, with delicate white flowers in her hair; like something pure and precious. He was so lucky to have her in his life. If she looks round at me before I'm level with the buffet table, I'll ask her to marry me, he thought, his heart thumping as he stepped further into the room.

But Jen didn't turn. As he watched, Marcia went over to her and whispered something into her ear. Then, the next moment, the two of them went off somewhere together.

Chapter Thirty-Three

Hannah and I are out in the garden with our coats on, stargazing. I've always loved the night sky, but ever since I moved in with Hannah, I've learned a lot more about it. She's taught me to pick out several different constellations, but I particularly like to see Venus.

"The goddess of love," Hannah tells me, but I just smile. "I just love its brightness."

Hannah's on the garden bench with a blanket wrapped around her legs. It's almost spring now, and for me, the warmer weather can't come fast enough. I've had enough of being cooped up indoors.

Hannah's voice is dreamy, like the stars we're drinking in. "Love's always easy when it's burning bright though, isn't it?" she says. "It's when it starts to get all hazy like the Milky Way that it gets more difficult."

"Are you trying to tell me something?" I ask, and she laughs.

"No, darling; not a thing. I'm sure you already know everything you need to know. You're so strong."

Am I? That's news to me, especially with my antenatal classes about to start. I feel so nervous about having to attend them on my own, I really do. I'm not looking forward to having to put on a brave face, as if I'm fine about being a single mum-to-be and getting paired up with the teaching assistant for any discussion activities because I'm not there with a partner.

"I know things haven't turned out as you wanted them to," Hannah says, "but I just want you to know that this time I've shared with you has been so very precious to me."

I put my arm around her, blinking away the seemingly ever-present tears. "To me too," I say. "I don't know how

I'd have got through it all without you."

Hannah smiles and pats my hand. "Listen, darling, you mustn't agree if you don't want to, but I've been thinking; that box room's just there, not doing anything. How about we ask Luther to decorate it for us? It could be a nursery for the baby. Just while you're here, you understand. I know you'll want to get your own place eventually."

Sometimes I don't think I deserve Hannah.

"D'you think he'd be up to that?" I say, expressing my gratitude for her offer by kissing her on the cheek.

Hannah smiles. "I daresay he'll moan a good deal, but you know Luther; when he gets on with it he'll insist on perfection – carefully rubbed down skirting boards; the lot."

"Well," I joke, "I should think so! My daughter will demand nothing less!"

At the antenatal class everyone's very friendly, but inevitably the couples gravitate towards each other, exchanging mobile numbers, arranging meet-ups. I'm not excluded – my own number is given and taken – but it's hard to imagine that I'll want to keep being reminded of their domestic bliss. Though maybe I need to get over that, because our children will be born within weeks of each other, so it's a chance for them to become childhood friends. Not that this is any guarantee of a lifelong friendship, as I should know. Marcia and I have only had very patchy contact lately. Ever since that telephone conversation where I all but told her to butt out, things have been distinctly cool between us.

In the class, there's a sort of glow about us pregnant women – even miserable-life me – all of us have an inner sizzle of excitement; of *expectation*, I suppose. Our bodies constantly do amazing things, only most of the time we don't think about it. But with our skin stretched tight, our bellies bulging and our babies moving inside us, we can't help but marvel at our mechanics.

The woman I'm sitting next to at the first session has a particularly huge bump. She also has a very friendly smile.

Poor woman; there are so many subjects it would be unwise to ask me questions about at the moment, but bless her, she picks one that is fine.

"D'you know if you're having a girl or a boy yet?"

"A girl."

"Me too! Isn't it great? I've been going crazy with the pink paint in the spare room."

"Not just the paint," her husband grunts. "I'd be surprised if there's anything pink left to buy in the whole of Norwich."

The woman lifts her eyebrows, ignoring him. "What about you?" she asks me. "Have you been decorating in pink?"

Ah, my housing situation. Another tricky subject. "Not yet, no," I say, thinking of Hannah's offer for her box room. It's a very generous offer, and one that I'll accept.

"The last minute type, are you?" asks the woman, but the session restarts after break at that point, so I get away with just smiling at her.

My phone rings after the class, when I've just finished easing my belly behind the steering wheel of my Fiat. Unclipping my seatbelt, I bend awkwardly to retrieve my bag from the floor, taking a quick look at the caller ID on my phone. It's Michael. What does he want?

"Michael?"

"Jen. Have you seen Kyle?"

"No, but I'm out at the moment. Is anything wrong?"

"Yes." The word's clipped, and it's obvious he's frantic with worry. "He took the bloody bike."

Oh my god! "Your motorbike?"

"Yes! We had a row; he stormed out. Only I didn't realise he'd actually left the house – I assumed he was sulking upstairs or something. Next minute I hear the bike engine start up. I'm sure he's on his way to you, but Rick's out tonight, so I've got no way of going after him."

"Why d'you think he's on his way to me?"

"Because he said he hates me and Diane, and he loves

223

you. He's going to ask if he can come and live with you at Hannah's."

My throat fills. I love Kyle too, and the thought of him lying by the side of a road somewhere in a tangled heap of metal is horrific.

"How long ago did he leave?"

"About ten minutes. I waited for a while because I hoped he might come back. But he hasn't. Shit, Jen, what shall I do?"

"Try not to worry. Ten minutes isn't long enough for him to have reached Hannah's yet. I'll come and pick you up. We can look for him together."

So I head over to Rick's house, and find Michael pacing up and down on the pavement. He rips open the car door as soon as I pull up, his hair all over the place where he's been running his fingers through it.

"Thanks for this," he says, clipping his seatbelt in, and we exchange a quick glance before I put the car into gear.

He looks haggard; older. "I'm sure he'll be all right," I say, though I'm not sure of anything of the kind, but the alternative can't be contemplated.

"Are you?" he says bitterly. "I'm not. We really went for it tonight. He's threatening to chuck his course in."

"What? The drama course? No! He loves it."

"Precisely. It's madness. He said…" Michael breaks off to look out of the window, away from me. "He says if I can give up on everything, then so can he."

"Oh, Michael…"

He sighs, looking back at me. "I've made such a sodding mess of everything, haven't I?" he says. "Us, the business, and now Kyle. Even Rick's had enough. He's hardly spoken to me all week."

"Rick's probably just stressed out. It's his department's turn for redundancies."

Michael touches my arm. "I know. Look, I heard about your job. I'm so sorry, Jen. I was going to give you a call, but…"

Each time I think it isn't possible for me to feel sadder

224

than I do, something happens to make me slip down another notch. "That's okay," I say, although nothing about our situation is bloody okay. But right now, Kyle's welfare has to be our priority.

I drive for a while, then Michael breaks the silence. "How are you, Jen?" he asks. "How's…?"

"Our baby? She's doing fine."

I can feel him looking at me through the darkness. "She? It's a girl?"

"Yes."

"Jeez," he says softly. "A girl. How about that?"

There's a slow-moving truck in front. However worried about Kyle I am, I'm not going to overtake it on a dark, winding road.

"Look," Michael says, "when this is over, I mean, after I've sorted out this business with Kyle, can we meet up? Talk?"

I want to ask what he wants to talk about exactly, but now's not the time. And besides, his mobile's ringing.

"Shit," he says. "It's Diane. Hello, Diane?"

I can't hear what she's saying, but I can make out the frantic, staccato tone of her voice, and it doesn't bode well.

"Jesus," says Michael, and I feel sick because instinctively I know Kyle must have crashed the bike. "Yes, all right, I'll come straight away." He ends the call. "Diane's just had the police on the line. Kyle crashed the bike in The Prince of Wales Road. They've taken him to the Norfolk and Norwich hospital."

"Oh, God! Is he all right?"

"She doesn't know; she's on her way there now."

"I'll turn round."

But it takes a while for me to find a suitable place to turn the car on the winding road, and when I do find somewhere, I end up stalling the engine.

"D'you want me to drive?" Michael asks, one hand already on the door handle.

The baby makes ripples inside me at that exact moment, warning me against allowing her fear-crazed father to drive

225

us recklessly around bends. "No, it's all right," I say firmly, restarting the engine. Then I head off.

At the hospital, I leave the car in a drop off zone and we tear inside. Someone tells us where to go, and we follow instructions, arriving on the ward breathless and frantic. Diane's already there, sitting on a chair in the waiting area, and she shoots us both an unwelcoming glare.

"How is he?" Michael asks.

"He's in X-ray at the moment, but they think he's got a broken leg and fractured ribs. Hell, Michael, what were you thinking of? He's sixteen, for God's sake! The police were involved! He's going to end up being banned from driving before he's even got a licence."

"He stole my keys, Diane," Michael tells her. "I didn't hand them over to him."

"Oh, yes, and why did he do that?" she spits right back. "Since when did our son become some sort of criminal tearaway? Since you stuffed up, that's since when!"

I'm hovering nearby, unsure what to do. It's a huge relief that Kyle seems to be all right, but the stress of it all has made me feel completely exhausted and I didn't get round to eating much before the antenatal class. Suddenly I need to sit down badly.

Diane glances towards me. "I don't think there'll be room for you at Kyle's bedside when they bring him back, Jenny," she says. "And you look as if you could do with heading home anyway." On the surface, her words are considerate, but there's nothing considerate about her 'fuck off' expression. But then she is worried sick about her son. I have to remember that.

Michael looks at me too. "She's right, Jen," he says. "It's late. You get off. I'll text you when I have any news."

But I'm not going to be pushed around by either of them. "Kyle was trying to make his way to me," I say. "So I'm going to stick around until I've seen him."

Judging by their matching expressions of surprise, I've probably allowed both of them to push me around in the

226

past, and it feels good to have stood up for myself. But my moment of victory is spoiled somewhat by my stomach giving a huge and highly audible lurch. When I clutch my hands to it, Michael gives me a glimmer of a smile. "Well, at least let me buy you a chocolate bar," he says, and heads off towards a vending machine, leaving me alone with Diane. It's the first time I've seen her since my redundancy, and not surprisingly the silence between us is awkward. Once I might have tried to fill it with nervous gabble, but now I just sit, half-watching Michael as he makes a selection on my behalf, grappling with the mechanics of the machine.

"I only told your work the truth you know, when they phoned up," Diane says at last. "But I'm sorry you lost your job. My residents had a good day out."

It's about the nicest thing she's ever said to me, even if her tone of voice was grudging. "I'm glad they enjoyed it," I say. "And it wasn't your fault about my job. You didn't ask me to organise it."

"Still, I suppose you'd have been finishing work soon anyway?" She nods towards my stomach. "When's the baby due?"

"The third of July."

"Well," she says, "make the most of the time till then. Once the baby comes, your life will never be your own again." When she swipes angrily at her cheeks, I realise she's crying. "Bloody little shit," she says. "Why did he have to do something so stupid?"

At this very moment, the 'bloody little shit' emerges from the lifts on a trolley, pushed by a porter who wheels him in our direction. Michael arrives with my chocolate bar just as they reach us.

Kyle's swathed in dressings, but save for a tiny cut above his eyebrow, his face is unscathed. He's pale and shell-shocked, but his smile's the same as ever, thank God. "Hi, Jen," he says. "It feels like a giant crushed my ribs, but I'm okay, don't worry."

Diane looks as if she wants to scream or yell, or both. For

227

that matter, so does Michael. If Kyle wanted to make a point that he's peed off with both of them, then he's certainly managed to do that by ignoring both of them to speak to me.

Taking his hand, I bend to kiss him on the cheek. He's been too old for me to do that for years, but with Diane and Michael watching, he tolerates it. "I'm very glad to hear it. I'm going to go home now, but I'll be back to visit you soon."

The porter wheels him off down the corridor with Diane and Michael following on. As they go into the ward, Michael turns to give me a last look. Then he lifts his hand, and he's gone.

With the brief warmth from my encounter with Kyle quickly fading, I start to leave, only to hear Michael calling after me. Looking round, I see him sprinting down the corridor. My heart starts to race. "I didn't give you this," he says. I look down, expecting to see something important, but see, instead, the chocolate bar.

Well, it was a nice thought, I suppose, but there are so many more things my baby and I would prefer to have from him. "Thanks."

"Speak soon," he promises, vanishing once again, and all at once chocolate is the very last thing I want to eat.

When I get back to the car I've been given a parking ticket and it seems so entirely appropriate for the end of this awful evening I just rip it off and slap it onto the dashboard, not giving it another thought. I'm so bone-weary I just don't have enough energy to get worked up about it, or to worry about how I'm going to find the money to pay for it.

Reaching for my phone, I call Hannah. I'll be back so much later than I expected to be, and I don't want her to worry about me. When there's no reply, I assume she's gone to bed; it is almost ten o'clock by now after all. But when I arrive home, the lights are still on in her bedroom, so I go up.

"Hannah?" As I cross the landing, I call out her name, but there's no reply. Expecting to find her in bed, asleep with her book still in her hand, I creep into her room. But although the covers are turned down on her bed, there's no sign of her.

"Hannah?" I come back out and go over to the bathroom. The door's closed, when I call again, there's still no reply. Frightened now, I knock on the door. Still nothing. When I push down on the door handle and it offers no resistance. I go inside. And there, lying on the floor by the sink, is Hannah.

"Hannah!" Hurrying over, I kneel by her side, taking her hand. Her lips are blue, her face grey, and although I can tell she's still breathing, I know she's seriously ill.

"Hannah, it's Jenny," I say, pushing her hair back from her face. "You've had a fall, lovely. I'm just going to get my phone to call for help, and then I'll be straight back. Stay there, won't you?"

It's a silly thing to ask, and yet it's not. For I'm crazy worried, and what I'm really asking is, *stay with me! Don't leave me!*

Quickly, I phone for an ambulance, then I open the front door for them and hurry back upstairs, grabbing blankets and pillows from the bedroom to make her more comfortable. "The ambulance is on its way, Hannah," I say, but tears are streaming down my face because I'm so worried it's already too late. Hannah can't seem to hear me – she's much too ill for that; and I know I ought to ring Luther. I *will* ring Luther. But just then the ambulance arrives and the paramedics take control, speaking to Hannah, giving her oxygen, using the defibrillator.

The paramedic tells me he thinks Hannah's had a heart attack, then casts a professional eye over my swollen belly and asks, "Sure you don't want to stay at home, love?"

His colleague, meanwhile, is readying Hannah for departure. I can't bear the thought of them leaving without me – of watching the blue, flashing lights until they fade into the distance. It fills me with blind panic. "No, I want to come."

"Up you get then; find yourself a place in the corner of the ambulance." The paramedic's tone is resigned, his actions quick and efficient, and these things signal to me the sheer gravity of Hannah's condition.

So I sit in the corner as I've been told, but nothing seems real. I have to keep on reminding myself that this is no Saturday night episode of Casualty; this is my Hannah's body jerking in that unnatural way as they perform CPR on her. It just doesn't feel possible that it can be, because she seemed so well today – there was more colour in her cheeks, her appetite was better and she even had more energy. I took her for a walk in Bacton Woods. It wasn't much of a walk – just a short one to a suitable bench for a picnic. But maybe the outing was too much for her after all?

"Stand clear."

They're trying CPR again, and I don't want to watch, so I cover my wet face with my hands, the tears dripping through my fingers. I wish I could stop breathing and turn time back. Not take Hannah to Bacton, but instead leave her in her cosy armchair listening to Desert Islands Discs on Radio Four. Not take her to Cuba. Not worry her with all my problems. Not fail to notice that all her flitting about to Paris and all those other places meant something.

Somebody touches my arm, and I take my hands away from my face to look at the kindly face of the paramedic. "I'm so sorry, love," he says. "She's gone."

And suddenly all the events I've tried to push away rush forward again into my mind like a fast-forwarded film, ending with Hannah at Bacton Woods, smiling her lovely smile as she takes in the sight of the freshly-opened leaves on the trees. So very beautiful. And gone forever.

Chapter Thirty-Four

Michael, October 2013

Michael was hanging an exhibition at the Norwich gallery. He was running late because the artist, who was something of a tricky character, had delivered his work at the very last minute. The private view was that evening, and with the artist now firmly ensconced in the pub for a pre-show celebratory drink, Michael was feeling slightly apprehensive about how the show was going to pan out.

He could really do with the show being a success too because, with the effects of the recession, profits on both galleries were right down. The paintings he was hanging were local scenes with a twist – the colourful beach huts against the pine trees at Wells-next-the-Sea and the fishing boats at Cromer – but with a flavour of pop art about them that set them apart from the norm. All being equal Michael thought they would sell, which would mean he'd be able to postpone a meeting with the bank manager, at least for a while longer.

When his phone rang, Michael had just finished hanging one room, and in the other, the paintings were stacked against the walls in the places he'd chosen for them. Normally the artist was on hand to be consulted, but this artist had been happy to leave the job to him. It made the job simpler really; although he suspected the artist was the type to complain about everything.

When his phone rang, Michael pulled it from his pocket, intending to ignore it. But one glance at the caller ID had him ignoring the paintings instead.

"Mum?" he said anxiously, with a premonition that

something bad had happened. Although he'd given her his mobile number a long time ago, she'd never used it until now. "Is everything all right?"

"He's gone," she said, sounding distraught.

"Who's gone? Ronnie?"

"Yes. He hit me. He hit me and then he left!"

The bastard! "Ronnie hit you? Mum, are you all right?"

"No…" she started to say, the rest of the sentence lost in a storm of weeping.

"Look, I'm on my way, okay? I'll be forty minutes at the most." Ending the call, Michael found his assistant June looking at him anxiously. "Sorry," he said to her, turning his back on the pictures propped against the walls. "I've got an emergency. Can you root the artist out of the pub and get him to help you finish up here? I'm really sorry about this."

Barely waiting to listen to her protests, he left; terrified at what he might find when he reached his mother. Thank God he'd got the bike so he could zip past the lines of traffic and slow-moving caravans. As he sped along the Acle Straight, a flock of lapwings rose up from a field, wholly inappropriate in their beauty. It was a relief when he finally passed Breydon Water to the ugliness of the industrial area. It meant he was nearly there.

The front door of number 47 was wide open. Michael went in quickly, making for Flat B. When she answered his knock, he still gasped with shock at the sight of her. Although the flat was in darkness, curtains drawn, he could still see that she'd been systematically beaten. This was no get patched up quickly at A & E job – she was going to have to be admitted to hospital. Not only that, but the police were going to have to be involved.

"Come on, Mum," he said gently, casting a quick eye over the ransacked flat. "Let's get you to hospital."

"No," she said, grabbing her hand from his. "No hospital."

"Mum," he said gently, "your injuries are serious. You have to go to hospital. Come on, the car's just outside." But then he remembered it wasn't; that he'd traded the car in for a stupid motorbike.

Much later, after getting his mum to hospital by ambulance and giving a statement to the police, Michael arrived home. The house was quiet; Jen had gone to bed. There were about a zillion messages and voicemails on his phone. Michael listened to the first one, from the artist. *I'm going to fucking sue your arse, Brandon.*

Then he switched the phone off, tossed down a stiff whisky, and went to bed. His very last thought was of his mother, when he'd returned to her bedside, having given a statement to the police. "Who are you?" she'd asked, her face showing absolutely no trace of recognition. "I don't know you! Get away from me! Nurse, tell him to go away!"

Chapter Thirty-Five

"You know the very worst thing about this," says Luther one night a week after Hannah's death. "With Mum gone, I lose my link to you."

We're sitting together on Hannah's sofa. There's a film on the TV, but neither of us has much heart for it. Luther's been so strong since Hannah died. Poor man; I've been so grief stricken, maybe I haven't allowed him to be anything but strong.

"It doesn't have to be like that," I tell him. "You can be Uncle Luther."

He takes my hand, staring straight ahead at the TV. "Can't I be more than that?" You know Mum would have been thrilled if we got back together."

But I can't agree with him there, because love him as much as she did, Hannah would have been completely horrified by the thought of me putting my trust in her son again. So, when my phone rings, buzzing noisily on the coffee table, I'm grateful for the excuse to take my hand back.

"I think really it's best to keep things the way they are, Luther," I say gently. "But you can always be a part of mine and the baby's lives if you want to. I promise."

He nods and gets up, taking his cigarettes to the back door and leaving me to answer my phone.

It's Michael. I texted him the news about Hannah a week ago when he sent me an update about Kyle's progress, and ever since then he's tried countless times to speak to me. But I've ignored all his calls and his messages because I just haven't felt strong enough to take them. Losing Hannah has been like losing my mother all over again. I've cried and cried in my room in Hannah's house, feeling like a lost, bewildered child; only emerging for Luther or Marcia's visits, doing my best to be strong for them.

"The funeral's on Thursday," I tell Michael now. "Yes, I know. I'm sorry. I just haven't been up to taking calls. Thank you. How's Kyle doing? Oh, good. Send him my love, won't you? Tell him I promise to visit him soon. Yes, Michael. I'll be in touch. Yes, thank you. Bye."

Another evening, and this time it's Marcia with me in front of an unwatched film. She's brought chocolate, and she's drinking tea even though she's staying the night, because I can't drink wine. Neither of us has brought up the subject of our falling out or her fling with Timothy in Cuba. Hannah's death has relegated both subjects to a lesser importance, and I'm glad I was able to turn to her when I needed her most. It shows me that whatever's happened, our friendship still means something.

Suddenly the baby moves inside me, swimming or playing football; joyously alive even though Hannah is dead.

"Marse," I say. "Will you be my birth partner?"

Marcia turns to look at me in full chocolate crunch, her cheeks bulging. "Are you kidding me?" she says. "Of course I will!" And we cling to each other and laugh and cry, and then she tells me all about her latest IVF treatment.

"So, right now I'm taking the drugs to thicken the lining of my womb, and then, if all goes to plan, the embryo transfer's scheduled for some time in June. They'll give me an exact date soon. Oh, Jen, I've got such a feeling it's going to work this time, I really have." She looks at me, her smile faltering slightly. "But I probably said that last time, right?"

She did. And the time before. "Not with such conviction," I answer, and she beams again.

The night before the funeral, Luther calls me up. "I just wanted you to know about the will. Mum left you a considerable amount of money. She also left a proviso about the house. Although it comes to me as part of the estate,

235

she's stipulated that you be allowed to live there for as long as you want to. As far as I'm concerned, that can be forever, Jen. I don't need the money."

I know this is an apology for all the hurts of the past, and I'm touched. I'm also very, very relieved. "Thank you, Luther," I say, the tears – which are never very far away – spilling over again. "Thank you."

"Don't thank me," he says. "Thank Mum. And yourself for loving her even though...well, despite everything I put you through."

And then it's time for the funeral, with a packed church and the hymns Luther and I picked out together. *All Things Bright and Beautiful*, because Hannah had the gift of being able to see the beauty in everything. *The Lord is my Shepherd,* because it gave her so much joy to see spring lambs. And *Jerusalem*, the Women's Institute anthem, because Hannah was a member of her local WI, but also because *Calendar Girls* was her favourite film and she was always jokingly trying to get the other women in her WI group to strip off to make a nude charity calendar.

I've cried so many tears since that dash to the hospital that my eyes remain dry throughout the entire service. But when we stand at Hannah's graveside and my daughter wriggles and kicks inside me, I'm suddenly caught out by the utter bleakness of her never knowing Hannah, and the tears come yet again. But I'm not alone, because we're all crying – all of us fortunate souls who knew her.

It's not a pleasant task, sorting out Hannah's belongings. Perhaps that's why it takes me so long to get round to doing it. Every time I go to her bedroom, I just stand there, looking around, and I want to weep all over again. All the things she collected on her travels – glittery Eiffel Towers, programmes for shows, antique earrings – they're the very essence of Hannah; the things that defined her life. If I get rid of them all, it's like getting rid of Hannah.

"You don't need to do this," Luther tells me every time he comes over. "I can get a house clearance company to come in. That's probably best. You don't want to be sorting through her stuff. I know I don't. It's too depressing."

I don't want to do it; he's right. But neither do I want impersonal strangers deciding everything Hannah loved is worthless, so finally, one morning in June, I make a start. Despite everything that's happened, I suddenly have boundless energy. Maybe it's because I've sat around so much since I lost my job – caring for Hannah, grieving for Hannah, I don't know. But anyway, suddenly I need to be doing something; taking some action. The baby books would call it the nesting instinct, and they're probably right.

I speak to Hannah out loud all the time, as if she can hear me. It's something I've done ever since the funeral, because it brings her near again. "I'm setting myself a challenge," I tell her now. "I'm going to pick five things that best express the essence of you to me, and I'm going to keep them. But I'm afraid the rest is going to have to go. It's not going to be easy to stick to five things, because you had so many passions, and I loved so many different things about you. But I'm just going to have to do my best."

As I finish speaking, the sun comes out, filling the bedroom with light, and it's as if Hannah has smiled at me. I smile too, feeling peaceful for the first time in months. Then I set to work, sorting things into four piles – Charity Shops, Tip, Ask Luther, and Keep.

It takes me several days. Luther comes backwards and forwards in-between working, ferrying things to charity shops and the tip, selecting a few things he wants to keep for himself, bringing takeaways and bags of shopping. I marvel at how we've become friends, and know that Hannah would have been pleased to see it.

By the end of the week the house is much clearer and I've chosen my five items. There's a photo of Hannah working in the garden with her flowers in full bloom, chosen because she loved her garden so much and I know her garden's not likely to ever look that good again. I'm no gardener, and in any case, it will inevitably fill up with the detritus of children – a sandpit, a mini trampoline, ride on

237

toys, abandoned balls and discarded play food.

I've also chosen to keep a pair of dancing shoes I found in the bottom of Hannah's wardrobe; I never saw her wear them, but I did see her face light up when she spoke of dancing with her husband, and the sparkle in her eyes when she was dancing salsa in Cuba. Even though that was the beginning of everything going horribly wrong, it's still a good memory.

And then there's the hat she was wearing for my intended wedding to Luther. It reminds me of the courage she displayed in coming to seek me out and pleading that we keep in touch despite everything. If she hadn't done that, my life would have been so very less rich these past five years.

There's also the baby bootie I found in her knitting bag, its partner so poignantly unfinished on the knitting needles. If I hold its softness to my cheek, I can still smell Hannah's perfume, and imagine the look of joy that would have been on her face when she first saw my baby.

And lastly, there's that sparkly, tacky Eiffel Tower which so symbolises the passion Hannah had for travel. One day I'll take my daughter right to the top of the Eiffel Tower, and we'll look out at the same view Hannah enjoyed – the whole excitement of Paris lain at our feet.

Emotionally, I find an old shoebox and place the five items reverently inside it, wrapped in tissue paper. I'll find a better box at some point, but for now the shoebox will serve as my memory box. With this job finally done, I start to clean, vigorously, thoroughly; even the places that are already clean, stopping only to go to an antenatal appointment. The midwife remarks that I've lost weight, but doesn't seem too concerned about it. Then she gets me to lie on the bed so she can feel my stomach. "Baby hasn't turned yet; she really ought to have done by now. It's looking as if she'll be breech."

A stab of fear passes through me. Nothing can happen to my baby; if it does, on top of everything else, that will be it for me. "Will she be all right?"

The midwife's smile is reassuring. "Yes, of course she will. It might just mean she's delivered by caesarean section if she doesn't turn, that's all." She looks at my notes. "Let's see; you have an appointment with the consultant gynaecologist coming up, don't you? If baby hasn't turned by then, she'll discuss the options with you and set a date for a caesarean if she feels that's the best option."

The baby doesn't turn, and the consultant does set a date for the caesarean. The third of July. Three weeks away. I phone Marcia to let her know, and also to wish her good luck. For tomorrow is June tenth – the date for her embryo transfer.

"That's perfect, Jen," she says. Marcia's voice is always so light and bright these days. She's a very different Marcia to the embittered girl I've shared my life with these past few years. I'm happy for her, and I so hope that events conspire to keep her positive and full of hope. "Who knows, I might be pregnant when you give birth!"

"I really hope so, Marse," I say. "I really do. Good luck for tomorrow. Are you nervous?"

"No, not really. Well, yes! I know it's silly; after all, I've been there, done it all before, haven't I?"

It's not silly at all, because so much is riding on the outcome of it, but I don't say that. I just say, "You'll be fine," instead. "We both will."

"Yes," she agrees determinedly. "We will." Then she asks, "Are you sorry you won't be having a natural birth after all?"

I have to smile to myself at that, because this is much more like the Marcia I know and love. If Marcia were going to have to have a caesarean, she'd mind terribly about it. Marcia will be the type of mother who insists on a natural, drug-free home-birth and will stand-up for the rights of women to breast feed at will. She'll also provide organic, all-healthy food for her toddler. No fish fingers or chicken nuggets for *her* child.

"No," I say honestly. "I don't mind about having a caesarean. The important thing is that everything goes smoothly."

"You're right," agrees Marcia, and, amazingly, leaves it at that. "Are you going to tell Michael the date?"

"Yes," I say. "Of course."

But I don't straight away. I so mean to, but somehow I keep putting it off. And then one afternoon the local newspaper comes through the door, and I read something in it that takes my breath away.

Every day I tell myself I should cancel the newspaper, but every day I quite enjoy sitting with a cooling cup of tea perusing its contents in the conservatory. It brings Hannah close somehow, because this is one of the things she always did after a hard afternoon's gardening, still dressed in her scruffy gardening clothes, her hands washed but not yet scrubbed under the fingernails.

Today I scan the front page, which leads with yet another story about a protested-against incinerator in West Norfolk. Then I turn to page 3, and there's a photograph of Michael, dressed in a suit, outside the law courts. The headline reads ARTIST SUES GALLERY OWNER.

"Oh, my God!" I say out aloud, bending to devour the article. Timothy Taylor, a local artist, has sued Michael for breach of contract because he failed to finish hanging the artist's exhibition on the day it was due to open. Michael, who is described in the article as the owner of the now defunct Brandon Gallery Chain, apparently upped and left with the exhibition only partly hung. As a result, the artist was caused significant embarrassment and loss of sales.

When questioned, former gallery-owner Brandon, 36, would only say that he was called away due to a family emergency.

My head suddenly throbbing, I read the staggeringly large amount of money in damages Michael has been ordered to pay the artist. Then I scrutinise the date, seeing that this so-called family crisis is supposed to have happened when Michael and I were still together. What family crisis? I can recall nothing of the kind. Was it something to do with Kyle? Something Michael didn't tell

240

me about? Or is he just lying about it being a family crisis? But why would he do that? Suddenly needing to speak to him, I get up to fetch my phone from my bag, but as I do so, a warm flood of water streams down my legs. I know what it is before the pains even start, which they do, almost immediately. My daughter doesn't want to wait another three weeks – she's coming now.

Chapter Thirty-Six

Michael, 2014

Rick was playing on his Xbox when Michael came in, the living room curtains drawn to heighten the experience. Michael hated the way his friend quickly shut the game down and came into the kitchen to put the kettle on – he shouldn't feel he had to do that; this was his home. Besides, Michael could do with some time on his own; it had been one hell of a day.

"All right?" Rick asked.

"Yes thanks," he answered, because he could hardly say, *No, I heard from my mum's social worker today that the git who beat her up is still at large, and what's more, he ran up a humungous bill on Mum's credit cards with his gambling habit. I told the social worker I'd cover it, but I've got no idea how I'm actually going to do that.*

"How about you? Any more news about your job?"

"Yeah; looks like I'm safe. For now, anyway." Rick smiled at him, his face lit up by relief. "Fancy coming out tonight to celebrate?"

"That's brilliant news, mate!" he said, slapping Rick on the back. "Fantastic! Of course I'll come out. Have you told Jen? She'll be so pleased for you."

Rick shook his head, handing him a cup of tea. "No, not yet. You seen her lately?"

"Not since I took her those flowers, no." Grimly, Michael remembered his visit to see Jen at Hannah's old house. The way she'd thanked him politely for the flowers on the doorstep before he'd gone inside to find the whole place was bursting with flowers already. Of course it was.

Hannah's garden had been her pride and joy.

"How are you?" he'd asked, worried by her pallor and the dark shadows beneath her eyes. He'd always said her friendship with Hannah was unhealthy, but what did he know? Since the business had gone bust, the majority of his friends had vanished into the woodwork. Hannah had always been there for Jen.

"Sad," she said, and the simple truth had chased away all the words he'd rehearsed on the way over – the apologies, the excuses, the declarations of love.

"How's Kyle getting on?" she asked, breaking the silence, and for the rest of his visit they talked about Kyle's health, his decision to stick with his course after all and a role he'd recently been offered with a local theatre group. Important stuff, but still top-layer stuff; and by the time Luther had turned up in his flash car, Michael still hadn't got round to mentioning the baby, despite the fact that Jen was, by now, very obviously pregnant. And when Luther breezed in as if he owned the place – which he did now that his mother was dead – Michael had taken it as his cue to leave, with nothing discussed, nothing arranged, nothing expressed.

Riding back to Rick's on the bike, jealously clamped around his heart. Were they a couple again, Jen and Luther? Or if they weren't now, would they become so? God, would Luther end up bringing up his child? But then, how would Jen even know he cared like hell about that? He'd as good as told her to get rid of it.

In Rick's kitchen, his phone rang. It was Jen – just as if he'd conjured her up with his thoughts. "Hi, Jen."

"Michael, it's started," she said, her voice panicky. "The baby's coming!"

His throat dried. "Jesus, are you sure?"

"Yes! And Marcia was supposed to be my birth partner, but she's got her IVF treatment first thing tomorrow, and I don't want to get in the way of that... Oh, God!" She broke off to moan with what was obviously extreme pain, instantly bringing images of the past pressing into his brain.

"I'll come and get you," he said, then remembered the bike. "Shit, I can't." He looked at Rick. "It's Jen; she's gone into labour. Can I borrow the car?"

"I'll drive you," said Rick, slamming his mug down on the worktop.

"Rick's bringing me, Jen," Michael told her. "We'll be with you very soon. Keep the phone next to you."

And very soon they were zipping along the country roads on their way to the Broads, Rick driving quickly but a whole lot more safely than Michael knew he would have done himself.

"She'll be okay, mate; don't worry."

Michael realised he was picking the side of his thumb and sucked at it, tasting blood. "D'you think she needs an ambulance?"

"It's not long since she went in an ambulance with her friend, is it? She'll be better off with us."

"I'm rubbish in hospitals," Michael confessed.

"You'll surprise yourself. Anyway, this is about Jen and the baby, not you." Rick sighed, shot him a glance. "That didn't come out quite right. Of course it's about you; it's your baby. You know what I mean."

He did.

"What if she's already gone? What if she called an ambulance herself?"

"We'll soon find out. Try not to worry."

Five more minutes and they screeched to a halt in Hannah's drive, sending gravel flying. It was Rick who got to the front door first, Rick who opened it. Rick who called out, "Jen?"

"I'm up here."

She was lying on the bedroom floor on her side, panting. Her eyes were wild, her hands clutching at her belly. Rick went over to her, offering soothing words of comfort, but it wasn't Rick she was looking at appealingly, it was Michael. With an effort, Michael pulled himself together. This was Jen; not his mother all those years ago. This was Jen, having his baby. He had to be here for her.

"Can you get up?" he asked. "We need to get you to the car. Or would you prefer an ambulance?"

"No!" she said. "No ambulance. I can get up if you help me."

He went one side, Rick the other. Together they helped her out to the car and settled her in the back. Michael sat next to her, and when the pain hit again, he held her hand tightly and stroked her hair, speaking soothing words that felt like words from a script.

"You'd better phone ahead; tell them we're on our way," Rick suggested, and between contractions, he did so, giving information, somehow making sense.

He'd never wanted this, but it was happening anyway. He ought to have resisted Jen at that party. Christ, he'd just split up with somebody – it's been way too soon to get involved again. Especially after he'd held her for the first time and something shifted inside him – something that told him this time, it was going to be different.

These past four years he'd been acting as if he and Jen were just the same as all the other relationships he'd ever had, when all along he'd known what they had was really special. And now it was too late for it to be any different. He didn't know what was going to happen after the baby was born, but whatever it was, it was unlikely to be anything that spelt happy ever after for himself and Jen. He'd seen that in her face when he'd said, "We can't keep it, can we? Not with all this on our plates."

But suddenly they were there at the hospital and the time for reflection was gone. Rick pulled up as close as possible to the entrance, and the two of them supported Jen inside. A nurse asked, "Which one of you is the daddy?" and Jen looked at him, maybe sensing his terror.

"Don't you dare leave me, Michael," she said, and so he nodded and told the nurse, "I am. I'm the daddy."

And Rick said, "Good luck, mate. Good luck, Jen." And left him alone to deal with it.

Chapter Thirty-Seven

The pain comes in pulsing waves – vicious, unbelievable; a livid, red-hot thing poking at me like a torturer, making me scream out loud. When it fades at the end of a contraction, I remember the way I screamed with pleasure that first night Michael and I made love, part of my mind thinking we might wake his son, the other realising there was nothing I could do to stop it.

I expected to be here with Marcia, getting sternly bossed about, given clear directions about what to do. But instead I'm here with Michael, which means I've brought along with me a quagmire of emotion and a list of unanswered questions. But when the pain comes again, I can't remember the questions or even why I wanted answers for them, and cling to Michael's hand as if it'll keep me in this world while others are trying to tear me out.

It's such a blessed relief to receive first, gas and air, and then secondly, the epidural. As numbness steals over my lower half, I turn to Michael, wanting to say, *"This is it! She'll be here soon!"* But I surprise such a look of bleakness on his face, the words die, unformed. Is the thought of becoming a father to my child really so hideous? So truly awful it makes him look like that? As if the world's about to end?

The look disappears quickly because Michael carefully adjusts his expression; but I can still remember it, and it gives me the strength to ask him one of my questions from the list that has surfaced as the pain recedes.

"Why didn't you tell me about that artist?"

"What artist?" But a flicker across his face tells me he knows exactly whom I mean.

"Timothy Taylor; the one who sued you. Why didn't you

tell me about it at the time? And what family crisis called you away that night? I don't remember any family crisis."

By the way his gaze slips away from mine, I know whatever he says next will be a lie. "I don't even remember now. And as for why I didn't mention it, I guess I just didn't want to worry you."

"But we were supposed to be a team!" I say, and tears spring to my eyes at my own use of the past tense.

Wordlessly, he hands me a tissue, and I blow my nose. "I didn't get pregnant on purpose, you know," I tell him. "I didn't deliberately trick you into becoming a father."

I don't realise we're not on our own any longer until after I speak the words – a midwife's come into the room, and I know she's almost certainly overheard me.

"Right," she says in an over-bright voice. "We just need to do a spot of shaving. They're almost ready for you in theatre now."

Michael stays with me while I get shaved. It doesn't take long. Afterwards, before we go into theatre, it's mostly silent between us. But then what is there to say? Whether or not he believes me about not deliberately trying to get pregnant, our daughter's about to be born.

We rehearsed having a caesarean at antenatal classes, taking it in turns to lie down on some large cushions while the rest of the group pressed in around us. This was supposed to give us an impression of how crowded the theatre would be, and it's true; it is crowded – there are at least eight people in there. Ten, with us. And theatre is most definitely the right word for it – with what's about to happen to me from the waist down the main act.

The obstetrician introduces himself to us, and we shake his hand like dinner guests. He's bluff, hearty and posh-sounding, and tells us his name is Mr Tinkle. *Mr Tinkle!* It's completely surreal, and I search Michael out to share a smile, but he's all grey looking with that bleak look back on his face, and doesn't even seem to have registered the ridiculous name.

As they put up a shield to block the horror of the action

247

from me, Mr Tinkle grins boyishly in Michael's direction. "Are you going to be at the sharp end, or d'you want to hold your lady's hand?" he asks.

I'm not desperate for Michael to see my insides and besides, something's telling me strongly that everything's not right with him. And suddenly I remember Diane saying, *Look, I'm telling you, his reaction was extreme. Really phobic.* "Hold my hand, please?" I say, and when he grabs it gratefully, I can feel his is shaking.

"Not a fainter, are you?" laughs Mrs Tinkle tactlessly, and suddenly I hate the man. If I could feel my legs and he weren't about to deliver my daughter, I'd kick him in the shins. Hard.

Michael's smile is grim. "I won't faint," he says, but he looks as if he's stealing himself to face his worst nightmare and just for a second, I experience a pang of hurt around my heart. But then I deliberately push it away because nobody's going to spoil this moment for me – not Michael, and not the ridiculous Mr Tinkle either.

But these brave thoughts are quickly followed by a wave of emotion because suddenly I really want Marcia here; Marcia with her no-nonsense support. Or my mother, even though I can't even remember her properly. Or Hannah. Oh, God, yes; I want Hannah.

"All right?" Michael asks me and I see they're all waiting for my reply; Michael, Mr Tinkle and all the green-garbed individuals I shall never remember the names of.

"Yes, I'm all right."

"Then let's get this show on the road!" says Mr Tinkle.

At the antenatal class, we were told that delivering a baby via caesarean section would feel a little like somebody doing the washing up in your abdomen. I doubt very much if Mr Tinkle has ever done such a thing as washing up in real life, in an actual kitchen; he just doesn't seem the type. But he's making a good job of it now, inside me, because much more quickly than I expect, Michael gasps and clutches my hand and something's being pulled from me.

"You have a beautiful baby daughter," Mr Tinkle tells us,

and Michael reaches down to kiss me, his grip on my hand relaxing ever-so-slightly, and I don't know whether to laugh or cry. Then a nurse with the biggest smile on her face brings my baby over to me, and I let go of Michael to take her. And here she is, my impossibly lovely daughter; a reality at last, looking exactly like her father.

"Congratulations," says the nurse. "She's exactly six pounds. She's beautiful."

And she is, she really is. She has a shock of black hair, bright blue eyes and the most perfect rosebud mouth.

"Have you chosen a name yet?" the nurse asks.

I tear my gaze away from my daughter for long enough to glance quickly in Michael's direction. "I thought of Hannah," I tell him, and he nods.

"That sounds just right."

Suddenly my eyes are awash with tears.

"I'm just going to deliver the placenta, then we can get you stitched up and you can spend some quality time with little Hannah," says Mr Tinkle.

"Do you want to hold her?" I ask Michael as the washing up feeling starts up inside me again.

"I'll get you a chair, the nurse tells Michael, and I wonder if, like me, she's seen how badly his hands are shaking.

He sits, and the nurse helps to place Hannah into his arms, and we both stare down at her. "She's perfect, isn't she?" I say; drinking her in, wondering what personality and future are locked into her DNA.

When Michael doesn't answer, I look at him and realise his eyes are filled with tears. For one empty, hollow moment, I realise I've got no idea what those tears mean. He didn't want this beautiful, perfect little girl; he wanted me to get rid of her. Is he crying out of guilt? Regret that she has, after all, been born? Or are they tears of love, all his doubts and reservations swept aside by the perfect reality that is our daughter?

"Yes," he says, as a tear overspills and runs down his cheek. "She's amazing."

And my heart sings, the smile on my face suddenly so broad it hurts my face. Maybe, just maybe, everything will be all right.

After Mr Tinkle has finished with me in theatre, they wheel me out to the recovery room, laying Hannah on my chest to help with bonding. Neither Michael or I speak very much; we just gaze down at Hannah. She's so warm, so real against my skin, but I still can't help reaching out to touch her because I can't quite believe she's there. It's a miracle, it really is.

Hannah snuffles and wriggles, then settles down to sleep. I'm completely exhausted, and could do with doing the same thing, but I know I'll never sleep.

"You'll have to tell Kyle in the morning," I say to Michael.

He smiles. "He'll be thrilled."

"Yes."

"D'you want me to let Marcia know?"

"Yes please; but not until tomorrow afternoon, after she's had her treatment."

"What about your dad?"

"Yes please."

"Okay."

Looking down, I see Hannah has her eyes open again. She's frowning slightly, as if to tell us to be quiet, because we're keeping her awake. Michael and I both smile. "She looks so much like you," I marvel. "D'you think there's anything of me in her?"

"I hope so," he says, and another wave of emotion comes for me.

"Michael?" I say, but at that moment the nurse comes in again – it seems we are fated to be interrupted at important moments today.

"How's it going?" she asks. "Someone looks comfortable! Shall we get you settled on the ward? I'm so sorry, Daddy; visiting hours for partners finish at nine o'clock in the evening. Tomorrow morning it's ten-thirty for dads, and two o'clock for everyone else."

"Right." Michael stands up, looking shell-shocked. I don't blame him; it's exactly how I feel myself. I don't want him to go.

He bends to kiss first me, then Hannah. "I'll see you tomorrow, okay? I hope you manage to get some sleep."

"Thanks. See you tomorrow." I want to add *I love you,* because I do, it's the truth, but I can't because we haven't talked about where *I love you* takes us now. So he stands there, watching as I'm wheeled away and despite all I've gained in the past hour – a daughter; a whole new way of life – I'm shrouded by a sense of loss.

Chapter Thirty-Eight

Michael, 11 June 2014

Michael woke up smiling. He had a daughter. A *daughter*. He couldn't wait to see her and Jen again, but he had to wait, because visiting hours didn't start for another two hours. But he could tell Kyle about it.

Smiling as he waited for the phone to be answered, Michael imagined his son holding little Hannah. He was sure to be smitten by her straight away; she was so tiny; so perfect. And hopefully it would help to smooth things over between the two of them. He hoped so, because he really missed his son.

Maybe he'd been wrong to fear having another child so much? Could Hannah, in fact, be the key to settling his demons for good instead of reawakening them?

Diane answered the phone, her voice typically grumpy.

"Hi, Diane, can I speak to Kyle please?"

"I don't think he'll want to speak to you, but I'll try."

Michael's smile faltered a little as he heard his ex-wife calling to his son. "Kyle, it's your dad for you!"

There was a pause, and then she came back on the line. "Sorry, Michael. It's no go. He's still angry with you."

Cow. She didn't have to sound so pleased about it.

Michael made himself smile again. Nobody was going to spoil this wonderful day for him, not even doom-deliverer Diane. "Okay," he said breezily, "can you pass on a message to him then please? Tell him his new sister was born yesterday."

"She's here already? But that's early, isn't it?"

"Three weeks early, yes. It all happened rather quickly

last night. But she's fine. Both her and Jen are fine."

"Well, congratulations then. I'll tell him."

Kyle rang back within minutes. "Is it true, Dad?"

Michael smiled at the obvious excitement in his son's voice. "Yes, it's true. You're now officially a big brother."

Kyle's laugh warmed Michael's heart. "Man, that's amazing! Does she look like me?"

"She looks like me. At least, that's what Jen said."

"Poor kid!" joked Kyle, and Michael laughed.

"Watch it. She's called Hannah; Jen named her after her friend."

"Cool. When can I see her?"

"I'm going down there this morning, but visiting hours for everyone else start at two. Want me to come and pick you up?"

"Yeah, please. I'll be at college."

"Okay; see you at the main entrance at one-thirty."

"Okay, Dad, but how am I going to travel on the bike with my leg?"

"I'll get a taxi."

"Right. Cool." Kyle paused. Michael had a good idea of what he was going to say next.

"Dad? Does this mean you and Jen are getting back together?"

He hoped so. He really hoped so. But it wasn't just his decision. Carefully, he stifled a sigh. "I'm not sure, Kyle. One step at a time, eh?"

When Michael arrived at the maternity ward promptly at ten-thirty, he found both Jen and Hannah asleep. Settling quietly in a chair by Jen's bed, he was content to watch them both – his two girls. Kyle's words were still ringing in his ears. *Does this mean you and Jen are getting back together?* God, why the hell had he ever let her leave in the first place? He was so stupid. Even at the time he'd known it was wrong. But the news about the baby, coming on top of everything else, had just been too much to cope with – like sand slipping through fingers he couldn't close. But it was time to stop that flow, if Jen would let him.

253

Hannah made a noise in her sleep, and instantly Jen woke up, opening exhausted eyes.

"Hi," he said, bending to kiss her cheek. "How are you feeling? Tired?"

She gave him a wan smile. "Beyond tired. And sore. It's pretty noisy in here; we didn't get much sleep last night."

Hannah stirred, properly this time, her tiny face puckering as she began to cry.

"She's hungry, I think," said Jen, instantly alert. "Shh, darling, Mummy's here. Can you pass her to me please?"

Carefully, he reached into the crib to lift his daughter.

"We haven't done do so well with feeding yet," Jen told him as he passed the baby to her. "She doesn't seem to be able to get the hang of it. The nurse said to give her one more go and then to try some formula if she doesn't take anything. I'm desperate for the loo though."

"D'you want me to help you get there?" he asked, but Jen grimaced.

"I've still got a catheter in."

Realising she was embarrassed, Michael smiled. "I'll have a cuddle of Hannah for a minute," he said, reaching to take the baby from her again.

Hannah gazed at him with blurred, grumpy eyes, snuffling and squirming as she considered him. Then she decided he was most definitely not what she needed right at this moment, and renewed her cries.

Michael laughed softly, gently rocking her and pressing the sweetness of her head to his face. He could remember doing exactly the same thing with Kyle all those years ago, and it felt as natural as breathing. Once again he thought how was ridiculous it had been of him to have been so scared of this.

"Here," Jen said, reaching out her arms for the baby, "I'm ready."

Michael transferred the precious cargo back to her and watched as Jen focussed her entire attention onto helping Hannah to latch on properly. Suddenly she looked up and grinned at him, her face alight with pleasure. "She's doing it! She's really feeding!"

"Of course," he smiled. "She's clever."

After Hannah was replete, they changed her nappy together and he gave her a present from Rick – a babygro with a cute cat picture on the front.

"I can't imagine Rick picking this out himself," she smiled, delighted with it.

"Nor me," he agreed, enjoying the special moment just as if he were like any of the other thrilled fathers in the ward enjoying special moments with their newborns.

Together they gave Hannah her first bath, smiling at the faces she pulled, and held their breath when she had a hearing test. He watched as Jen rummaged gleefully through the free bag of goodies in the Bounty pack a woman brought round, and while she fed Hannah again. And if the smell of Hannah's head had reminded him of Kyle's first hours, then none of this shared activity did. All he could remember about Diane's brief stay in hospital was her disapproving mother and the way he hadn't been able to do anything right.

By the time he had to leave to meet Kyle, Michael was feeling optimistic about the future. He and Jen hadn't talked about any of the big stuff they needed to talk about yet; it was true. He'd just wanted to enjoy the moment, and imagined Jen felt the same. After all, there would only ever be one first morning of their daughter's life. But it had been so good to share it all together, and surely she could tell how he felt now?

"I'll be back in an hour," he told her, kissing her cheek. "Why don't you have a rest while I'm gone?"

"If madam lets me," she smiled. "See you in a bit."

But when he returned with Kyle, Marcia was there, holding Hannah in her arms. When she looked up at him, her expression was typically unfriendly.

"I was just going to call you," he said, wondering if she had ever smiled at him properly, in all the years he'd known her. He didn't think she had.

"Jen texted me this morning," she told him. "I came just

as soon as I finished my treatment."

"Sorry, Michael," Jen said. "I forgot to mention it before. Kyle! Come on, come and meet your sister. Hand her over, Marcia."

Standing at the end of the bed, Michael watched as Kyle, having hobbled over on his crutches and settled in the other chair, prepared to take the baby from Marcia.

"Make sure you support her head," Marcia told him. "That's it."

"Wow!" said Kyle, looking adoringly down at Hannah. "She's gorgeous! Oh, wow, Jen!"

"I think he's in love," said Marcia wryly.

"You betcha," said Kyle, bending even closer to examine every little detail of his sister's face.

"Sorry, folks," said a nurse, bustling over. "Not more than two people are allowed at a bedside at any one time. It gets like Liverpool Street station in here otherwise."

Kyle and Marcia both looked in Michael's direction, and there could be absolutely no mistaking their meaning. *You've already had your turn.*

"I guess I'll go and get a coffee then," he said. "Be back to get you in thirty minutes, Kyle."

"Yeah, Dad," Kyle said vaguely, but Michael could tell he was already lost in his little sister's eyes once again.

Chapter Thirty-Nine

"It's a pity they don't allow flowers on the ward," Marcia said, staring down into Hannah's face. "Although you're the best flower of them all, aren't you, sweetie?"

Michael's taken Kyle back to college, but Marcia's still here, still doting on Hannah. I'll have to claim her back soon though, because my boobs are starting to hurt. But first of all I need to go to the loo, which, although it's only on the other side of the corridor, is a major undertaking because my operation scar's so sore. But it's a whole lot better than the humiliating catheter, which I had removed half an hour ago.

"D'you know what I'd like more than flowers?" I say, preparing to swing my legs ever so gently off the bed.

Marcia speaks vaguely, not looking up from Hannah's gorgeousness. "What? Chocolate?"

"Big knickers. The bigger the better. They have disposables here, but I'd love some of my own, and my usual ones are going to dig into my scar. You couldn't nip into Primark and get some for me, could you?"

Marcia's expression says, *Buy big knickers? Me? Never!* But her mouth says, "Sure. How many pairs?"

I smile. "Get lots. Then I won't need to do any washing for a while. And don't worry; nobody will think they're for you. You're not a big pants kind of a girl."

Her expression goes all dreamy. "I might be though, mightn't I? In nine months' time."

"Let's hope so." Having succeeded in getting my feet to the ground, I commence the painful shuffle to the toilet.

By the time I return, Hannah's wailing to be fed again, her little face bright red; but I knew that anyway. All those babies in the ward, and I could pick out my daughter's cry if

I were blindfolded.

Marcia waits while I prop myself up with pillows then passes Hannah to me. My daughter snuffles like a puppy then latches expertly on, feeding hungrily.

"Nobody would think she found it difficult at first," I say fondly, smiling and stroking the impossible softness of her hair. When I look up, Marcia's expression tells me she's wondering how she'll cope if the pregnancy test's negative in two weeks' time. I want to tell her it'll be all right, but since I don't know any such thing, it seems better not to do so.

"When do you get out of here?" she asks. "Three days is it?"

"Yes, on Thursday."

"I'll come and get you, if you like."

"Oh," I say, taken aback, because I suppose I assumed that Michael would be the one to take us home.

"Well," says Marcia. "*He* can't do it, can he? Not now he's only got that ridiculous motorbike."

Which is completely true. Smiling very carefully so she won't see how disappointed I am, I accept her offer. "Thanks, Marcia. That's kind of you."

"No problem. I don't suppose he's bothered to speak to you about the future yet, has he?"

I think about the blissful morning Michael and I have just shared, and shake my head reluctantly. "Give him a chance, Marse," I say. "We were busy with Hannah this morning."

Her expression says it all, but amazingly, she manages to restrain herself from launching into a diatribe against Michael.

"I'd better go now, I suppose; let you get some rest. I'll pop in and see you tomorrow in my lunch break, okay?"

She bends to kiss first me, then Hannah; and Hannah, who is mid-suck, kicks one arm and one foot in the air.

"Look," says Marcia. "She's going to be a dancer!"

When Michael comes back later, I tell him Marcia's prediction for our daughter's future career. "She can be whatever she wants to be, just so long as it's legal," he says, and I smile because when he talks like that, it shows me he means to play a part in Hannah's life. Exactly how this will happen I still don't know, if we never talk about it. But this just isn't the right place to do so, not with only curtains for walls.

"The nurse on the reception desk said you should be discharged on Thursday," he says.

"Yes, all being well."

"I'll ask Rick to lend me his car," he says, then stops, seeing the expression on my face. "What?"

"I've just arranged with Marcia for her to take me home."

"Have you? Oh."

"Sorry, I didn't think. Well, I did, but only about the motorbike."

"You ought to have guessed I'd sort something out for you both."

Ought I? My gaze slips away to Hannah's enthusiastic sucking. It's an awkward moment, and who knows? We might actually have started talking then, curtain walls or no curtain walls. Only just at that moment, Luther arrives. Or rather, a giant teddy bear balloon with Luther behind it.

"Hi, Luther."

I can tell he's taken in both my exposed breast and Michael's glowering presence in one glance by the way he quickly puts the bear balloon in front of his face. "Hi, little Hannah, I'm Birthday Bear, and I've come to wish you a very happy birthday," he says in a daft voice, and I see Michael give a kind of *give me strength!* shift on his chair.

"Hi, Birthday Bear," I say, hiding a smile. "Can you tell Luther he doesn't have to be embarrassed about me feeding and it's very nice to see him?"

Luther sits; still ludicrously holding the birthday bear balloon, and acknowledges Michael with a nod. "Michael."

They've only met once, and that was by accident. Since Michael's always loathed me even mentioning Luther, it comes as no surprise when he limits his response to Luther's greeting to an answering nod and gets swiftly to his feet.

"Want anything from the shop, Jen? A magazine? Book? Sweets?"

"Surprise me," I say, and he smiles wanly at me before walking off.

Luther pulls a face but somehow manages to restrain himself from making any smart comments. "How are you?"

I smile weakly. "Exhausted. Happy. I hope you didn't mind that I named her after your mum?"

I'm watching his face carefully, so I can tell he means it when he says, "It's an honour."

Hannah unlatches from me and I lift her off my breast and quickly cover myself up. Then I put her over my shoulder and pat her back to make her burp.

"You look like a natural," remarks Luther, and I smile.

"I still feel like I'm following instructions," I say. "The thought of doing it all at home on my own is terrifying."

"You won't be alone though, will you?" he says, and I shake my head.

I smile. "No, I'm sure I won't. I'll have lots of support."

"From him?"

I don't pretend I don't know who he's talking about. "Of course." And if wanting something is enough to make it happen, then Michael's going to be right there by my side the way he was this morning; the two of us looking after Hannah together. I'm just going to have to wait and see.

Going home is a very emotional experience. After we've been discharged, I wait by the hospital exit with Hannah in her car seat, while Marcia goes to fetch the car. Hannah's wide-awake, and it's as if she's drinking everything in. I can't help smiling at her, or reaching out to stroke her perfect cheek with my finger. It's as if I have to keep touching her to check she's really real, and suddenly my heart swells with so much love, I'm not sure I can contain it. It's probably the hormones, but I'd like to blub, right there in the reception area, I really would. I'm so happy, and yet I'm also sythingly sad. Hannah's house is a haven for us, but I don't want to go back there. I want to go home, to Michael's old house. I want to show Hannah the copper beech trees and have Michael rub my back and make me a cup of tea the way he knows I like it. For us to curl up together on our bed – the three of us, just delighting in being a family.

Marcia gets out of her car. "They're really going to have to sort out more parking for this place. Three people practically ram-raided each other to get to my parking spot first. Come on, let's get the baby strapped into the back."

I know how to strap a car seat in, but with my scar still throbbing it's easier to let Marcia take over. I can't help checking the seat's in right though.

"She's fine," Marcia tells me, and I smile bravely and settle down in the back of the car next to my daughter for the journey home.

Chapter Forty

Michael

Jen had said he could go over any time he liked, but the first time he went she was in bed, getting some rest while the baby slept, and he'd felt awful, disturbing her. The second time Marcia was there, taking care of Hannah while Jen was in the shower. And on his third attempt, when he tried ringing before he went over, Jen's phone just kept going through to voicemail. It seemed hopeless.

"You need a plan, mate," Rick told him. "You and Jen need to sort out how you want things to work. That way you'll both know where you are."

Rick – tree officer extraordinaire, committed bachelor and Xbox addict – giving him advice. Good advice, as it happened, but easier said than done. He'd always loved Jen, and as for little Hannah, she'd scooped out his insides right from the very first second he'd held her. His mind was completely and unequivocally changed on the subject of becoming a father again. All he had to do was convince Jen of the fact. But how? Some sort of big gesture was required.

Suddenly, an idea popped into his head; an idea that could really make a difference, if it worked. Hell, he would *make* it work. Excitedly, Michael went about making plans, and one evening when for once, he, Jen and Hannah were actually alone together, he broached the subject.

Earlier he'd made a casserole with jacket potatoes, and the fragrant smell of the meal was still pervading the house. They were in the conservatory; Jen in her favourite armchair, feeding Hannah, and Michael on the sofa with the newspaper. All was quiet and peaceful, the evening stretching pleasantly before them. Then Michael realised Jen was crying.

"God, Jen; what's wrong?" he asked, immediately slinging the newspaper down and hurrying over to her.

She put up the hand that wasn't cradling Hannah's head to wipe away her tears. "Nothing," she sniffed. "Just hormones, I expect."

The easy option would be to just nod and accept what she said, but Michael knew he couldn't afford to take the easy option; not if he wanted things to work out for them. "But it's not just hormones, is it?" he asked.

"I don't know," she said miserably. "I'm just exhausted all the time, that's all. Don't get me wrong, I love her *so* much, and she's everything I've always wanted, but it's such a pain not being able to drive yet. I can't go anywhere or do anything; I have to wait for people to come to me. And everyone's been so brilliant, but... Oh, God, I don't mean to whine; I'm not really unhappy. It's just that when she came, I'd only just lost Hannah..."

When Little Hannah shifted in her arms, Jen moved her expertly to the other breast, not speaking again until she was settled.

"I think you're doing brilliantly," Michael said. "You only have to look at her to see that. The midwife said she's thriving, didn't she?"

She sighed. "Yes. And I know it's true. But the thing is..." She kept her face down, watching Hannah. Suddenly, he knew what was coming and his heart began to race. "I don't know where I am with you."

He took his courage into his hands and asked, "Where do you want to be with me?"

"I don't know that either," she said, her hand gliding over Hannah's downy head.

She sounded so completely tired and hopeless, Michael instinctively knew that whatever words he chose right now, they wouldn't be enough. He was useless at speaking about his feelings at the best of times, and now, with Jen at such a low ebb, it just didn't seem like a good time to talk.

"Listen," he said, "there's something I want to show you. Have you got any appointments on Friday? Any midwives or friends visiting?"

Jen shook her head, frowning. "No, I don't think so."

"Then I'll come and get you both at nine o'clock. We're going out somewhere."

She looked up at him as if he were an idiot. "How are we going to do that, when you haven't got a car?"

He shrugged. "I'll borrow one. Or we can use yours, if that's okay."

"Well, does it have to be so early? It takes me an age to get Hannah ready in the morning."

"Yes," he said firmly. "It does. Any later than that and it won't work. Don't worry, I'll help you, and you can always feed her in the car." He reached out to stroke a hand down her hair, urging her to agree. "Please say 'yes', Jen. I promise you it will be worth it."

"All right," she sighed. "We'll come."

At dawn on Friday morning, the sky was cloudless. Arriving at Winterton beach, Michael smiled. It was the perfect day for what he had in mind, and that had to be a sign. This was going to work out; he knew it was.

Chapter Forty-One

On Friday morning, I wake early. Of course I wake early; these days there is nothing but early. My daughter, bless her, wakes every few hours throughout the night, demanding to be fed. I swear she sleeps better during the day than the night. At six a.m. I hold her, gazing down at her face. "You're nocturnal, you funny girl," I say, and she stares back at me thoughtfully, as if considering the truth of this statement.

"Mummy doesn't know if she's going to be able to stay awake today for whatever it is Daddy's got planned for us; she really doesn't."

Suddenly, I remember speaking to baby Luis with exactly the same bright tone of voice in Cuba, upstairs from the crazy paladar restaurant. When I've got through these precious, difficult weeks, when I can drive again, when I know what the hell's happening between myself and Michael; then I must make sure Hannah meets other babies like Luis. I'll join baby groups; have some structure to my days. A life.

"What has your daddy got planned, eh?" I ask Hannah, sighing because it would be so much easier just to go back to sleep.

I refer to Michael as Daddy when I speak to Hannah, but only when we're alone. To do so in front of Michael would seem like a huge step, even though it is what he is. Maybe – if we ever manage to have that highly necessary conversation about our future – it will seem more natural to call him Daddy when he's there.

And suddenly, despite the total exhaustion in every particle of me, a tiny flicker of excitement about the day ahead tingles into my brain. Whatever it turns out to be, at least it's a day out. And after almost two whole weeks of being indoors, that's a very exciting prospect indeed.

When Michael arrives, I try to get him to tell me where we're going, but he won't.

"I told you," he says. "Wait and see."

But when we reach a familiar dogleg crossroads on the way to Martham, it's easy to guess. "Winterton-on-Sea?" I say disbelievingly. "You're taking us to Winterton-on-Sea?"

"Might be," is all the reply I get.

"Why?"

"I told you—"

"I know; wait and see." Sighing, I give up, closing my eyes. "Wake me up when we get there then."

And I do doze for a few minutes, but wake as soon as the car stops, because that's what Hannah does. Immediately I reach to open the door, intending to go to her.

"Wait!" Michael stops me. "Let me help you out. You need to move carefully with your scar."

He means well, and besides, it's true, I definitely do need his help. My operation scar still hurts, and sleep-deprivation has robbed me of all strength. So it's illogical of me to feel irritated. But somehow I can't help it, because I'm just so sick of being so helpless and dependent. Every time Hannah cries, an overwhelming feeling of panic rises up inside me and I just have to do something – anything – to stop it as soon as is humanly possible.

"I'll have to sit in the car and feed her," I say, but Michael frowns.

"Didn't you just feed her before we came out? She's only crying because the car's stopped; babies like motion. When we start walking, she'll be fine."

That's another thing that's unfairly aggravating; the fact that Michael knows more about babies than I do. As a first-timer, I'm tense about everything, whereas he takes it all in his stride. When he's there, that is. I'm the one who deals with Hannah twenty-four-seven.

Michael's watching the conflicting emotions pass over my face. "Come on, Jen," he says persuasively. "There are already quite a lot of people here. It'll be too late soon.

266

Come and see. Please. Hannah will be fine."

Once again, my curiosity's piqued. What can he want me to see? A wrecked ship? A beached whale? But how could he have arranged either of those things so specifically for nine-thirty on a Friday morning?

He has Hannah in his arms by this time, and her eyes are already closing as he rocks her.

"All right," I say ungraciously, "but I hope you don't expect me to walk very far."

"Just to the dunes; not far."

Very grudgingly, I begin to walk slowly beside him. "Why's it so busy here today?" I ask, because normally on a Friday morning during term time I'd only expect a few dog-walkers' cars to be parked in the car park. It's different in the summer holidays, but we're still only in June.

"Careful!" Michael warns as I half stumble down the step from the beach café terrace. Then he looks away, something distracting him. "Oh, God," he says. "The TV's here. They must have had a tip off."

I turn to look, and sure enough, two men are unloading equipment from a van emblazoned with the logo of our local news programme. "Michael?" I ask. "What's going on?"

He smiles, reaching over to kiss me. "Just a little further and you'll find out."

There's a crowd grouped on the cliff, and they're all looking down at something on the beach. It's frustrating as hell not knowing what it is, but as we get closer, excitement begins to flutter in my tummy. Excitement mingling with something else. Apprehension. A part of me wants to risk blinding pain from my operation scar and to run the rest of the way to the cliff top. The other part wants Hannah to wake up and start demanding her feed to give me an excuse to delay the evil moment.

But my daughter stays fast asleep, and in any case, the cliff top is drawing me like a moth to a flame.

As we get closer to the people already gathered on the cliff top, a man nudges his companion, pointing at Michael.

"That's the artist," he says. "I saw him on the beach earlier."

Artist? When I quickly glance in Michael's direction, I notice his eyes are feverish; furtive even, and the squashy feeling in my tummy increases.

"Excuse me, everyone," Michael says to the crowd, "can we get through please?"

"That must be her," a woman holding a Jack Russell dog on a lead says in a loud whisper. I want to grab her by her jacket lapels and give her a good shake, demanding she let me in on the secret.

"Aah," says her friend soppily, looking at me as if I'm some sort of curiosity. "Aah…"

Then, at last, we're on the edge of the cliff, and Michael looks down at me. There's an intensity about his expression that makes me want to keep looking at him forever. I can't remember him ever looking at me quite like that before.

"Shh," someone in the crowd says, and then Michael speaks.

"I did this to show you how I feel about you," he says, his voice sounding thick and dark with emotion. "I've never been good at putting that into words. So, I thought this might help." Then he smiles, reaching out to wipe away my sudden tears. "Look, Jen."

Very fearfully, I turn my head to look down onto the beach. And what I see there makes me gasp, bringing shocked hands up to my face. It's amazing; unbelievable. Incredible.

Down on a large area of the beach, somebody – Michael – has drawn a giant paisley pattern of interlocking droplets in the sand. And inside every droplet, there's a perfectly drawn ladybird. And just in case I don't realise what those ladybirds mean, there are some words written in artistically-looped writing in the centre of the piece.

I love you, Jen. Marry me? Michael. XXX

I can feel his gaze burning on my face as I stare and stare down at the work of art. It's the most romantic thing anyone has done for me ever, and I can feel the crowd around us shifting restlessly. At the back, someone says, "What's she going to say?" And someone else, "Oh look! Maybe we'll be on television!"

Finally I manage to speak. "Can we go closer?" I ask Michael, and my voice doesn't sound like my own.

"As long as you think you're up to it," Michael says, and when I nod, he starts to lead the way through the crowd, still holding Hannah in his arms.

As we walk away, I hear a mumble of conversation starting up behind me. I know my reaction's not what they were all hoping for; God, I'm sure it's not what Michael hoped for. But it's all I've got to give just now.

Close-up, it's possible to see the full skill of his work. "Did you really do all this yourself?" I ask, stunned and moved to my very core at the thought of him beavering away, totally focussed, arranging all this just for me.

"Yes. This morning. I started at first light. I'd planned exactly what I wanted to do beforehand. I've decided… well, I'm going to start making art again. I haven't done any, not for years."

"Not in all the time I've known you."

"No," he agrees, then shrugs. "Well, as I say, I'm going to get back into doing it. I'm not sure why I stopped really; pressure to make a living, I suppose. Though obviously, that's still an issue. I'm still going to need a job as well."

"I'm very glad," I tell him, my gaze still on the wonderful swirling patterns. "Really glad you aren't going to waste your talent anymore."

Michael's standing with the sea behind him, our daughter contentedly asleep in his arms. His eyes are the same greeny-blue as the sea, and I love him so very much. I always have.

"Thank you for doing this beautiful thing for me," I say emotionally. "It's totally incredible. I can't even begin to find the words to describe it."

His lips twist, and he looks down at Hannah. A pair of seagulls squawk above our heads. Somewhere in the distance, a dog barks.

"There's a but though, isn't there?" he says quietly. "You

269

aren't going to say 'yes'."

Everything I've ever wanted is within my reach. It's not even at arms' length – it's right there waiting for me to gather it in. I can't believe I'm going to say what I'm about to say.

"No, it's not a 'yes'. Not yet anyway."

He swallows, nodding. "But it could be, in the future?" His eyes are hungry; a little desperate. They remind me of how I felt the day I took the pregnancy test and stood in the kitchen, waiting for him to come home.

"You'd need to convince me," I tell him, and he half turns to look out at the paisley ladybirds.

"And this doesn't?"

"It's so very beautiful, Michael. Completely moving. But no, it doesn't quite, no. I'm sorry."

The dejection on his face brings clawing panic into my brain, and it's hard to ignore the voice that's shouting inside me, ARE YOU COMPLETELY CRAZY? But I know I have to, for Hannah's sake.

"That's okay," he says and starts to walk up the beach. "I guess I've only got myself to blame. Shall we get back to the car?"

There's a sandy slope to negotiate on the way, and each movement of my legs sends a stabbing pain through my scar. There are crowds of onlookers and watchful eyes. A TV microphone shoved in my face and ignored. Cameras clicking. Michael helps me through it all, his face impassive, and Hannah sleeps on, oblivious.

We journey home in almost complete silence, and when we arrive, Michael helps me and Hannah out of the car. Then he deposits the changing bag by the front door. "I'm going to get off now, okay? I'll call you soon. Bye."

He returns to the borrowed car, gets in and starts the engine. A skilful turn in the drive, a hand lifted in farewell, and then he's gone. Leaving me feeling more alone than I've ever felt in my entire life.

Chapter Forty-Two

Michael

Rick called to him from the sitting room. "You're on the national news, Michael!"

With a sinking heart, Michael went to look. And saw himself, walking back from the beach, holding Hannah and trying to keep it together. Jen, pale-faced, eyes down, enduring the attention of the crowd.

"The art installation was apparently part of an elaborate plan by thirty-six-year-old Michael Brandon to propose to his girlfriend," the newsreader told viewers, and Michael groaned.

What a stupid, stupid idea it'd been. His phone had been ringing all day long, and social media had gone mad with it. Someone had posted a film of his artwork on YouTube and thousands of people had watched it. If he'd set out to become famous, then he couldn't have thought of a better plan to achieve it. But that hadn't been his aim, and the whole thing had gone badly wrong. He was a laughing stock, his grand action reduced to being the fun item at the end of the news, just before the weather forecast.

But at least Kyle had been impressed. "I can't believe you actually did that, Dad," he'd said to Michael on the phone earlier on. "It was so totally cool!"

"Well," said Rick now, "I said you should show Jen how you felt, and you certainly did that. Well done, mate. I'm only sorry she didn't go for it; can't believe she didn't, I must admit. Still, I guess you know where you stand now."

But he didn't though; that was the thing. Jen had said it was 'no' for now; that he still needed to convince her. But convince her of what? And how?

Chapter Forty-Three

Michael

The week after the Winterton proposal, I arrange to meet Marcia in Norwich. It's the first time I've ventured into the city since Hannah was born, and it feels slightly surreal to be inside the bustle of the Forum café. I've braved the bus to get here, successfully manhandling buggy, baby and changing paraphernalia inside. Marcia offered to come and fetch me, but I wanted to manage by myself. And now that I have, I wish I'd done it earlier, because it was fine. Everyone was so helpful, and Hannah's thoroughly enjoyed been cooed over by an entire busload of passengers.

She's awake now, but still in the buggy, content for the moment, so I have both hands free to hug Marcia when she arrives. After we've kissed, I look intently into her eyes. "Well?" I ask, but by the way her eyes are sparkling, I'm already pretty sure what her answer's going to be.

Sure enough, she nods, grinning. "Yes!" she whoops, punching the air. "The test was bloody positive! I'm pregnant!"

"Congratulations," says the woman at the next table, and Marcia and I clutch each other and laugh.

"That's so great, Marse," I say. "Fantastic."

She sits down at the table, grinning all over her face. "I know! After all this time. I can't believe it; but it's true. It's early days of course; I'm not going to go around telling everybody, but wey heh, eh?"

"Wey heh indeed! It's fabulous; really fabulous. This calls for a celebratory cappuccino. Keep an eye on Hannah, and I'll go and get you one."

"And a croissant," demands Marcia. "With butter and

jam. I'm eating for two now!"

When I return with the tray, Marcia's goo-gooing down at Hannah, who she's holding in her arms. I smile to myself, carefully placing the tray on the table. Motherhood's going to soften my friend somewhat, and love her as I do, that can only be a good thing.

"She smiled at me!" Marcia crows, and I quash any comments I might have made about wind or it being too early. Since Hannah was born, everything's been about me. But today's Marcia's day.

I hold out my hands to take my baby from her, saying, "Here; you'll need both hands to butter your croissant."

Reluctantly she passes Hannah to me and starts talking happily about Gary's reaction to her news.

Finally the subject's temporarily exhausted, and she asks, "How about you? Have you got over your dramatic proposal yet?"

"Oh, don't," I sigh, instantly feeling guilty. "I've only seen Michael once since then, and things were really awkward between us."

"I must admit," Marcia goes on, "I was really surprised when you knocked him back."

I gape at her. "Were you?"

"Of course," she answers simply. "It's all you've ever wanted, isn't it? To live happily ever after with Michael? And what he did; well, it was just amazing."

I just can't believe what I'm hearing. Marcia's always been so dead set against Michael, and now, because she's pregnant; because he made a grand, romantic gesture, she's completely changed her tune.

"D'you think I was wrong to turn him down then?"

She shrugs. "I'm not saying that at all; I'm sure you had your reasons."

I look down at Hannah, lying in the crook of my arm. "Everything's different now I've got her. Michael's always...well; I've always felt he's held something of himself back. If I was going to marry him, I'd have to feel he was completely mine, that's all." Hannah squirms in my

273

arms and starts to make little sucking noises with her mouth, reminding me it's time for her feed.

"Fair enough," says Marcia brightly, but some of the sparkle's gone out of the morning for me, and I only half listen when Marcia changes the subject, talking about the way her mum reacted to the news of her pregnancy.

I glance around the café, trying to judge whether I'll get away with feeding Hannah here, in such a public place. If I do, it will be my first go at feeding Hannah anywhere but in the hospital and at home, and I'm a little self-conscious about the prospect. I could really have done with a more discreet table than this, but it was the only free one when we arrived.

Suddenly, I notice a group of women just leaving a comfortable leather sofa across the café. "Marse? D'you mind if we move over there so I can feed Hannah?"

"Of course not," she says, but before we can move, a strange-looking man comes over to us.

"'Scuse me," he says, and the slurred way he speaks, together with the way he's weaving about slightly, speak to me of high-strength beer drunk at an inappropriately early hour. "You're Michael Brandon's girlfriend, aren't you?"

Bloody hell! How does he know that? I stare up at him, speechless, with Hannah wriggling and protesting in my arms. The man's face is ultra pale, and his clothes are grubby. He's also standing way too close to Hannah for my liking. Yet he seems to know who I am. How can that be?

I hold Hannah protectively to my chest, unsure how to answer him. But he doesn't seem to need a reply anyway. "Saw you in the newspaper the other week," he explains. "And on the telly. Michael's little stunt on the beach. You really knocked him back, didn't you?"

I flush. "I'm sorry," I say, "I don't—"

"No need to apologise," he says easily, plonking himself down, uninvited, onto a spare chair. "Can't help it if you don't want to marry the guy, can you?"

Hannah doesn't want to be pressed against me; she wants to be fed and she's making sure I know it. Suddenly the man

274

reaches out a hand as if to touch her, and I flinch, moving her away, unintentionally giving him a good view of her face.

"Ah, isn't she sweet?" he remarks. "Dead spit of Michael. Can't help feeling sorry for the poor sod, getting turned down so publicly."

"I'm sorry, how do you know Michael exactly?" I ask.

At the same time Marcia says, "You're making the baby cry. Move back a bit, will you?"

The man swivels round to look at Marcia, his gaze suddenly hostile as it rakes over her. "What's the matter? Contaminating the air she's breathing, am I?"

Yes, is the non-politically correct answer; not that Hannah's aware of him or anything else but her desperate need to be fed. She's stretching her tiny body out now; the bleating cries a prelude to the hungry bellows I know will shortly follow. But it's quite impossible to unfasten my top in front of the man at our table. I want him gone, but I also need to know how he knows Michael.

Slowly, with Marcia temporarily silenced, he turns back in my direction. "Michael and I go way back," he says. "At school together, we were. Lost touch for a while after high school, but met up again a few years ago. Turns out I live in the same street as his mum."

By now, Hannah's cries are so loud they're turning heads.

"Shall I take her, Jen?" Marcia asks, holding her arms out. "Or do you want to leave?"

But I hardly hear her. "Michael's mother lives in New Zealand," I say, but the man just laughs as if I've said something extremely funny.

"That what he told you is it? And you believed him?" He laughs some more, then he shrugs. "Suppose I can't blame him under the circumstances. But no, Mike's mum's still very much alive and over here. She lives in Edward Street, Great Yarmouth. Two doors down from me."

Marcia's on her feet now, gathering our belongings together, fetching the buggy. "Come on, Jen," she says.

"Let's go."

Automatically, I stand, my movements dazed and clumsy. Although Hannah's cries are almost loud enough to deafen, I still hear what the man says when he shouts after me.

"Number 47B Edward Street – that's her address. I'm sure she'll be very pleased to have a visitor."

Marcia and I head off towards Chapelfield Gardens to find a shady bench for me to feed Hannah.

"He was off his face," Marcia says on the way. "I'm sure it was all bollocks."

"Are you?" I ask, my voice filled with doubt; because instinctively, I believe what that horrible little man's just told me, and suddenly it feels as if the man I've loved these past four years is a complete stranger.

"Well, you could always call Michael and ask him about it," suggests Marcia. "Though I suppose there's no guarantee he'll tell you the truth. Pity; I was just starting to come round to him as well."

My brain's buzzing. "I need to go to Yarmouth to check this out," I say. "Will you take me?"

She frowns. "Really? Jen, he was just some wasted tosser trying to stir up trouble. Looks like he's succeeded too. And what about Hannah?"

"You can look after her in the car. I won't be long."

"If that guy lives in the street, God only knows what it's like."

"Please." If she says no, I'll have to do it by myself somehow, but I really don't want to have to take Hannah in with me.

Marcia sighs, her expression resigned. "Oh, all right," she says, "I'll take you. But I still think—"

"I know you do. But I have to see for myself."

We set off just as soon as Hannah's finished her feed. All the way there my brain's working overtime, trying to think of any earthly reason why Michael would lie to me about his mother. It just doesn't make sense. If it turns out to be true, then obviously he didn't want me to meet her. But why not? Especially now she's a grandmother. A grandmother. If

276

it does turn out to be true, then Hannah has a grandmother.

In Yarmouth, we park along the sea front. I've looked up Edward Street on my phone; it's just across the road. As I get out of the car, my nostrils are assailed by a strong smell of fish and chips. "You've got fifteen minutes," Marcia tells me sternly. She's sitting in the back of the car, next to Hannah, who's fallen asleep. "Then we're coming to check up on you."

"Okay. Wish me luck."

I walk quickly away from the car, crossing the road and turning up Edward Street, looking for number 47B and wondering what number does the guy from the Forum live at. At least I know I'm unlikely to bump into him here. Just the thought of him makes me shudder; unpleasant little man. It's difficult to believe Michael ever knew him, and I really hope I never see him again.

As I reach number 47, a young woman's just coming out of the front door. She holds the door open for me. "Are you going in?" she asks in accented English.

"Yes, please. I want 47B."

She points into the darkness of the interior. "At the back," she says and leaves.

"Thanks very much…" My words follow her down the steps, but she doesn't turn to acknowledge them. For a second, I stand to watch her click clacking on her way. Then I take a deep breath and venture inside. There's a large pile of post strewn on a table in the shared hallway, and I walk past it to reach the door at the far end of the hallway. Number 47B. Oh, God, this is it.

Raising my hand, I knock gently, the sound pathetic in the emptiness. Nothing. I knock again, harder this time, and at last I hear shuffling footsteps. The door opens – just a crack, but far enough for me to see part of a woman's face.

"Hello," I say, my eyes busily comparing the glimpse of nose, eye and mouth with Michael's. "Can I…speak to you for a moment?"

"I'm still taking the tablets, if that's what it's about," she says, pulling the door open a little further and turning her back on me to return to her flat.

I'm not sure what to do. Follow her? Clearly she's mistaken me for someone else, but who? Some sort of health professional?

I venture along the hallway and into her flat, closing the door behind me. It smells of cigarettes and stale air. "Are they doing you any good?" I ask, improvising. "The tablets?"

She turns, giving me my first good look at her face. It's a shocking experience. Because I can see Michael in her features – they share the same cheekbones; the same jaw line. But Michael's eyes are green, and this woman's are dark; so dark, they're almost black. And more than that, they're suspicious and furtive, sizing me up in a way that reminds me of the man at the Forum.

But her eyes aren't the only disturbing things about her; her face is covered in wounds and bruises at various stages of recovery. Clearly she's been in a car accident, or somebody's attacked her; something traumatic. And yet she's just let me – a total stranger – into her home.

"You lot tell me they do me good," she says, and it takes me a moment to remember she's speaking about the tablets. Suddenly I'm ashamed to have given her a false impression.

"Look," I say, "I'm not sure who you think I am, but my name's Jenny. I …know Michael."

"You're not from the Social?" She stares at me, sizing me up.

"No. I know Michael, your son."

"I know who Michael is," she says, and there's an edge of hostility in her voice now.

I have to be totally sure that this is Michael's mother and not some kind of sick, freaky coincidence, so I reach for my bag, taking my purse out. "I've got a photograph of him, look." I fumble in the purse and find the photo, tucked between a discount card for the local cinema and my driving licence. "This is him," I say, showing it to her.

She seems reluctant to take it, her face suddenly sulky and uncooperative, so I go over with it. "Is this your

Michael?" I ask.

She looks at the photo, but doesn't take it from me, her lank, grey hair flopping forward as she moves her head. "Yes," she says. "That's my son. At least, I think so. Sometimes he's here, and sometimes he's not."

My head starts to throb. Does she mean that Michael's sometimes physically here? Or that he's sometimes in her mind, and sometimes not? I don't know, and neither do I know what to say next. I came here to find out the truth about that horrid little man's claims, but seem only to have found more questions.

Why has Michael kept this frail, vulnerable woman a secret all this time? It makes absolutely no sense. All these years I could have been caring for her alongside him, making sure her hair is washed and she wears clothes that fit her properly. I'm willing to bet this woman has mental health issues, but is that any reason for her to be hidden away like some shameful secret?

An hour ago, I told Marcia I've always felt Michael was holding something back from me. Now I know how right that instinct was. What hope did we ever have of building a successful relationship when he was hiding something as big as this from me? And what about Kyle? Does the poor woman even know she has grandson? And a granddaughter now too…

Thoughts of Hannah instantly bring milk oozing from my breasts. The feed in Chapelfield Gardens was a hurried affair, with me desperate for us to be on our way. The damp breast pads pressing against my bra tell me she's hungry again, and I know I can't stay here much longer. Yet I can't drag myself away either. Somehow I feel compelled to form some sort of a relationship with this woman, though I don't know why. Michael and I have split up; it's too late to make any kind of difference. And yet I can't help myself. I just feel so sorry for her.

"What's your name?" I ask, and she answers straight away.

"Linda. But they call me Lin."

The room's so fusty and stale; I long to throw open the windows and get stuck into a good clean. I can't do that now, but I can come back, if she'll let me.

"Lin?" I ask her. "How would you like me to wash your hair for you?"

Chapter Forty-Four

Michael

Michael was washing up. Rick was at work, and Michael had the radio on to fill the silence. Another long day stretched out emptily before him. He couldn't go on like this, sponging off Rick; he had to get his own place sorted out, and he also urgently needed to find a way to make a living. But, fundamental as both things were, they both felt out of his reach just now. Before he could really apply himself to either of them, he needed to sort things out with Jen. Unless he could do that, he just wouldn't have the energy or the mind-space to make plans for the future.

On the radio, a woman was talking about her husband's affair. "The thing that hurt the most was knowing he'd concealed the truth from me for so long; that he'd just let me cruise along, thinking everything was all right with our marriage, when the truth was very different."

"Honesty is everything, isn't it?" said the presenter, and suddenly, with his hands submerged in the washing-up water, Michael knew what he had to do. Maybe he'd known it all along, and just hadn't been able to face it.

He had to tell Jen everything – the whole truth about his mum and the way he'd gown up. What shc did with the information after that was entirely up to her. She was hardly unlikely to be thrilled that he'd lied to her all this time. Perhaps she'd even pity him. He hoped not, because he didn't want her pity. And neither did he want her to choose to be with him for the wrong reasons.

Hell, who was he kidding? He just wanted her with him, helping to make his life make sense. They could sort anything else out if they were just together, couldn't they?

Quickly drying his hands, Michael reached for his phone, dialling the number of Hannah's house. When it rang and rang, he tried Jen's mobile instead. But that went unanswered too. Frustrated, he grabbed his helmet and bike keys, needing to take some action. Now he'd decided to tell her the truth, he had to do it, because if he thought about it too much, he might just lose his nerve.

Should he ride over to the house? Maybe she was taking a rest and she'd unplugged the phone. As he stood, still uncertain, his phone rang. It was a number he didn't recognise, but some instinct told him to answer it.

"Michael? It's Marcia."

Marcia? Ringing him? Hell hadn't frozen over, so something must be badly wrong. "What's wrong?"

"It's Jen. She's not answering her phone."

He could only just about make Marcia out over the sound of a crying baby. Hannah.

"Where are you?"

"In Yarmouth. I'm looking after Hannah while Jen—" Marcia broke off, but Michael didn't need the rest of the sentence anyway. As soon as she said Yarmouth, he knew where Jen was.

"She knows about my mum, doesn't she?"

"Yes. Look, she went to see her, about twenty minutes ago. And now she's not answering her phone, and I can't remember the number of the house."

"Hold on," he said. "I'm coming."

Chapter Forty-Five

There's no shower, only a bath, and no shower attachment that I can see, so I find a wooden chair and set it in front of the bathroom sink. Lin sits on it, and I put a towel around her shoulders, speaking brightly all the time about the difference it makes to the way I feel when my hair's clean and shiny. I'm like some kind of manic hairdressing trainee, but Lin just lets me rabbit on, accepting it all without comment. In fact she doesn't speak again until I'm arm deep in shampoo lather.

"They took him away from me, you know, when he was a little boy." Her words are so entirely blank, that at first I think I must have misunderstood her.

"You don't mean Michael, do you? They didn't take Michael away from you?"

I detect the movement of her nod beneath my fingers. Jesus. "Who took him?" I ask. "Social Services?"

"Yes," she says. "Who else would it be?"

"That's...terrible." What's even more terrible than what she's just said is the fact that there's still such a shocking lack of emotion in her voice. But then, surely that's just a front, isn't it? A defence mechanism against the utter awfulness of the event? "How old was Michael when it happened?"

She shrugs. "Four, five. Can't remember now."

Hannah's only a few weeks old, but already I love her more than my own life. What must it be like to have your child taken away from you? And Michael! Oh, poor Michael. However did it feel to him? And what happened to him?

Lin's eyes are closed now, and she seems relaxed beneath my massaging fingers. I, on the other hand, am not relaxed at all. It's taking a supreme effort of will not to communicate my churned up feelings through my fingertips.

"That must have been so very hard for you," I say at last, feeling how very inadequate the words are.

Lin shrugs. "Don't remember much about it really. Almost feels like it happened to someone else; like a story I heard once." She pauses for a moment. "Then he turns up here and I have to remember it all over again."

What does she mean? That she wishes Michael didn't come to see her? That she'd be happier forgetting?

The silence between us stretches on as my fingers work the shampoo into her scalp. I can't get the image of a distressed little boy being dragged away from his mother out of my head. And suddenly it hits me all over again that I've never seen photographs of Michael as a child. I asked him about it once, and he said something about them all being in New Zealand with his parents. But in reality, there probably aren't any.

I want to ask Lin what happened to Michael after he was taken, but don't quite have the courage. Besides, she might not even know. "I've just had a baby," I say instead, though I have no idea why. Maybe I just want to show her I understand the bond between a mother and a child, but in any case, if that was my intention, it doesn't have the expected affect on Lin, because she shudders; really shudders. The movement's so strong it almost knocks my fingers from her scalp.

"Don't talk to me about babies," she says. "I don't like babies. That's when the trouble really kicked off, that was, when I got pregnant."

Any images I might have had of this woman smiling down into Hannah's face are instantly erased. What trouble? What does she mean? But there's no time to ask, or even to fully process the information. Because now she's telling me something else – something equally shocking.

"His father wrote to him, every week after he left. But I never told them about the letters."

There's something so chilling about the satisfied way she says it, it makes me wish I'd never come here.

"Who?" I whisper, hardly daring to hear the answer. "Who didn't you tell?"

"The social workers of course; the do-gooding, we're better than you bloody social workers. Always saying, "Has Mr Brandon been in touch at all?" Useless shit of a man. Michael was better off without that bastard pitching up and disrupting everything. So I told them I hadn't heard from him."

Automatically, I put the plug into the plughole and turn on the taps to fill the sink, speaking as casually as I can. "A letter a week, you say? That's a lot of letters. Whatever did you do with them all?"

Lin's face stays blank for a moment, and then, as I watch, the same furtive look I saw before crosses her face. Despite my best efforts, my question probably came out a little too eagerly.

"Don't know," she says casually, but she's lying; I know it. "They're somewhere about, I think. Or I might have burnt them. Can't remember."

Turning off the taps, I pull the long strands of Lin's hair into the water and immerse the cup I brought from the kitchen. As I rinse her hair, my mind suddenly fills with the memory of a childhood dream. There was a music box with a ballerina inside it; every time I opened the lid, the ballerina danced around to the music. In my dream, the dancer was real – performing just for me; making me feel completely special. When I woke up, I suddenly knew the music box– albeit without a performing ballerina – had been real. It was my mother's, and when she was alive, I asked her over and over again to show it to me.

I was eight years old when I had the dream, home from boarding school for the summer holidays, staying with my father and stepmother. When I went down to breakfast, I asked dad about the music box, but he didn't know what had become of it. But Olivia, my stepmother did. Quick as a flash, always pleased to snuff out any little bit of pleasure I could experience in life, she said, "Oh that old thing. I gave it away to charity with some other junk. It's long gone now."

The water in the basin needs changing if I'm to make a good job of rinsing Lin's hair. But my hands are shaking and useless. I feel as if I've awakened a snake from sleep, and I keep thinking about a little boy – Michael – waiting to hear from his absent father, never knowing that his dad had, in fact, been writing to him week after week.

Why did Lin act so cruelly? And what else did she put Michael through? It must have been something pretty bad for Social Services to take him away from her, and I'm ashamed of how ready I was to believe Lin was somebody to be pitied and cared for. Why didn't it ever occur to me that she might be also someone to be feared?

Suddenly, there's a knock at the door. Straight away I know it's Marcia, come to check up on me, because even in the bathroom I can hear my daughter's hungry cries.

God, Hannah; I don't want her here. Not that I think Lin's going to do anything to harm my daughter, but I still haven't forgotten her instinctive shudder of dislike when I mentioned having a baby, and I don't want anyone to look at my Hannah that way.

Lin sits up straight, soaking the towel with water.

"It's okay," I say quickly. "You wait here. I'll go and see who it is." And I put the rinsing cup down on the side of the sink and hurry out.

"Are you all right?" Marcia asks when I open the door. "Only she started screaming, and for the life of me, I couldn't remember the house number."

My daughter's bright red in her desperation for me, and I take her from Marcia, ashamed to have let her get into this state.

"Shh," I say, resting my cheek against her head. "Shh, darling, I'm here now. It's all right."

I only realise Lin's followed me from the bathroom when I see Marcia looking over my shoulder. Very reluctantly, I turn to her. "I'm sorry, Lin, I've got to feed my baby now.

286

She's hungry."

My bag's in the living room, next to the armchair I was sitting in before we went into the bathroom. I need to get it, but I don't want to take Hannah into this flat with its cigarette stink, and the recent revelations of cruelty and despair.

"Jen? What's wrong?" Marcia asks.

Along the corridor, the front door's wide open. Someone clumps up the steps – a man wearing a leather jacket, holding a bike helmet. Michael. Oh, God, it's Michael. Tears of relief spring to my eyes.

"I phoned him when I couldn't remember the house number," Marcia explains. "Then it just popped back into my head a few minutes ago, so I came."

Michael strides towards us down the corridor, strong and sure. When he reaches us, he ignores everybody but me, his beautiful eyes searching my tear-streaked face. "Are you all right, Jen?" he asks, and I nod, sniffing back the tears, because now he's here I am all right.

"Yes," I say, "I'm fine."

Chapter Forty-Six

Michael

She was sitting by the window – in the same seat he'd sat in when he first met Ronnie – feeding their baby. It felt surreal to be here with her, in his mother's flat, and yet at the same time it was the most natural thing in the world. He needed to speak; to make a start at unravelling and explaining everything, but he didn't have any idea how to begin.

Jen was waiting, giving him time, her fingers gently stroking Hannah's toes, curling them up like flower petals. When Hannah suddenly kicked her foot, dislodging her hand, Jen looked up to share the moment with him, and he couldn't believe they were smiling together, while Marcia was in the bedroom with his mum, finishing off her hair with a hairdryer. All those years of pretence; all the years of lonely numbness, and it could have been like this instead.

"Hey." He didn't realise there were tears in his eyes until Jen spoke, taking her hand from Hannah's foot to reach out to him.

Brushing the tears away, he sat on the arm of her chair, listening to the laughter coming from the bedroom. "Am I really hearing Marcia and my mum laughing together?" he asked.

Jen smiled. "There are sides to Marcia you know nothing about," she said. "She can have a very good bedside manner. Or in this case, a dressing table manner."

"Obviously," he said.

But when she laughed, he couldn't join in. He didn't feel as if he deserved to laugh. "I'm so sorry you had to find out like this."

Jen's smile became more forced. "It doesn't matter."

"Of course it does. Jason's a total prick. I hope he didn't scare you. He can be…intimidating."

"Marcia was a match for him," she said.

"Huh! I can believe that," he said, and had a sudden flashback to the playground, with Jason and his mates surrounding him. Your Mum's a looney! Your mum's a looney! What he'd have given to have someone like Marcia on his side back then.

"You know, the irony is, I'd just made up my mind to tell you the truth about Mum. I hoped… I hoped you'd realise I was giving you my all by finally opening up about it."

Jen was the one with tears in her eyes now, and he put his arm around her shoulders, burying his face in her hair.

"Is that what you want to give me?" she asked shakily. "Your all?"

"If that's what you want, yes."

"Oh, yes."

They held each other silently for a moment, and Michael was aware of a feeling of deep peace beginning to settle over him. They still needed to do a lot of talking; he still had to share all those things he'd kept to himself for so long with her; but somehow he knew it would be all right.

"I ought to have asked you about it all first," Jen said. "Instead of rushing straight here like some crazy woman on a quest for the truth."

Michael sighed, moving so he could look into her eyes. "I don't suppose I've ever made it very easy for you to talk to me about important things."

She kissed him. "No. But it sounds as if there was a good reason for that."

It was his cue to start spilling the gory details, but Marcia came into the room just then, bringing his mother with her.

"Hey, lovebirds," she said. "What do you think of Lin's lovely hair?"

Michael looked. His mother's hair was a perfect, shiny bell, expertly blow-dried under at the neck. She was standing there, holding onto Marcia's hand, the very beginnings of a shy smile on her face as she waited for their reaction.

"It's beautiful, Lin," Jen said.

"Yes," he agreed, his voice cracking slightly. "You look beautiful, Mum."

Marcia drove Jen and Hannah home, and Michael followed on the bike. Hannah was fast asleep in her car seat when they got there, and didn't stir when Michael lifted her out of the car.

"D'you want me to watch Hannah while you two talk?" Marcia asked.

"No, we'll be fine," Jen said. "But thanks so much for all your help."

"Yes," Michael agreed. "Thanks. It was really good of you to be so nice to my mum."

"You're welcome." Marcia smiled at both of them, then gave Jen a hug. "Phone me later, yeah? Good luck, you two."

He watched her drive away. "It's kind of strange to have her being nice to me," he said.

Jen laughed. "Enjoy it while you can!" she advised. "You know Marcia. But you've definitely gone up in her estimation ever since your beach art gesture. She was very impressed."

For a moment Michael remembered the salt wind in his hair, the press of the crowd of onlookers and the bleak devastation when he'd seen the answer to his proposal in Jen's face. Then he pushed the memories away. "So," he teased. "It worked on her, but not on you?"

She put her arms around his neck, her face growing serious. "It did work on me; very much so. It would have been so easy for me to get swept off my feet. But...I just sensed something still wasn't quite right between us. And now I've got Hannah to consider, I had to be completely sure of you."

"You know, you've changed this past year," he said, cupping her face with his hand. "You've grown much stronger."

She nodded. "Yes," she agreed. "I have. But then I needed to, didn't I?"

"No. You've always been perfect in my eyes."

She kissed him. "The me who first found out I was pregnant was quite a needy, insecure person. But I'm not like that now. With everything that's happened, I've had to be strong. I know I can deal with whatever life throws at me now."

He nodded, watching her swallow back her emotion. "I'm sorry I never gave your friend Hannah a chance," he said. "I was jealous, I suppose. I didn't like the way she continued your link with Luther. He treated you so badly, and I hated to think of you still seeing him." He sighed. "Not that I've got any right to judge him, after the way I've behaved lately."

She reached up to stroke his face. "Luther never had anything to do with my friendship with Hannah," she said. "Though he isn't all-bad, you know. In fact, he's been really good to me since she died. We've helped each other through it."

Michael kissed her. "Good. Come on; let's get Hannah inside. I don't know about you, but I could murder a cuppa."

Indoors, he made the tea and took it to the conservatory. Jen was settled on the cane sofa with Hannah's car seat next to her, on the floor, and a quick glance told him the baby was still blissfully asleep. He sat down next to Jen, aware of the serious nature of the conversation to come, but suddenly, he was ready for it. He wanted to get everything out into the open. Then they could move on.

But before he could dive in, Jen surprised him by saying, "Your mum's the reason for all the unexplained absences everyone's been mentioning, isn't she?"

He frowned, not understanding. "Who's everyone?"

Suddenly she didn't seem to want to meet his gaze. "Well, Diane and Rachel. I did meet Nita too, at the shop where she works, but...we didn't speak. You see, I thought... Well, I thought if I could find out why you split up with them, I might be able to stop the same thing happening to us."

She'd been to see Diane and Rachel? Spoken to both of them about him? Jesus. It was all too easy to imagine the dirt that pair had shared about him. It was a wonder Jen was here, right now, wanting to try and build a future with him.

"It was a stupid thing to do," she said, looking at him now. "I know that now. I'm so sorry, Michael. See? I told you I was needy and insecure back then."

"That's why you went to Cuba, wasn't it?" he said, suddenly realising it. "To meet with Rachel. I'd heard she was working over there."

Jen nodded. "Yes."

She sounded so ashamed, but Michael knew he only had himself to blame. If he hadn't been so closed off, she'd never have had the idea in the first place. "What did Rachel have to say about me?" he asked. "Nothing good, I'm sure. We didn't exactly part on good terms."

"She said you were talented."

"Good of her. What else?"

Jen traced a crease on the leg of his jeans with her finger, her eyes avoiding his. "She said…she said you're a commitment phobic, and you always keep a part of yourself out of reach."

He sighed, knowing he had no right to feel resentful. "Well, she's right. At least, she's partly right. Mum's health always went up and down a lot, you see. After I'd been taken away from her the first time, she got well again after several months. So I was sent back to live with her. But then she got ill again, and I was taken away. After that had happened a few times, Social Services finally accepted it wasn't going to work out. But by then, I was too old for people to want to adopt me. I suppose you need to grow a tough skin to survive something like that. Maybe you start to lose yourself too, I don't know."

He risked looking at her, afraid he might see pity on her face. But all he saw was compassion and a huge amount of love.

"Hannah will help us to find you, if you let her," she said, and the tears returned to his eyes as he looked down at their contentedly sleeping daughter.

"I'm so very sorry I ever said...well, what I said about not keeping her," he said brokenly. "I don't know what Diane told you, but, I've got rather an extreme phobia about childbirth."

Jen smiled at him. "I was there the other week, remember? When Hannah was born?"

"Were you?" He smiled, wiping away his tears on his sleeve, and reached out a hand to stroke her hair. Then he sobered, readying himself to talk about the really bad stuff. "I had a brother, you know, but he was stillborn. He was born at home – I was there, and...well, I had to deal with it all. I thought my mum was dying. That's... Well, that's when they first took me from her."

Jen's eyes were full of tears as she looked at him. "Oh, Michael," she said. "That's so awful."

"It wasn't the best of times, no. I was only four, but I know I'll never forget it."

"Of course not," she said.

Suddenly Hannah began to make little sucking movements in her sleep, and they smiled down at her. "It might have been different if my dad hadn't gone off the way he did. I've got a photo of him somewhere; I'll have to show it to you. Hannah's got a real look of him."

When Jen looked suddenly troubled, Michael frowned. "What?"

"Your father wrote to you."

"What?"

"Lin told me so today; your dad wrote to you. Oh, Michael, I think she still has the letters somewhere. She said he wrote to you every week; I don't know how long for."

Suddenly Michael felt sick. So many dark years, feeling lonely and abandoned, and all the time his father had been writing to him, presumably wanting to arrange to see him. "God," he said, reeling from the pain of it.

Jen gripped his shoulders, her gaze compelling him to

293

believe her. "We'll have to get the letters from her, Michael. And I'm sure it's not too late to trace him."

Michael closed his eyes, the image of a beach beginning to form in his mind. But somehow, the image was shaky and wouldn't quite come into focus. It was all such a long time ago. "I can only remember him very vaguely."

"Why would your mum do such a cruel thing?" Jen asked. "Why would she keep those letters from you?"

He shrugged. "She's ill. And I've no idea what happened between the two of them, after all. Maybe, in her own way, she was trying to protect me. Who knows?"

"What's wrong with her?" she asked. "Has it got a name?"

"She has schizophrenia. I was always terrified I'd develop it myself, but so far so good."

Jen stared at him. "That's why you were so reluctant to have another child, wasn't it? It wasn't just the birth thing. It was because you were afraid they might inherit your mum's illness."

He nodded. "Partly, yes. It skipped me, and so far anyway, it seems to have skipped Kyle." He looked down at their perfect baby, and felt Jen take his hands.

"Listen, our daughter's not going to develop schizophrenia, okay? She's not."

"No," he said, turning his face so he could kiss her hand. "I'm sure she won't."

"And if she does…" Jen's voice wobbled, and she broke off.

"Hey," he said, knowing it was his turn to comfort her now. "If she does, we'll be there to help her through it. Listen, Mum never had anyone to support her; nobody. And attitudes to mental illness were so different back then. Her life's been really difficult; maybe that's why she's inclined to latch on to people who might not always be good for her."

And he told her about Ronnie's attack.

Jen was horrified. "Oh, God; that's so terrible! Poor Lin. She must have been so frightened."

"Yes. Though one thing about her illness, she does seem to be able to push reality from her mind." He smiled. "Maybe I am a bit like her, eh? I've been good at hiding the truth, anyway. Though from the first moment I met you I wanted it to be different. But it was just easier to carry on living a lie."

"The timing was very bad, when I broke the news about being pregnant," she said after a while. "What with the business and the house. And...I shouldn't have kept it from you. I ought to have told you as soon as I found out. Marcia said I should."

"There she goes, surprising me all over again," he said, attempting to be flippant.

Jen smiled. "I think she's mellowing, actually. Keep it to yourself, because it's very early days, but she's pregnant."

Well, thank the lord, he thought, imagining Marcia if things hadn't turned out the way she wanted them to. It just didn't bear thinking about, it really didn't; but he was also genuinely pleased for her. "That's great; really great. I'm glad for them. Gary's a good bloke."

"Marcia's good too, underneath it all," she said.

He nodded. "So you keep on telling me. No, I'm sure she is. I've just never liked the way you let her push you around, that's all."

"I'm not going to let her do that anymore. From now on, I'm not going to let anyone push me around."

At that very moment, Hannah woke up and began to cry.

"Not even our daughter?" he asked, smiling.

Jen laughed, reaching down to unfasten the car seat straps, her nose crinkling as she lifted Hannah out. "It's not me she needs this time," she told him, her smile wicked. "It's her daddy."

Michael took his daughter from her without complaint, more than happy to deal with a smelly nappy.

When he was elbow deep in filthy wipes and flailing legs, Jen spoke again.

"Michael," she said, "will you marry us?"

He looked up, his heart suddenly racing. "Us?"

"Hannah and me." She was grinning all over her face as she looked at him. "Will you marry us?"

Michael laughed, filled with pure joy. "What?" he teased. "Aren't you even going to make me an art installation?"

"Don't push it," she warned him, and he laughed again, finishing off Hannah's nappy and picking her up.

Then, with the baby cradled close to his heart, he looked at Jen more seriously. "Are you really sure this is what you want?"

She nodded. "Of course," she said. "I love you."

A lump appeared in his throat. He swallowed. "And I love you," he said. "So very much."

He thought back over the last six appalling months, unable to quite believe they could lead to this. "But...I've made a complete mess of things lately – us, the business, the house..."

"We'll get through it," Jen said, dismissing all obstacles and curling her arms around his neck. "After all, we are Tom and Madonna."

He laughed, bending to kiss her. "You're right," he said. "We are."

THE END

Great Authors
Fantastic Books

CROOKED
CAT

Meet our authors and discover our exciting range:

- Gripping Thrillers
- Cosy Mysteries
- Romantic Chick-Lit
- Fascinating Historicals
- Exciting Fantasy
- Young Adult and Children's Adventures

Visit us at:
www.crookedcatpublishing.com

Join us on facebook:
www.facebook.com/crookedcatpublishing

14732798R00178

Printed in Great Britain
by Amazon.co.uk, Ltd.,
Marston Gate.